LOVERS' TRYST

Rising to her knees, Jasmine slipped her arms around Barrett's neck and played the tip of her tongue about the corners of his mouth until he parted his lips and met it with his own. A wave of unbearable desire coursed through her, taking her breath away.

"Jasmine," he whispered, his lips moving against the base of her throat, "oh, my sweet, sweet Jasmine!"

Near to swooning with the need of him, Jasmine lost all thoughts of vengeance on her mother and the faceless man in France to whom she had been promised. Her body pleaded for—demanded—release from the fever of passion burning within her.

"Love me, please, Barrett," she urged. "Please!"

Barrett's lips claimed hers in an ever-deepening, ever more demanding kiss as he lowered her gently to the ground . . .

Whispers of Passion

Sandra DuBay

Book Margins, Inc.

A BMI Edition

Published by special arrangement with Dorchester
Publishing Co., Inc.

Copyright© 1984 by Sandra DuBay

Printed in the United States of America.

Part 1

Virginia

Spring
1756

Chapter 1

The great plantations of Belle Glade and Paxton Hall overlooked Mobjack Bay near the mouth of the North River. The mansions themselves were similar, being of the same red brick trimmed white shutters and tall dormers that ringed their steep roofs.

The rolling lawns that ran from the mansions to the water's edge were divided by Paxton's Creek, which formed a natural boundary as it ran between the two plantations. The creek was spanned by a stone bridge, and geese and ducks swam with effortless grace in its cool shade. At the mouth of the creek, a small copse of willow grew; their long, trailing branches floated in the cool, clear water of the creek and bay.

Jasmine DuPré—daughter of Jean-Baptiste DuPré, Master of Belle Glade—lay in the shade of the willows, hidden from view to the inhabitants of the mansions. She smiled as she looked toward the young man who lay beside her.

Barrett Paxton—son of Samuel Paxton, owner of Paxton Hall—was the picture of utter contentment as he lay there with the sun sending shadows of leaves dancing across his face. One lock of his dark hair had escaped from the ribbon that bound the queue at the nape of his neck and it lay in a lazy curl along his lean cheek. His cravat had been tossed aside and, at the base of his sun-browned throat, Jasmine could see the steady thump-thump of his heartbeat.

She reached out to touch him. "Barrett?" she whispered. "Are you asleep?"

He opened his dark eyes and smiled. "You keep me in such a torment, I can't sleep at night—how can you expect me to sleep here with you beside me?"

Jasmine blushed, her black-lashed, gray-green eyes sparkling. Barrett was two years her senior, having turned eighteen the previous winter, and she could not remember a time when she'd not been in love with him. Even as a child, when his first loves were horses and shooting, when the sight of the little copper-haired girl from the neighboring plantation who watched him with what his amused parents called "calf's eyes" was enough to send him into moans of annoyance, she had followed him wherever she could hoping for a kind word or a smile.

And then, like a miracle, she had grown suddenly from a gawky little girl into a stunning young woman and Barrett, already a man, no longer groaned in vexation when he saw her approaching. For him it was a fascinating discovery; for Jasmine it was the long-awaited answer to a thousand girlhood prayers.

Now, with only the willows as witnesses, Jasmine's eyes never left Barrett's as he leaned over her, and she shivered when she felt his practiced fingers unfastening the hooks concealed beneath the ruching on the bodice of her gown. As his hand slid inside and moved over the alabaster silk of her skin to caress the firm and

8

agonizingly sensitive flesh of her breasts, her tiny gasp of pleasure was matched by one of his own.

Lifting the material of her bodice aside, he captured one coral nipple with his lips, and he could not be sure if the shudder of desire he felt had coursed through his body or hers.

His lips left her breast and traveled over the pale flesh of her bosom to the hollow of her throat where her pulse raced wildly.

Jasmine held him close and cursed the skirts and many-layered petticoats that separated their bodies. As she felt the eager yet infinitely tender touches of his hands and the gentle, fervent caresses of his lips as they moved up the long ivory column of her throat, she knew sheer happiness. Given her way, she would have asked nothing more of life than to be allowed to remain forever in the shade of the whispering willows and in the circle of Barrett Paxton's arms.

His lips moved to her ear and he murmured softly: "Jasmine, I love you. I swear I do."

"And I you," she replied ardently.

"Then please, let me love you. You know that I would never hurt you. You know it was meant to be."

Jasmine felt her resistance melting beneath the warmth of his lips and hands. Surely, she told herself, he was right. Her mother had asked her to promise that she would allow no man to touch her outside the sanctity of marriage and she'd been warned of the hazards of love-making, but Jasmine was convinced that they were destined to marry. If a child resulted from their tryst beneath the willows, the wedding would merely be sooner than anyone expected.

But they both heard the voice that called from the direction of Belle Glade. It was Norah, one of the housemaids, and she was calling to Jasmine.

Barrett moaned as he allowed Jasmine to leave his embrace and mopped his brow with the wrist-frill of his shirt. He watched, his ardor reluctantly cooling, as she walked to the edge of the clearing.

"What it is, Norah?" she called, her fingers smoothing the ruching over the refastened hooks.

"Madame wants to see you, Miss," Norah replied.

"Very well. I'll be along directly."

The maid returned to the mansion and Jasmine sighed as Barrett slid his arms about her once again. "I have to go home," she told him. "Maman wants to see me."

"Kiss me once more before you go," he asked.

She heard the pleading in his voice and marveled at the newly discovered power she held over him. In a sudden mood of coquettishness, she shook the willow leaves out of her auburn curls. "I will not!"

"Jasmine, please!"

"You take me for granted, Barrett Paxton; I truly believe you do! You think that because there are no other young men about for miles I am your private property." She lifted her chin haughtily. "If you want a kiss you shall have to earn it!"

Before he could reply, she lifted her satin skirts and ran away from him. They were on the Paxton Hall side of the creek and she had to go to the bridge to cross for it was spring and the creek was too wide to leap over.

"Jasmine," Barrett called as he started after her, "wait—slow down!"

Jasmine glanced over her shoulder and laughed at the growing distance between them. In spite of the rippling skirts and heavy petticoats that she held away from her flying feet, it was obvious that Barrett was putting forth no great effort to catch her. Deliberately but not blatantly, she slowed her pace and tossed a dazzling smile back at the darkly handsome man behind her.

Barrett returned her smile. He could have caught her easily but he enjoyed the sight of her ahead; a slender silhouette against the finely manicured green of the lawns. She reminded him at times of the skittish thoroughbreds in which his father took such pride. In the drawing room she seemed so fragile, giving the impression that she would break like fine crystal if touched too harshly, and yet she harbored within her a strength that could carry her through times of trouble.

"Jasmine!" he called. "Wait on the bridge!"

The gap between them narrowed as they approached the bridge that spanned Paxton's Creek. Leaning on the balustrade, Jasmine pressed a hand to the place in her side that ached with the exertion of the chase.

Barrett watched her remembering a time when she had not been so biddable; a time when she would no more have obeyed him so meekly than she would have offered to help one of the maids scrub a floor. Even now he knew that, should she take the notion into her head, she could easily be within the solid walls of Belle Glade before he had crossed the broad expanse of lawn and garden at the side of the mansion. Lord knows she'd done it often enough before she grew up and learned the fine art of coquetry.

Jasmine watched Barrett approach and the sparkle in her black-lashed eyes were heightened by the roses that colored her cheeks. Her full, deep pink lips parted as she breathed.

Barrett reached the bridge and Jasmine turned away and leaned over the balustrade to watch a duck and five ducklings paddle from under the bridge.

"I fear you'll be the death of me," he told her,

tugging at one coppery curl. "I suppose when we're old and gray you'll still be leading me a merry chase."

Jasmine turned around and lowered her eyes knowing that the bright sunshine would cast feathery shadows from her thick black lashes across her cheeks.

"I suppose so," she agreed. "I'm afraid I shall never learn to be a proper lady."

Barrett slid a finger beneath her chin and tipped her face toward him. "You may never learn to be a proper lady," he said softly, "but you are all the woman any man could want."

She tilted her head and allowed the corners of her mouth to curve into a smile that was at once innocent and seductive.

"Why, Barrett Paxton! How familiar you've become! Take care lest my father feel obliged to defend my honor and reputation!"

Barrett smiled and wound one of her auburn curls around his finger. "Your reputation! Jasmine, there isn't another plantation for miles! Exactly who is going to be put off by your soiled reputation?"

She pouted, thrusting out her lower lip, and turned her back on him. That was not at all the remark he should have made. He took her too much for granted.

When she felt his lips touch the soft, creamy flesh of her shoulder, she shuddered but refused to look around. She was no stranger to his kisses and knew well that if she made no protests he would soon be emboldened enough to make tentative forays with his tanned, work-roughened hands.

She stepped away and put out a hand to ward him off. "Not here, Barrett, Maman might see us. She's been corresponding with my grand-maman in Paris and has suddenly become unreasonably strict."

She glanced toward Belle Glade and wondered if her mother was even then watching with a disapproving frown while she "dallied shamelessly with that young rogue, Barrett Paxton."

She was. From the windows of the parlor at the end of Belle Glade, Isabeau DuPré scowled as she watched the two young people on the bridge. It was not that she disliked Barrett. He was a handsome young man and the heir to a great plantation—for anyone else's daughter he would have been a wonderful catch. But not for her Jasmine. She had other plans for Jasmine.

Reluctantly taking her eyes away from her daughter and her beau, Isabeau crossed the room and tugged at the bell pull. Almost immediately, the door opened and her maidservant—Lotte—entered the room and curtsied.

"Lotte," Isabeau said, her French accent apparent even in the single word, "go out to the bridge and bring Mademoiselle Jasmine back."

Lotte curtsied again. "Yes, Madame."

When the girl was nearly out the door, Isabeau called to her. "And Lotte? Do not bring Master Paxton."

"Maman," Jasmine complained as she sat in the parlor. "Why did you send for me? Barrett and I were . . ."

"I saw what Barrett and you were doing," Isabeau interrupted sharply. "And that is precisely why I sent Lotte to bring you back. You should have come back when Norah called for you and not dawdled with Master Paxton."

"Why does it matter to you? You never objected to my spending the afternoon with Barrett before."

"That was before. You were children then. You are growing into a woman, ma petite. You have just passed your sixteenth birthday. Barrett is eighteen now. You are too old to play together as children and I do not want to risk your playing together as adults.''

Jasmine blushed wondering what her mother would think of their trysts beneath the willows. ''But, Maman, what difference does it make? Barrett and I will be married one day. Everyone has always said so.''

''You will not marry Barrett Paxton!'' Isabeau saw the startled look on her daughter's face and caught herself. ''You will not marry Barrett Paxton,'' she said more softly.

''But . . . but,'' Jasmine stuttered anxiously, ''Maman, I thought you liked Barrett.''

Isabeau took a deep breath to calm herself and sat down next to her daughter on the bright yellow brocade of the sofa. ''My darling, of course I like him. And he will make a marvelous husband for someone someday. But not for you—not for my beautiful Jasmine.'' She reached out and stroked her daughter's cheek. ''You know, you look like I did at your age. My hair was once the same rich auburn as yours before I began to find strands of silver in it. What a marriage I could have made with the proper opportunities.''

''Maman! You made a wonderful marriage! Papa loves you so and you have me and little Armand and Belle Glade.''

''But it isn't France!'' Isabeau rose and went to the window to lean her forehead against the cool glass. ''It isn't France!'' Choked sobs wracked her slender body and with one long-fingered hand she covered the wide, gray-green eyes that had been part of her legacy of beauty to her daughter.

Stunned, Jasmine went to her mother. ''I thought you loved Virginia.''

Madame DuPré's tears fell to the window sill. "I never loved Virginia—I love France. I never wanted to leave."

"You knew Papa was leaving France when you married him. Why did you marry him if you didn't want to leave?"

"What choice did I have? My father, the Marquis, was dead—all of his money and lands went to pay his debts. What dowry could I have offered a nobleman?" Isabeau stared out the window at the garden which was just then coming into bloom.

"You never loved Papa?" Jasmine asked quietly. "He worships you."

Isabeau frowned at the note of rebuke in her daughter's voice. "I have been a good wife to your Papa! I have given him a beautiful daughter and a son to inherit Belle Glade. I have never given him cause to regret his marriage to me."

A tense silence filled the room and reigned until Jasmine broke it to demand:

"Tell me what this has to do with Barrett and me."

"I want more for you, Jasmine." Isabeau touched her daughter's hair. "You are lovely and your Papa will give you a large dowry. You will be able to marry a man worthy of you."

"A Frenchman?"

"Yes! A Frenchman! And, what is more, a French nobleman! I have written to your grand-maman in Paris and she has replied to assure me that she is looking for a prospective husband for you. When she finds one, you and I will go to France for your wedding."

"You would force me to marry a man I've not even seen?" Jasmine cried, horrified. "A man I do not love?"

"Ungrateful child! You will trust your grand-maman's judgment as I do. She would not choose a man who was unsuitable in any way.''

"But Maman!"

"No! Go to your room and do not leave it until you can be respectful to me!"

Jasmine looked up as her mother's maidservant tapped at her bedchamber door.

"Come in."

Lotte appeared in the doorway. "Pardon, Mademoiselle. Madame has sent me to help you undress."

Jasmine climbed off the elaborately carved, Tudor fourposter which dominated her bedchamber. The hangings of rich, green and white brocade matched the draperies, and the color was repeated in the walls of the room and in the rich carpeting.

"Undress? But am I not to go downstairs for supper?"

"Supper is finished."

"Finished! Are you sure?"

Abandoning her carefully cultivated manners, Lotte planted her fists into her hips. "Of course, I'm sure! I helped Momma clear the table!"

Lotte, whose real name was Charlotte, was the daughter of Sarah and John Yunger, the housekeeper and overseer of Belle Glade. She'd been carefully trained since childhood to be a proper lady's maid and had entered service with Madame DuPré when barely old enough to know how to serve her mistress. As Jasmine was considered too young to need a full-time maid of her own, Lotte was often pressed into service as a maid to both.

"I was not accusing you of lying, Lotte!" Jasmine snapped. "I was merely surprised that I was not called down to eat."

"Sent to bed without supper, eh?" Lotte's smile was

catty. She enjoyed seeing Jasmine treated as a child.

Of an age, they had played together from earliest childhood; but they were not friends. Their continued companionship stemmed from the fact that there was no alternative for either of them. The only other young women their age on either the DuPré plantation or neighboring Paxton Hall were slaves who were allowed no time to be the companion of anyone. At sixteen they had long since been put to work in the fields or in the mansions.

But forced companionship had not bloomed into camaraderie for Jasmine and Lotte. Each was all too aware of the differences that would forever separate them. Jasmine was the daughter of the master; she was to be deferred to in all matters. Lotte was a servant and her resentment against cruel fate grew every time she was forced to cater to Jasmine's whims.

Jasmine unhooked the front of her blue satin gown and then held up her arms while Lotte lifted it over her head. While the maidservant took the gown to the clothespress, Jasmine began untying the ribbons of her petticoats.

As she passed the pier glass, Lotte held the blue gown up before herself. Her own gown was of gray poplin and had been her mother's. It had been passed to her only when it became too shabby to be seen on the housekeeper of Belle Glade. Her hair, though blonde rather than auburn, was every bit as lustrous and luxuriously thick as Jasmine's. But it was not brushed and polished to shine like gold; it was hidden beneath a cap of white muslin. Her bosom, as creamy and full as Jasmine's, was covered by a fichu instead of being displayed for the admiration of gentlemen. Her hands, as long-fingered and elegant as Jasmine's, were red and

17

work-roughened instead of soft and whitened with lemon. While Jasmine was out in the afternoon sunshine being courted by Barrett Paxton, she was in Jasmine's room or Isabeau's sorting stockings or hanging petticoats in the clothespress.

"Lotte?" Jasmine said from the edge of the bed where she waited for her nightdress. "Lotte? What are you doing?"

Lotte looked around, jerked out of her reverie. Quickly she put the gown away and brought the linen nightdress.

Jasmine pulled her chemise over her head and dropped it atop her shoes and stockings near the bed. While Lotte gathered them, she pulled on the nightdress.

"Lotte," she said as she climbed into the wide bed. "Did Maman tell you why she sent you for me this afternoon?"

"No, she didn't," Lotte replied as she put the shoes away. "Why did she send me to get you?"

"It's none of your business!"

Lotte shot her a look of distaste. Without a word, she jerked the bedcurtains closed and pinched out the candles in the ormolu candelabrum on the mantel. When only one was still burning, she lit a candle in a small pewter candlestick. Blowing out the last candle in the candelabrum, she left the room using her single candle to light her way.

Behind her, in the pitch blackness of her bed, Jasmine wondered about what kind of man her grandmother would consider suitable for her to marry. Doubtless rank and wealth would be her prime criteria. It wouldn't matter if he was handsome, as Barrett was; or kind and gentle, as Barrett was; or if he would love her, as Barrett did. And that she could not possibly grow to love a man who was none of those things mattered least of all.

Jasmine stubbornly shook off the sinking depression that threatened to take possession of her. "Ah, well," she told herself as she turned on her side and snuggled farther beneath the scented sheets, "I can always hope she doesn't find anyone!"

Chapter 2

"Papa?" Jasmine peeked around the edge of the door to her father's study.

Jean-Baptiste DuPré looked up from his ledgers and smiled at his daughter. "Come in, come in, child," he said. "What can I do for you?"

Jasmine leaned over the desk and kissed his worry-furrowed brow. She hated to add to his troubles; he worked so hard to make Belle Glade the success it was, but she felt she had no other choice.

She sat in the red-leather upholstered chair. "Papa," she began tentatively, "has Maman spoken to you on the subject of my marriage?"

"Your marriage?" His blue eyes, set in a long, lean face beneath gray-flecked brown hair, widened. "Why no she hasn't. Has that young scamp, Paxton, offered for your hand without speaking to me?"

"No, Papa. In fact, Maman has said I must not see Barrett any more."

"She has? Why ever not? And what has this to do with your marriage?"

"She says Grand-maman is going to find me a husband . . ."

"In France," Monsieur DuPré finished for her. He laughed wryly. "So she is going to use you to achieve her own goals, is that it?"

"Oh, Papa, I don't think . . ."

He held up a hand. "Yes, child, it is true. Your Maman has obviously determined to get you the husband she wanted." He saw the surprised look on his daughter's face. "Yes, I knew I was not the kind of man your mother would have chosen for herself. But she was a beautiful woman and has been a good wife, and most marriages are not love matches at any rate."

"But can you not ask her to forget the notion of finding me a French husband, Papa?" she begged, her fragile composure deserting her. "I don't want to leave Belle Glade. I've always believed I would marry Barrett and live just across Paxton's Creek. It's all I want."

Jean-Baptiste walked around his desk and sat on its edge near her. His eyes were kind but his expression was sad. "I cannot ask her to do that," he replied. "I cannot ask her to give up her dreams when she's given up so much to make my dreams a reality. She has given me Armand to inherit Belle Glade and continue the line of the DuPrés. I cannot refuse her the opportunity to re-establish the honor of her own family through her daughter."

Jasmine stood. "I understand, Papa," she lied.

"Good." He patted her shoulder. "You will become accustomed to the notion, chérie. We cannot expect to have our lives exactly the way we want but often we find it is not so bad as we imagined it would be. Barrett is the only young man you have ever spent any amount of time near—it is natural that he should be your first love. But mayhap he will not be your last.''

Forcing a wan smile, Jasmine kissed his creased cheek and left the room quickly lest he see the tears that welled into her eyes.

Jasmine lay across her bed lovingly studying Barrett's recent birthday gift to her.

It was a small, hinged, leather case. Into one side of the case was fitted a gold-framed minature of Barrett painted on ivory. In the other side of the case, coiled beneath a delicate crystal, a lock of his dark hair shone softly.

"Master Barrett is coming!" Lotte cried excitedly. She had abandoned her work and leaned against the sill of Jasmine's bedchamber window watching the tall, lithe man striding toward the mansion.

Jasmine looked sharply at the maidservant, disliking her tone of voice. She looked at the half-filled ash scuttle near the fireplace. Lotte had been shoveling ashes from the grate, a task that normally might have been delegated to some lackey if it were not that Isabeau refused to allow any man to enter her daughter's bedchamber for any reason.

"Finish your work!" she ordered, sliding off the bed.

"I can look if I've a mind to!" Lotte retorted. She smiled slyly. "And who knows? Perhaps after you've left Belle Glade, I might do more than that!"

Eyes blazing, Jasmine lashed out at the scuttle sending it rolling over the unprotected carpeting. With a delighted smirk she saw the anguish in Lotte's eyes, for it was she who would have to clean the carpet with a bucket and brush on her hands and knees.

"Oh, Lotte!" she cried in mock chagrin. "I am sorry!"

"You did that on purpose!" Lotte hissed. "I'll not clean it! You can lick the ashes off the floor!"

Without bothering to curtsy, she strode across the filthy floor and left the room.

Jasmine smiled, unperturbed. She hurried to the window and saw that Barrett was nearly to the door. Just before leaving her room, she tugged the bell cord to summon Sarah Yunger, the housekeeper. One look at the carpet and, Jasmine knew, Sarah would be after Lotte with a vengeance.

Leaving her room, Jasmine went to the balcony that overlooked the entrance hall. A manservant answered Barrett's knock and she heard Barrett say:

"I've brought a letter for Madame DuPré from Yorktown. Will you see that she receives it?"

The manservant bowed and, taking the letter, disappeared into the depths of the house in search of the mistress.

The moment he was gone, Jasmine hurried down the stairs and out the front door. She frowned as she saw Barrett not far away speaking with Lotte, who punctuated her conversation with bold caresses of his hand.

"Barrett!" Jasmine called as she started toward them. "Why ever didn't you send up word that you were here?"

Reaching them, she took his arm as she stepped between him and the maidservant. Scowling at Lotte, she said: "You've hardly begun your chores, Lotte. Don't you have the chamber pots to empty or, perhaps, a carpet to scrub?"

Lotte's blue eyes narrowed with hatred but she had no choice but to curtsy and return to the mansion.

"Good morning, Jasmine," Barrett said, smiling.

"Had I known you were up and about already, I would have asked to see you."

"What was that you brought to Maman just now?"

He shrugged. "Only a letter. Father went to Yorktown yesterday and the letter was there so he brought it back with him."

"Do you know who it was from?"

"Certainly not. Jasmine, do you think I would read someone else's correspondence?"

"No, no, of course not. I'm just afraid it was from my grand-maman in Paris."

He lifted one eyebrow. "Do you dislike your grandmother?"

"Actually, I've never met her." She saw the quizzical look on his face and went on: "But you see, she might have sent bad news."

"Bad news?"

She took his arm and they walked across the lush green lawn toward the small cluster of willows at the bay shore. Heedless of the morning dew's effect on her pale green lute-string gown, she sat down and waited for him to join her.

"You see, Barrett," she began uncertainly, "Maman has taken the notion into her head that I should marry a French nobleman." She refused to look up to see what effect her words were having on him. "She has been corresponding with my grand-maman on the subject and my grand-maman is searching out prospective husbands for me."

Barrett sagged against the trunk of one of the willows. "Is there nothing you can do to prevent this? Cannot your father keep you here at Belle Glade?"

She shook her head, biting her lip. "No. He cannot do anything; will not do anything. He says Maman must have her way in this.'' She took a deep breath as her throat began to close. ''Oh, Barrett,'' she whispered, ''I don't want to leave Belle Glade. I don't want to leave you! But I don't see what can be done to prevent it.''

Leaning toward him, she pressed her forehead against the soft cloth of his coat. He held her gently but there were no words that could lessen their grief or express his astonishment.

''Pardon, Mademoiselle?'' Leon, one of the DuPrés' footmen, stood nearby. ''Madame wishes you to return to the mansion. She said . . . that is . . .'' He looked wretchedly uncomfortable.

''What did she say, Leon?'' Jasmine demanded.

''She said you were not to bring Master Paxton with you.''

''I see. Thank you, Leon. I shall be along shortly.''

The buff-and-blue-liveried manservant returned to the mansion and Jasmine watched him, her hopes sinking. She looked at Barrett sadly.

''I'm afraid to go back,'' she said softly. ''I'm afraid that Grand-maman has succeeded in finding me a bridegroom.''

Barrett got to his feet and offered her his hand. Wordlessly they embraced, and suddenly the whispering of the willows and the lapping of the water on the shore seemed mournful and lonely.

''I must go,'' she sighed at last. She forced a bright smile. ''Perhaps we are mistaken. Perhaps Grand-maman has discovered that there is not a gentleman in all Paris who would care to marry me!''

Barrett didn't smile. ''Do you think that's likely, sweet Jasmine?''

''No,'' she admitted. ''There are doubtless many men who would marry any woman with breath in her body provided her dowry was large enough. And Papa has provided me with a very generous dowry." She looked toward the mansion. "Maman will be coming after me with fire in her eyes." She reached up and touched his cheek and he caught her trembling hand and kissed it. Reluctantly, she moved away and started toward the house.

Her skirts swished over the grass as she walked slowly toward the mansion. When she was nearly halfway, she turned and looked toward Paxton Hall. Barrett stood on the bridge watching her and, resisting the overwhelming temptation to run to the comforting shelter of his embrace, she raised her hand in a dispirited wave. He returned her salute half-heartedly and then started toward the mansion in the distance.

"Where is she?" she asked Leon who held the door for her as she entered.

"In the Green Parlor, Mademoiselle," he replied.

The Green Parlor overlooked the gardens at the rear of the mansion. With its pale green walls and furnishings upholstered in shades of green, it seemed almost an extension of those gardens.

Jasmine found her mother sitting on a gilded chair; the letter delivered by Barrett was in her hand.

Isabeau frowned as her daughter entered the room. "Where have you been?" she demanded. "I sent Leon to find you long since."

"I was outside, Maman." Jasmine stood just inside the door.

"With Barrett Paxton, I suppose," Isabeau muttered, a hint of disgust in her tone. "Well, no matter, come and sit down. I've wonderful news from your grand-maman and I will not allow your disobedience to spoil

26

my good mood." She patted the chair facing hers. "Come Jasmine, I have asked you to please sit down."

She waited impatiently until her daughter was sitting down and then unfolded the letter.

"Your grand-maman," she began, a bright smile curving the corners of her mouth, "has remarried."

"Remarried? Grand-maman?"

"Really, Jasmine! Because a woman is old enough to be a grandmother does not mean she should lock herself away from life. Now listen—quietly, if you don't mind. Your grand-maman has married Alexandre d'Aubois, the Marquis de Mareteleur. He is very rich and she writes that he has a magnificent hôtel in Paris and a château in the country."

"That's very fine, Maman," Jasmine said dutifully.

Isabeau sighed. "You don't realize what this means, do you? This means that your grand-maman is now the Marquise de Mareteleur. She will have entrée at Court and access to many handsome, noble, rich young gentlemen. Not that that matters now, of course."

Jasmine's interest perked up. "Doesn't matter?" she repeated eagerly, her heart seeming to flutter in her bosom. "Maman, does that mean you're given up the notion of my marrying a French gentleman?"

"Of course it doesn't, goose! I'm more eager than ever to go home and see you properly married. But Grand-maman will not have to search out a man now. The Marquis de Mareteleur has a son who is unmarried."

"Oh, Maman, no!" Jasmine wailed. "Grand-maman wants me to marry her stepson?" She got up and went to the windows.

"He is a Marquis, I will have you know!" Isabeau cried in annoyance. "He is the Marquis de Saint-Antoine, and your grand-maman assured me that he is rich enough to make a grand life for any woman lucky enough to marry him.''

"Then surely he should be able to find a wife in France!"

Isabeau was offended. "I will not have you entertaining childish notions about Barrett Paxton any longer, Jasmine! Henri d'Aubois is rich and titled and you will be his wife. If you cannot learn to ignore this infatuation you have for Master Paxton, I will have to forbid him this house until we have departed.''

Jasmine turned from the window, her face pale. "Please, Maman! Do not forbid me to see Barrett! You could not be so cruel!"

"I will not—if you promise to try and resign yourself to the marriage with the Marquis de Saint-Antoine."

Returning her gaze to the window, Jasmine nodded. "I will try," she lied, hoping only to keep her mother from barring Barrett from Belle Glade. Perhaps, her inner voice told her, something can be done to prevent their traveling to France. Perhaps together she and Barrett could concoct a plan. Perhaps . . . perhaps . . . It all seemed hopeless. Not only was her mother determined that she leave Belle Glade, her father was equally determined that his adored wife should be indulged.

In the face of such odds, she was unable to suppress the sobs within her. With a furious frown, Isabeau noticed the shaking of her daughter's shoulders.

"Jasmine! Stop it this instant!" She threw the letter to the floor. "I have said it before and I will say it again. You are the most ungrateful child I have ever seen! Now you are going to France and marry Monsieur le Marquis de Saint-Antoine and that is an end to it! Go to your rooms and begin sorting your possessions. We sail at the end of the week.''

Jasmine spun from the window and grasped the draperies. ''The end of the week? So soon? Can we not wait a little longer, Maman, please?''

Isabeau stamped one pink-satin-shod foot. ''Enough! We will sail at the end of the week and you will go if I have to bind you hand and foot and have you carried aboard! Now leave me!''

Without waiting to be told again, Jasmine hurried from the room. In the hallway outside the door she paused to catch her breath, but she could hear her mother crossing the parlor and feared her wrath should she find her still downstairs. Lifting her skirts, she ran up the stairs and went to her room.

As she entered, she found Lotte on her hands and knees lathering the carpet with a brush dipped in a bucket of ox-gall and water.

''I'm not doing this for you, you swine!'' the maidservant hissed.

Unable to hold back her tears any longer, Jasmine ignored her and ran across the bedchamber to the comparative privacy of her sitting room.

Lotte watched as the door closed behind her and wondered what could possibly be so terrible that it would keep Jasmine from rising to a quarrel. Then a slow smile replaced the puzzled frown. The only thing more powerful than their rivalry was Jasmine's fear that she would be taken away from Virginia or, more precisely, taken away from Barrett Paxton. That was it! It had to be! Madame DuPré had found Jasmine a French husband!

Hearing the sobs from the adjoining room, Lotte threw

back her head and laughed. What exquisite revenge! The one thing Jasmine wanted more than anything in life was to be denied her!

Humming a merry little tune, Lotte dipped the brush into the bucket and went back to her work.

Chapter 3

Jasmine slapped at the soap bubble as she reclined in her bath. The gilded wooden tub which hung like a hammock between two scrolled pillars had been brought into her sitting room and was surrounded by towels to protect the rich carpet.

"Claudette," she called to a housemaid who was on her knees beneath the tub wiping away stray splashes of water. "Come wash my back."

"Yes, Mademoiselle," the girl agreed meekly. She climbed to her feet and soaped a cloth while Jasmine leaned foward in the tub.

"Has Madame DuPré said anything to you about accompanying her to France?" Jasmine asked while the maid washed her back with comforting, circular strokes.

"Oh, yes, Mademoiselle! Madame says I am to come along and work as your maidservant."

"And will you be happy to be returning to France?"

Claudette thought of the last time she'd seen France and her mother, who was a lady's maid to Madame DuPré's mother, now the Marquis de Mareteleur. When

Madame DuPré had written complaining of the trouble involved in attempting to train the slave girls to be proper lady's maids, the Marquise had dispatched Claudette on the next of the DuPré ships to make a voyage to France. It had not mattered that the child was barely ten years old.

"Yes, Mademoiselle," Claudette replied. "I shall be most happy to return to France."

Jasmine examined her fingernails, frowning to force back the tears that constantly seemed to hover near the surface. "I'm glad someone is happy about it."

Claudette said nothing knowing that it was not her place to state an opinion. If she had, however, it would have been to tell Jasmine that she considered her a fool to pine for Virginia and Monsieur Paxton when she was being offered a life in France and marriage with a noble gentleman.

"Give me the cloth," Jasmine said, taking the sudsy cloth from the maidservant, "and go into the bedchamber to see if Lotte has my gown ready."

Claudette curtsied and left the room while Jasmine sponged water over her soapy back.

"Jasmine," Lotte said, entering the sitting room from the adjoining bedchamber, "are you nearly finished? If I am to help you dress before I go to help Madame, it must be soon."

Jasmine sighed and swung her legs over the edge of the tub. "Very well, I'm coming."

Claudette caught the wet towel Jasmine tossed to her and took it back to the sitting room where footmen had already been admitted to drain the tub and dismantle it for shipment to France the next morning.

"Have the Paxtons arrived yet?" Jasmine asked Lotte as she held up her foot so that the silk stocking could be rolled on.

"No—it will most likely be some time before they will arrive."

Jasmine adjusted the buckle of one of her garters which were woven with her initials interlaced among flowers. "I suppose you're right. Has Maman told you when we sail tomorrow?"

"At first light."

"So I will not have an opportunity to say goodbye to . . ." She let the sentence trail off as she lifted her chiffon chemise over her head.

"To Barrett?" Lotte supplied, smirking.

"Master Paxton to you! I will have to say my goodbyes tonight."

Lotte let the remark pass but she would remember it and repeat it to Madame DuPré when she went to help her dress. Doubtless Madame DuPré would be interested to know that her daughter had not completely given up on Barrett Paxton.

"You will be able to say goodbye to Monsieur Paxton as well as his Mama and Papa tonight," she said idly as she brought Jasmine's corset.

"I don't care about saying goodbye to Monsieur Paxton's Mama and Papa," Jasmine told her churlishly. "I care only about Monsieur Paxton. And I do not want that corset. I will not wear it."

"Not wear it?" Lotte was shocked. "Not wear your corset? What will your Mama say?"

"How will she know? My gown has a boned bodice and I don't need so very much corsetting." Lotte started to protest but Jasmine glared at her. "Lotte," she said imperiously, "get my gown and stop with your questions."

The gown, sent from Paris by Isabeau's mother, was of pale blue satin. Its round neckline was cut fashionably low exposing most of her bosom. Only a narrow lace "modesty piece" across the deepest point of the décolletage prevented her being in constant danger of indecency. A collar of cream lace, widening toward the back of her neck, was wired to stand up and framed her shoulders and throat.

"Careful!" Jasmine cautioned from inside the gown as Lotte lifted it over her head. It was settled around her and she began to hook the tiny fastenings which were concealed by a trimming of lace ruching. When the gown was fastened, she turned to and fro before the pier glass.

"You see?" she demanded of Lotte who eyed her jealously. "The lack of corsetting makes no difference."

"Your mama would not approve."

"Lotte! I don't care if Maman approves or not."

"But . . ."

"You are excused, Lotte. You may attend my mother."

Lotte curtsied. "Yes, Miss," she said coolly.

Jasmine called to her before she reached the door. "Send Claudette to me before you go to Maman. She will have to dress my hair. Well? What are you waiting for?"

Lotte shrugged. "I was just thinking. Barrett Paxton is a mighty handsome man, don't you think so?"

Jasmine eyed her warily. "And?"

"There isn't another plantation for miles and I'm sure he'll be lonely after you leave. But don't you worry—I'll do my best to see that he's not too lonely."

"You little bitch!" Jasmine growled. She started toward the girl but Lotte was poised for flight and was out of the room and down the corridor before Jasmine reached the door.

Slamming the door with a resounding crash, Jasmine

34

seized a delicate blossom from among the bouquet of flowers in a crystal vase and tore it apart wishing it were Lotte.

The Paxtons—Samuel, tall, lean, and dark; his wife, Dulcie, short, plump, and blonde; their pretty, pale daughter, Susannah, who was of an age with Jasmine's young brother, Armand; and Barrett—arrived just as Claudette was placing the last of the gold-headed hair needles in Jasmine's hair.

"What do you think, Claudette?" she asked, patting the chignon atop her head.

"It looks very fine, Mademoiselle," Claudette told her.

Leon, the footman, tapped at the bedchamber door. Jasmine signaled for Claudette to answer his summons.

"The guests have arrived, Mademoiselle," the footman announced.

"Thank you, Leon," Jasmine said over her shoulder. The footman bowed and Claudette closed the door. "Claudette, you may retire. I don't believe I'll need you tonight. Get to bed early for there will be much to do tomorrow."

The maidservant curtsied and left and Jasmine reexamined her appearance in the pier glass. "There will be much to do tomorrow," she repeated to her reflection, "and much to do tonight." Smiling cryptically, she picked up her fan and left the room.

The entrance hall of Belle Glade was two stories high and the grand staircase, whose lower flights flanked the front door, swept up the side walls. A balcony on the second floor overlooked the entrance hall and Jasmine stood there watching as her father and mother welcomed their guests.

"Come in, come in," Jean-Baptiste urged. He patted

Susannah's head and kissed Dulcie's round cheek. When Barrett and his father entered, he shook their hands heartily.

Isabeau and Dulcie carefully took stock of one another's gowns and, as usual, Isabeau smiled sweetly knowing that her Paris gown was more fashionable than Dulcie's, which had been made by a local mantuamaker.

"Jasmine is not down as yet," she said as they started for the drawing room. "Armand, show Susannah to the drawing room."

Armand, nine years old and auburn-haired like his mother and sister, groaned as he saw the unbridled admiration in Susannah's shy smile. To his way of thinking, Jasmine was fortunate to be escaping from Virginia. He liked life on the plantation and did not long for the luxuries of Paris and the Court, but he would have been glad to sail away from Susannah Paxton. Reluctantly, he offered her his arm and rolled his eyes when she giggled.

Isabeau's skirts of dove-gray watered silk merged with the pale pink grosgrain of Dulcie Paxton's as they left the entrance hall followed by their husbands, who looked decidedly uncomfortable in their silk coats and breeches and embroidered waistcoats. Samuel Paxton handed his hat to a manservant and tugged impatiently at his white-powdered wig.

Only Barrett remained in the entrance hall and Jasmine smiled as she watched him look into the gilt-framed mirror. He shunned the powdered wigs which were so fashionable, and his own lustrous, dark hair was pulled back and tied with a black ribbon. The claret-colored silk of his coat and breeches was matched by the embroidery of his beige grosgrain waistcoat.

Leaning over the railing, Jasmine laughed. "Vanity," she said loudly enough for him to hear, "thy name is Man."

As Barrett looked up, she spread open her large, blue satin fan. It was not so much flirtatiousness that prompted her to do so, it was a fear that the force of gravity might cause her scantily covered bosom to leave what little protection it enjoyed.

"Jasmine!" Barrett started up the stairs as she started down.

They met halfway and he took her into his arms. Their lips met in a crushing, desperate kiss and their passion was made more urgent by the knowledge that they would soon be half the world away from one another.

"I can't believe that you're leaving," Barrett said, pressing his face against her hair to hide his grief.

She pressed a finger against his lips. "Shhh. Don't let's talk about tomorrow, Barrett. Let's concentrate on tonight."

"Jasmine?" Armand stood at the front of the stairs regarding his sister and Barrett with a look of mixed wonderment and distaste.

"What is it, Armand?"

"Maman says for you and Barrett to come into the drawing room immediately."

After one last hurried kiss, Jasmine took Barrett's arm and they walked down the stairs and followed Armand to the drawing room where their parents waited.

Dinner was finished and while Isabeau, Dulcie, and Susannah retired to the Green Parlor, Jean-Baptiste, Samuel, and Armand started for the study. Jasmine waited until her mother had dissappeared into the parlor and then approached her father.

"Papa," she said sweetly, smiling up at him, "may I go out for a walk with Barrett? It's such a fine night."

Jean-Baptiste embraced her. "Of course, chérie. But do not stay out too late. Your Maman will worry."

Standing on tiptoe, she kissed his cheek. "Thank you, Papa."

As their fathers and young Armand went to the study, Jasmine linked her arm with Barrett's and they left the mansion.

The night air was cool and a gentle breeze blew across the lawn from the bay. Jasmine leaned her head against Barrett's arm as they walked toward the bridge. As they disappeared into the darkness of the wide lawn, neither saw a side door of Belle Glade open and a lone figure start after them.

Lotte had seen them leaving and knew that Isabeau would not appreciate their being alone together in the night. Stepping down from the latticed side porch, Lotte strained her eyes into the darkness. A huge, black cloud obscured the moon and when it moved away and the moonlight once more illuminated the lawn the couple had vanished.

Jasmine ducked beneath the thick branches of the willows in the copse at the bay's shore. The breeze made the long, trailing branches undulate and whisper softly and the moonlight through the branches made dark, feathery patterns on the ground.

"Sit beside me, Barrett," Jasmine said quietly. She waited until he was seated on the ground near her and then she wrapped her arms about his neck and pressed her lips to his.

"Jasmine," he said warily. "Perhaps we should not."

"But why not? Tomorrow I will sail away—I cannot

know if I will ever see you again. Surely you do not begrudge me a few memories.''

"But you belong to someone else now—to the Marquis de . . . What was his name?''

"The Marquis de Saint-Antoine.'' Jasmine shook her head. ''My mother can give me to whomever she pleases and I can do nothing to prevent it; but that is in the future. For tonight, I can give myself to whomever I choose.''

"You cannot mean . . .''

She nodded and reached around behind him to untie the bow that held his hair. As the dark waves fell about his face, she reached up and removed the pins that held her chignon.

"Your future husband will expect to find you a virgin bride,'' he protested. ''Honor demands it.'' But the breathlessness in his voice convinced Jasmine that his noble intentions were wavering.

"The Devil take honor!'' she murmured. ''If my . . .'' she paused, hating to say the words, ''if my future husband finds me unacceptable, then my future husband may divorce me and I will gladly return to Belle Glade . . . and to you.''

She reached beneath his coat collar and unfastened his stock. Laying it aside, she slipped his claret silk coat from his shoulders and then began on the buttons of his waistcoat.

He gripped her wrists. ''You cannot be serious about this Jasmine. This is only impulse. You will regret this in the cold light of morning.''

"I will never regret this, Barrett,'' she whispered. ''And I have never been more serious.'' She pulled her wrists from his hands and looked into his dark eyes as she worked at the hooks beneath the lace ruching of her bodice. As the last of them yielded to her fingers, she rose and slipped the satin gown from her shoulders. Still watching him, she unfastened the waistband of her petticoat and let it fall to the ground. All that remained were her chemise, stockings, and shoes and she kicked her shoes off and pulled her chemise above her knees before she sank once again to the ground.

Barrett watched her, fascinated. His lips were parted and his short, staccato breaths were audible above the sigh of the breeze through the willows. As Jasmine's fingers began working on the buttons of his waistcoat, he made no move to stop her.

She slipped the grosgrain waistcoat from his shoulders and smiled as she laid it aside. Her fingers seemed thick and clumsy as she worked at the buttons of his shirt but at last they gave way and she pressed her lips to the warm flesh of his chest.

"Jasmine?" he whispered.

She raised her eyes and saw the dark light of desire in his. Rising to her knees, she slipped her arms about his neck and played the tip of her tongue about the corners of his mouth until he parted his lips and met it with his own. A tiny hiss of pleasure and triumph escaped her as she felt his hands rise, as though with a will of their own, and caress her breasts through the delicate chiffon of her chemise.

A muffled groan welled into his throat and, lifting the fluttering skirt of her chemise, his hands cupped her rounded buttocks and he pulled her hard against him. With only the thin silk of his breeches separating their bodies, she could feel the swollen proof of his arousal. A wave of unbearable desire coursed through her, taking her breath away.

"Jasmine," he whispered, his lips moving against the

base of her throat, "oh, my sweet, sweet Jasmine!"

Near to swooning with the need of him, Jasmine lost all thoughts of vengeance on her mother and the faceless man in France to whom she had been promised. Her body pleaded for—demanded—release from the fever of passion burning within her.

"Love me, please, Barrett," she urged. "Please!"

Barrett's lips claimed hers in an ever-deepening, even more demanding kiss as he lowered her gently to the ground.

Their surroundings faded and they were conscious only of one another. They did not hear the wind through the willows or the slapping of the bay against the shore. They did not hear the occasional call of the night bird high in the trees nor the chirruping of the crickets in the darkness. And, most of all, they did not hear the footsteps of Lotte, muffled in the thick grass, as she ran back across the lawn toward Belle Glade.

Chapter 4

"Barrett!" Jasmine cried as he leaned away from her. But she smiled when she saw that it was only a brief respite while his fingers fumbled with the stubborn fastenings of his breeches. Lying on the soft cushion of willow leaves, she watched him, eager for the secrets of his body to be revealed to her; eager for the awsome aching of desire within her to be quenched. She held out her arms to him but he looked away, peering through the branches of the willows toward Belle Glade.

"Jasmine," he said quietly, "someone is coming."

"Oh, Barrett, no!" She sat up and looked toward the mansion. The flickering flame of a torch was visible and she reached for her petticoats in the tangled pile of their clothing.

But it was too late and the intruders were upon them before either was dressed.

Isabeau ducked under the willow boughs while Lotte, who held the torch, waited beyond the trees.

Jasmine fumbled with the fastenings of her petticoat but her effort was stayed when her mother's hand closed over the tangled masses of her hair and jerked her head back sharply. With her free hand, she lashed out and caught her daughter across the face.

Barrett, abandoning his own dressing, caught her wrist as she drew her hand back again.

"Take your hand off me!" Isabeau hissed. "Is it not enough that you dishonor my daughter? Must you compound your wickedness by preventing me from chastising her?"

"It was not her fault, Madame," he said. "She does not deserve to be punished."

Isabeau released her hold on Jasmine's hair. Her smile was skeptical. "Am I to believe, then, that you forced your attentions upon my daughter? Are you become a rapist, Monsieur Paxton?"

"He did not force me, Maman," Jasmine insisted, reaching for her crumpled gown. "It was I who seduced him."

Isabeau looked from one to the other. "I see. Which of you shall I believe? Is Monsieur Paxton a rapist or is my daughter, whom I have worked all my life to make a lady, now become a whore?" She looked at Barrett. "I believe I know the answer. Monsieur Paxton, I will thank you to leave Belle Glade and not return until my daughter and I are safely aboard ship bound for France. It is not because I blame you for this incident that I make this demand—it is merely to spare you any further attentions from an ungrateful girl who would fain become a slut." She waited for a moment and when Barrett made no move, went on: "Well, Monsieur? I have asked you to leave. I will make your excuses to your parents."

Barrett looked as Jasmine and she nodded. "Go on, Barrett," she insisted sadly. "There is nothing you can do."

Gathering his waistcoat, stock, and coat, he took his reluctant leave of them and disappeared into the darkness.

Isabeau watched silently while Jasmine worked at the hooks of her gown. When she was dressed, Isabeau took her by the arm.

"Come, we will go in by the side entrance that your father might be spared the shame of seeing his daughter brought home from her assignation."

Jasmine said nothing during the long walk back to Belle Glade. They entered by the side entrance and she was whisked up the back stairs and pushed into her room.

"Lotte," Isabeau said, "help her off with her clothes. I will return to deal with her after the Paxtons leave."

The house had grown quiet during the hour after the Paxtons had taken their leave. Jasmine sat at her window in her nightdress and taffeta wrapper and watched Samuel and Dulcie Paxton walking across the lawn with Susannah. As they disappeared into the night, and only the flickering light of the torch which was carried by a young, black link boy was visible, she began to wonder what punishment her mother would inflict upon her.

The hour passed with agonizing slowness and, when she heard the click of the door latch being depressed, Jasmine stiffened and cast a wary glance toward Lotte, who had remained in the room to prevent her leaving the house again.

Isabeau entered the room and it was obvious to Jasmine that her rage had not diminished. Dismissing Lotte, she closed the door and turned the key in the lock.

"Well, Mademoiselle, our guests have gone and your father is sleeping soundly in his bed. It is now the time for your punishment."

44

Jasmine stood. "I have done nothing to deserve punishment."

Madame DuPré laughed unpleasantly. "Are you now a liar as well as a trollop? Lotte heard you begging Barrett Paxton to make love to you and I myself found the two of you nearly undressed."

"But nothing had happened. You arrived too soon."

Isabeau frowned impatiently. "Enough of your protests of innocence. Take off your wrapper."

"What are you going to do?"

"Do as I say! I am your mother, though tonight you have made me ashamed of the fact. I will be obeyed!"

Her eyes never leaving her mother's face, Jasmine cast the peach taffeta garment aside.

"Go to the bedside and kneel," Isabeau directed. "Grasp the bedpost. If I see your hands leave it, I will bind you to it."

Jasmine did as her mother demanded and was surprised when Isabeau untied the ribbons of her nightdress and drew it off her shoulders. She parted Jasmine's thick curls and tossed them over her shoulders, baring her daughter's back.

As her mother left the bedside and crossed the room, Jasmine watched with growing curiosity. When Isabeau opened a drawer of the clothespress and pulled out her daughter's riding crop, Jasmine's eyes widened in horror.

"Maman! No! Please!" she begged. She started to get up but her mother brandished the crop.

"Stay there! Stay there or I swear I will bind you to the bedpost!"

Jasmine bit her lip as Isabeau brought the whip down across her daughter's back. She heard the hiss as it cut through the air and felt the searing pain of the angry red welts it raised on the delicate alabaster skin. As her head began to reel, she willed herself to faint but, maddeningly, remained all too conscious. Burying her face against her arm, she tried in vain to stifle the cries which she feared would only spur her mother on.

When at last Isabeau dropped the riding crop to the floor, she sagged against the side of the bed.

Isabeau touched one of the red welts on the pale flesh of her daughter's back and, in spite of herself, grimaced as Jasmine twisted away from her touch. She fell to one knee and hissed into her ear:

"Was it worth it, Jasmine? Were a few brief moments of passion worth this pain?" Jasmine did not reply and she went on: "Would it not have been more prudent to keep yourself pure for a noble man, a man worthy of you, rather than to squander your innocence in the dirt beneath the willow trees?"

Jasmine lifted a tearful face to her mother. "But nothing happened, Maman," she insisted. "I am still a virgin."

Madame DuPré gazed into her daughter's eyes as though searching for some sign that would tell her if Jasmine was telling the truth.

Rising, she summoned Lotte to the door and instructed her to go to the nursery and bring Marguerite. She looked at Jasmine as the maidservant, who had tried unsuccessfully to look past Isabeau at Jasmine, hurried off. "We shall soon see if you are telling the truth, Mademoiselle. And if you are not, you may look foward to another bout with the riding crop for lying. Now come, tie your gown and bathe your face. I will not have the servants gossiping about your condition."

Marguerite, the Frenchwoman who had come to Belle Glade at Isabeau's behest many years before because Madame DuPré did not trust the local midwives to deliver her children, was well into middle age. She had been a young woman upon her arrival, just before Jasmine's birth, and had been the childhood nurse of both the DuPré children. She was still Armand's governess despite his protests that he was much too old to be as yet under the authority of a woman.

"Yes, Madame?" she said as she entered Jasmine's bedchamber followed by both Lotte and Claudette.

Isabeau took Jasmine's arm and drew her close. "Marguerite," she said pleasantly, "as you know, Mademoiselle Jasmine and I are leaving in the morning to return to France. My daughter will be married shortly after her arrival."

Marguerite pressed her hands to her shelf-like bosom. "Ah, yes, Madame. I had heard of it. Only to imagine, the little baby I delivered into this world, a bride!" She used her knuckle to wipe away a tear that glistened on one plump cheek.

"Yes, well, what I want of you is that you examine Mademoiselle. If there is some problem that would prevent her from becoming a proper wife and mother, I would want to know of it before she is married. If there is some defect, it should be discovered now."

"Of course, Madame. Mademoiselle, if you would be so good as to lie on your bed."

Jasmine's eyes pleaded with her mother but Isabeau's returning gaze was icy—insistent. She climbed onto the high bed and lay down gingerly. The contact of her bruised back and the satin coverlet caused her to gasp.

But Marguerite did not notice. She brought a stool to the bedside and directed Lotte and Claudette to hold candelabra as closely as they dared. "This is much easier in the light of day, Madame," she told Isabeau.

"Just examine her, if you don't mind," Madame DuPré insisted.

Jasmine closed her eyes and clenched her teeth as she

felt her nightdress being lifted and her knees pushed up and apart. The hot blood rushed to her face as Marguerite's plump fingers prodded and poked her. When at last her skirt was pulled down, she was nearly in tears.

"She is perfect, Madame," Marguerite told Isabeau. "There are no problems of any kind."

"And she is intact?"

The nursemaid seemed startled by the question. "But . . . but of course!" she stuttered. "Absolutely untouched!"

"Thank you, Marguerite. You may go."

Marguerite curtsied but her glances from Jasmine to her mother and back betrayed her intense curiosity. When she hesitated, Isabeau snapped:

"Thank you, Marguerite! You may go!"

"Yes, Madame. Good night, Madame; good night, Mademoiselle." She hurried from the room and Lotte closed the door behind her.

"You are dismissed as well, Claudette," Isabeau said. "You will need your rest."

Claudette curtsied and left the room, excited by the prospect of returning to her homeland. Behind her, Lotte eyed Jasmine looking for tell-tale clues as to the punishment Isabeau had meted out. Her eyes met Jasmine's and locked until Isabeau said:

"Lotte, go to my room and turn down my bed for the night."

Reluctantly the maidservant left the room. As the door closed behind her, Jasmine turned her eyes toward her mother. "Are you satisifed now?" she demanded defiantly.

Isabeau smiled. "Yes, and you may thank your guardian angel that I am for the second beating would have put the first to shame! You may also thank heaven that I am taking you to France to be married. I have little respect for Monsieur Barrett Paxton—no Frenchman worth the name would have allowed you to keep your virginity under those circumstances.'' Her laughter was derisive as she went to the sheveret for a pot of salve for Jasmine's back.

Jasmine's eyes blazed as her mother came to the bedside and, untying the ribbons of her nightdress, drew it away from the ugly welts with their pinheads of blood.

''Sweet Jesus in Heaven!'' Jasmine could not stifle the cry of pain as her mother spread the salve over her back. ''Barrett is a man of honor,'' she managed to hiss.

''Honor!'' Isabeau sneered. ''You will learn that honor will not warm you when you are cold nor will it put a child into your belly!''

''I don't care to bear any child but Barrett's!'' Jasmine declared and then cried out as her mother's fingers pressed into the injured flesh of her back.

''You will bear a child for your husband!'' Isabeau growled. Then, recovering herself, she smiled. ''You are a passionate young woman, Jasmine. Once you are married and properly bedded, you will forget about Barrett Paxton and his honor!''

There was a knock at the door and Isabeau bade Jasmine tie the ribbons of her gown while she replaced the salve in the sheveret.

''Come in,'' Isabeau called.

Lotte appeared. ''Your bed is turned down, Madame, will there by anything else?''

''You may tuck Jasmine into bed, Lotte, since I have dismissed Claudette. And then you may go to bed. In the meantime, I shall look over your sitting room, Jasmine, to be sure you have not forgotten anything that should have been packed.''

Isabeau left the room and Lotte came to Jasmine's bedside. Her close scrutiny did not overlook the way Jasmine's nightgown adhered to the sticky salve.

"She beat you, didn't she?" Lotte asked, smiling wickedly. "And all for nothing. Oh, yes, I heard Marguerite telling Madame that you were still a virgin." She laughed, ignoring Jasmine's glare of hatred, and tucked the bedclothes around her. "Well, perhaps I will write to you in Paris and tell you what you've missed."

"What do you mean?" Jasmine demanded. "Barrett would no more touch you than he would touch one of the kitchen sluts!"

"Wouldn't he? He is a man, as you so nearly discovered tonight. And with you safely in France, I will be the only white woman older than his sister and younger than his mother for miles around. Think about that in your château, Madame le Marquise!"

Jasmine's hand shot out but Lotte was too quick and it flew through the air missing its target. With a smirk, Lotte curtsied mockingly and started for the door just as Isabeau was entering the room.

"Lotte, wait," Jasmine called, suddenly calm. "Maman, won't Grand-maman think it strange if we arrive in Paris with only Claudette?"

"What do you mean?" Isabeau asked.

"Well, Papa is a wealthy man and we are anxious to impress Grand-maman's new husband, are we not? I should think it would create a poor impression if it were thought that we were too poor to each have our own maidservant."

With a thrill of triumph, Jasmine saw the fury in Lotte's eyes which grew when Isabeau said:

"You're quite right, Jasmine. I hadn't thought of it in

50

that way. Lotte, you must pack your belongings. You shall accompany us to France.''

''But . . . but Madame,'' Lotte protested frantically. ''My mother and father . . .''

''No arguments, Lotte. Your maman and papa will be delighted. Why, only today your maman was telling me how much she envied people who traveled throughout the world. Think how excited she will be to learn that her own daughter will travel to Paris and live among the nobility.'' She raised one eyebrow, noticing Lotte's stupefaction. ''Come along, Lotte. Don't act the dunce. Extinguish Mademoiselle's candles and then go about your work. We sail at daybreak, you know.''

Passing Lotte, Isabeau left the room. As the door closed behind her, Jasmine smiled in the face of Lotte's rage.

''You miserable bitch!'' Lotte snarled as she began angrily pinching out the candles about the room. When she was finished, she paused in the doorway. ''I hope this Marquis of yours is fat, foul, and ninety-five!'' She started to close the door and then thrust her head back inside. ''And impotent!''

Jasmine laughed as the door crashed and she heard Lotte stomping off to pack her bags. But the laughter died away and she lay in the cool, darkened room wondering if Lotte was right. Would she be torn from Barrett's arms and thrust into the embrace of some decadent, vice-ridden old roué who would use her as his whim decreed with no regard for her feelings? She shuddered and the pain of her back mingled with her rising nausea at the thought of being bedded with such a man as Lotte had described.

She did not regret her actions; she did not wish that she had remained in the mansion during the visit of the

Paxtons. If there was anything she regretted about the evening, it was that she and Barrett had not had time to accomplish what they had set out to do. She would go to France and to the Marquis de Saint-Antoine as a virgin. But though she might well lose her maidenhood in some marriage bed in a château in France, she had already lost her heart beneath the willows of the shore of Mobjack Bay.

The day dawned bright and clear and the wind, to Jasmine's dismay, was perfect for their departure.

"Hurry, Jasmine," Isabeau ordered, peering around her daughter's bedroom door. "Everything is ready—everyone is waiting."

Her throat closing with emotion, Jasmine took one last look around the room that had been hers since leaving the nursery. Claudette waited at the door and returned Jasmine's half-hearted smile.

"Are you ready to leave, Claudette?" she asked.

"Yes, Mademoiselle," the maidservant replied.

With a final, mournful glance at her room, Jasmine and Claudette left the room and the mansion.

The docks of Belle Glade were bustling with life as the crew of Jean-Baptiste's largest ship, the Saint-Brieuc, named as were all the ships belonging to Belle Glade after a city in France which had played a prominent part in the family history of the DuPrés, prepared to sail. The ship rocked against its moorings as though impatient to begin the journey.

Jasmine walked slowly from the mansion toward the dock. She could see her mother and father standing on the dock with the Paxtons and Armand clambering over the deck besieging the sailors with questions.

When she reached her parents' side, she put on a brave smile for her father's sake and tried to hide the pain his embrace caused her.

"Goodbye, Jasmine," he said, not bothering to conceal the grief her leaving gave him.

"Goodbye, Papa," she whispered.

Both Samuel and Dulcie Paxton kissed her cheek and Susannah pressed a tiny doll into her hand.

Jasmine smiled. "Thank you, Susannah," she said softly. "I'll keep it with me always."

She moved a little toward the ship and found herself standing before Barrett. Glancing toward her mother, she could see that Isabeau was enraged by Barrett's presence but she could not have ordered him away without a lengthy, and embarrassing, explanation.

"Goodbye, Jasmine," Barrett said, his dark eyes holding hers. With little regard for the others, he lifted a hand and caressed her cheek, catching the tear that glistened there.

Jasmine closed her eyes against the agony of her grief. "Barrett," she whispered, "I . . ."

"Come, Jasmine," Isabeau interrupted, taking her daughter's arm firmly. "We must leave—the hour grows late."

"Goodbye, Barrett," Jasmine finished.

Isabeau tried to pull her away but not before Jasmine stretched up and kissed him. They strained toward one another and their lips were crushed together for a long moment before Isabeau succeeded in separating them.

She pulled Jasmine toward the ship but Jasmine, seeing Barrett take a few tentative steps toward her, broke away and ran to him, throwing herself into his embrace.

"I love you, Barrett," she murmured against his

caressing lips. "Nothing will ever change that."

"And I love you," he replied, crushing her to him although he knew, to his anguish, that she was promised to someone else.

"Jasmine." Jean-Baptiste Dupré laid a hand on her shoulder. "You must go now."

"Papa, please," she entreated, hoping against hope that he would take pity upon her and let her stay.

For the first time in her life, she saw a tear coursing down her father's cheek as he shook his head.

"You must go now," he repeated. "I have given my word to your mother."

Through her tears, Jasmine saw Samuel Paxton lay a restraining hand on Barrett's shoulder and she felt herself being led away toward the ship that would take her to France.

Jasmine stood at the railing of the Saint-Brieuc as the mooring lines were cast off. She waved to the group on the dock—her father and brother, Samuel, Dulcie, and Susannah Paxton, and to the group of servants from Belle Glade who had gathered behind them. But most of all, she waved to Barrett, who raised his hand in a half-hearted salute.

"The damp wind is not healthy for you," Isabeau told her. "Come, let us go below."

"A few moments more, Maman," she pleaded. "Only a few moments more."

Isabeau took her arm and tugged her away from the railing. "Now, Jasmine," she insisted.

The ship was moving away from Belle Glade— moving well out into Mobjack Bay. As the distance between them grew, Jasmine pressed a hand to her lips and then waved sadly to Barrett, who was by then little more than a silhouette against the dark dock. But before she left the deck for the cabin which would be her home until they reached France, she saw him press his hand to his own lips and return her kiss.

Part 2

France

Summer
1756

Chapter 5

The inn was dingy, its furnishings worn and shabby from use by the innumerable, nameless travelers who had passed the night within its walls and then moved on to their destinations.

Jasmine stood, her back carefully toward her mother, before a grimy window that overlooked the courtyard. But though she might have appeared to be staring at the bustle in the courtyard, she was really studying the smiling face of Barrett Paxton in the leather-cased miniature she'd been careful to smuggle out of Belle Glade.

One reverent finger traced the smooth spiral of the lock of hair beneath the crystal and her mind—and heart—went back across the cruel Atlantic to Virginia and to Barrett's arms.

"Jasmine!" Isabeau snapped, and her tone made it plain that it was not the first time she had addressed her.

Returning the case to its place of concealment in the pocket of her voluminous skirts, Jasmine turned from the window.

"Yes?"

"Mooning over Barrett Paxton again, I suppose," Isabeau grumbled. "Put on your bonnet and come along. We will be leaving soon."

Jasmine sighed as she tied the ribbons of her hat beneath her chin. "Will we reach Paris today, Maman?"

Across the small room she and her mother had shared the night before, Isabeau nodded. "Yes, perhaps by late afternoon."

"Late afternoon? Maman, we've ridden in that awful diligence for days! Surely we must be close to Paris."

"We are, by my reckoning, nearly eight hours away." She took Jasmine's arm and steered her out of the poorly furnished, ill-lit room and downstairs to the dining room of the inn.

"Eight hours!" Jasmine cried as they joined the other Paris-bound passengers of the diligence which was even then being hitched up outside. "Why did we have to land at Brest? It makes the journey to Paris so long! Why couldn't we land at Le Havre? At least the ship wasn't bouncy and the sea wasn't dusty!"

"Pardon me, Mademoiselle," Madame Giroux, a formidable lady of three score and ten years who was their fellow passenger, interrupted, "but I believe I can explain. France, you see, is currently engaged in a conflict with England. Had your ship sailed to Le Havre rather than landing at Brest, you would have run an increased risk of encountering English warships. Certainly you will agree that a long overland journey through France is preferable to capture by English barbarians."

Jasmine nodded. "Certainly, Madame, that is true."

Isabeau learned toward them. "My daughter," she explained to Madame Giroux, "is merely overly anxious to reach Paris. She is to be married shortly after our arrival, you see."

The elderly lady in her black and white mourning raised on black-painted eyebrow. "Indeed? How fine! I'd wager your bridegroom is a handsome man."

"I've never seen him, Madame," Jasmine replied diplomatically. "He is my maman's stepbrother."

"He is the Marquis de Saint-Antoine," Isabeau informed Madame Giroux proudly. "My stepbrother is the Marquis de Mareteleur."

"Aha. I see. I believe I have heard the names. They are both very rich."

"Oh, yes!" Isabeau agreed gaily. "Very, very rich!"

"Hmmm, yes," Madame Giroux said between bits of her pastry. "A pity they are out of favor at Court."

Jasmine smiled as she saw the stricken look which transformed her mother's face.

"Out of favor at Court?" Isabeau repeated. "Surely you are mistaken, Madame!"

"By no means, Madame. I was in Paris a few weeks since and it was all the talk. Something about Madame la Marquise de Pompadour, as I recall. It seems to me that the Marquis de Saint-Antoine insulted her and the King sent him from Court."

Isabeau was horrified. "Banished from Court for insulting the King's mistress? But that is impossible! Surely the King would not banish a high-ranking nobleman from Versailles for insulting a low-born whore like La Pompadour!"

"He is very fond of his Marquise de Pompadour, Madame; she is a beautiful, charming woman."

"But still, Madame," Madame DuPré insisted, "she is little more than a glorified harlot. Doubtless your image of her is better than she deserves. Perhaps if you knew her . . ."

"Madame de Pompadour," Madame Giroux interrupted, "is my grand-niece. I have known her since she was a child."

For once Isabeau was speechless. Dabbing at her lips with her napkin, she stood. "Come, Jasmine, I believe the diligence is almost ready."

She started away and Jasmine took a last bite of her pastry. She looked over and saw her mother leave the room and went back to Madame Giroux.

"Pardon, Madame," she whispered. "But, is Madame de Pompadour really your grand-niece?"

Madame Giroux smiled. "Indeed she is, child."

"Is she really as beautiful as I have heard?"

"She is very, very beautiful—but, alas, not well."

"Not well? What malady does she suffer from?"

Madame Giroux waved one gloved hand. "Who knows? A weakness. At any rate, she is delicate and the rigors of being the favorite wear heavily upon her."

"But still she remains the King's favorite?"

The grande dame dabbed her wrinkled lips daintily and stood. Waving aside the arm offered by her maidservant, she leaned instead on Jasmine. "Oh, yes, she is the favorite," she said as they walked slowly toward the diligence which was waiting before the inn, "but not in every sense of the word. The King has many other ladies to see to his—oh, my, this is really not a subject for the ears of an unmarried child, but then you are to be married, no?—his sensual needs which, it is no secret, are considerable. The Bourbon temperament, you see. Reinette, Madame de Pompadour, caters to his more aesthetic tastes."

"She is his favorite but not his mistress?"

"Oh, she may still be his mistress upon the odd occasion, but the pretty little light o' loves who reside at

Parc aux Cerfs see to his other needs.''

''Parc aux Cerfs? What is that?''

''It is a beautiful hôtel in the village of Versailles where the King's young ladies are brought . . .'' She looked up and saw Madame DuPré glaring out the window of the diligence. ''Oh dear, I am afraid your Maman does not appreciate our speaking together.''

''I suppose not,'' Jasmine agreed. ''But I find it fascinating. Perhaps I will meet Madame de Pompadour someday. That is, if my future husband is ever allowed to return to Court.''

''Oh, pish, you need not worry on that score— the King rarely invites both the husband and the wife to Court at the same time. If your grand-mère, the Marquise de Mareteleur, has entrée, she could introduce you to the right people and you could go to Versailles in spite of your husband's disgrace.''

''But that is wonderful, Madame! Perhaps I will see you at Versailles.''

''Alas, child, I have not entrée at Court—Madame de Pompadour did not become a Marquise until after she became the King's favorite. Her father has been given many estates and her brother is now the Marquis de Marigny, but I am related through her dear, departed Maman and the King's generosity has not extended quite that far as yet.''

''But surely you visit Madame de Pompadour!''

''Oh, naturellement, but usually in her apartment, never at Court entertainments.''

''Then per—''

''Jasmine!'' Isabeau called, leaning out of the coach window, ''for heaven's sake get in! We shall never reach Paris if you insist on standing out there prattling all morning!''

Jasmine glanced at Madame Giroux and was surprised

at the broad wink the old lady directed at her. "Coming, Maman," she replied, unable to keep the giggle from her voice, "coming."

The Hôtel de Mareteleur stood in the Faubourg Saint-Germain on the Rue de Lille. The courtyard was visible from the street through the iron gates set into the massive archway. Built around three sides of the courtyard, the hôtel was two stories high with a steep mansard roof. Behind the hôtel a garden stretched down to the Seine.

Inside the hôtel, the Marquise de Mareteleur reached up to pat the cheek of her husband's young valet.

"Eh bien, Michel, is everything ready?"

The tall, blond valet nodded, smiling slyly. "Of course, Madame la Marquise."

"And you have given Alexandre his drops?"

Michel's smile faded. "I don't know if we should give him more, Sofie. Madame Beauchesne said too much might kill him."

Sofie laughed setting her plump, painted cheeks to quivering. "What does it matter? Once my dear granddaughter marries Henri, we will not need him any longer. His money will pass to Henry and Jasmine, and into the waiting hands of Jasmine's dear, dear grand-maman."

"And to her dear grand-maman's dear, dear Michel?" the valet prompted.

Sofie looked deeply into his pale blue eyes. She wondered if it was wise to enlist his help. He was attractive, there was no denying that, but he was also her equal in cunning. She had no doubt that he would get his share of the profits or the world would know about the "medicine" she gave her husband in his goat's milk or chocolate every morning—medicine which was bought in the darkened salon of Madame Beauchesne, the leading provider of poisons, philters, and potions to the fashionable world of Paris.

She smiled uneasily and looked into the gilt-framed mirror. Straightening the powdered wig which covered her own gray hair, she laughed a little too gaily. "But of course to dear Michel," she replied. "Would I forget my handsome Michel?"

His face appeared in the mirror beside her. "You had better not, Sofie, my darling." He pressed his face against her cheek. "You had better not."

Jasmine, Isabeau, Lotte, and Claudette were crowded into a fiacre riding through Paris on their way to the Hôtel de Mareteleur.

"Maman, I think it was rude of you not to allow me to say goodbye to Madame Giroux when we left the diligence."

Isabeau shot her a sour look. "I do not like that woman!"

Jasmine rolled her eyes. "You do not like Madame Giroux because she gave you your comeuppance with regards to Madame de Pompadour."

"She was probably lying; she is probably merely a mad old woman who suffers from delusions."

Turning her attention to the city of Paris through which they were riding, Jasmine did not comment on her mother's opinion.

The fiacre stopped before the gates of the Hôtel de Mareteleur and the coachman hailed the concierge.

"Yes, yes," the man replied, leaning through a window of the gatehouse. "What is it?"

"Open up for Madame DuPré and Mademoiselle DuPré!"

"Very well, wait a moment."

The man emerged from the gatehouse pulling on his coat of brown cloth. Lifting the heavy latch of the gates, he swung them wide and stepped back to allow the hired coach to enter the courtyard of the hôtel.

Jasmine stepped down into the courtyard and looked up at the impressive facade of her grandmother's home. "Oh, Maman!" she breathed, her dread of what awaited her there momentarily forgotten, "isn't it beautiful!"

Isabeau's eyes glittered as she looked at the tangible proof of her mother's new-found status. "Yes," she replied excitedly, "it is very beautiful!"

The front door of the hôtel opened and Sofie hurried out toward them followed by several brown and buff clad footmen who began unloading their baggage.

"Isabeau!" she cried, throwing her arms wide to her daughter. "Isabeau, my own darling! How long it has been!'"

Tears trickled from Madame DuPré's eyes as she fell into her mother's embrace. "Maman! Maman! How I have missed you and France! It is wonderful to be back in Paris!'

Over her daughter's shoulder, the Marquise de Mareteleur looked at Jasmine. "Who is this lovely woman?" she asked, extricating herself from Isabeau's embrace. "Surely this cannot be my little granddaughter, Jasmine? But she is a woman—and such a beauty! You have done yourself proud, Isabeau."

Jasmine smiled shyly as she was enveloped in a musky embrace and crushed against a jutting bosom barely restrained by aqua satin. "How do you do, Madame la Marquise," she said quietly.

Sofie held her at arm's length. "No ceremony, please,

my darling. Soon you and I will share the rank. You must call me Grand-maman. Come into the hôtel, you must be tired and you are certainly dusty. We will get you a bath and a rest and then you must meet the Marquis, my husband.'' She started toward the mansion. ''Come, Isabeau, bring your maids.''

Hand in hand, Jasmine and Sofie entered the hôtel and Jasmine was dazzled by the magnificence of the furnishings and the breathtaking ceiling paintings that made the rooms seem to soar to the very heavens. Though her heart ached for Belle Glade and her life there, and though she trembled when she remembered the feeling of Barrett's caresses, Jasmine had to admit that she had entered a new and fascinating world and she wondered what secrets it might hold for her.

Chapter 6

The villa of Parc aux Cerfs stood in the village of Versailles. Its entrance discreetly hidden in an enclosed courtyard, it was a handsome building whose elegant furnishings were of a much better quality than would ordinarily be found in such a modest residence.

A black coach without identifying armorial bearings turned off the Rue Saint-Médéric and rolled through the gateway. It drew up before the front door of the villa and a satin-liveried footman hurried out to open the door.

In an upstairs bedchamber of the villa, a young girl was being tucked into a splendid bed whose hangings were of the finest lace.

Dominique-Guillaume Lebel, Concierge of Versailles, fluffed up the lace trimming of the silk nightdress the girl wore and artfully draped one of her long, blonde curls over her bare shoulder.

"What is your name, Mademoiselle?" he asked.

"Henriette," she replied, "Henriette Beaujean."

Lebel jotted it into his book. "Very well, Henriette Beaujean, how old are you?"

"Fourteen, Monsieur."

He noted it. "You are not a virgin?"

She lifted her chin. "Certainly not! I know my business!"

"Of course, of course. I meant no insult. It is merely that the gentleman you are about to entertain is a very important personage and it would not do for him to be disappointed."

Henriette's blue eyes sparkled. "Important? Who is he, Monsieur?"

Lebel smiled. "Discretion, Mademoiselle, is a virtue. Should you please the gentleman you will shortly meet, you may be asked to reside here at Parc aux Cerfs. However, if you prove to be the kind of young woman who asks too many questions, that offer will not be forthcoming."

Henriette surveyed her exquisite surroundings. Born the child of a Paris prostitute and an unknown father, her only escape from poverty was through her mother's profession. Parc aux Cerfs was a far cry from the Paris brothel in which she had been born and raised and she knew she could not allow her curiosity to destroy her chance to rise to the height of her profession.

But her quizzical expression betrayed her intense curiosity and Lebel took pity upon her.

"Let us just say, Mademoiselle Beaujean, that the gentleman in question is someone very close to Her Majesty the Queen. He is a very close relation."

"Ah!" Henriette breathed, impressed.

A footman entered the room and whispered to the Concierge.

"Thank you," Lebel replied. Closing his book, he took one last look about the room. "The gentleman has arrived," he told Henriette, "and has been prepared to join you. You are to address him as 'Monseigneur' and ask no questions. Do you understand?"

Henriette nodded. "Yes, Monsieur."

"Good. If you will excuse me, I must see to our gentleman." With a nod, he left the room.

Henriette waited nervously. The opportunity which was being given to her overwhelmed her. She hoped desperately that all the delicious tricks she'd used so often to please so many would not desert her.

The door opened, and a handsome, middle-aged man entered the room. Clad in a dressing gown of purple silk shot with gold, he was tall with regular, strong features and large, black-lashed eyes.

The dark eyes were kind as he discarded the dressing gown and joined Henriette in the grand bed.

"Good afternoon, ma petite," he said in a voice that was curiously husky but terribly attractive.

"Good afternoon, Monseigneur," she replied shyly.

He drew the silk gown over her head and stroked her while she, instinctively, turned her attentions to his already formidably aroused manhood. Shuddering, he slid further down on the bed and drew her over him.

Henriette sighed and writhed in practiced abandon. Men were men, she realized, be they kinsmen to the Queen or fishmongers in a Paris bordello. As the aristocratic gentleman beneath her released a long murmur of contentment, she saw a glittering future opening to her.

Jeanne-Antoinette d'Étoiles, the Marquise de Pompadour, reclined on a chaise lounge in the red-lacquer paneled salon of her apartment. On the ground floor of Versailles, it was fit for a queen and there were many at Court who were scandalized by the honor accorded a woman of such bourgeois origins.

She twisted her delicate features into a sour grimace as she drank the contents of a tall glass. She grimaced again as her maid, Madame du Hausset, entered the room.

"What are you drinking now, Reinette?" she demanded.

Madame de Pompadour smiled at the maid's use of her childhood nickname. Reinette—little Queen. Her family had given it to her when, at the age of nine, a gypsy fortune-teller had read her palm and announced that she would grow up to be the King's mistress.

She looked at the empty glass. "Vanilla, truffles, and garlic ground and mixed in honey and goat's milk."

Madame du Hausset curled her lip. "Why do you torment yourself so?"

"You know why, Louise. I was told that it was a great aphrodisiac."

"Aphrodisiac! When will you stop trying to discover new aphrodisiacs? You do not need them."

Madame de Pompadour's dark eyes filled with tears. "But you know I do! I am so frightened that the King will leave me. You know how . . . how . . . amorous he is. And I am cold by nature."

Louise du Hausset sat down beside her. "The King will not leave you, chérie. He loves you; he adores you."

"But he sets such store by lovemaking. And I am not equal to his desires. He exhausts me."

"Still, he would never forsake you. He cares more about you than about making love."

La Pompadour shook her head. "If that were true, he would not need to maintain a private brothel at Parc aux Cerfs."

"Most of those women do not even know who he is!"

"If I could satisfy him, he would not need them at all!"

Madame du Hausset drew her into her arms.

"Reinette, Reinette," she cooed. "You do satisfy him. You satisfy his soul—you calm him, you cheer him. You take his mind off the awesome responsibilities of sovereignty. Surely that satisfaction is more precious than a few moments of physical pleasure."

The Marquise shook loose from the maid and got up to pace the magnificent room.

"But it means so much to him! It means so much!" Her voice quavered and she was near to the tears which seemed to come more often of late. "The lowliest harlot of Paris can drive him to ecstasy, but I . . ." She sank into a gilded chair. "Louise, do you realize that some of the girls Lebel brings to him are mere children? Girls of twelve and thirteen! How old I must seem to him after them!"

"Pish, Reinette, you have never been lovelier!"

"But I am thirty-five! Thirty-five! He comes to me after making love to girls young enough to be my children!"

"Young enough to be his grandchildren," the maid added disapprovingly.

"Now Louise, the King is only forty-seven."

"Many children are married at fifteen or younger. Many man are fathers by fifteen or sixteen. Why, Their Majesties' oldest children were born when the King was only seventeen! These twelve-year-old girls could be his granddaughters."

"Very well!" La Pompadour conceded. "They could be his grandchildren! That only illustrates my point. Little girls can fulfill him while I cannot! I . . ."

She stopped suddenly and leaned foward in her chair, her hands covering her face.

Immediately Madame du Hausset was on her feet and calling for help.

"Guilbert! Pierre! Come help Madame! Vivienne! Bring Madame's drops!"

The footmen swept Madame de Pompadour from her chair and carried her through the splendid apartment to her bedchamber. Madame du Hausset turned back the coverlet and they laid her down gently.

"Guilbert, fetch Doctor Quesnay," the maid ordered.

"No, Louise," the Marquise protested, "I do not need the doctor."

"Nonsense. The King would never forgive me if I allowed harm to come to you."

Vivienne entered the room with a bottle of medicine in her hand. The Marquise turned her face away when Madame du Hausset poured a serving into a silver spoon.

"It tastes so foul," she complained.

"Fouler than truffles, vanilla, and garlic in honey and goat's milk?" du Hausset asked skeptically.

While the footman went for the doctor and Madame du Hausset administered the medicine, Vivienne loosened the Marquise's stays.

"Pierre!" Madame du Hausset called to the footman who had left the room when Guilbert had gone for the doctor. "Go lock the apartment door; we do not need any unexpected visitors."

Doctor Quesnay arrived by way of the little secret staircase which connected Madame de Pompadour's bedchamber with the King's private bedchamber a floor above. A kindly, country-bred man of sixty-three, he was more than Madame de Pompadour's doctor, he was her friend and admirer. His gentle eyes were filled with a genuine concern as he came to her bedside.

"Reinette, what have you done to yourself?" he asked as he felt for her pulse.

"She got herself into an agitation," du Hausset

supplied in spite of the annoyed look on her mistress's face.

"An agitation? What kind of agitation? Has someone upset you?"

"The usual subject, Doctor," the maid replied when Madame de Pompadour remained stubbornly silent. "She has been drinking 'aphrodisiacs' once again."

François Quesnay frowned. "We have discussed this before, Reinette," he said sternly.

"But, Doctor . . .!" she began.

"No, calm yourself!" he commanded. "Or I will give you a sedative. You know how you hate that." He took her hand in his and his tone was serious. "Reinette, you are not a strong woman. Your health is delicate and your system easily unbalanced. You cannot allow yourself to destroy that balance. There are many in this palace who would be happy to see your health fail and force you away from Court. You cannot contribute to your own destruction."

Reluctantly, Madame de Pompadour relaxed into the pillows, but a fire of defiance shone in her eyes. Doctor Quesnay and Madame du Hausset recognized the look and exchanged an exasperated glance. This was not the first time their dear Reinette had worked herself into such a state that she had to be confined to her bed. Neither of them deluded themselves by thinking that it would be the last time.

Henriette Beaujean curtsied deeply as the gentleman, now fully dressed in emerald satin with the Cordon Bleu across his chest, re-entered the room.

"You gave me great pleasure, ma petite," he said softly.

"Merci, Monseigneur," she replied demurely.

"You will be well rewarded," he continued. "However, I want to give you something extra." Fishing in his capacious pocket, he extracted a handful of louis d'or and pressed them into her hand, folding her thin fingers over them. "Bless you, ma petite." With a fond smile, he turned and left the room.

Henriette opened her hand and stared at the gold coins that lay there. Five louis d'or! The most she'd ever received in Paris was a few francs—and that from an elderly—and infinitely grateful—merchant.

She turned the coins over in her hand and gasped. A profile of Louix XV adorned the obverse of each coin and she instantly recognized him.

Running to the window, she caught a glimpse of him stepping into the unadorned black coach. A close relation of the Queen indeed! Henriette danced across the room and threw herself across the rumpled bed. She, Henriette Beaujean, was the King's mistress! The lips that had touched the Queen had touched her lips! The fingers that had caressed the legendary Marquise de Pompadour had caressed her! She giggled. That she, the brothel-bred daughter of a Paris prostitute, should pleasure the Body Royal was nearly incomprehensible and she was awed by the magnitude of it all.

As he rode back through the town of Versailles, the King frowned and blushed as a passerby recognized him and shouted, "Vive le Roi!" He disliked having his rare moments of privacy disturbed.

Basically a shy and retiring man, Louix XV accepted the public life into which he had been born. He'd become King upon the death of his great grandfather, the glorious Sun King, at the tender age of five years. He accepted the duties of kingship as a matter of course but

75

that did not mean he enjoyed being constantly on display. He coveted his privacy and for that reason he'd constructed the exquisite Petits Apartements at Versailles to which he could retire with a few carefully chosen friends.

There were few people with whom he was totally at ease. The Queen—Marie Leszczyńska, daughter of the deposed King of Poland—was not one of them. Seven years older than he, she had done her duty by presenting him with ten children in nine years and then had respectfully retired from the marriage bed. But she was dull and, he considered, overly pious. He sought her company infrequently.

Madame de Pompadour, on the other hand, was a different case entirely. His frown faded as he thought of her. Beautifully mannered, she never embarrassed him and never forced him into a difficult situation. With Madame de Pompadour he could drop his mantle of royal reserve and allow himself to relax completely. If only she were capable of passion on a level equal with his own, she would be perfect—their life together would be complete.

At the thought of passion, his mind returned to Parc aux Cerfs. The little girl Lebel had brought for him that afternoon had been charming. Perhaps he would have her brought to the palace and lodged in one of the attics until he tired of her. It would not matter—she knew who he was, he was sure of it. Oftentimes the girls were kept in ignorance; it helped him avoid the usual petitions for help to families spread throughout France or titles for the children he begat upon them. He wondered occasionally how many children he had. Dozens, he supposed. The Queen had borne him ten children. Madame de Pompadour had had at least as many miscarriages during the early years of their liaison when he still went frequently to her bed. Oftentimes Lebel would mention that this girl or that girl who had been at Parc aux Cerfs was with child.

He shrugged as the coach entered the first of the three courtyards which stretched before the front of the palace. It didn't really matter. Lebel had orders to present each of the girls with a handsome pension upon their departure from the Parc aux Cerfs and the King's life. He doubted that any child in whose veins ran the blood of the Royal Bourbons was going hungry.

He stepped from the coach and started toward the palace. His little respite from sovereignty was over and he felt the heavy mantle of kingship descending upon his shoulders as he entered the palace in which he had been born.

Chapter 7

"Only to imagine, Claudette," Jasmine said in wonderment, "an entire room just for bathing."

Claudette nodded looking around the room whose walls were panaled in pale blue with lavish and heavily gilded scrollwork. "It is beautiful, Mademoiselle."

Stepping from the marble bath, Jasmine wrapped her wet hair in a towel and took another to wipe the droplets of scented water from her body.

"It certainly is," she agreed. Tossing the towel aside, she slipped into a satin robe which was embroidered with fanciful designs of mythical beasts. "The Marquis de Mareteleur must be very rich!"

Leaving the bath chamber, Jasmine went to her bedchamber, which—though it scarcely seemed possible—was even more elegantly appointed than the bath.

The walls were paneled in ivory with borders of gilded carvings; the ceiling was painted in a gentle scene of evening full of reclining gods and goddesses in exotic settings. Jasmine often found herself gazing up at the magnificent painting and blushed whenever Claudette caught her at it; certainly no mansion on Mobjack Bay would have been decorated with renderings so blatantly sensual.

She sat on the edge of the fourposter and unconsciously rested her hand on the round bottom of one of the four gilded cupids who supported the canopy. The hangings of crimson silk shot with gold thread were drawn back at the bed's corners and at the tall windows which overlooked the front courtyard.

Kicking off her mules, Jasmine dug her toes into the deep pile of carpet. "I wonder," she said aloud to Claudette who sat on the bed behind her drying her hair, "what I should wear. I fear my gowns will seem a trifle plain in these splendid surroundings."

"Doubtless you will have to have a new wardrobe made before you go to Court, Mademoiselle."

Jasmine smiled. "Yes, I must admit that there are advantages of being the step-granddaughter of a rich Marquis. If only I didn't have to marry his son!"

"Well, Mademoiselle, were I to have to marry a man I didn't love, I would as soon marry a rich man as a poor one. Surely I could find some comfort in so much luxury!"

"I would I could find comfort so easily," Jasmine murmured, her eyes wistful.

"Which gown will you wear, Mademoiselle?" Claudette asked when she'd finished buckling the garters which held Jasmine's cream silk stockings up.

She toyed with the ribbons which were laced about the neck of her chiffon chemise. "I think the pale green silk with the ivory lace. It needs the wide hoop."

As Claudette went to the next room where large armoires held many gowns, Jasmine examined the furnishings of her room. There were gilded sofas, Boulle cabinets, an elaborately carved writing desk and the silk-and-lace-draped toilette table. Sitting on the stool, which was shaped like an enormous sea shell, she smiled into the mirror of the toilette table and ran a silver-backed brush through her shining curls.

A movement in the mirror caught her eyes and she jumped to her feet as the bedchamber door swung open.

The Marquise de Mareteleur entered the room and held out her hands to her granddaughter. "Come, my little darling," she said. "I wish to become better acquainted with you."

Jasmine hurried toward the bed to retrieve her discarded dressing gown but, to her dismay, the Marquise caught her hand and stopped her.

"Now, now, child, you need not be so over-modest. Why, there are ladies at Court who think nothing of appearing in public little more covered than you are at this moment. You should not be ashamed of your beauty." Holding her granddaughter at arm's length, she surveyed her figure through the diaphanous chiffon with such close attention that Jasmine blushed hotly. Noticing her embarrassment at last, the Marquise laughed. "Oh, very well," she said, releasing Jasmine's arm, "cover yourself if you've a mind to. A few weeks of marriage will cure you of such timidity. Your husband, you realize, will expect to see what he is receiving in exchange for his title."

Jasmine lowered her eyes. "Yes, Grand-mère."

"Good, I see you understand your duties as a good wife. Love cannot always be expected in arranged marriages, to be sure it is a rarity these days, but even apathy can sometimes be turned to passion if the lovemaking is not regarded as a chore. Tell me, child, have you experience in the pleasures of love?''

"I . . . I . . .'' Jasmine was unaccustomed to such frankness. "I am a virgin, Grand-mère,'' she managed.

The Marquise laughed. "To be sure, to be sure, my dear, but there is much a man and a woman can do without ever crossing that fragile threshold.'' Seeing the shielded expression in her granddaughter's eyes, she patted her hand. "Never mind, it can remain your secret.''

"Tell me, Grand-mère,'' Jasmine said quickly, seizing the opportunity to change the subject, "will I meet the Marquis de Saint-Antoine today?''

"Now, now, you must think of him as Henri—he is your fiancé, you know. But no, you will not meet him today. He is not in Paris.''

"Not in Paris? But where . . .''

She was interrupted when Claudette opened the bedchamber, Jasmine's gown draped over her arm. She stopped suddenly and curtsied when she saw the Marquise there.

Sofie stood. "Come in, girl, help your mistress dress.'' She leaned over and pecked at Jasmine's cheek. "Hurry and dress, chérie, and come downstairs. You will want to meet your new grand-père.''

"Yes, Grand-mère. I will be down shortly.''

The door closed behind the Marquise and Jasmine rolled her eyes at Claudette. "They are very different here than in Virginia, Claudette. I fear I have much to learn.''

Jasmine descended the grand staircase of the Hôtel de Mareteleur slowly. She was on her way to meet her grandmother's husband and her nerves were ajangle. At the bottom of the marble staircase, she paused, unsure of which of the many salons was her destination.

"May I help you, Mademoiselle?"

She started and turned to find Michel standing behind her. "Who are you?" she demanded.

He bowed. "I am Michel, Mademoiselle, Monsieur le Marquis's valet."

"Oh, I see. Then, could you direct me to Madame la Marquise? She is going to present me to your master."

"Certainly, Mademoiselle, if you will follow me."

The valet started off down the corridor. In spite of herself, she found herself watching the play of muscles beneath the satin livery he wore. He was a handsome man, even Jasmine—who prefered dark hair to blond—admitted as much. He had a way of looking at her which made her want to look away and blush.

Michel stopped before a set of doors and turned to wait for her to join them. "Madame la Marquise and Madame DuPré should be here, Mademoiselle," he said softly.

"Thank you, Michel."

The valet bowed and, for a moment, Jasmine thought he was going to try to kiss her. But he did not; his eyes only looked deeply into her own for a fraction of a second and then he straightened and walked off down the corridor. At the corner of the hallway, he glanced back over his shoulder and she blushed when he caught her watching him. Hurriedly, she tapped on the door and in response to her grandmother's "Entrez!" stepped out of his sight and into the salon.

Still standing at the corner of the corridor, Michel's full lips curved into a smile. They were handsome women, these DuPrés. The Marquise was still attractive, though well past what were considered a woman's best years. Madame DuPré still retained much of the beauty evident in the portrait he had seen which was painted when she was a new bride of twenty. And Mademoiselle

DuPré, well—in spite of the fact that life in Virginia had kept her rather unsophisticated when compared to Parisian girls of her age, she was beautiful enough to turn any man's head. He wondered if it would be possible to charm his way into her bed. If she was a true DuPré it would not be too difficult. The Marquise had practically ordered him into hers not a fortnight after her wedding after she'd found that old de Mareteleur could not satisfy her desires. Already he had been the target of admiring looks from Madame DuPré—he was sure of success with her. But the little Mademoiselle—he shrugged—eh bien, that was in the future. The Marquise had assured him that the girl was innocent. In fact, she had almost warned him of it as thought saying, "She is not for you, Michel. She belongs to another." And so she did, for the present, at least. But he knew the Marquis de Saint-Antoine; he knew his tastes. The Mademoiselle would get little affection from that quarter. By the time her honeymoon was ended, she would be experienced enough to appreciate the pleasures of love and yet unfulfilled, eager to taste the full range of delights to be had. He smiled as one of the Marquise's maidservants passed and reached out to pinch her ample backside. He could wait—he would not go hungry waiting for the little Mademoiselle, of that he could be sure!

Jasmine stepped into the parlor and curtsied to her grandmother, who sat with Isabeau on a sofa near the windows.

"Come in, child," Sofie invited. "Don't you look lovely! Your new grand-père will be delighted."

"Thank you, Grand-mère," Jasmine replied. She joined them near the windows and kissed her mother's cheek.

"Did you sleep well, Jasmine?" Isabeau asked.

Jasmine nodded as she gazed out the window toward the gardens and the Seine, which was just visible in the gathering dusk. "Yes, Maman, very well," she answered.

"Good, a nap and a bath were exactly what you needed after a long journey. We want you to be rested and refreshed for your wedding."

"My wedding?" She looked from her grandmother to Isabeau and back. "Is it to be so soon, then?"

Sofie reached out and took her hand. "The sooner the better, child."

"I see." Jasmine felt the nervous fluttering in the pit of her stomach. "When do I meet the Marquis de Saint-Antoine?"

"Henri," Sofie corrected.

"Henri," she repeated. "When do I meet him?"

"Tomorrow. We will leave Paris tomorrow."

"Leave Paris? But where are we going?"

"Sit down, Jasmine," Isabeau said. "Your grand-mère will explain."

Sofie waited until her granddaughter left the windows and was seated and then, taking a deep breath, began: "You see, my dear, Henri has gotten himself into a bit of trouble. Nothing serious, you understand, but, well, he is a bit impetuous and cannot always keep his opinions to himself. But, let me start at the beginning. You have heard of Madame de Pompadour?"

"Oh, yes! She is the King's mistress! Madame Giroux says she is kind and beautiful!"

"Who is Madame Giroux?" Sofie demanded of Isabeau.

Isabeau dismissed her with a wave of her hand. "An old busybody on the diligence who claimed to be La Pompadour's great-aunt."

Sofie sniffed. "I see. Well, regardless of Madame Giroux, La Pompadour is nothing! She has been honored by the King to the extent that his courtiers are ridiculing him behind his back! Do you think that is kingly behavior?"

"No, Madame," Jasmine replied, abashed.

"No, indeed!" Sofie agreed. "At any rate, Henri was at Versailles a few weeks ago and La Pompadour's father, a most disagreeable little man who still positively reeks of his origins—he was a steward, you know—tried to push his way in front of Henri when they were entering a room. Of course, Henri has precedence and tried to assert his right. La Pompadour, however, told Henri to stand aside for her father. Such an insult could not be tolerated and Henri told her to her face that he would never allow a mere steward to take precedence over a true aristocrat. Well! La Pompadour was incensed! She complained to the King and the King was furious! He would rather you insulted the Queen than upset his precious Pompadour! The upshot of this was that the King told Henri to go to his château in the country where he would not have to worry about precedence. He was banished to the country for one year."

"A year! And this began only a few weeks ago?" Jasmine felt near to tears. All her visions of frequenting the glittering Court of Versailles vanished before the dread reality of a long, cold winter in a draughty old château in the depths of the forest. "Oh, Maman!" she wailed. "An entire year!"

"Now, Jasmine," Sofie soothed, "it is not so bad. After all, your husband will be with you. Perhaps your marriage will be stronger for the long time you will have to get acquainted."

Jasmine did not reply. A year in the country with a

man she had never so much as laid eyes upon was not what she'd imagined her life in France would be.

"Who knows, chérie," Isabeau said happily. "Perhaps by the time you get back to Paris, you will be huge with child and contented as a cow!"

Jasmine tried to hide the revulsion she felt at the thought of bearing the child of any man other than Barrett Paxton. Suddenly she had visions of herself being presented to King Louis XV and his beautiful Madame de Pompadour looking like a brood mare in satin and lace. Instead of the looks of admiration and compliments she had dreamt might be hers, she would hear whispers of, "My, doesn't she look contented!" In spite of the questioning looks of her mother and grandmother, she thrust a fingernail between her teeth and bit it sharply. If this was any indication of what surprises lay in store for her, she had no doubt she'd have them all to the quick by her wedding day!

Isabeau shook her daughter gently by the shoulder.

"Jasmine, Jasmine! Where is your mind? Come along, we are going to meet your new grand-père. Come now."

Shaken out of her reverie, Jasmine followed Sofie and Isabeau out of the salon and down the corridor to another parlor.

The drapes were drawn and several silver candelabra were placed around the room, their candles ablaze. In spite of the warmth of the summer evening, there was a fire in the fireplace and the room seemed stifling.

"Alexandre?" Sofie said cheerfully, as she entered the parlor and went to a high-backed chair near the hearth. "Alexandre, I have brought Isabeau and Jasmine to meet you." She gestured for them to join her.

Jasmine's eyes widened as she circled the chair and

caught her first glimpse of the Marquis de Mareteleur. Bundled beneath a satin quilt, the Marquis was enveloped in a brocade dressing gown. Wisps of gray hair showed from beneath his nightcap of green satin. He looked from Isabeau to Jasmine and back again and nodded his head.

"Charming, charming," he said, and his lips parted in a smile which revealed teeth which were surprisingly white and even. "Do you have a kiss for your old stepfather?" he asked Jasmine.

Never losing her smile, Isabeau leaned over and pecked at the man's wrinkled cheek.

Jasmine watched. The Marquis, instead of the three score and ten years of her grandmother, had to be nearer four score and five. He was of an age to be her mother's grandfather! If the father was this old, she realized with a feeling of rising panic, how old must the son be! She looked back to find the ancient Marquis looking at her appraisingly.

"So, you are to be my little daughter, are you?" he asked.

She curtsied. "Yes, Monsieur le Marquis."

"But no, child," he said, waving a crablike hand. "No ceremony—you must call me 'Cher Papa.' Can you do that?"

She forced a little smile. "Yes, Cher Papa."

His blue eyes twinkled in the wrinkled face. "Charming, enchanting. Come, little girl, give your Cher Papa a kiss, eh?"

Steeling herself, Jasmine leaned over but, as her lips touched the ridged brow, she felt the gnarled fingers close over her breast and squeeze it sharply. Gasping, she stepped away with her face blushing hotly.

"Alexandre," Sofie chided, "you must not touch

Jasmine. That was not good of you."

The elderly man chuckled. "Leave me alone, Sofie. Leave me to what few pleasures I have remaining to me."

Behind them, someone rapped on the door and Sofie called, "Entrez!"

Michel appeared with a tray on which was a tall class of chocolate and a small bottle of white liquid.

"Ah, here is your medicine, Alexandre," Sofie said.

"I don't want it," the Marquis insisted. "I feel better without it."

"Nonsense!" As Michel placed the tray on a table and unstoppered the little bottle, Sofie started toward the door. "Come, Jasmine; come, Isabeau. Dinner should be ready. I left orders for it to be served at nine. Michel will see to Alexandre's medicine."

Jasmine followed her mother and grandmother out of the room and, when the door was shut behind her, Sofie patted her cheek.

"You must not mind Alexandre, my darling. He is a sick old man and must be forgiven his peccadilloes."

Jasmine touched her breast and the blush returned to her cheeks. She would remain out of "Cher Papa's" reach from then on! He didn't seem so sick to her! "Yes, Grand-mère," she replied dutifully. But there were many questions still in her mind as she went into the dining room to eat.

Isabeau and Sofie had returned to the Marquise's suite to discuss wedding plans and Jasmine, not being privy to their discussions, left the dining room to wander about the hôtel discovering its many delights.

She paused as she passed the door of the parlor in which she'd encountered the Marquis. For a moment she hesitated but then tapped lightly. Surely she could learn something about her prospective husband from his father. She was sure it would be all right, as long as she remained at arm's length from the old man.

There was no answer and, thinking that perhaps the Marquis had been taken upstairs to his suite, she pushed down the latch and opened the door.

The fire still burned and the candles which illuminated the room were still lit. At the bottom of the Marquis's chair, she could see the satin quilt which had been tucked around him.

She approached the chair. "Monsieur le Marquis?" she said. She kept her voice low in case he slept. "Monsieur le Marquis?" There was no reply and she crept closer. "Cher Papa?" Reaching the chair, she stepped around it and caught her breath.

The Marquis sprawled in his chair. Instead of the twinkling blue eyes which had swept over her only an hour before, his eyes were half-shut and seemingly staring off into space unseeing. His hand lolled to one side and his mouth gaped open with a trickle of saliva dribbling from the corner. His hands, which had been so dexterous earlier, hung uselessly in his lap.

Jasmine reached out cautiously and touched the slack cheek. "Monsieur le Marquis? Cher Papa? Are you all right?" He made no answer and she looked past him at the tray which was placed on a marble table nearby.

The glass which had contained the Marquis's chocolate was empty but the bottle of medicine seemed as full as it had before. Leaving the chair, she went to the table and examined the glass. There was no foul odor, no suspicious residue. She picked up the medicine bottle and tried to pry the stopper out. A click caught her attention and she looked up to see the door open to reveal Michel.

"Good evening, Michel," she said pleasantly. But her smile faded when he hurried across the room and snatched the bottle from her.

"You must not touch that, Mademoiselle!" he said.

"And why not?" she demanded. "And who are you to tell me what I must do?"

He smiled ingratiatingly. "Pardon, Mademoiselle, but I speak with your best interest in mind. This is very powerful—and very dangerous!"

"I can see its effect on the Marquis. He seemed much more healthy before his medicine."

Michel shrugged. "Well, Mademoiselle, how can we say? We are not doctors, you and I."

"That is true, Michel," she agreed. "But I cannot see the sense in taking medicine which has an ill effect on one's health."

"As you say, Mademoiselle," he agreed condescendingly. "As for me, I only follow Madame la Marquise's orders." He dropped the bottle into his pocket. "May I escort you to your rooms, Mademoiselle? Surely you will be wanting to get a good night's sleep before your journey to the Château de Saint-Antoine tomorrow."

"Are you telling me to get out, Michel?"

"By no means, Mademoiselle. I was only interested in your well-being."

She placed her hand on his proffered arm and they left the parlor. "Will the Marquis be joining us tomorrow?"

"Absolutely."

"He does not seem equal to a long coach ride."

"He will be recovered in the morning."

Aware that he would not tell her anything, she did not press him. They mounted the stairs and walked down the corridor towards her suite.

"Tell me, Michel," she asked as they walked. "What is the Marquis de Saint-Antoine like?"

"He is a consummate nobleman, Mademoiselle."

"But what does he look like? How old is he?"

Michel laughed. "I do not think Madame la Marquise de Mareteleur would appreciate my gossiping about my superiors."

Jasmine pouted as they paused outside her door. "That is scant comfort," she told him.

"Eh bien, Mademoiselle, I think you will find that many women have done worse in an arranged marriage."

Jasmine sighed, shaking her head. "You are doing nothing to help me, Michel. You sound as though you are trying to make the best of a bad situation. That thought is even less comfort!"

"Comfort," he said softly, "can be found under any circumstances. There are always those who are willing to comfort a beautiful woman."

She tilted her head and lowered her lashes. "And are you one of those who are willing, Michel?"

"I appreciate beauty, Mademoiselle," he replied, stepping closer.

"Do you think I am beautiful?" she could not resist asking.

"Very beautiful," he answered.

She reached up and stroked his cheek and saw his nostrils flare. He leaned toward her but, before his lips could touch hers, she reached back and pressed the latch of her door.

"Thank you, Michel," she said softly as she shut the door in his face.

Outside, in the corridor, Michel leaned against the wall and laughed. Oh, she was a hellcat all right, this little DuPré! Suddenly he was eager for the trip to Saint-

Antoine. She would be disappointed in her husband, he was sure. And, isolated in that château so far from Paris, who would she turn to for comfort? Who would she turn to to slake the fires of passion when the Marquis did little more than fan the banked coals? Why, who would be there for her to turn to? Who except dear, concerned Michel?

As he returned to the stairs and the parlor where his master waited, he felt a little tremor of anticipation and his full, sensuous lips parted in a broad grin.

Chapter 8

The great coach jolted over the rough road causing the occupants to catch hold of the seats to steady themselves. Inside the coach, sunk into sullen silence, rode Jasmine and Isabeau, the Marquise and Marquis de Mareteleur, and Michel, who was acting as the Marquis's valet and nurse.

Jasmine tapped a finger against the gleaming brass fittings of the coach window. They'd set out from Paris at first light and now it was nearing evening and there was no indication that they were near their destination. Of course, it had not helped when the other coach, carrying their baggage and the women's maidservants, had overturned. They had had to wait until the coachmen and their company of outriders righted it. It was fortunate that the vehicle had not been damaged so badly that it could not be driven. Still, the delay had cost them nearly two hours.

The coach rocked as it turned from the main road onto a less well-traveled highway which was cut through a forest.

"Are we going uphill?" Jasmine demanded as the coach seemed to slow down.

"Yes," Sofie replied. "The château is at the top of the hill. Watch out the window now, in a moment we will pass a clearing and you will be able to see it."

Jasmine peered out the window and, when the coach slowed to negotiate a turn, saw the Château de Saint-Antoine through a break in the trees.

Perched precariously on the edge of a cliff, the château seemed to brood. Tall watchtowers rose at the four corners and smaller turrets broke the line of the roof haphazardly. Its gray mass was unlivened by any hint of color as the only vegetation nearby was on the lower level of the cliffside, far below the bottom of the great, heavy walls.

"Well?" Sofie demanded. "It is impressive, is it not?"

"Magnificent!" Isabeau breathed, leaning from the window of the coach to try to catch a last glimpse before the forest hid it from view.

"Stunning," Jasmine added unenthusiastically.

She leaned back against the high, tufted seat. That gloomy gray pile was going to be her home for the next year, she thought dejectedly. Suddenly, her spirits, which she'd imagined could not fall any lower, plummeted. She glanced across the coach and her eyes met those of Michel. The valet looked over at the Marquise and her sleeping husband, and at Isabeau. Finding them all preoccupied, he looked again at Jasmine and threw her a slight smile and a broad wink.

Taken by surprise, Jasmine used a corner of her lace-edged fan to hide her smile. She felt his foot nudge hers beneath the cover of her spreading skirts and, without fear of detection, nudged his in return. As Isabeau glanced their way, both composed their features and gazed passively out the window at the passing scenery.

"Here we are!" Sofie cried at last.

Jasmine opened her eyes. It had seemed, when they'd sighted the château through the clearing, that they were nearly upon it. But the road wound its way slowly up the steep incline and it was actually many miles away by coach.

She leaned out the window and looked toward the castle as they approached. An iron grille was being raised and the gateway stood open like a gaping mouth waiting to swallow the coach and its inhabitants. For some strange reason, Jasmine closed her eyes as the coach passed through the gateway and rolled up to the front doors of the château. It was as though she could not bear to see the grille being lowered behind them, sealing them inside the massive fortress.

A lackey hurried out the doors of the château and opened the coach door. He lowered the steps and stepped aside as Michel climbed down and prepared to help the Marquis from the coach.

From where Jasmine sat, she could not see the iron-bound doors and, when they opened and closed for a second time and Michel paused in his labors to bow and say, "Good evening, Monsieur le Marquis," she could not see the man he was greeting.

"Good evening, Michel," the man replied. His voice was deep and of a similar timbre as her own father. But it gave no clue as to the man himself.

"Henri, how good it is to see you again!" Sofie exclaimed as she joined Michel and the Marquis in the courtyard.

Isabeau was the next to emerge from the coach but she

moved away from the door and Jasmine could not see the expression on her face when she met her future son-in-law.

Sofie peered into the vehicle. "Come, Jasmine," she urged.

Warily, Jasmine moved across the coach and took the hand of the lackey who reached out to help her down the tiny steps. She stood at last in the courtyard and, as the coach was driven off toward the stables, raised her eyes to her fiancé.

The Marquis de Saint-Antoine was a large man with a stern visage and eyes of a steel-blue which seemed to cut through her. Dressed in black velvet, his appearance, from the jeweled buckles on his shoes to the black ribbon tying his powdered wig, was impeccable. He was not unhandsome though she might have added, "for a man of his age." Had she have hazarded a guess, Jasmine would have given him at least a dozen years on her mother's age. He was, she would have supposed, very near the end of his fourth decade or possibly in the beginning of his fifth. At any rate, there was little doubt that he was at least thirty years her senior.

She dropped him a little curtsy and, when she rose, found him studying her as though she was an object he was considering buying.

"Mademoiselle, I trust your journey was pleasant?" he asked.

"Yes, Monseigneur," she replied softly. "I . . ."

"Good," he interrupted. Turning away from her, he offered his arm to Isabeau and gestured for Sofie and the Marquis de Mareteleur to precede them into the castle.

As they walked away from her, Jasmine stood rooted to her spot in the courtyard. She was confused. Was he so little interested in her? After all, she was to be his wife, did he not care if she had the sense to reply to a simple question? She could have been a prattling idiot for all he knew—or seemed to care.

The Marquis de Saint-Antoine and Isabeau paused as they reached the door of the château, and the Marquis looked over his shoulder with an expression of impatience.

"Well? Come along, child!" he snapped.

Lifting her skirts, Jasmine hurried to the château and followed them inside.

The stone walls and floors of the château were covered with tapestries and carpets which did little to allay the chill present even on the warm, midsummer evening. A small fire burned in the hearth of the great hall and they dined beneath candlebeams which were hung from the high-vaulted ceiling.

The Marquise de Saint-Antoine sat at the head of the table while Sofie occupied the place at the opposite end in lieu of her husband, who had been taken to his room to rest after the long journey. Jasmine and Isabeau faced one another across the table and Jasmine cast a sharp look at her mother when she said:

"When is the wedding to take place, Monsieur?"

The Marquis sipped his wine. "Tomorrow. The priest will be here in the morning. I would thank you to tell the maidservants to have the child ready. I would not like there to be unnecessary delays."

"Of course, Monsieur."

Jasmine rolled her eyes. "The child," he called her! On the eve of her wedding and her fiancé referred to her as a child! She looked up as the Marquis spoke.

"You need not refer to me as 'Monsieur,' Madame DuPré," he said. "After all, are you not to be my belle-mère?"

Isabeau giggled. "Of course! And after tomorrow you

97

shall be my son-in-law.''

The Marquis laughed and Jasmine thought it an incongruous sight. "Never, Madame," he said, "never! You are far too young to be anyone's mother."

Isabeau bridled, flattered, and Jasmine's eyes opened wide. It was as though they were courting! He was the gallant swain, fawning his way into her good graces, and she was the demuring maiden eager to be wooed. She glanced toward her grandmother at the far end of the table but Sofie's eyes were on her daughter and stepson.

She approves! Jasmine realized in amazement. She does not care which of us the Marquis wants so long as one of us captures the heart of her husband's heir! It is only because I am unmarried that I am to be his bride! The realization made her sag in her chair, and her mother noticed her inattention to her food.

"Jasmine, if you are finished, you may be excused. Go to your room; you will need your rest for tomorrow will be a long day."

"But Maman . . ." she began.

The Marquis cleared his throat loudly. "Mademoiselle, I disapprove of disobedience."

Her eyes met the steely gaze of her fiancé and she felt like a naughty little girl. "Yes, Monsiegneur," she said quietly.

Sofie rose at the same time. "I will take Jasmine to her room," she said. "She would not want to be lost in this rambling old château. Come, darling, bid your Maman and Henri good night."

Walking around the long table, Jasmine leaned down and kissed her mother. "Good night, Maman," she said softly.

"Good night, Jasmine," her mother said. "Sleep well."

She looked shyly at the Marquis not knowing if he expected her to kiss him as well, but he merely nodded.

"Good night, child," he said coolly.

She curtsied. "Good night, Monseigneur," she replied.

Returning to her grandmother's side, she left the room. As they started down the hall toward the stairs, the sound of laughter could be heard from the great hall.

"I'd wager he wishes it was Maman he was marrying tomorrow," she said aloud.

"Why, Jasmine!" Sofie exclaimed. "What a thing to say!"

"It's true! He did not even speak to me. He had eyes only for Maman."

"Now, you must not think he disliked you, chérie. How could anyone dislike you? You are a charming and beautiful young woman. It is only that Henri has been a soldier all of his life. He has never married and has no brothers or sisters. He is really quite unacquainted with . . ." She let the sentence trail off.

But Jasmine knew what she had been about to say. "He is quite unacquainted with children!" she finished.

Sofie nodded. "Yes, that was it. But never mind, my darling, after tomorrow evening, you will no longer be a child. You will be a woman!" She kissed Jasmine's cheek as they stopped before her door. "And then things will be better."

"Yes, Grand-mère," Jasmine agreed. But she did not believe it. As she opened the door and went into the bedchamber where Claudette waited to help her undress, she shuddered at the thought of being put to bed with the Marquis de Saint-Antoine. She could not even bring herself to speak to him; she was afraid to call him anything more familiar than Monsieur le Marquis or

Monseigneur. How would she be able to hide her terror when they were alone together and he had her at his complete mercy? How would she feel when those steel-blue eyes filled with lust?

"Mademoiselle?" Claudette came to her as she stood inside the bedchamber door. "Are you ill?"

"No, why do you ask?"

"You are so pale; you were deathly white when you came through the doorway."

"I am just nervous, Claudette. That is all. I would imagine that most women are nervous on the eve of their weddings."

"Yes, Mademoiselle, I am sure that they are."

As Claudette helped her off with her gown, Jasmine looked at the huge bedstead which dominated the room. The bed itself, with its elaborately carved head- and foot-boards, stood on a raised platform. At the four corners of the platform, carved posts a foot thick rose from the floor to the ceiling and were surmounted by a wide, carved entablature. Curtains of rich brocade were caught back to the posts and hung in graceful folds to the floor. It was in that bed that the Marquis would come to her. It was in that bed that she would have to come to terms with the apprehension which quaked within her.

As she climbed into the high bed, Claudette unfastened the curtains and let them fall, enclosing her in the darkness of the small room within a room. She lay back against the pillows and listened as the maid went about the tasks she had to complete before she could go off to her own bed.

As happened with torturous regularity, her mind was suddenly filled with thoughts of Barrett. It should have been he to whom she was to be married on the morrow; it should have been he with whom she would be put to bed after the ceremony. With all her being, she raged against the cruel fates which had decreed that she must come to France and be married to the old and aloof Marquis who seemed so much more interested in her mother than herself.

The clock across the room struck the hour and Jasmine suddenly wished it would stop—she wished time would cease to pass and that night might never come to an end.

Chapter 9

Jasmine wandered through the cavernous rooms of the château while all about her preparations were being made for her wedding. Everywhere were servants bustling from room to room and most did not seem to realize that the girl they passed on their errands was their soon-to-be châtelaine.

She entered a parlor whose tapestries told the story of Diana the Huntress. The tall windows looked out over the rear of the château where a little forest stretched along the edge of the cliff. Paths led away from a gateway in the château wall and disappeared into the forest. As she stood at the window, moodily staring at the trees and the blue sky above, the door of the parlor opened and Michel entered the room.

She looked around as his footsteps thudded on the thick carpeting.

"Michel!" she said in surprise. "Why are you not attending to my Cher Papa?"

The valet laughed. "Your 'Cher Papa' is asleep. Doubtless he needs all the rest he can get so he will have the strength to give his new little daughter a kiss. And perhaps a friendly squeeze or two as he did yesterday?''

Jasmine frowned. "I could do without Cher Papa's squeezes, thank you. Do me a favor, will you, Michel?"

"Anything!" he cried melodramatically. "You have only to name it!"

"Give Cher Papa a double dose of his medicine tonight!"

Michel chuckled, but his smile faded as he glanced out the window toward the forest below. Puzzled, Jasmine looked toward the forest and saw the figures who had just emerged from it.

The Marquis de Saint-Antoine and Isabeau DuPré reined in their horses and leaned close, deep in conversation. While Jasmine and Michel watched from above, the Marquis touched Isabeau's cheek gently and bent toward her. Their lips met in a brief kiss and then Isabeau spurred her horse forward. The Marquis laughed and urged his own horse on in pursuit.

Jasmine turned away from the window. Her brow was creased in a frown and she felt faintly embarrassed that Michel had witnessed her mother and fiancé in such a tender moment. But, when she gathered her courage enough to look up at him, his face was impassive; he seemed not in the least surprised by what he had seen.

She forced a smile. "Well, in-laws should get along, I suppose."

The valet smiled sympathetically. "Do not fret, Mademoiselle. It is only that some men prefer older, more worldly women."

"Then why did he agree to marry me? Surely he knew I was young and unworldly. Is that my fault?"

"Of course not. I, for one, am delighted that you are young and unworldly."

Jasmine grinned. "But you are not the Marquis de Saint-Antoine and it is that gentleman to whom I must be a dutiful wife."

"The Marquis does not realize what a fortunate man he is," Michel said softly. He took Jasmine's hand and raised it to his lips. His blue eyes holding her gray-green ones, he parted his lips and nibbled gently on her fingers.

Against her will, Jasmine shivered and quickly pulled her hand away. But Michel was encouraged and he bent toward her. When she leaned a little away, he pressed a hand to the back of her head and held her while their lips met. She drew a deep breath as his lips left hers and moved to her cheek and then her throat. Her pulse pounded and she slid her hands around his satin-liveried waist.

"Michel," she whispered against the blond hair he kept tied in a long queue. "Michel, no, this is wrong."

Michel chuckled low in his throat. "It is wrong for you and me, but it is right for your mother and the Marquis?"

"No!" She pushed against him and he stopped away. "It is wrong for them as well! It does not make it right for us simply because we have their example to follow."

He shrugged. "As you say, Mademoiselle. But the long winter months stretch their icy fingers before us. We will still feel this way when the wind is howling about the château and your bed is cold because your husband is warming that of your mother?"

"How dare you!" Jasmine cried. Lashing out, she caught him across the face. As she brought her hand back for another blow, he caught it and pinioned it behind her back.

"You may dislike what I am saying, Jasmine," he told

her seriously, ''but you will find that I speak the truth. And I want you to know that I am ever ready—nay—I am ever eager, to give you the affection and, I may say without fear of contradiction, the satisfaction you may find lacking in your marriage.''

Jasmine raised her chin haughtily. ''You sound very sure of yourself, Monsieur. How do I know you are not merely a braggart whose amorous capacity in no way equals his boasts?''

Michel smiled slyly. ''Were there not so much chance of discovery and did I not know you to be a virgin, I would take you onto that carpet and prove my 'amorous capacity' to you. As it is, I can only refer you to my mistress for verification. Though I daresay she would hardly confirm our liason to you.''

''Your mistress? And who might your mistress be, Monsieur? Some lovesick chambermaid?''

''I need not waste myself on lovesick chambermaids, Mademoiselle. No, I refer to Madame la Marquise de Mareteleur—your grandmother.''

Leaving Jasmine to stare after him in stunned silence, Michel bowed grandly and left the room with a self-satisfied swagger.

Jasmine and Henri de Saint-Antoine knelt before the priest in the chapel of the château and were married. Though they had been told that the wedding was the cause of celebrations in the village at the base of the cliff, they did not ride down to visit the celebrants, nor were there any of the local village squirearchy invited up to the château. It was a quiet ceremony and a quiet evening of dining and listening to music played by the Marquis's own musicians followed it.

Jasmine plucked nervously at the painted roses on her

white taffeta gown. It seemed she could hear every chime of the clock over the soft music and, as the hours passed, her tension grew. It was growing closer and closer to the time when she would be taken to her room and dressed in the white satin and lace nightgown in which she would wait for her husband to take what she had never imagined giving to anyone except Barrett.

She glanced at her mother, who smiled and nodded her head in time to the tinkling minuet. Could Isabeau tell her what she could expect in her marriage bed? Had her mother already sampled the amorous talents of the stern and forbidding Marquis? She blushed as she realized the gravity of her thoughts. It was true that he and Isabeau were no blood relation, but still they were mother and son in the eyes of the Church. Any affair between them would be incestuous. She should be ashamed, she told herself, to sit beside the man to whom she was bound in the eyes of the law and the church, no matter how she loathed him, and accuse him and her mother of incest.

"Jasmine?" Sofie was standing beside her. "Jasmine, it is time."

She blinked and looked up at her grandmother. Beyond her, on the other side of the room, Michel sat near the Marquis de Mareteleur. Was her grandmother really the valet's mistress? But . . . no! She chided herself on the direction her thoughts were taking.

"Jasmine?" Sofie leaned down to touch her shoulder.

"It is time?" she asked.

The Marquis nodded. "Come, darling, I am to escort you to your room."

Jasmine stood and smiled uncertainly as Isabeau came to kiss her cheek.

"Do not fear, my sweet child," she whispered in her ear. "Do not fear."

"No, Maman," Jasmine replied uncertainly. She looked toward the old Marquis de Mareteleur but he was sound asleep and she wondered if Michel had really given the old man a double dose of his medicine.

Sofie took her hand and led her from the room. As they walked up the stairs, she brushed a curl back over Jasmine's shoulder.

"The Marquis . . . that is . . . your husband, will retire to his room by another staircase. The door connecting your room with his has been unbolted and he will be able to come to you without the prying eyes of the servants upon him."

"Yes, Grand-mère," she replied absently.

They arrived at Jasmine's door and the Marquise ushered her inside. Claudette and Lotte were waiting but Sofie dismissed them.

"I will call you when you are needed," she told them. She waited until the maids were out of the room and then took Jasmine's hands. "My darling, you know that your family's honor is at stake tonight, do you not? You must do your duty to your family and to your husband tonight. No matter what Henri desires, you must oblige him for he is your master as much as he is the master of the lowliest scullery in the kitchens. Do you understand me?"

Jasmine nodded. "Yes, Grand-mère," she whispered, her fear growing. "I understand."

"Good."

The Marquise summoned the maids and Jasmine stood like a little child while Claudette and Sofie removed her clothing. Lotte turned back the coverlet on the bed to reveal white satin sheets over which she sprinkled attar of roses.

Jasmine stood naked in the candlelight, shivering with apprehension. She raised her arms above her head as the two maids slid the white satin nightdress over her head and let the full skirt fall to the carpet. It swirled about her feet and Sofie sighed as she walked around her.

"How beautiful you look!" she exclaimed, watching as Claudette brushed out her auburn curls so that they gleamed against the stark white satin. "Henri will not be able to help falling madly in love with you!"

Jasmine walked to the bed and sat on its edge while her grandmother went about the room snuffing out the candles until only one burned on a table beside the bed. Coming to the bedside, Sofie kissed her cheek.

"I will bid you good night now, my darling. Your husband, I doubt not, will be coming to you soon and he will expect to find you alone. Come, Lotte; come, Claudette." Herding the two maids before her, she bustled out of the room leaving Jasmine to her fate.

Watching the door which connected her suite with her husband's, Jasmine rose and walked to the opposite side of the bed. She feared it would not be long before the door opened for she had seen the glow of light beneath the door and had heard the sound of movement in the room beyond.

When at last the doorlatch was depressed and the door swung open, she took a step backward as though she could escape through the thick, stone walls.

The Marquis looked about the room and then saw her standing beside the bed. Her white satin nightdress gleamed in the candlelight. He crossed the bedchamber and cast aside the brocade dressing gown which covered his linen nightshirt.

"Remove your gown and get onto the bed, if you please," he said sternly.

"Pardon me, Monseigneur?" she asked.

He looked at her exasperatedly. "I said, remove your

gown and get onto the bed. I have little patience with such fripperies.''

Going to the bedside table opposite her, the Marquis pinched out the lone candle flame and climbed onto the high bed. Afraid to disobey him, Jasmine pulled the long, full nightdress over her head and joined him.

Immediately his hands were upon her and she gasped and pulled away from him in surprise. He exhaled in a long hiss.

"Come now, child," he said grimly. "Let us have none of this. I realize that you are inexperienced, but certainly you are not totally stupid. I do not intend to spend the entire night at this."

"But, Monseigneur . . ." she began.

"Have you any idea of why you and I were married?" he demanded. "I will tell you why. I am not in the first bloom of youth as you, doubtless, have noticed. I am without an heir. Should I die childless, both my estates and those of my father will pass to the crown, which is, by my reckoning, quite wealthy enough. Consequently, I must provide myself with an heir. It is therefore necessary that I take a wife; preferably a woman with many years of child-bearing before her. There were, of course, many young women here in France who were well connected and had much larger dowries than you, but I had no need to make a marriage with social or financial concerns in mind. Your grandmother told me of you and you were chosen for one simple reason. Your grandmother is something of a spendthrift and I do not care to see my father's estate totally depleted. In marrying you, I hoped that your grandmother would decide to cease her wild extravagance in order that her descendents through you might have the opportunity to spend some of it themselves. Do you understand?"

Jasmine nodded in the darkness. "Yes, Monseigneur."

"Good. Now, if you will kindly give over with your maidenly bleating and lie down, we will attempt the business of providing ourselves with an heir."

Too intimidated to refuse, Jasmine lay back against the pillows and made no further protests. His hands ranged over her, not in the tender, gentle caresses she'd known with Barrett, but roughly, prodding her and squeezing there. When they moved lower, over the firm flesh of her belly, to assault the very center of her womanhood, she gasped and writhed away from him.

"Madame!" he growled, seizing her knees and forcing them apart.

Jasmine closed her eyes as he moved over her and, with one brutal thrust, tore her delicate maidenhead asunder. A cry of pain and shame welled into her throat but she stifled it by biting into her lip.

"There now," he said a surprisingly few minutes later when he moved away from her and tugged his nightshirt into place, "that wasn't so bad, was it?"

"No, Monseigneur," she replied, trying to hide the quavering of her voice.

He climbed off the bed and pulled on his dressing gown. Retracing his steps across the dark room, he paused at his bedchamber door. "Good night, child," he said, almost as an afterthought.

"Good night, Monseigneur," she returned softly.

The door closed behind him and she slid off the bed and felt about in the darkness for her satin bridal nightdress. Pulling it over her head, she felt her way to the dressing table and opened a drawer to find a handkerchief. But instead, her hand touched the leather case that held Barrett's portrait and hair. She slammed the drawer shut. She could not look into Barrett's eyes after what had just happened—she felt befouled and ashamed.

Returning to the bed, she straightened the rumpled coverlet that was stained with the proof of her defloration, and slipped between the sheets. Snuggling into the thick softness of her pillow, she thrust a knuckle into her mouth and bit it to keep the tears at bay.

But she could not and, as she saw the light beneath the Marquis's door go out, the first of her tears fell from her cheek to the scented satin sheet.

Chapter 10

Jasmine stared morosely out the window as she sat curled on the window seat of her bedchamber. Rain poured down on the Château de Saint-Antoine and she could see the little streams of water falling over the side of the steep cliff. At least, she told herself with scant comfort, the weather is too foul to allow Isabeau and Henri to go out riding as they usually did. Not that it mattered—the Marquis was teaching Isabeau to play chess and they spent hours together in the parlor which overlooked the forest hunched over the chess board laughing and flirting.

In the weeks following their marriage, Jasmine had seen the relationship between her husband and her mother blossom from the mutual attraction which had existed from the moment of their meeting into a full-blown love affair. The Marquis came to her bed only when a midwife brought from the village assured him that the time was right for her to conceive. When, during the first month of their marriage, the woman's predictions did not prove correct, she was dismissed and his visits became even less frequent. There had been nights when she'd lain awake and heard him return to his room in the early hours of the morning. She hadn't had to guess where he'd been—the radiant glow of her mother's face at breakfast told her all she needed to know.

She couldn't help wondering, during all those sleepless nights, how different he must be with her mother than with her. He had not changed since that first night—their encounters had an unmistakable air of an unpleasant duty and then she was ignored in the cold light of day. She felt as though the Marquis was her stepfather instead of her husband. And, in spite of the fact that she could not feel anything but repugnance for the cold Marquis, she resented her mother's having taken him from her without even a struggle.

She looked around as a knock sounded at the door. "Come in," she called disinterestedly.

"I've brought your petticoats up, Madame," Claudette said as she entered the room. "The laundress said she managed to get the wine stain out of the quilted satin." She spread out the white quilted satin petticoat for Jasmine's inspection.

"It's fine, Claudette."

As the maidservant went about putting the petticoats into the clothespress, she hummed a happy tune.

"I'm glad someone has found a reason to be cheerful," Jasmine muttered sourly.

"Has the weather gotten the better of you?"

"Would that were my only complaint!" She frowned at the thick rivulets which ran down the window panes. "I wish I were away from this place—away from this sham marriage my mother has coerced me into."

"Monsieur le Marquis is a fine, handsome man, Madame."

"Oh, yes. He's handsome enough, I suppose."

Jasmine allowed as she slipped off the window seat. "But looks are not the most important attributes of a good husband. Now, Master Paxton was also handsome—more handsome than the Marquis, younger I daresay—but he was a good man as well. He would have been a kind, considerate husband. And, what is more important, he loved me."

Claudette said nothing, knowing it would not have done for her to contradict her mistress. But she was overjoyed to be back in France. The Château de Saint-Antoine was exactly what a noble household should be and the Marquis de Saint-Antoine was a fine example of an aristocrat.

The situation remained static for several weeks and it was just after the first frosts of winter had begun coating the trees outside the château that Jasmine's resentment became apparent to her husband.

He entered her bedchamber one night when she sat near the fire reading a novel she'd found in the château's dusty, seldom-used library. Discarding his dressing gown, he sat on the edge of the bed and kicked off his slippers.

"Come child," he said, using the hated epithet which had almost replaced her name, "come to bed."

Gripping the book tightly, she steeled herself. "No, thank you, Monseigneur," she said quietly.

"Child," he said in a firmer tone, "come here. I wish to be with you tonight."

She refused to look up from the book. "No, thank you, Monseigneur," she repeated.

Rising, he came to her and snatched the book out of her hands. He cast it into the fire and reached for her but she leaped from the chair and stepped away from him.

His icy gaze swept over her from the waves of the rich auburn hair which fell over her shoulders to the toes of her embroidered mules which peeked from beneath her blue muslin nightdress.

"You've the very devil in your eyes tonight," he told her, amused by her angry stance. It was the first time he'd detected any spirit in the girl he regarded as a docile child. "Has something vexed you? It can't be the weather. The rain has stopped; the stars are shining. What can it be that has troubled you?"

Jasmine gathered her courage. "Did you think I wouldn't learn the truth, Monseigneur?" she snarled.

"I've little patience for riddles, Jasmine," he said, using her name for the first time. "If you've some grievance against me, for heaven's sake, tell me what it is and be done with it."

"I'm talking about my mother and what has been going on between you two."

"Aha!" He laughed. "So she told you, did she? The vixen!"

"She said nothing—but I've the wit to realize what is happening under my very nose. Give me that much credit at least!"

He walked past Jasmine and lounged on the edge of her bed, his back supported against the tall footboard. "Well?" he asked with an unconcerned lift of his shoulders. "What about it?"

"What about it!" She was aghast at his nonchalance. "I won't have it! You are my husband and I will not tolerate your philandering. I will not tolerate . . ."

Coming to her, he caught her arm and pulled her back toward the bed. She gasped as he pinioned her arms behind her back.

"You will not only tolerate it, you will accept it

without comment. Or you will regret your shrewishness. I will not be ruled by a snippet of a girl barely out of the nursery.''

''Well, then, Monseigneur,'' she said defiantly, her teeth clenched against the pain in her arms, ''if you can play the whore, so shall I. A pity there are not many handsome manservants in the château. Perhaps there are peasants in the village who show promise.''

His pale eyes narrowed and, with a swift motion, he loosed one of her arms and struck her across the face with his free hand. Jasmine felt her head snap to one side and, in her shock, could not manage to catch herself as he released her and she fell to the floor.

She half lay at his feet staring up at him. She knew he was difficult; she knew he had none of the gentle kindness she had so admired in Barrett Paxton, but she'd never dreamt that he possessed such a capacity for violence. She saw the look of triumph in his eyes as he recognized the fear in hers. He reached a hand toward her and, warily, she took it and allowed him to pull her to her feet.

''Sit down, Jasmine,'' he said softly. ''Sit here beside me.''

Afraid to disobey, she perched on the edge of the bed.

''You understand,'' he told her, his eyes holding hers, ''that I cannot have a wife who lays with peasants and lackeys. I cannot abide it; I will not abide it. If you make a fool of me with your indiscretions, I will be forced to discipline you harshly. Do you understand?''

She nodded, afraid to anger him. ''Yes, Monseigneur.''

''Good.'' He smiled and entangled his fingers in her hair. For a moment she expected him to yank her head to the side, but he let the strands slip between his fingers and caressed her cheek. ''You are a beautiful child,'' he said. "But I could destroy your beauty if I chose." He let his hand slide down her throat. "You've an exquisite throat—so long. What a pity it would be if it were broken."

"Please, Monseigneur," she begged, thoroughly frightened.

He smiled at her fear, feeling his power over her as though he were the conqueror and she the vanquished enemy. "Oh, do not fear," he told her. "I will not harm you—unless you anger me."

"I will not anger you. I promise."

"That is wise of you, child." His hand slid lower, across the wide neckline of her nightdress and then still lower. His fingers traced the curve of her bosom beneath the thin muslin of her gown and, in spite of her fear, she caught her breath.

Her lips parted and the Marquis smiled as he saw her involuntary response.

"Oh, child," he whispered, "you do have much to recommend you."

Jasmine licked her lips and made no move to stop him as he untied the ribbons which fastened her nightdress. Frightened as she was, she was also curious—tantalized by his touches. In spite of her loathing for him, she suddenly wanted to feel his fingers against her skin rather than through her nightdress.

She heard the Marquis's breathing quicken as he parted the front of her gown and pushed it off her shoulders. Looking down, she watched as he reached out and touched her flesh, stroking and caressing her, but he only took her by the shoulders and pushed her backwards, pressing her deeply into the soft mattress.

"Henri," she whispered, as though to remind him of her presence.

But he ignored her and fumbled with his nightshirt.

117

She reached up and stroked his face but he seemed not to notice.

"Henri," she said once again, a little more loudly. She had been aroused by his caresses to a pitch she'd never before reached with him but her passion was fading in the face of his indifference toward her.

He threw off his nightshirt and she, almost desperate to be treated with some tenderness, opened her mouth to call out to him. But her words were muffled as he abruptly gathered the skirt of her nightdress and threw it over her head.

Furiously, she kicked at him and fought the yards of fabric to find her way out. But his strength was far superior to hers and she was powerless against him.

When at last he moved away from her, she emerged from the tangle of her skirt and tied the ribbons of her nightdress with shaking fingers. Tears of anger and frustration welled in her eyes and she sniffled loudly.

The Marquis's head appeared as he pulled his nightshirt on and he threw her a sour look. "For heaven's sake, child, you've shown some spirit for the first time—please do not revert to your former, immature behavior."

Jasmine ignored him, huddling on the far side of the bed. She heard him sigh with exasperation and then his footsteps crossed the floor. It was not until she heard the door to his bedchamber open and close that she looked up, her eyes ablaze with fury.

Leaving the bed, she went about the room blowing out the candles. When the room was illuminated only by the glow of the fire, she climbed into bed and stared at the ceiling. She would pay him back, she vowed to the darkness. She would have her revenge, even if she was the only one to know of it. Smiling, she went to sleep eager for the next day to arrive and, with it, opportunities to exact vengeance.

She smiled at herself in the pier glass while Claudette fastened the back of her gown. Of gold taffeta trimmed with black lace, it was fit for a Court reception. Her hair was pulled into a chignon and diamond-headed hair needles sparkled in it.

"What do you think, Claudette?" she demanded as she turned slowly in a circle.

"It is very beautiful, Madame," the maid confirmed, "but I do not understand. Is today a special day?"

Jasmine laughed as she picked up a black lace fan. "Oh, yes, Claudette! I think today will be a very special day!"

Leaving the maid in puzzlement, she left the bedchamber humming a little tune.

Chapter 11

"I don't like it, Maman," Isabeau said as she popped a sweetmeat into her mouth. "I don't like it at all." She chewed the delicacy thoughtfully and then swallowed. "It has been nearly four months since Jasmine was married and there is not a hint of a pregnancy."

"In either of you," Sofie added significantly.

Isabeau shot her a petulant glance. They sat on opposite sides of a small, gilded table near the fireplace in Isabeau's sitting room. Both women wore velvet cloaks to ward off the chill of the morning and Sofie shivered a little as she noticed the fluffy snowflakes falling past the windows.

"It is going to be a hard winter. I do believe Alexandre and I should be returning to Paris soon."

"Please do not change the subject, Maman. It is rather important, you know."

Sofie poked among the sweetmeats for one which appealed to her. "Very well," she agreed peevishly. "I only happened to notice the snow."

"At any rate, though I think it rather crass of you to

point it out, it is true that neither Jasmine nor I have exhibited signs of pregnancy. I begin to wonder if Henri is capable."

"Perhaps if he were more amorous with Jasmine. From what you say, he is inclined to be rather abrupt."

"Abrupt!" Isabeau laughed and choked on her sweetmeat. "Henri is a soldier, Maman. He makes love as though he were laying siege to a town—he is anxious to subdue his victim and then ride away from the ruins."

"Well, then, perhaps that is his trouble."

Isabeau shook her head. "No, I do not think so. I have heard many women with very large families complain about their husbands' technique."

"Still, there must be a child. There must be! Alexandre is failing—I have a strong suspicion that he will not live much longer. And then Henri will be the Marquis de Mareteleur—by then Jasmine must have a son to become the new Marquis de Saint-Antoine. She must!"

"Or, suffice to say, someone must."

Sofie considered this. "Do you mean to say that Henri would accept a child who was not his wife's?"

"Henri is desperate to have an heir—if I had a child and Jasmine did not, it would be no great task to convince him to own the child. Jasmine could be persuaded to claim the child as her own."

"It would be better if she bore the child herself," Sofie pointed out, "then she would be more inclined to care for it."

"It doesn't really matter," Isabeau said with a sigh, "all this talking is a waste of time if Henri is incapable. We cannot wish a child into a womb."

Sofie smiled. "No, we cannot. But there may be a way—there just may be a way."

Jasmine tapped the Marquis de Mareteleur on the shoulder as he sat before a fireplace in a parlor of the château. But there was no response. The wrinkled face held the same vapid expression she'd seen at the Hôtel de Mareteleur in Paris and on most of the occasions she'd seen him since coming to the country.

"May I help you, Madame la Marquise?"

She started and whirled to find Michel standing behind her. "You startled me, Michel," she chided. "However did you come into the room without my hearing you?"

"I was here all the time," he replied. "I was sitting there, on the window ledge behind the draperies. I heard you enter and then slipped from the ledge and tiptoed across the carpet."

"Well, shame upon you! One should not startle people—it's very rude."

"I beg your pardon, Madame. I was so dazzled by your beauty that I temporarily forgot my manners."

Jasmine giggled. "Michel! You are incorrigible!"

Seizing her hand, he kissed it making loud, smacking sounds. "And you, Madame," he said between kisses, "are gorgeous!"

"Oh, Michel, I . . ." She stopped as the parlor door swung open and a footman stood there. "Yes?"

The footman bowed. "Pardon me, Madame la Marquise. Madame la Marquise de Mareteleur wishes to see Michel at once."

"Thank you." When the door was closed once again, Jasmine pouted. "I fear you must go, Michel."

The valet's sigh was exaggerated. He pressed her hand to his heart. "I shall not be gone long, I promise you!"

As the door closed behind Michel, Jasmine went to a

chair beside the old Marquis and sat down. "Monsieur le Marquis?" she said softly, tapping his withered hand. "Cher Papa?" She looked up as the door opened once again.

The Marquis de Saint-Antoine stood there. "Oh, Jasmine," he said. "I thought perhaps your Maman was here."

Jasmine sulked. "I am sorry to disappoint you, Monseigneur. When last I heard, Maman was in her suite with Grand-mère."

He chose to ignore the sarcasm in her voice. "I am pleased to see that you are taking an interest in my father. Where is Michel?"

"Grand-mère asked to see him. He should return shortly."

"I see. Then I shall leave you. A messenger has arrived from Paris with correspondence from Virginia."

"From my Papa?" she asked eagerly.

"I would presume so. I really haven't read it—it is not my habit to read the correspondence of others."

"I did not mean to imply . . ."

"Of course you didn't. Now, I must be going. Good morning, child."

Jasmine frowned at the door which had just closed behind him. He really was the most exasperating man!

"Did you miss me, Madame la Marquise?" Michel asked as he peeked around the edge of the door.

"Terribly!" Jasmine replied, her good humor restored.

"I nearly collided with your illustrious husband on my way down the stairs."

"Yes, he was here. He said he had some correspondence for Mama. A letter from my father, I believe. I will ask her later if I may read it."

Taking her hand, Michel led her away from the somnolent Marquis and to an alcove which was in reality a small turret. Reclining on the tufted-velvet settle, he drew her down beside him.

"Really, Michel," she scolded playfully, "you are a bit bold. Aren't you afraid my illustrious husband, as you call him, will discover us?"

"No. You forget, dearest Madame, that he is with your mother."

"Ah, but you forget that my grandmother is there as well."

Michel laughed. "But your grandmother would leave if she thought your mother and your husband wanted to be alone."

Jasmine giggled and then pulled a mockingly sober face. "That isn't funny, Michel," she said severely. But then, unable to maintain her somber demeanor, she dissolved into laughter once again.

Her laughter was muffled as Michel pressed his lips against hers. Taken by surprise, she struggled but then, tantalized and profoundly curious, she allowed him to take her into his arms and made no further resistance against his lips or the arms which encircled her.

When he released her, she was breathless. "Michel," she whispered, "that was very reckless. Someone could have come in at any moment."

With gentle fingers, he stroked her face. "I would risk everything for you."

She gazed into his blue eyes and the passion she saw in them was such a welcome change from the cold indifference to which she had become accustomed that she trembled. She shook her head. "It is too dangerous."

His only answer was to draw his tongue along her

124

shoulder above the lace edging of her gown's neckline. She felt her resolve ebbing away with every beat of her pounding heart.

"What about Grand-mère?" she demanded. "Won't she be cross with you if you dally with me?"

Michel felt success within his grasp. "How can you imagine that I would ever touch her again if I'd once held you in my arms?"

"But how, Michel? How could we avoid detection?"

"Leave that to me, dear Jasmine," he breathed into her ear. "Leave it all to me."

The snow continued throughout the day and into the night and Jasmine lay in her bed in the darkness watching it fall past the window of her room.

The curtains of her bed were drawn back on the side facing the fire to catch the heat and the flames illuminated the room with a flickering light.

Beneath the door of the communicating door, she could see a light burning in her husband's room and she prayed that Henri would not decide to join her.

She climbed off the bed and went to the dressing table. Lifting out the leather case, she went back to bed and lay down, her eyes fixed on Barrett's portrait. Suddenly she heard the sound of a door latch being depressed and she thrust the case beneath her pillows. The door that led to her sitting room opened and Michel stood there.

"Shhh," he warned as she was about to speak. He crossed the room to the bed and sat down. "I told you it could be managed."

"You must be insane!" she hissed, raising a shaking finger to point to the sliver of light under Henri's door.

"But he's not there," Michel told her, unconcerned.

"How do you know?"

"I saw him going to your mother's suite when I returned from putting your Cher Papa to bed. I've no doubt he'll be there till dawn. What was that you were looking at?"

Before she could stop him, he had reached beneath the pillows and pulled out the leather case. Opening it, he studied Barrett's portrait.

"This is the man you were in love with?" he asked. "The young man from Virginia?"

Jasmine took the case from him and put it into a drawer of the bedside table. "He is the man I am in love with," she corrected defiantly.

Michel regarded her seriously. "And yet he was not your lover." He saw her wondering glance and nodded. "I know that you were a virgin on your wedding night." He smiled. "You're blushing. Tell me, chérie, what do you think of the pleasure of love?"

"I find no pleasure in what my husband calls love," she spat.

Michel struggled to keep his triumph from showing. "No?" he asked innocently. "And would you have found pleasure with Monsieur Paxton?"

Jasmine's eyes grew wistful. "I know I would have."

Michel discarded his dressing gown and untied the black velvet ribbon that held his hair in a long queue of silky blond curls. Facing Jasmine on the bed, he nodded.

"Yes, chérie, I suppose you would have. You have passion in your eyes, I can see it." He laughed as she dropped her gaze. "No, it's too late to hide it." Slipping one finger beneath her chin, he tilted her face toward his. "Let me help you find your pleasure, Jasmine."

She gazed into his blue eyes, fascinated. All her senses screamed for his touches and she was amazed at the intensity of her desire for him.

126

Michel lay down on his side and drew her down to face him. He kissed her, gently at first, and then more deeply as she parted her lips for him.

"Don't be afraid of me, Jasmine," he murmured. His fingers loosed the ribbons of her nightdress and, lifting her, he pulled it over her head and let it fall to the floor. Again he saw the bright flush rise to her cheeks.

"Don't be embarrassed," he whispered. "You're beautiful. Don't be afraid of the light."

Under his hands, Jasmine found herself reaching heights she'd never known existed. Michel was skilled enough to have long ago recognized her need for gentleness and care and he took his time, prolonging her pleasure and delaying his own until she was near to weeping. Nevertheless, when he parted from her long enough to pull his own nightshirt over his head, he saw that she'd closed her eyes.

"Jasmine, Jasmine," he soothed, "you're like a little virgin despite your marriage. Has your husband never allowed you to see his body?" She shook her head and he cursed the Marquis for the brute he was. Lying by her side once again, he kissed the tip of her nose. "I am not so modest as he," he told her softly, "but I don't want to add to your fear. There will be time for exploration in the future."

Trembling, Jasmine pressed her body to his and gasped at the sensation of his warm skin against hers. Her hand caressed the smooth, hard-muscled flesh and, with a groan of desire that would no longer be denied, Michel poised himself over her and sought his own release.

When at last he held her quietly against his chest, he smiled as she stretched up to kiss his cheek and caress his still-perspiring body.

"Are you happy, my little Jasmine?" he asked.

"I never thought I could be so happy in France, Michel. I never thought I could find such joy except with . . ." She stopped, afraid of having offended him.

But he laughed. "Except with your Monsieur Paxton, no? Ah, chérie, you are new to all this but you will learn. Love is a rare and priceless emotion but sometimes lust can do quite as nicely."

Jasmine opened her mouth to speak but paused as Michel held a finger to her lips. Listening, she stiffened as she heard movements in her husband's bedchamber. She was terrified that Henri would come in and find them. She could not have borne the sight of Michel being beaten or even put to death as was Henri's right. He was precious to her—he was her only link to the life she'd desired; to the passion and ecstacy she'd thought were lost to her.

But the light went out and the sounds ceased and she sagged against Michel in relief.

"I must leave," he said, swinging his long legs over the side of the bed.

"Michel, no!" she pleaded. "Stay a little longer!"

He laughed lightly and kissed each finger of the restraining hand she had placed on his arm. "I cannot, chérie," he said fondly. "It is not long before dawn. I must awaken in my own bed."

"Then tonight. Please say you will return to me tonight!"

"I will return when it is safe, my darling," he promised. "We must take care."

Watching sadly, Jasmine saw him draw on his nightshirt and pull on his dressing gown. His slippers were beneath the bed and she pinched him as he knelt to retrieve them.

"Until morning," he said, tying his hair back. He kissed her and started out the room.

"Until morning, cher Michel," she replied.

Michel hurried down the corridor and let himself into Sofie's suite. The Marquise dozed in her chair, both her chins resting on her ample bosom, and she started as he jostled her.

"What?" she muttered. Opening bleary eyes, she peered at him in the dim light of the dawn. "Oh, it is you. What time is it? I waited up for you to return. It is morning!"

Michel shrugged. "She wanted me to stay with her."

Sofie smiled slyly. "She enjoyed herself, eh?"

"She is eager for our next meeting," he confirmed.

Sofie laughed and chucked him beneath the chin. "How could she help it, you are a magnificent lover and, believe me, I have a basis for comparison!"

Michel accepted the compliment with a slight nod. "Thank you, Madame. Now, if I may, I would like to sleep for a few hours—I am very tired."

"I've no doubt you are. When will you bed her again?"

"When can Madame DuPré manage to keep Saint-Antoine occupied for a few hours?"

"Oh, she will, she will. She is willing to give her all to our cause—like you, no, Michel?"

Michel smiled. "I will make the supreme sacrifice and make love to our little Jasmine at every opportunity."

"Thank you, Michel," Sofie said sarcastically. "But I hope you will be able to find an hour or two for me occasionally as well."

"How can I? I must save my strength for Jasmine!"

"You rogue! I begin to feel the pangs of jealousy already! Whenever I see her radiantly happy face I will." She saw him yawn. "Oh, very well, go to bed."

She reached out and patted his bottom as he turned to

leave and then hoisted herself out of her chair to go to bed. The sky toward the east was turning to the light gray of morning and she was stiff and sore from spending the night in her chair. But it had been worth it. If Jasmine did not conceive under the skillful attentions of the handsome and virile young valet, she would begin to believe that she was indeed a barren wife.

Chapter 12

"Did you sleep well last night, dear?" Sofie asked with a careful air of innocence.

Jasmine shot her a startled look but then, deciding that her grandmother could not know about Michel's presence in her bed the night before, replied:

"Oh, yes, very well, Grand-maman. And you?"

"Oh, very well, indeed."

Looking up at the manservant who took her empty breakfast dish away, Jasmine missed the conspiratorial look that passed between Isabeau and Sofie. By the time she looked back toward them, they were intent upon their meals.

"By the bye, Maman," Jasmine said. "What did Papa have to say in his letter?"

Isabeau and Sofie exchanged an uneasy glance. "Papa and Armand are well and send their love," Madame DuPré replied.

"And?" Jasmine prompted.

Seeing the determined look in her daughter's eyes, Isabeau nodded. "All right, Jasmine. But please, sit down. You must understand . . ."

"Understand what? Maman, what's happened?"

"It's Barrett." She held up a hand to stay Jasmine's exclamation. "You see, darling, some relatives of the Paxton's have come to stay at Paxton Hall and Barrett has become enamoured of their daughter, one Octavia Dashwood."

"No!" Jasmine cried. "It's not possible!"

Isabeau sighed with exasperation. "Really, Jasmine, did you expect him to enter the priesthood?"

"No, but . . ."

"You are a married woman," Sofie reminded her. "You must forget the past. Get on with your life and accept the fact that Barrett will do the same."

Unable to hide her pain, Jasmine bolted out of her chair and out of the room.

A cold drizzle that was half rain and half snow was falling when Jasmine awoke. In spite of the gloom of the winter morning, she smiled.

Her plan was succeeding—as the days passed, she grew more and more sure of it. Every symptom was becoming apparent; every sign seemed to point to the probability that she was with child. And, in spite of the fact that she'd had to admit her husband to her bed on more than one occasion in the past two months, she was sure that the child within her had been fathered by Michel.

She frowned as she thought of him. He had returned to Paris with the Marquis and Marquise de Mareteleur— Sofie wanted to be in the capital before the celebrations of Christmas and New Year. She missed him—but he had served his purpose! She laughed aloud and hugged herself. What exquisite vengeance! How delighted Henri would be when he discovered her condition. How Sofie and Isabeau would rejoice! And how delicious it would be to watch them exult over the heir of the noble Marquis de Saint-Antoine while she alone knew he was the child of a valet.

Throwing back the coverlets, she leapt out of bed. "Oh, my!" she cried, clutching the bedpost. She would really have to be more careful—she was getting dizzy every time she moved too quickly. But it seemed a small price to pay to be avenged.

"Claudette!" she called down the corridor as she leaned from her sitting room door. "Claudette!"

She danced across the bedchamber while she waited for the maidservant to arrive. When she turned back toward the door, she found Claudette watching her with a curiously puzzled look on her face.

"Are you all right, Madame?" she asked.

Jasmine laughed gaily and made the maid a graceful curtsy. "I am perfectly all right, Claudette. In fact, I am even better than right!"

She stood quietly while Claudette hooked up the back of her gown.

"Pardon me, Madame," Claudette said, tugging at the hooks, "I fear you have gained weight. I can scarcely pull these hooks together."

"I know, Claudette. Isn't it wonderful?"

The maid seemed puzzled but then an astonished light dawned in her eyes. "Oh, Madame, are you enceinte?"

"Shhh!" She cast a look toward her husband's bed-chamber door.

"Monsieur le Marquis is not there, Madame. He went out earlier."

"Good! Then yes, Claudette, I believe I am going to have a baby. But you must promise not to breathe a word to anyone! I am not completely sure and I do not want to raise unfounded hopes."

The maidservant nodded. "As you say, Madame." She smiled shyly. "I am very happy for you, Madame."

Jasmine embraced her. "Thank you, Claudette, but remember, not a word to anyone!"

"I promise!"

Leaving Claudette to direct the housemaids in changing the linen of her bed, Jasmine went downstairs and asked for something to eat.

"Nothing heavy," she directed, being all too familiar with the standard fare usually presented in the mornings. "Perhaps some pastry; is there any pastry?"

When the manservant brought the pastry, she asked: "Has Madame DuPré already eaten?"

"Yes, Madame, she has."

Dismissing the servant, Jasmine sat alone at the long dining table. It was lonely at the Château now that the Mareteleurs and Michel had returned to Paris. She would be glad when the year of Henri's exile was over and they could return to Paris and, perhaps, to Court. Of course, she would be unable to be presented to the King and Queen immediately upon their return. She would not yet have borne her child and she had no desire to waddle into the royal presence like a great Flanders brood mare.

Finishing her pastry, she left the dining room and went upstairs to her mother's suite. Perhaps she would reveal her news to Isabeau—doubtless she would want to tell Henri. Not that she should—what business was it of Henri's anyway?

She chuckled as she let herself into her mother's sitting room. It was empty. Passing through the splendid room, she cautiously entered the bedchamber.

"May I help you, Madame la Marquise?" Lotte asked

from the floor where she knelt straightening the fall of Isabeau's bedhangings.

"May I help you, Madame la Marquise?" Jasmine mocked. "My mother is certainly training you to be a proper French maid. I doubt anyone would suspect that you'd been born on the banks of Mobjack Bay."

Lotte glared at her. "Is that supposed to be a compliment, Jasmine?" she snarled, sounding more like herself.

"Take it as you please. I am not here to bandy compliments with you. Where is my mother?"

"With your husband," Lotte replied, a sneer in her smile.

Jasmine smiled patiently. "And where is my husband?"

"They went out this morning. The Marquis ordered the sleigh brought out of the stables and he and your mother went for a sleigh ride."

Jasmine glanced toward the window and saw that the half rain, half snow of the early morning had changed to a steady, fluffy snow. "Did they say when they would return?"

"No." Lotte raised an eyebrow. "But then, perhaps they stopped somewhere to get warm. I understand there is a hunting lodge in the forest. I'm told it is very secluded and romantic; the kind of place lovers find useful for assignations."

Ignoring her, Jasmine went to her mother's study. There were several layers of paper spread over the top of the desk and Jasmine wondered if the letter from her father was there.

There had been no further word from Belle Glade and, as Isabeau had refused to show her the letter, she had begun to think that her mother had invented the story about Barrett and Miss Dashwood to discourage her.

She poked among the papers. One fluttered to the floor and she bent to pick it up.

"Are you looking for something in particular?" Lotte asked from the doorway.

"Yes, Lotte," Jasmine replied sweetly, "I am looking for a little privacy. If you don't mind . . ."

"If you are looking for privacy, may I suggest you look for it in your own suite?"

"That is enough, Lotte!" Jasmine snapped. "You go too far! That will be all; you may leave me."

They glared at one another for several moments before Lotte dropped her an abrupt curtsy.

"As you wish, Madame la Marquise!" she growled. Leaving the room, she slammed the door violently.

Jasmine looked at the paper which still lay face down on the floor. Picking it up, she turned it over to find that it was an unfinished letter.

"My dear Master Paxton," she read. "Master Paxton!" Going to the sofa, Jasmine sat down weakly. Taking a deep breath, she read on:

My dear Master Paxton:

Jasmine has asked me to respond to your kind letter. Naturally, she would ordinarily have done so herself. However she finds it difficult to tear herself away from her husband's side long enough to tend to the simplest of chores. It is for that reason that I have remained at the château. Having been married only six months, Jasmine has not yet settled herself enough to become a proper châtelaine. Of course, it is so difficult to convince oneself to handle the mundane tasks when one is so very much in love.

In answer to your letter, Jasmine is overjoyed

to learn that you have found someone to care for and she wishes you good luck and hopes that you and Miss Dashwood find as much happiness as she and Henri have.

There the letter ended and Jasmine sagged against the back of the sofa. Barrett had written to tell her about this Octavia Dashwood who threatened to come between them! No wonder Isabeau had seemed uneasy when she'd pressed her for details! Barrett was concerned for her happiness and Isabeau was going to tell him that she was so ecstatically in love with Henri that she could not even be bothered answering his letter!

Tossing the letter onto the desk, she rummaged through the papers in search of Barrett's letter.

"Oh, damn!" she cried in frustration. "Where could she have put it?"

Her eyes wandered toward the fireplace where a low fire burned. Starting off the desk chair, she stood dejectedly in the middle of the floor. It would be just like Isabeau to burn the offending letter. Jasmine knew that if she had, indeed, burned it, it was long since consumed in the flames.

Feeling near to tears, Jasmine collapsed onto the desk chair once again. Idly, she drew open one of the desk drawers and fumbled in it, though she knew it was much too obvious a place for her mother to have hidden such an incriminating piece of evidence. As she pushed the drawer closed, the lace ruffle of her sleeve caught in the drawer pull. She worked to release the delicate lace and the drawer pull turned, a hidden spring released, and the bottom of the drawer opened.

Jasmine paused in surprise as a sheet of paper fell to the floor. The drawer had a false bottom!

Impatiently, she tore the lace free and slammed the

false bottom shut so she could close the drawer. Picking up the paper which had fallen out, she opened it and tears filled her eyes as she recognized Barrett's handwriting.

My dearest Jasmine:

I pray you forgive me for my boldness. I know it is improper of me to write thusly to another man's wife, but I do so with the best of intentions. Your father has had precious little news of you since your marriage and I am concerned for your happiness. Madame DuPré assured him that you are well and deeply in love with that fortunate man, the Marquis de Saint-Antoine. I pray this is so, but long to hear it from you yourself.

As you may have heard, some of my mother's cousins have come to Paxton Hall bringing with them their daughter, Octavia. She is a gentle creature, docile and agreeable, and I have come under great pressure to offer for her hand. I would not consider it if I thought there was any chance that you might be mine one day. If there were no chance, it would not matter to me how or with whom my life was spent. If you could spare me a few moments and a few lines to tell me if I might continue to hope, I would be grateful. If you are, in fact, as happy as Madame your mother paints you to be, I will retire from your life, my concerns laid to rest. I will yield to the pressures and marry Miss Dashwood knowing that Paxton Hall must have heirs and that if you are not my wife, I care not who is.

I am, sincerely, your humble servant and devoted admirer,

Barrett Paxton

Jasmine wiped a tear from the corner of her eyes. She

had only to say the word and he would not marry his cousin; and her mother was going to lie to him! He must know the truth; he must know how desperately she missed him. How terribly much she wished she had never left Belle Glade and the comforting circle of his arms.

Hiding the letter inside her garter, she left her mother's suite without a glance for the obviously curious Lotte who lounged in the sitting room awaiting Isabeau's return.

Chapter 13

"My darling Barrett . . ."

Jasmine paused, brushing the tip of her quill against her chin. She had to take stock of her own emotions. It would not do to alarm him—it would serve no purpose when they were separated by such a distance. She had to let him know that she still loved him and that her mother's assurance would be lies.

Her heart pounding, the quill raced over the paper releasing her emotions in a great rush. The past six months faded away in the remembering of the sweet days she'd spent with Barrett—of the promises and vows they'd made in the shade of the willows on the shore of Mobjack Bay.

When she finished, she sanded and sealed the letter and a great feeling of relief swept over her.

"How will I get it to him?" she wondered aloud. Certainly Henri would never consent to send it to the village below to be dispatched on the next diligence. If she wanted it dispatched, she would have to do it herself.

She hurried down the corridor to the head of the stairs.

Below, she saw a housemaid passing.

"Marie?" she called.

The little housemaid curtsied. "Yes, Madame la Marquise?"

"Do you know where Claudette is?"

"I believe she is in the kitchen, Madame."

"Fetch her, if you please. Tell her I wish to see her immediately. And send someone to the stables—I want two horses saddled at once."

The housemaid curtsied once again. "Yes, Madame."

Returning to her room, Jasmine went to the clothespress and pulled out her riding habit and the small black tricorne that went with it. Tossing the garments on the bed, she returned to the press and got her black riding boots.

"You sent for me, Madame?" Claudette stood in the doorway watching her with a confused expression.

"Come in, Claudette, and help me change. I want you to ride down to the village with me."

"Now, Madame? The road is terribly slippery."

"Had I wanted a report on the weather, I could have asked Marie. Now, come unhook my gown."

While she waited for the maid to dress to go out, she took a silver letter opener and slit the seam of her hat's lining. Slipping the folded missive inside, she fastened it with a hat pin and carefully set the tricorne atop her head. Then she waited, impatiently slapping her riding crop into the palm of her hand.

"Are you almost ready?" she asked Claudette.

"Yes, Madame," the maid replied harriedly, "almost."

Jasmine shook out the crease in the skirt of her dark blue velvet riding habit. Worn over an oblong hoop, it jutted out on either side and hung nearly flat in the front

141

and back. The tightly fitted jacket was trimmed with gold braid and a small black velvet bow was tied beneath her chin above the ruffles of her cream-colored lawn shirt.

Claudette buttoned the last button on the jacket of her grey cloth habit. Though similar in cut to that of her mistress, the maid's habit lacked the elaborate braiding and ruffling. Seeing them together, one would never mistake which was mistress and which servant.

Leaving her suite, Jasmine hurried down the corridor with Claudette close behind. They started down the steep stone staircase but, when they were less than half-way to the bottom, Jasmine stopped and clutched the railing.

"What is it, Madame?" Claudette hissed.

"Shhh," Jasmine hushed. She listened, a frown creasing her forehead. Then she relaxed. "I must have imagined it."

Starting once again, they had gone down only a few more steps when Henri de Saint-Antoine appeared at the foot of the staircase.

"Where are you going?" he asked, his bulk blocking her way.

Jasmine looked down at him and at her mother who had appeared behind him.

"I am going riding," she told them. "Claudette is coming with me."

"It is too slippery to ride. You will injure yourself," Henri told her.

"It was not too slippery for you two to be out," she countered.

"We went in the sleigh," Isabeau said.

"Then I shall go in the sleigh."

"I have had the sleigh put into the stables," Henri said.

"Then I shall have it brought out of the stables."

The Marquis shook his head. "I think not."

Jasmine brought her riding crop down on the stone balustrade. "Why am I a prisoner here? You may go out; my mother may go out. But I may not!"

"Jasmine," Isabeau reasoned, "we are only concerned with your welfare."

Jasmine's laugh was cruel. "My welfare! You were concerned about yourselves! Tell me, Maman, is the hunting lodge beautiful? Is it a good place for your assignations?"

"Jasmine!" Henri's tone was threatening.

"No! I will say what I have to say! I know what is between the two of you; I would have to be a complete dolt not to know! It is unnatural! It . . . it is incestuous!"

Henri bounded up the stairs and the back of his hand caught Jasmine across the cheek sending her hat flying over the balustrade. Gasping, Isabeau ran to them and caught at him.

"Henri! Take care! You will harm her!"

"I will teach her respect!" he growled.

Jasmine cowered against the balustrade feeling stunned and dizzy. She felt her mother's hands grasping her arms.

"Are you all right?" she asked.

Jasmine pressed a hand to her cheek and her eyes met and held her mother's. "Why didn't you tell me?" she asked softly.

Isabeau stepped back. "What do you mean?" she asked.

"I mean the letter—Barrett's letter. Why didn't you tell me it had arrived?"

The color drained from Isabeau's cheeks and she glanced up at Henri. "How do you know about that?"

"I went to your room looking for you this morning

143

and I found the reply you were writing. And then I found Barrett's letter."

"You should not pry, Jasmine. It was wrong of you."

"Why were you lying to Barrett? Why were you telling him that I was happy; that I was in love?"

"It is for your own good. You must put Barrett Paxton out of your life. I was doing it for you."

"You were doing it for yourself! Are you afraid he will tell Papa what you are doing? How you are having an affair with your daughter's husband?"

Isabeau caught Henri's arm as he was about to strike Jasmine.

"Chérie, you are distraught," Madame DuPré said patiently. "Come back to your room—we will put you to bed and after a nap you will feel better."

"No!" Jasmine shouted. "I will go out!" She started down the stairs but the Marquis caught her by the shoulder. "Leave me alone!" she shouted. "Let me go!" Twisting, she pushed his hand away but her sudden movement put her off balance and, when she tried to catch herself, the sole of her riding boot came down on a piece of ice which had been tracked in on the Marquis's boot. She felt herself slipping and felt the Marquis's hands grabbing for the soft, slippery velvet of her sleeve. But his hands were too late and she screamed in pain as she hit the first of many stone risers. While Henri and Isabeau watched in frozen horror, she fell toward the flagstones of the floor at the foot of the tall staircase.

"My God!" Isabeau shrieked. "Henri, save her!"

The Marquis took a step down and then paused as though fascinated by the sight of the blue velvet-clad woman rolling in a tumble of skirts. It was only when she lay on the flagstone foor that he was able to move.

As Claudette stood transfixed at the head of the stairs,

the Marquis and Isabeau ran down the stairs and knelt at Jasmine's side.

"Henri," Isabeau whispered, "is she alive?"

The Marquis unbuttoned Jasmine's jacket and pressed his ear to her breast. He clasped her wrist with one hand and felt for a pulse at the base of her throat with the other.

"Yes," he replied at last. "She is alive."

Isabeau looked up at the maidservant, who stared with frightened eyes. "Go to her room," she ordered, "and turn down her bed."

"Wait!" the Marquis commanded. He looked at Isabeau. "We cannot carry her up the stairs. Marie!" The housemaid, who had been watching with several other servants, came forward and curtsied. "Take quilts and pillows to the Silver Salon and prepare a bed in the alcove. Claudette, bring your mistress's nightdress and wrapper."

Lifting her carefully, the Marquis carried Jasmine to the Silver Salon, which was so named because the various tables and ornaments furnishing the room were wrought of solid silver.

In one corner of the room a rounded alcove, which was in fact the base of one of the château's smaller towers, contained a small couch bed which was one of the few which survived from the days when the château was the scene of glittering balls to which hundreds of guests were invited. Such accommodations were necessary for there had not been enough bedrooms for everyone, but now Versailles was the place for balls and the beds had fallen into disrepair. Most had been broken up and burned.

The Marquis lowered Jasmine onto the hastily made-up bed and felt again for her heartbeat. He stepped aside while Isabeau undid the buttons which fastened the tight waistband of her daughter's skirt.

"Lift her again, Henri," she asked. "You must undress her."

The Marquis shook his head. "She should not be lifted again or jarred too violently. I have seen grievous injuries result from lifting a person who has suffered a bad fall."

"Then how will we remove her clothing? She cannot lay there in her hoops and corset."

Henri turned to a footman. "Bring me a knife."

Little by little, Jasmine's riding habit was cut away and tossed aside. By the time a trembling Claudette arrived with Jasmine's nightdress and wrapper, Jasmine wore only her petticoat and chemise. The Marquis hacked at the ruffled linen of her petticoat and Isabeau gently but firmly tugged the shredded fabric from beneath her.

Isabeau gasped as the petticoat finally gave way and pulled free from beneath Jasmine's body. It was stained —smeared with a large, ugly blotch of blood.

"Oh, no!" she moaned. "Oh, dear Lord!" She watched in horror as the Marquis cut through the thin chiffon of Jasmine's chemise.

Like the petticoat, the chemise was stained and, as it was pulled free, they saw that the bright red blood was smeared over the pale, cool skin of her thighs.

Isabeau looked at Claudette, who stared in horror at the blood. "Claudette," she said softly, "was your mistress with child? Did she tell you she was enceinte?"

Claudette said nothing and Henri clasped her arm and shook her roughly. "Answer Madame DuPré," he ordered, "was your mistress with child?"

The maidservant bit her lip and nodded. "Yes, Monsieur le Marquis," she whispered. "She told me this morning."

Isabeau covered her face with her hands. "What have

we done?'' she moaned. Her eyes sought those of the Marquis. "Henri, what have we done?"

Thanks to the thick padding of her riding habit and the petticoats and hoops beneath it, Jasmine's injuries were largely superficial. She was stiff and sore and several large bruises spotted her body, but it was not long before she was moved to her own room.

She had been saddened by the loss of her child. She had felt herself so near to completing her vengeance on the Marquis and her mother. But as she saw their contrite faces day after day and the way the Marquis brooded over the loss of his heir, she was not at all sure that the child's loss was not more of a punishment to them than its birth would have been.

Both Isabeau and the Marquis came to her rooms several times a day and tried to sooth her and amuse her. The Marquis spoke often of how she would soon be well and then they would spend all of their nights together. She would be enceinte once again very soon, he promised to her great distaste. She feigned weakness and dizziness to delay his return to her bed. It seemed that since she had proven herself capable of conceiving, he was eager to try again for the much-desired heir.

She smiled as he left the room and reached beneath the pillow for the letter she'd written to Barrett. Claudette had retrieved the hat while Henri and Isabeau were tending Jasmine on the day of her fall. The letter, secured within the silk lining, had gone undetected. She would see that it was sent to him, she vowed. She would see to it herself! As she lay in her bed "convalescing," she began to plan for her escape from the Château de Saint-Antoine.

But she would not have Claudette to aid her in her

escape. Once they were sure Jasmine would live, Isabeau summoned the maidservant to her suite.

"Claudette," she said sternly, "it was wrong of you to encourage Madame de Saint-Antoine to ride when you knew she was enceinte."

The maidservant studied the floor. "I did not encourage her, Madame."

"You did not discourage her."

"But I did! I did! I told her it was very slippery outside. She insisted on riding!"

"Then you should have sent someone for me or for Monsieur de Saint-Antoine. But you did not and now Madame de Saint-Antoine has miscarried her child."

Claudette wanted to shout that it was not her fault. She had not struggled with Jasmine on the stairs; she had not tracked in the ice on which Jasmine had slipped! Instead she murmured, "Yes, Madame."

"You realize that you will not be able to remain in Madame de Saint-Antoine's service?" Isabeau saw the girl's stricken eyes and continued: "Do not fret, I am not turning you into the street. You will be taken to the village and put aboard the next diligence for Paris. I believe your Maman is in the service of the Marquis de Mareteleur?" The child nodded. "Then you will enter their service. Go to your quarters, then, and pack your belongings. You will leave in the morning."

Tearfully, Claudette curtsied and turned to leave the room.

"Maman," Jasmine said as her mother entered her bedchamber, "has Claudette gone?"

Isabeau sat on the chair beside the bed and brushed a curl back from her daughter's cheek.

"Oh, hours ago. She left for Paris on the diligence this morning."

"What will I do for a maidservant?"

"I have given that some thought. The only housemaid in the château suitable to become your maidservant is Marie but she is a scatterbrained little baggage. While the maître d'hôtel was in the village, he went to visit the home of Gaspard Dunault, who is the richest burgher there. His wife was only too happy to allow her favorite maidservant to return to the château to enter your service."

"And when do I meet this favorite maidservant?"

"I did not bring her in immediately because I feared you would be too tired to receive her."

"I feel very well, Maman. Please bring her in."

As Isabeau went to get the maidservant, Jasmine smiled. Claudette had been safely seen off on the diligence to Paris. But not before she'd come to bid a tearful farewell to her mistress. And not before Jasmine had given her the letter to Barrett Paxton. Claudette had hidden the letter inside her garter and promised to post it immediately upon her arrival in Paris. How perfectly Isabeau had played into her hands. Sending the maidservant to Paris was the best thing she could have done!

She stifled her smile as the door opened and Isabeau led the new maidservant into the room.

"Jasmine, this is Solange Lancour. She will be your new maidservant. She comes highly recommended. Solange, this is your new mistress—the Marquise de Saint-Antoine."

Solange came forward and dropped Jasmine a deep curtsy. She seemed about Jasmine's own age—sixteen—and was visibly impressed by the luxury she saw about her. Gaspard Dunault had been a rich man by the rather meager standards of the village of Saint-Antoine, but all his wealth could not have purchased the precious objects which furnished one suite in the château.

Jasmine saw the girl's dark eyes sweep around the room. "Good afternoon, Solange," she said.

Solange's eyes came to rest on her. "Good afternoon, Madame la Marquise," she replied.

"I hope you will not be sorry you have come to us."

The maidservant pushed a strand of dark blonde hair over her ear and her eyes dropped to the diamond-studded wedding ring Jasmine wore.

"I am sure I will be most happy here, Madame la Marquise," she said.

"I'm sure you will. That will be all, Solange. You may go and acquaint yourself with the château and the staff."

Solange dropped her another curtsy and backed from the room.

"Well?" Isabeau asked.

Jasmine shrugged. "She will do."

Perhaps, she thought, she will more than do. In fact, the girl was so obviously impressed by beauty and wealth that it might just be terribly easy to induce her to help her escape. Greed, she reflected with a smile, was sometimes a wonderful thing.

Chapter 14

Jasmine frowned as the communicating door closed behind the Marquis de Saint-Antoine. Since her miscarriage, he had become obsessed with the idea of a child. It was as if, being convinced that he'd gotten her pregnant once, he was sure his much-longed-for-heir was within reach.

In pursuit of his goal, the Marquis had almost abandoned Isabeau's bed in favor of his wife's. He came to her every night without fail and sometimes spent the entire night at her side.

But if the Marquis was enchanted with the notion of his wife's bearing him a child, Jasmine was less than happy. With every passing day—with every new demonstration of his increased interest in her—she grew more determined to leave the Château de Saint-Antoine, Isabeau DuPré, and the newly amorous Marquis behind.

Jasmine stood with her hands on her hips while her new maidservant, Solange, hooked the back of her gown. "Well, Solange," she said, "you have been with us for nearly a fortnight, how do you like it here?''

"Oh, Madame! It is so beautiful here!'' Solange replied, her voice filled with wonderment.

"You should see my grand-mère's hôtel in Paris. It makes the château look positively shabby!''

"Pardon me, Madame la Marquis,'' the maid said shyly, "but I cannot believe that to be true.''

"That is because you have never been to Paris. You would like Paris, I think.'' She looked down at the maid's print cotton skirt and black bodice laced over a white cotton shift. "If we were in Paris, I would dress you in silk—a grand lady must not be seen with a dowdy maidservant, you know.''

Solange's dark eyes shone. "It sounds wonderful! I wish we were in Paris now!''

"So do I, Solange, so do I.'' Jasmine heaved a great, exaggerated sigh. "Unfortunately, the Marquis's banishment will not end until summer. We will have nearly six months left here.''

The maid's smile faded. "Six months! Such a long time!''

Jasmine bit back a smile. It was not going to be too difficult to convince Solange to help her! "Of course, I am not banished. I could stay at the Hôtel de Mareteleur with my grand-mère if Henri would give me permission to leave the château.''

"Would he, Madame?'' Solange asked eagerly. "Would he give you permission?''

Jasmine shook her head sadly. "No, I fear not. He wants me to remain here and have a child. He cannot get me with child through the mails, you know.''

"But you are young! Surely there will be many opportunities for children after the Marquis is back in Paris!''

"Yes, that is quite true. But Henri is determined that

I give him a child as soon as possible."

Solange thought for a while. "Madame," she said at last, "what if you were to steal away? Surely you would be forgiven if there was naught your husband could do about it."

"Oh, Solange," Jasmine said, feigning hesitancy, "I do not know. Disobeying one's husband is a serious matter."

"Would Madame your grand-mère take you in if you returned to Paris without Monsieur le Marquis?"

"I am sure she would," Jasmine allowed, "but still . . ."

"Think of Paris, Madame," the maidservant urged. "Think of Paris and Versailles."

"Versailles! That is a long step, Solange. What do you know of Versailles?"

"My former mistress, Madame Dunault, was there once. She went to see the King eat his dinner. She says it is a grand place!"

"I'm sure it is. But don't you think that we should try to decide how we will get to Paris before we worry about how to get to Versailles?"

Solange chewed thoughtfully on a stand of her dark blonde hair. "I suppose you are right, Madame, but I don't know how we are going to go about it."

"First we would need the help of a coachman. Neither you nor I are capable of driving to Paris and we cannot take the diligence."

"There is someone," the maid said. "One of the younger coachmen." She smiled impishly. "He is very handsome and he pinches my botton whenever we meet."

"Oho! It sounds serious!" Jasmine teased.

Solange giggled. "I do not think it would be difficult

to convince him to help us.''

"In fact," Jasmine laughed, "I think it might even be fun trying!"

"I think it might, Madame," Solange agreed. "I think it very well might!"

"Well, have you spoken to your coachman yet?" Jasmine asked her maid a few days later.

She spoke over the howling wind which swirled the snow around the thick walls of the château. They were in Jasmine's bedchamber and, for lack of better entertainment, Jasmine was dressing Solange in one of her grand gowns.

Solange was captivated by her own image in the pier glass and it was several moments before she realized that she had been spoken to. "Yes, Madame, I have spoken to him." She fingered the lavender ruching which trimmed the gown of violet watered silk.

"Well?"

"Oh! He says he would gladly drive us to Paris if you could guarantee that he would not be punished for it."

"I could guarantee that. Even if the Marquis dismissed him, I could assure him that my grand-mère would engage him in her service."

"Then he would have no objection." Solange touched the ruffle of organza gathered into a lavender ribbon which encircled the base of her throat above the deep décolletage. "You are so fortunate, Madame, to be a grand lady. I would give anything to wear such gowns every day! But of course, no one would take me for a great lady."

"Now, Solange, you are too modest! Dressed that way anyone would take you for a lady of the Court! Where were you born? Were you born in Saint-Antoine?"

"No, Madame. I was born in Auligny; it is a small hamlet not far from here."

"Very well then, Solange. I christen you Madame la Comtesse d'Auligny."

"La Comtesse?"

"Here now! Do not be greedy! I cannot be outranked by my own maidservant, can I?"

Solange chuckled. "I suppose not." Turning sideways, she admired her reflection. "La Comtesse d'Auligny. I like that, Madame. But do you think anyone would believe it?"

"I am sure they would! You could fool the King himself!"

"Oh no, not the King?" Solange's dark eyes widened.

"Yes. The King himself."

"Imagine that!" the maidservant mused, examining her reflection. "The King himself!"

Once Jasmine had convinced Solange that great adventure awaited them in Paris, the maidservant badgered her to formulate their plans for escape. Luc, the young coachman who'd allowed himself to be drawn into their scheme, promised that he could have a coach ready at a moment's notice. There was nothing for them to do but wait for an opportunity to slip away and be well on their way to Paris before they were missed.

Jasmine tucked a velvet bag containing a good part of her jewelry collection into the false bottom of a trunk filled with gowns and accessories.

"Why are you hiding them, Madame?" Solange asked.

"If we were stopped by highwaymen, the jewels would be more safe here. I will keep just enough in my other trunk to satisfy them."

"Do you think we will be robbed?" the maid asked worriedly.

"No, I don't think so. But it is not an unknown occurrence these days." She sat on the top of the trunk while Solange fastened the clasps. "Now, I want you to tell Luc to take this trunk and the other down to the coach house and hide them in one of the coaches. Then we will not have to wait while the coach is loaded and we will not have to lose precious time."

"When do you think we will be able . . ."

Jasmine sighed. She'd heard the question so many times she'd lost count. "I don't know, Solange, but I hope it will be soon!"

"What do you mean you are not going to the village?" Henri demanded as he stood next to his wife's bed. "It is the custom that the Marquis and Marquise de Saint-Antoine attend the Christmas Mass at the cathedral. The villagers will expect it—they will be greatly disappointed."

"I do not want to go, Henri," she replied. "I do not feel well—I have a cold."

"But it is expected. It is the duty of the family to set an example of piety for the villagers."

With an angry groan, Jasmine threw back the coverlets. "Oh, very well! Enough of your lectures! I will go to the village and attend the Mass, but if I take a chill and die it will be on your head. You know, Henri, I have been feeling poorly these past few days."

The Marquis's cold blue eyes lit up. "Jasmine! You don't think . . . So soon?"

Jasmine shrugged. "How can I know? As you say, it is doubtless too soon. Call Solange, if you please. I must dress if I am to attend the Mass."

The Marquis studied her for a long moment. "No," he said at last, "I think not. I will call Solange, but only to help you back into bed." Reaching out, he took her into his arms. "We must not risk your health," he said, his face pressed against the top of her head.

But, standing with her back to him, Jasmine noticed his hands resting lovingly over her abdomen where, she knew, he was imagining a tiny seed flowering into a beautiful son for the house of Saint-Antoine.

"Have they left yet?" Jasmine called from her bed.

Solange, keeping watch for the window of Jasmine's sitting room, shouted back: "Not yet . . . wait! The grille is being raised. Yes! The coach has just left. I can see it on the road beyond the walls of the château."

Jasmine kicked the coverlets back and climbed off the bed. "Quickly, Solange! Help me dress! No, wait! I'll wear the black velvet—it hooks up the front and I can manage it myself. Go and tell Luc to bring the coach out of the coach house. We will leave as soon as possible."

Enveloped in a pelisse of black velvet lined with red fox fur, with her hands stuffed into a muff of the same materials, Jasmine left the warmth of the château for the snowy courtyard. Solange leaned from the door of an ancient berlin and held out a hand to help her up.

"Is this the best coach available?" she asked the coachman who held the door open.

Luc shrugged his shoulders. With one gloved finger, he pulled away the scarf which covered his mouth. "It was the only one which had not been used in a while, Madame la Marquise. I was afraid to use another—Monsieur le Marquis might have decided to use it and then your baggage would have been discovered."

"All right, then. Let us get underway. We will never make it to Paris before nightfall as it is."

Helping her into the coach, Luc slammed the door and climbed up onto the box. With a crack of his long coach whip, he slapped the reins and the six horses started off.

Jasmine felt the coach lurch as it started out and she held her breath. She heard the clanking as the grille was raised in the gateway. As they passed beneath the spiked bottom of the raised grille, she exhaled in a long hiss of steam.

"At last," she whispered. "At last!"

"I beg your pardon, Madame?" Solange said from across the coach.

Jasmine waved a hand. "Nothing, nothing. I am merely delighted to be leaving Saint-Antoine. Soon we will be in Paris. Won't that be marvelous?"

"It will be!" Solange agreed. "Madame la Marquise de Saint-Antoine and Madame la Comtesse d'Auligny in Paris!"

Jasmine laughed. "Well, Madame la Comtesse d'Auligny, why don't you come to this side of the coach and share my lap robe? I've a feeling we'll need all the warmth we can get before we get to Paris!"

Solange moved to the other side of the bumping coach and slipped beneath the wolf-skin and velvet lap robe. As they reached the bottom of the hill and drove through the small town of Saint-Antoine, they passed the cathedral, whose magnificent windows were ablaze with light. Jasmine saw the black coach which had taken the Marquis and Isabeau to Mass and watched it until they were out of sight.

"Is something wrong, Madame?" Solange asked.

Jasmine shook her head. "No, Solange, nothing.

Nothing at all. At least nothing that will not be cured by our arrival at the Hôtel de Mareteleur!''

But, as the berlin rolled on through the tiny town and into the forest beyond, Jasmine felt an unexplainable shudder of apprehension. As a sudden chill ran up her spine, she burrowed farther under the fur-lined robe and dug her fingers into the soft fur lining of her velvet muff. In a pocket inside, she had placed the leather case from Barrett and she fingered it lovingly as though it were a kind of talisman that could protect her from harm.

Chapter 15

Jasmine started from a fitful sleep as the coach bumped
to a halt. The vehicle swayed as Luc climbed down from
the box and came to the door.

"Why have we stopped?" she demanded.

He pulled his scarf from in front of his mouth. "It's
getting very dark, Madame, we should stop at the inn in
the next town."

"What is the next town?"

"Sommeville."

"Is that near Paris?"

"It would take another two hours at least to reach
Paris, Madame."

Jasmine pursed her lips. "It didn't take this long to
reach Saint-Antoine from Paris."

"The roads weren't covered with snow then either,"
Solange pointed out.

"I suppose that's true. Can't you drive in the dark,
Luc? The moon is very bright."

Luc shook his head. "It is difficult to see the edge of
the road now because of the snow. When the darkness is

complete . . ." He shrugged.

Jasmine shivered as a gust of wind blew snow from the trees into the coach. "Oh, very well, if the inn in Sommeville looks habitable we will stop for the night."

The Golden Griffin lay just without the limits of the village of Sommeville. As the berlin turned into its courtyard, Jasmine realized that she was eager to be inside a warm room rather than half-frozen in the rattletrap coach.

Climbing off the box, Luc went into the inn to discover whether or not it was a proper place for Jasmine to spend the night. He returned after a short while with the innkeeper.

Dressed in a sleeveless waistcoat of blue and white stipes over a white cotton shirt, the rotund innkeeper rubbed his hands over his arms. His long white apron covered breeches of grey and, as he stamped his feet, snow covered his black leather shoes and caked in the steel buckles.

"Madame la Marquis?" he said. "I am Renard Brousseau. Welcome to my inn."

"Thank you, Monsieur Brousseau. Do you have rooms for me and accommodations for my maidservant and coachman?"

"Indeed I do, Madame la Marquise, indeed I do! Please, come inside."

Giving the innkeeper her hand, Jasmine climbed down from the berlin and followed him into the inn. She turned in the doorway and saw Solange standing beside the coach.

"Solange, are you coming?"

"Yes, Madame."

"Luc? Please bring my trunks inside. I don't care to

have them left in the coach overnight.''

Luc tipped his black tricorne. ''Right away, Madame la Marquise.''

The inn seemed clean and pleasant as Monsieur Brousseau led her into the dining room.

''It's very quiet, Monsieur Brousseau, do you have a tap room?''

''I do, Madame la Marquise. But it is nearly empty tonight—most of the people of Sommeville have gone to Beauvais for Mass in the cathedral there.''

''Ah, yes, this is Christmas.''

''Yes. My wife has gone with my son and his family. Will you excuse me now, Madame? I will set someone to building a fire in your rooms. May I get you something to eat or drink while you wait?''

''Anything warm, Monsieur Brousseau. Some warmed wine, perhaps. And pastry—do you have any pastry?''

''I believe so, Madame. Will you excuse me? I will return shortly.''

Jasmine nodded and, while the innkeeper went to see to the rooms, she and Solange went to the fireplace where a roaring fire did little to warm much of the room.

A rather shabby armchair faced the fire and, after draping her pelisse over a table, Jasmine sank into its softness with a sigh.

''Oh, Solange, I thought I would never sit down again!'' she said as the maidservant sat on a footstool near the armchaim. ''I wish Luc could have found a coach with a little more padding on the seats!''

Solange nodded as she looked around the room. The dark paneling of the walls and heavy, old-fashioned furnishings caused her to wrinkle her nose. ''I wish Luc could have found a better inn!'' she sniffed.

''What is wrong with this inn? Monsieur Brousseau

seems very nice. The inn seems clean."

"Still, after the château . . ."

Jasmine laughed. "You know, Solange, you are beginning to sound like a real aristrocrat! You are beginning to sound like the Comtesse d'Auligny."

Solange pouted a little. "You should not have told Monsieur Brousseau that I was your maidservant. We could have fooled him."

A young maid came to Jasmine and, with a pretty curtsy, handed her a large mug of hot mulled wine.

She sipped it and sighed at the feeling of delicious warmth it produced. Solange accepted a mug with a haughty nod of her head.

"To what purpose?" Jasmine asked when the maid had gone.

"Pardon?"

"I said, to what purpose should we have fooled Monsieur Brousseau?"

"What difference would it have made? He is merely a peasant—a stupid innkeeper."

Jasmine sipped her wine thoughtfully and smiled as the maid returned with a dish of pastry.

"May I remind you, Solange, that you are not actually the Comtesse d'Auligny? You are no better than Monsieur Brousseau."

Solange's glare was murderous. "Of course, Madame, just as you say." She swallowed the last of her wine and stood. "If you will excuse me, Madame la Marquise, I will go to your rooms and see that everything is ready for you to retire."

Jasmine dismissed her with a wave of her hand and then stared into the crackling fire wondering what she had done to create such an attitude in the maidservant.

The suite to which she had been shown consisted of two rooms—a salon and a bedchamber. Monsieur Brousseau was quick to point out that it was the best suite in the inn and had recently been completely refurbished. In fact, she had to admit, they were handsome rooms. The salon was paneled in white with trimming of pale pink and the bedchamber was pale green with trimming of emerald green. In both rooms the furnishings were of dubious quality but fashionable design. The hangings in both rooms and on the fourposter in the bedchamber were of moreen, an imitation watered silk.

"I hope you will find these rooms satisfactory, Madame la Marquise," he said eagerly.

"They are very nice," Jasmine assured him.

"I have given your coachman a room over the stables." He looked at the two large trunks on the floor of the salon. "Would you like these brought into the bedchamber?"

"No, they will be fine, Monsieur Brousseau. Anything I require can be brought from here."

"Very good, Madame la Marquise. Good night, Madame. If you require anything . . ."

Jasmine nodded. "I will send for you. But I warn you, Monsieur, I will be famished in the morning. I hope your dining room will be open in spite of the holidays."

"Oh, yes, Madame; of course, Madame. My wife will be back from Beauvais tomorrow. She is an excellent cook."

Folding his bulk nearly in half, Monsieur Brousseau made her a courtly blow. Suddenly he grasped her hand in his beefy red one and kissed it making a loud, smacking sound. With a delighted smile he turned and left the room.

As the door closed behind him, Jasmine smiled. She

was glad Solange had not seen the incident—Monsieur Brousseau was a kind, charming man and she would not have liked to see him ridiculed.

"Solange?" She went into the bedchamber to see if the maidservant had taken her night attire from the trunk and warmed it by the fire in the bedchamber.

"I am here, Madame." The maidservant replied from the bedchamber. There was a frostiness in her voice that had not existed there before.

She is getting entirely too enamoured of her role as the Comtesse d'Auligny, Jasmine thought. She seems to really believe she has been transformed into Madame de Pompadour herself.

"Help me undress, Solange. I believe I will go to bed now."

While Jasmine unhooked the front of her gown, Solange stepped behind her and began unpinning her hair. "If you don't mind, Madame," she said as Jasmine stepped out of the gown, "I will sleep on the sofa in the salon tonight."

"If you want to," Jasmine agreed with a shrug. "But it will be warmer in here. The fireplace in the salon smokes and is rather too far from the sofa."

"I would rather, Madame."

While Solange held Jasmine's nightgown before the fire to warm it, Jasmine unbuckled her garters and rolled her stockings off. She raised her arms above her head and leaned over to allow Solange to pull the loose gown over her. Taking Jasmine's garters, stockings and shoes, she made as if to take the gown and petticoats to the salon.

"Leave them, Solange," Jasmine said. "I want them warm in the morning."

"As you say, Madame la Marquise," Solange replied coolly. With a deep curtsy, she left the bedchamber for her bed on the sofa of the salon.

Casting a dismayed look after her, Jasmine climbed into the bed and pulled the coverlet up under her chin. If Solange was going to behave so irksomely she might have to dismiss her when they reached Paris.

It would be a shame for Solange was a good maidservant who did her work well. But if she was going to effect such haughty airs and behave with such total disregard for their respective ranks she could not expect to remain in anyone's service for long.

A gust of wind whistled beneath the edge of the window sash and Jasmine snuggled further beneath the warmed coverlet. It would be good to reach Paris in the morning, she told herself. It would be good to return to her own room in the Hôtel de Mareteleur. Most of all, she told herself with a smile, it would be good to escape from the arrogance of the counterfeit Comtesse in the salon and into the gentle, quiet company of her former maidservant, Claudette.

Jasmine shivered as she sat up in the wide bed. A weak winter sun was peeking through gray clouds and the icicles sparkled on the eaves of the inn. The fire in the fireplace of the bedchamber had died and Jasmine's teeth chattered as she climbed out of bed and hopped from one foot to the other across the room.

"Solange!" she called, her breath making puffs of white steam in the cold room. "Solange! Get someone to build up the fire in here and please find my fur-lined mules in the smaller trunk!"

She tiptoed to the fireplace and poked at the dying embers. She looked toward the salon door but there was no sign of the maidservant.

"Solange!" she called again, wrapping herself in her

166

fur-lined pelisse. "Did you hear me?"

There was no sound and, preparing to give the tardy servant a good dressing-down, Jasmine crossed the room and wrenched open the door.

But the salon was empty. There was no sign of Solange and even the two trunks containing her belongings were nowhere to be seen.

She tugged the bell rope and waited, rubbing one foot against the other, until Monsieur Brousseau arrived.

"Good morning, Madame la Marquise," he said with a bright smile. "My, it is cold in here. Let me start the fire for you."

Following the stout innkeeper into the bedchamber, Jasmine watched him deftly start a crackling fire in the fireplace.

"Monsieur Brousseau," she said, sitting on a sofa and drawing her freezing feet up into the relative warmth of her pelisse, "have you seen my maidservant this morning?"

"Why, yes, Madame," he replied, dusting his hands on his apron. "I saw her early this morning—barely after dawn. She and your coachman loaded your trunks into the coach and left."

"Left!" Jasmine was stunned. "What do you mean they left? What did they say?"

"They said . . . that is . . . actually, Madame, their story was a bit odd."

"What was their story?"

"Your maidservant said she was not actually your maidservant."

Jasmine groaned. "She didn't tell you that she was the Comtesse d'Auligny, did she?"

Monsieur Brousseau nodded. "Yes, Madame, that is exactly what she told me. She said she was your sister."

He started as Jasmine gasped and hurried on: "She said you were taking her to Paris to marry an ancient Duc or something. She said she and the coachman were in love and were going to elope."

"She and Luc have left! They have taken my belongings and left!"

Monsieur Brousseau seemed puzzled by her anger. "She said you would take the diligence to Paris."

"The diligence! How am I to take the diligence when she has taken all my money!"

"All your money? But, Madame la Marquise, the Comtesse said you would pay for the night's lodging."

"First of all, Monsieur Brousseau, she is not a Comtesse! And, second of all, I cannot pay for the lodging when I haven't any money."

The innkeeper seemed troubled. "This is a serious matter, Madame. Have you no jewels? I will accept jewels."

"I have no jewels. They were in my baggage."

"What of a wedding ring? Surely a Marquise must have a very fine wedding ring."

She thrust her bare hand toward him. "I have a beautiful, diamond-studded band, Monsieur, but, fearing highwaymen, I left it in the false bottom of my trunk."

Renard Brousseau's florid face lost its cheery subservience. "You are married but have no wedding band. Your sister is not your sister. The Comtesse d'Auligny is not a comtesse but a maidservant. You are a marquise but have no money. Or are you a marquise? There have been many lies told here, Madame Whoever-you-may-be. I don't know what to believe, but I do know one thing. I don't run this inn for charity. I expect to be paid for lodging."

"I will pay you, Monsieur Brousseau. Once I get to

Paris, I will send a messenger back with . . ."

"Heigh ho, my girl!" he cried. "Do you think I'm a complete fool? You will not leave until your debt is paid. If you try to leave before I have any money, I will set the constables after you and see you clapped into jail."

"But, Monsieur Brousseau . . ."

"Enough. What is your name, girl?"

"Jasmine."

He laughed. "Jasmine! Indeed! Very well, Jasmine, dress yourself and present yourself downstairs. We will find work for you to do."

"Work?"

"Yes! Work! You will do an honest day's work for your lodging, I promise you that! Now, dress yourself. I do not run the kind of inn where young women earn their keep by lolling about in their nightclothes all day."

Jasmine stared after him in alarm. "But . . . but . . ."

Monsieur Brousseau waved a hand at her. "Hurry, girl. If you are not downstairs soon, you will miss the morning meal. You won't eat again until evening so I'd advise you to hurry!"

As the door closed behind him, Jasmine threw off her pelisse and pulled the nightdress over her head. Her stomach, which had had nothing in it except pastry and hot, mulled wine for almost twenty-four hours, was growling loudly. She could not afford to miss breakfast.

Hurriedly she dressed herself, her cold fingers fumbling with the hooks of her gown. She felt the knots of apprehension start within her. She'd gone from Marquise to tavern wench in one night and she was not anxious to begin her new occupation.

Chapter 16

"I want to thank you, Madame Brousseau, for lending me these clothes," Jasmine said as she tugged on the laces which fastened the black corset-bodice over her white cotton shift. A white apron covered the front of her striped cotton skirt and the toes of her black leather shoes peeked from beneath the hem. Her auburn hair was barely visible, the majority of it being coiled inside a white mob-cap, and a white cotton fichu filled in most of the low, wide décollectage of the shift.

"Never mind your thanks, Marquise," Madame Brousseau said. "Their cost will be added to your bill. I couldn't have a fine lady in velvet and lace scrubbin' my floors, you know." The plump innkeeper's wife looked Jasmine over with a critical eye. "Though you are pretty enough to be a marquise. You've good breedin', that's clear. I expect that's why Renard was taken in by your story. He ever did have an eye for a handsome woman. And that's somethin' else—don't try to charm your way out of your bill. Renard might well be easy enough for you to get around, but it's I who does the books around here and I won't be cheated of a sou. Do you understand me?"

"Yes, Madame Brousseau. But as I was telling your husband, my grandmother—the Marquise de Mareteleur, would be happy to give you the money . . ."

Madame Brousseau waved a silencing hand. "Now your grandmother's a Marquise too, eh? And who's your great-uncle? The King? Or perhaps you're Madame de Pompadour's favorite niece?"

"Of course I'm not!" Jasmine insisted. "But I did meet her great-aunt, Madame Giroux, once."

Agnes Brousseau burst out with a great guffaw. "You're a treat, Marquise! I'll give you that! Next you'll be tellin' me you're the long-lost bastard child of the Cardinal de la Rochefocauld. But never mind, enough of your stories—there's work to be done. You can come up here later and move your things to room number eight. It is usually rented out but business is slow this time of year."

"Why can't I stay in these rooms if business is so slow?" Jasmine asked.

"You want to keep the best suite in the inn? Fine! And every day you stay I will add three louis to your bill."

"Three louis!"

"Take it or leave it, Marquise."

Jasmine grimaced. "Where is number eight?"

Madame Brousseau laughed. "I'll send Vignette up with you later. The room is upstairs."

"Upstairs! In the attic?"

"Not exactly Versailles," Madame Brousseau admitted, "but a penniless Marquise is no greater guest at an inn than is a beggar from the gutters." She gave Jasmine a good swat on the backside. "Come now, you won't pay off your bill standin' here talkin'."

Jasmine scooted away as Vignette slopped another bucket of water on the taproom floor.

"Whew! It is almost time for supper?" she asked the buxom, black-haired Vignette.

Joining her on the floor, Vignette took a brush and started scrubbing the floor. "It's not near time, Marquise. We've still a good three hours."

Sitting back on her heels, Jasmine brushed a bead of perspiration from her nose. "I can do no more, Vignette. My hands are a mass of blisters."

"Haply Madame Brousseau will let you go into the kitchen and help with the cookin'."

"I don't know how to cook."

"You'd only have to peel vegetables."

"I've never peeled vegetables."

Vignette laughed as she moved the brush in a circle with a loud "whoosh, whoosh." "You're good at your story, Marquise, I'll give you that! You could almost make me believe that you're a real aristocrat!" She shrugged. "If you can't peel vegetables, Monsieur Brousseau might let you serve drinks to the customers. There's usually a lot of 'em after supper."

Jasmine heard footsteps and hurriedly bent over and went to work with her brush. "That sounds easier than this!" she said, feeling one of her blisters break on the hard wooden brush.

"Oh, yes! It's easy work! The hard part comes in tryin' not to spill the drinks when one lout has his hand down your bodice and another has his up your skirt!"

Jasmine shuddered at the thought of some farmer's dirty hands on her skin. "I believe I'd rather learn to peel vegetables!"

172

With an aching back and hands rubbed raw by the scrub brush, Jasmine climbed the stairs to her room in the attic of the inn. She carried a pitcher of warm water for her evening ablutions. In the few days she'd been working at the inn she had learned that Monsieur Brousseau's tavern wenches did not ask for a warm bath before bed. She'd made the request on the first evening of her employment and, after a long moment of astounded silence, everyone within earshot, from Monsieur and Madame Brousseau to the last stragglers in the taproom, had burst into shouts of laughter.

"Marquise," Monsieur Brousseau said, wiping his eyes, "I ought to take a louis a day off your bill for the entertainment you provide!"

Jasmine blushed at the memory. Wincing, she plunged her hands into the basin of warm water. It was a mystery to her how she was ever going to pay her debt to the Brousseau's. Every day her room and meals were added to the bill and Madame Brousseau had shown her a ledger where her debt was added in one column while her payments were deducted in another. It had seemed that the debt column was lengthening rapidly while the payment column's progress was dishearteningly slow.

She hissed as the pain in her aching back overcame her. Her bed was an old one with threadbare hangings and lumps in the thin mattress. But it felt good to lie down—it felt good to close her eyes and relax, allowing the day's labors to drain from her knotted muscles.

A soft rapping sounded on the door. "Marquise?" It was Monsieur Brousseau. "Marquise? Are you awake?"

Groaning, Jasmine climbed out of the bed and went to the door.

"What is it, Monsieur Brousseau?" she asked through the door.

"Open the door, Marquise, I need to talk to you."

"One moment, please, Monsieur."

Going to the small armoire, she took out her pelisse and pulled it around herself to cover the thin silk of her nightdress. "I'm coming, Monsieur!" she called as he rapped on the door once again.

She opened the door a crack and saw Monsieur Brousseau standing in the hallway. His portly body was wrapped in a green dressing gown with a linen nightcap askew on his head.

"What is it, Monsieur Brousseau?"

He shifted from one leather slippered foot to the other in the cold hallway. "Could I not come into your room, Marquise?" he asked, eyeing the fire in the small fireplace.

"I do not think that would be wise, Monsieur," she said. "Madame Brousseau . . ."

His eyes twinkled. "Madame Brousseau is sound asleep in our bed downstairs. You need have no worries about her."

"Still . . ."

He rolled his eyes. "Very well, Marquise, if you're no more desire to hear what I have to say than that . . ."

Still distrusting him, Jasmine stepped out into the hallway. With one hand behind her on the doorlatch, she raised an eyebrow. "Well, Monsieur?"

"None of your airs, Marquise. I've a proposition to make. I've a way for you to get out of your dilemma without spending your days on your hands and knees."

"Oh? And what would that be?"

Monsieur Brousseau smiled. "I think you've an idea, Marquise. You're a damned pretty woman and I'm not braggin' when I tell you I've had no complaints from women I've bedded.''

Jasmine's mouth dropped open. ''Are you . . . are you actually suggesting that I become your mistress to pay off a five-louis debt? I'm not one of Sommeville's two-franc whores, you know!''

''Oh, no? And what is your price, Marquise? How much do you think I could get for you? I would be within my rights, you know, to auction you off to any man in the taproom who is willing to pay your debt.'' His smile turned into an evil leer. ''Of course I doubt any one man would have the money to pay the entire debt—more likely a dozen of 'em would pool a few livres each for a turn with you.''

Jasmine pressed herself against the door, trying to put as much distance as possible between them. ''You wouldn't . . .''

He shrugged. ''Haply I might—then again I might not. Better to bed with one old innkeeper than with a dozen farmers with a month's dirt under their fingernails and a year's manure caked on their boots, wouldn't you say? Think about it, Marquise. I'll abide by your decision and, to prove what a good sort I am, I will even provide you with that hot bath you've been talking about should you choose the auction. After all—you'd need it. I doubt there's more than a handful of the lot of 'em who're not crawling with lice.''

With a shudder, Jasmine depressed the latch and stumbled backward into her room. She started to close the door but Monsieur Brousseau caught it and held it open.

''Think carefully, Marquise. I don't enjoy your looking at me as though I were not fit to breathe the same air as you. I'm not squeamish but I wouldn't want to be a woman at the hands of a drunken mob of men who've never been within spitting distance of a woman like you. Men who have paid hard-earned money for the privilege of using you as they pleased.'' He stuck his face close to hers. ''They will want their money's worth, Marquise, I guarantee you that!''

As he moved away, Jasmine slammed the door and twisted the key in the lock. She was trembling with fear and a knot of nausea was forming in the pit of her stomach.

She climbed back into bed and pulled the worn coverlet tightly around herself. She had no money—her debt was decreasing by only a few livres a day. Would she be driven to admitting Monsieur Brousseau to her bed? She shuddered at the thought. But the mere suggestion of being at the mercy of the men she saw in the taproom made the bile rise in her throat.

She lay awake long after Monsieur Brousseau was sleeping soundly in his bed. When at last she did fall asleep, it was a troubled slumber filled with frightening dreams.

Jasmine started as she felt a sharp pinch through her skirt and petticoat. Turning, she found Monsieur Brousseau standing behind her.

''Well, Marquise?'' he said. ''Have you decided?''

She shook her head. ''No, Monsieur, I have not. You must give me more time.''

''I will give you until tomorrow. If you have not made up your mind to accept me by tomorrow morning—I shall offer you at auction in the taproom tomorrow night.''

''Monsieur Brousseau, I beg of you . . .''

''Pleading will do you no good, my pretty aristocrat.

Now, I want you to go to the taproom and help Avice serve the drinks. That way you will have a better idea of your choices.''

''But Madame Brousseau told me to finish scrubbing these pots.''

Renard Brousseau took the pot and scrub brush from her and slammed them onto the sideboard. ''Go! Now! I am still the master here!''

Taking her by the shoulder, the innkeeper propelled her to the door and the crowded taproom and pushed her inside.

''My friends!'' he called above the hum of conversation in the room. ''My friends! We've a new wench here —we call her the Marquise. A worthy title, is it not?''

Jasmine raised her chin as the men turned to stare at her. She heard their appraising comments and stepped aside as a large, hairy man in a farmer's long linen smock and brown felt hat reached toward her.

''She's a handsome piece of goods, Renard,'' he said loudly, eliciting laughter from his neighbors. ''Is she as handsome in the dark?''

Jasmine felt the hot blush rising into her cheeks. As Renard gave her a sharp slap that propelled her across the room, she felt the eager hands of the men grasping her.

''If she doesn't behave herself,'' Renard Brousseau called, ''you may have a chance to find out for yourself!''

The hairy man chortled and his neighbor clapped him on the back.

As Jasmine stumbled toward the bar at the rear of the dimly lit room, she tried in vain to escape the hands of the men at the long wooden tables. By the time she reached the bar it seemed there was not a part of her which had not been pinched, prodded, or poked.

Avice, a plump blonde who worked solely in the taproom because the men enjoyed her cheery laughter and pliant nature, leaned toward Jasmine.

"Well, Marquise? How do you like the taproom? The gentlemen seem to have taken a fancy to you!"

Jasmine fought to retain her haughty disdain. "I hate it here! And any resemblance between those savages and gentlemen is beyond my comprehension!"

Avice laughed and poured a tall mug of ale. "I miss about half of whatever you say, Marquise," she said with a shake of her head. "You do have some big words in your mouth. Here," she shoved the mug toward her, "take this to Hugues Aubel over there."

"Which one is he?"

Avice nodded toward a near table. Following her gaze, Jasmine saw a young man with disheveled hair flowing to his shoulders and a rumpled, long-tailed coat. His woolen breeches were stained and dirty and his waistcoat was missing most of its buttons.

Reluctantly, Jasmine took the mug and carried it to him. Setting it down before him, she moved away but her arm was caught in his grasp. He pulled her down onto the bench beside him.

"Don't be in such a hurry, Marquise," he breathed into her ear. He didn't seem to notice the wrinkle of her nose as she smelled the aroma of stale ale and sweat which surrounded him. He drank deeply of the ale and wiped his mouth on the back of his grimy hand.

Jasmine pulled away from him but his arm was tight around her waist. As she strained against the restraining arm, his calloused hand moved up toward the swell of her breast beneath her corset-bodice.

He smiled at her discomfiture. "Yes, you're a comely chit—no question about it. Renard told me you're in debt to him." He took another mouthful of the ale. "He told me he's of a mind to sell you for your debt. I've a mind to pay your debt and take you for myself.'' He laughed as her distaste showed plainly in her face. ''Yes, you're a dainty one, all right. I'm not likely to find a woman like you in my bed again. Here, girl, give us a kiss.''

He pressed his lips to hers and she struggled to free herself from his grasp. When at last she broke away, she gagged and ran behind the bar.

The men in the taproom laughed loudly and called their compliments to Hugues Abel. Hugues, obviously pleased with himself, waved one beefy hand.

Avice held a glass of ale out to Jasmine who sat on a bench behind the bar.

''Drink this, Marquise. It helps to be as drunk as they are.'' She watched while Jasmine choked down the golden ale. ''Let me give you a piece of advice,'' she said softly. ''Broussneau has given you until tomorrow to make up your mind. When tomorrow comes, welcome him into your bed. Wouldn't one man who admires you be better than a dozen like Hugues who know only that they have the use of a woman who, if nothing else, looks like she could be one of the titled sluts who pass through and toss them a sou for licking their boots?''

Jasmine sighed miserably. ''There must be another way! There must be!''

''Listen to me!'' Avice sat beside her and shook her by the arm. ''Take Brousseau! I know him! I have been in your shoes, Marquise. At worst it will last only a few minutes—at best old Brousseau will not be able to do you any harm, or himself any good!''

''You have slept with Brousseau?''

The plump maidservant shrugged. ''Every woman Brousseau hires is obliged to service him. It is his way.''

"Why? Can you not refuse?"

"Refuse? Bedding with Brousseau is a small price to pay for a roof over your head and food in your belly! Sometimes I really believe you are an aristo, Marquise. You don't know any more about life than any one of them."

The shouts of the men demanding service were growing louder and Avice patted her shoulder.

"Come, Marquise, we'd better get to work." She smiled and tucked a strand of Jasmine's hair into her cap. "Think about what I've said—will you?"

Jasmine nodded glumly. "I will, Avice. I will."

Chapter 17

"Marquise! Marquise! Wake up!" Madame Brousseau shook Jasmine roughly. "Wake up!"

"What? What is it?" Jasmine mumbled.

Opening her eyes, Jasmine saw that it was still dark in her attic room. A candle burned on a little table and the fire was burning brightly. Shivering a little, she sat up and squinted toward Madame Brousseau.

"What is wrong, Madame? Is it morning already?"

"No, you dolt!" the innkeeper's wife growled. "It is not morning. You've only been in bed an hour! A diligence has broken down outside and we need this room. Get up and straighten the bed."

Confused, Jasmine slid from beneath the coverlet. "But Madame Brousseau, where will I go?"

"Go to Avice's room. She will let you sleep with her."

"I'm paying for this room, you know," she snarled as she pulled her pelisse around her shoulders.

"I am charging you five sous a night for this room, Marquise," Madame Brousseau reminded her. "The gentleman waiting in the hall is paying me ten sous for tonight. Unless you are willing to have me add ten sous to your debt tomorrow, you had better finish making the bed and get out!''

Jasmine glared at the avaricious woman but she knew she could not afford to add unnecessarily to the money she owed the Brousseau. Without a word, she started to straighten the bed.

"Hurry with it," Agnes Brousseau urged. "I have to see to the others. When you are finished with the bed, put some more wood on the fire and then show the gentlemen in."

"Yes, Madame," Jasmine sighed.

As she pulled the coverlet over the freshly plumped pillow, Jasmine heard Madame Brousseau speaking to the gentleman who was waiting for her bed.

"She'll have the room ready for you presently, Monsieur . . . er . . . Monsieur . . ."

"De Seingalt, Signora," a heavily accented masculine voice replied. "I am Giovanni Giacomo Casanova— Chevalier de Seingalt."

"Just as you say, Monseigneur," Madame Brousseau agreed, apparently loath to try and pronounce the name. "Your room will be ready for you as soon as the Marquise is finished making the bed."

Madame Brousseau's footsteps thudded away into silence as she went to supervise the accommodations of the other stranded travelers. Jasmine knelt before the fire and prodded the newly added logs to those already burning. She stopped as she felt a pair of eyes upon her and looked over her shoulder.

The man who stood in the doorway was tall, slender and swarthy. A white powdered wig contrasted with his suit and black velvet and a waistcoat of white satin embroidered with black showed from beneath a snowy white stock. A small leather-bound trunk sat at his feet.

"You are the Marquise Signora Brousseau was speaking of?" he asked.

Jasmine nodded. "And you are the Chevalier de Seingalt?"

"Yes." He crossed the room and tossed his heavy coat and tricorne on a chair. Sitting on the sofa, he tugged off his boots. "I am the Chevalier de Seingalt. I rather like the title—I bestowed it upon myself, you know. Who bestowed the title Marquise on you, my angel? Some admirer?"

"Actually, it was bestowed upon me by my husband— the Marquis."

"He should have settled for Chevalier or Comte at the most. The law has a way of catching up with too ambitious imposters."

Jasmine frowned and drew her pelisse more tightly about herself. "You're just like them!" she cried. "You don't believe me either! But I am a Marquise! I am! And I don't care if you believe me—it is true!"

He seemed surprised by her outburst but, as she would have stormed from the room, he caught her wrist and drew her down onto the sofa beside him.

"I believe you," he said softly, his black eyes looking deeply into her gray-green ones.

"No, you don't," she said miserably. "No one does. If Solange had not stolen everything I had I would be in Paris now with my grandmother."

"And who is Solange?"

"My maidservant."

"And why did she steal everything you had?"

"Because she is going to go to Paris and impersonate a Comtesse."

"You were traveling to Paris from where?"

Jasmine looked up suspiciously but the gentleman's eyes seemed alight with kind interest. "From Saint-Antoine—my husband is the Marquise de Saint-Antoine."

"Why was he not here to protect you?"

Jasmine dropped her eyes. "I was running away from him." She looked up and found him smiling. "Do not laugh at me, Monsieur. It isn't funny!"

"I was not laughing at you," he assured her. "I only find it amusing that people are the same everywhere. I have been to many different places, from Venice, where I was born, to Constantinople, and I have found that husbands and wives should be separated after the wedding night and reunited on their fiftieth anniversary."

"Better yet," Jasmine corrected, "they should never marry at all."

"But if they never married, who would inherit great titles and estates?"

"Oh, someone will ever be near to relieve a man of his riches."

He smiled. "True, true. But tell me, my adorable Marquise, why are you working in the inn?"

"Monsieur Brousseau will not allow me to leave until my debt is paid. He says . . ." She lowered her eyes and felt a blush rise in her cheeks. "He says I must become his mistress or he will auction me to the men in the taproom for the money."

Casanova touched her cheek with a gentle finger. "He would not do that!"

"He insists he would."

"He says that only to frighten you into taking him into your bed. Do you think he would stand by and let other men have you? If he wants you badly enough to threaten you, he would not be able to see you given into the hands of another; not even if it meant your debt would be paid.''

Jasmine shuddered. ''I don't want him to touch me.''

''I have seen Monsieur Brousseau,'' he said with a chuckle. ''I cannot fault you in your distress.''

Jasmine smiled into the deep, black eyes which sat above an aquiline nose and a full-lipped mouth. ''You understand,'' she said in surprise. Remembering herself, she rose from the sofa. ''If you will excuse me, Monsieur, I will leave you to your room and your rest.''

''It grieves me to see you put out of your own room for my sake,'' he said.

She shrugged. ''You are a paying customer—I am merely a lowly tavern wench.''

He laughed and took her hand. She winced as he raised it to kiss and he turned it over. The soft skin of her palm was reddened and dotted with blisters. Some were broken, some were not, but all were red and angry looking.

''Poor little angel, they have hurt you.'' He pressed a kiss into the painful flesh of her palm. ''Sit down—don't leave me. I would know more about you.''

''But you must be tired after traveling,'' she said, hoping he would say he was not.

''Shall I tell you a secret? My traveling companions are as boring as a maiden aunt's nights! I slept all the way from St. Dizier. So you see, I am not tired in the least! Now, will you stay? It has been a long time since I have had a beautiful lady to talk with.''

Jasmine felt herself falling beneath the spell of his charm and she sat down. ''For a little while, perhaps,'' she agreed demurely.

''Excellent! But first, I believe I will make use of that

screen in the corner to change my clothes.''

Leaving the sofa, he took the small trunk from beside the bed and went behind a battered lacquered screen which stood in the corner near the bed. While Jasmine watched, he removed his powdered wig to reval a head of shining black hair which he unfastened and allowed to fall around his shoulders.

''Tell me, my lovely Marquise, what is your name?''

''Jasmine.''

''Ah! Perfect! It fits you!''

Attired in a dressing gown of red and gold brocade, he returned to the sofa and sat beside her.

''So! Now we may become acquainted in comfort, eh? You must tell me everything about yourself.''

Jasmine stroked the worn velvet of the sofa, avoiding his eyes. ''I have told you everything, Monsieur.''

''Giacomo,'' he corrected. ''Or, if you prefer since we are in France, Jacques.''

''Giacomo then; it suits you better. But I have told you everything there is to know about myself.''

''Alas!'' he cried. ''You wound me to the quick, cruelest girl!''

''But, Monsieur—Giacomo—what would you want to know about me?''

''Everything! You do not love your husband, else you would not have fled from him. What sort of man is he?''

Jasmine grimaced. ''He is a soldier.''

Casanova nodded sympathetically. ''And has no time to romance a beautiful young woman?''

''He has time if he wishes; he has time for my mother!''

''Is he an old man or has he merely a taste for matrons?''

''He is more than thirty years my senior.''

"Poor darling! And have you never known true love?"

Jasmine looked past him toward the orange flames in the fireplace. "Oh, yes," she replied quietly. "But he was not a Frenchman and not a nobleman—in short, he was everything my mother did not want in a husband for me."

"And where is he now, this love of yours?"

"He is in Virginia. He lives on a plantation called Paxton Hall near my father's home—Belle Glade."

"In America! I will have to go there someday if all the ladies are as beautiful as you."

Jasmine giggled at his flattery but her smile turned to a yawn. "Pardon me, Giacomo, it is only . . ."

"Hush, my beauty, it is I who should beg your forgiveness! Monsieur Brousseau makes you work until your pretty little hands are raw and blistered. You must be sleepy, and I am keeping you awake. I will let you go to your rest but first, you must allow me to treat your hands."

"Are you a doctor?"

"Not by profession, no. But I have some skill in the art of keeping feminine skin soft and delicate."

He went to his trunk and returned with a small pot. "Hold out your hands now." She complied and he began to apply a pink lotion which smelled delicious.

"What's in it?" she asked as she watched his long, thin fingers gently massaging the lotion into the broken flesh of her palms.

"That is my secret. Suffice it to say that I learned of it while I was a guest of Yusuf Ali, a very rich man in Constantinople. This lotion is prepared to anoint the bodies of houris. Yusulf Ali keeps a most impressive harem."

"A harem!" Jasmine was impressed. "And tell me,

Giacomo Casanova, how well acquainted with these houris were you?''

His smile was fond. ''I was most generously treated. In fact, Yusuf Ali offered me the hand of his favorite daughter in marriage.''

''And why did you not accept?''

''I would have had to become a Moslem. I may be a poor Christian, but I've no great wish to change.''

''But then you . . .'' Jasmine stopped as another yawn overtook her.

''Enough! Enough!'' he insisted. ''You must sleep.''

''Yes,'' Jasmine agreed sadly. ''I must go and find Avice's room.''

''You are welcome to spend the night here, dearest Marquise.''

Jasmine looked at him suspiciously. ''Monsieur de Seingalt . . .'' she began sternly.

His expression was pained. ''How cruel you are! Do you really think I am the kind of man who would extend my hospitality to a lovely woman merely in order that I may relieve her of her virtue?'' He stood and went to lean on the mantel with his back to her. ''Go then, heartless girl, if your opinion of me is so low!''

Jasmine hesitated and then went to him. ''I'm sorry, Giacomo,'' she said softly. ''I did not mean to accuse you of anything. I will stay here.''

He turned with a smile. ''Splendid! But, since you cannot trust me completely, I will take a pillow and quilt to the sofa.''

''Oh, that wouldn't be right; you are the guest. You must sleep in the bed. I will sleep on the sofa.''

His smile faded once again. ''I was right! You do not trust me! Cruel fate that I should find such beauty containing so pitiless a heart!''

"But I do trust you, Giacomo," she hastened to assure him. "I swear I do!"

Catching her hands, he covered their backs with kisses. "I knew it! I knew it! Come then, let us go to our slumber."

The lone candle was extinguished and the room was lit only by the flickering light of the fire as Jasmine cast aside her pelisse and slid beneath the coverlet. On the opposite side of the bed, Casanova discarded his dressing gown and joined her.

"Are you sure you want me to stay here, Giacomo?" she asked.

He touched her cheek. "I have seldom been more sure of anything, my angel. Exquisite torture though it will be, my heart would break to see you walk out the door. Sleep now, sweet Jasmine."

Jasmine closed her eyes and it was not long before the labors of the previous day led her into an exhausted slumber. Casanova lay beside her. He had not lied when he had told her it would be torture for him to lay with her and not taste the luscious pleasures she seemed to promise. But he knew it would endear him to her—it would make her eventual surrender more complete. Taking care not to wake her, he slipped from the bed and went to his trunk. Extracting a leather pouch, he weighed the hundred sequins it contained. Approximately equal to forty-five French louis d'or, it represented all the money he possessed. He wondered what Jasmine's debt amounted to—could he afford to take her to Paris with him? He shrugged. She was a Marquise—surely she had access to at least a small estate. Surely she had family who missed her and would be willing to reimburse him for returning her. And, more importantly, surely she would be delighted to thank him for helping her to escape the lecherous desires of Monsieur Brousseau.

Replacing the leather pouch, he returned to the bed. Her body was warm against his and she snuggled against him in her sleep causing him the most unbearable torment. Perhaps, he thought, watching the rise and fall of her breasts beneath the thin silk of her nightdress, he would wait until he had sampled her charms before deciding whether to return her to her family. Involuntarily, one hand reached out to touch the gentle curve of her hip and, just in time, he withdrew it. Great heavens! he thought, as he tried to concentrate on something other than the woman sleeping beside him, it was going to be good when he did not have to play the good Samaritan any longer!

With a slight shiver, he moved a little away so that their bodies were not touching and tried to will himself to sleep.

Chapter 18

Jasmine awakened to the feeling of lips gently kissing her cheeks, forehead, eyelids and mouth.

"Stop!" she cried between giggles. "Stop!"

"You must get up," Casanova told her softly. "You must dress. The diligence will not wait forever."

"Oh, Giacomo," she said sadly, "don't remind me that you will soon be leaving. You have made me happier than I have been since I left Virginia."

Smiling cryptically, he took her hand and helped her out of the bed. Clad in brown velvet, he went to sit on the sofa where a small mirror had been propped on a battered table.

"What are you doing?" Jasmine asked as she ran a brush through her hair.

He grinned into the mirror revealing sparkling white teeth. "Cleaning my teeth."

"With what?" She went to the sofa and peered at him.

Holding the brush under her nose, he allowed her to smell the substance he was using.

"It smells like violets!"

"It is orrisroot. It comes from the stalks of irises."

Satisfied that his teeth were perfect, he reached for the powdered wig which lay on the table. "I detest this wig," he said as he drew it over his own black hair.

"Then why do you wear it? Your own hair is beautiful."

He turned his head to the right and left, making sure his own hair was invisible beneath the two horizontal ringlets on either side and the black-bowed queue in the back.

"As you may have noticed," he replied, "I have no valet or hairdresser with me. It would be impossible to dress my own hair properly."

Leaning back on the sofa, he examined her critically. "You really must dress, my angel," he told her, "the time for departure is drawing near."

Jasmine made a pretty moue. "Very well, Giacomo," she agreed.

Crossing the room, she stepped behind the screen but, instead of her tavern wench's garb, she found the black velvet gown in which she had arrived at the inn.

"Well?" Casanova stood leaning on the screen.

"What does this mean?" she asked.

With a laugh, he came around the screen and swung her into his arms. "It means that you need never see those old rags again! Oh, my angel, do you think I could ride away and leave you at the mercy of old Brousseau and the clods of his taproom? Could you imagine that I could be so brutal?"

Jasmine stared up at him in disbelief. "But . . . but, Giacomo! My debt!"

He spread his hands wide. "Has been paid!"

"You have paid my debt?" He nodded. "Then I am free to go?"

He consulted his watch. "Yes, but if you do not dress there will be no diligence for you to go in!"

With a cry of delight, she threw herself into his arms. He lifted her until their faces were level and she covered his swarthy face with kisses.

"Easy! Easy, my own darling! Else it will be my fault that we miss the diligence!" He pinched her bottom and set her on her feet. "Now, into your gown—we must hurry!"

Jasmine pulled her nightdress over her head and felt a delicious sense of voluptuousness as she heard his sharply indrawn breath. She pulled her chemise over her head and picked up her stockings and garters.

Casanova took them from her and bade her sit down on the stool behind the screen.

"I will be your maidservant, Madame," he offered, falling to one knee.

Jasmine laughed and held out her foot to him. With an expertness that made her suspect that he'd had a great deal of practice, Casanova slipped the silk stocking over her foot and rolled it up over her knee. Fastening the garter about her leg he bent and planted a light kiss on the soft skin of her thigh.

"Giacomo," she warned when he would have ventured further, "we must be ready for the diligence."

He sighed and looked up at her, his cheek resting on her knee. "You are right, sweet Jasmine, though I curse the barbarous Fates that make my heart bleed so." With another light kiss, he started on her other stocking.

When her stocking were at last in place, Jasmine stuck her feet into her shoes and held out her arms for

193

Casanova to lace her stays.

"They are loose, Giacomo," she complained. "Can't you draw them tighter?"

"No. You must have become thinner during your stay." He held her petticoats for her and then lowered her gown over her head.

"Even my gown is too lose," she pouted.

"Never mind. Once we get to Paris, you shall have a new wardrobe fit for a Queen!"

"Goodbye, Monsieur Brousseau!" Jasmine called from the window of the diligence. "Goodbye, Madame Brousseau! Goodbye, Avice! Goodbye, Vignette!"

Settling back against the seat, Jasmine nestled against Casanova, who smiled down at her. Her happiness seemed complete. She was going to Paris, away from her husband and away from Monsieur Brousseau. She would never scrub another floor, never serve another tankard of ale. And, above all, she hoped she would never have to stir from the side of the fascinating man who had been her rescuer.

Casanova helped Jasmine out of a fiacre in the courtyard of a handsome mansion in the Rue Croix des Petits Champs.

"Who lives here, Giacomo?" Jasmine asked while she waited for him to pay the driver.

"We do, my little seraph," he answered. "I sent word to the propriétaire that I would be arriving."

"How did you know who to notify?"

"I have been in Paris before. Several years ago. I have many friends in this marvelous city."

The grand front door to the hôtel opened and a tall, thin woman with greying hair drawn into a chignon atop her head bustled toward them.

"Jacques!" she cried. "Jacques! How good it is to see you! Welcome back to Paris! It has been so long!"

Casanova raised the woman's hands to his lips. "Indeed it has, dearest Madame Sauveur. Indeed it has. Too long. Have you reserved rooms for me?"

"But of course! I would throw another tenant into the street if it was the only way I could vacate a suite for you."

"You are too kind," he murmured modestly. "Madame, I would have you meet my companion." Taking her hand, he drew Jasmine forward. "This adorable creature is the Marquise de Saint-Antoine. I made her acquaintance during my journey and she will be my guest—at least until she chooses to seek out her family here in Paris."

Madame Sauveur's brown eyes slipped over Jasmine and she dropped her a shallow curtsy. "Welcome to my home, Madame la Marquise," she said coolly. Incredible as it seemed, the woman seemed annoyed at the presence of a young female in Casanova's presence.

"Thank you, Madame," Jasmine replied. "Giacomo told me you were an old friend of his."

Madame Sauveur's eyes narrowed slightly at the way Jasmine's voice caressed Casanova's name and at her stress on the term "old." She said nothing but turned her attention quickly to her more welcome guest.

"Come into the hôtel," she said. "It is too chilly to stand out here in the courtyard." Turning toward the hôtel, she slipped her arm through Casanova's and called loudly: "Cosme! Cosme!" A young man appeared in the doorway. "Come and bring our guest's trunks into the hôtel!"

The apartment to which Madame Sauveur led them consisted of four rooms—a drawing room furnished with elegant furniture which, if not of the best quality, was well crafted and handsome, a dining room in which a great chandelier hung over the table, a dressing room with two brocade upholstered chaise lounges, and a bedroom in which a great dome bed dominated the room.

"Oh, my!" Jasmine breathed as she entered the room whose walls were hung with scarlet silk.

The great bed, which required the presence of a set of bed steps on either side, had posters which sported carved vines and flowers. High atop the domed canopy of the bed, lovebirds reposed, carved of wood and painted realistic colors.

"It is very nice, Mathilde," Casanova said, removing his coat and tossing it over a chair. "Very nice, indeed."

"Thank you, Jacques," the landlady replied. But her eyes were looking past him toward Jasmine, who was sitting on a little velvet-covered stool before a brocade-draped dressing table on which gilded cherubs supported a mirror and a canopy above it.

Casanova, never loath to find a lady jealous of his attentions toward another, smiled at the naked resentment on the older woman's face. "Madame Sauveur?" he prompted. The look vanished and the lady smiled at him. "Mathilde," he continued, having regained her attention. "The little Marquise will require new gowns and the accompanying paraphernalia. Do you know of a good mantau-maker who would be able to oblige me immediately?"

"Of course," the landlady replied. "There is Madame Thibault. She is honest and does very good work."

"Would you be so kind as to summon her as soon as possible? I am interested in having Madame de Saint-Antoine's wardrobe replenished as soon as possible."

"Yes, Jacques."

The lady hesitated and Casanova looked over her

shoulder as Cosme entered the room followed by two other young men. Each bore a leather-bound trunk which they deposited in the center of the room and each bowed as Casanova tossed them a franc for their troubles.

"Will there be anything else?" she asked as she watched Jasmine place her pelisse and muff in the armoire.

"One other thing. Does your son still practice the fine art of hairdressing?" Madame Sauveur nodded. "Then I would appreciate his services." Taking the wig from his head, he tossed it aside. "I can abide that piece of shammery no longer! I will have my own hair dressed before I go out to pay calls on important friends."

"Shall I send him up immediately?"

Casanova glanced toward Jasmine, who sat on a gilded sofa covered with Beauvais tapestry. She smiled and he shook his head. "No, not immediately. Perhaps in an hour—or two. On second thought, I will send for him when I want him."

"Very well." Mathilde Sauveur dawdled. She was not eager to leave the room for she read his intentions plainly in the glances he cast toward the young girl on the sofa. She remembered the last time he had been a guest in her home. He had made her feel like a girl of sixteen or seventeen. But now he was back and with him a girl who was actually only sixteen or seventeen and now she felt every one of her forty-seven years.

With no other excuse to keep her there, Madame Sauveur curtsied to Jasmine and smiled at Casanova. "Eh bien! I shall leave you. I will tell my son to stay in the hôtel and wait for your call. And I will send for Madame Thibault."

"Thank you, Mathilde," Casanova said. Leaning over, he kissed her cheek and held the door as she left.

Turning the key in the lock, he went to the sofa and sat beside Jasmine.

"And so," he said softly, "we are alone."

"Yes," she agreed, "we are alone." She reached up and loosened his dark hair, which was fastened up to hold it under his now-discarded wig. She fluffed it about his shoulders and he caught her hand and kissed the blisters on her palm and the place where her pulse raced in her wrist.

"Giacomo?" she said quietly.

"Yes, my angel?" He kissed the inside of her elbow and slipped out of his brown velvet coat.

"Were you Madame Sauveur's lover?"

He nibbled on the lobe of her ear while working at the buttons of his gray satin waistcoat. "Yes," he answered.

Jasmine caught her breath as his fingers began to work at the hooks of her gown. His head was bent to her bosom and she kissed the shining crown of his head. "Giacomo?" she said as she unfastened his stock.

In one fluid movement, he slipped her gown from her shoulders and his waistcoat from his own. "What is it, my adorable darling?"

"Did you have many mistresses when you were last in Paris?"

He reached around her and adeptly unlaced her stays. "Yes," he replied. "I am cursed with an attraction for ladies and a weak will."

Jasmine worked at the buttons of his white lawn shirt. She caught her breath and paused momentarily as he cast her stays away, drew her chiffon chemise off her shoulders, and pressed his lips to her breasts.

'Giacomo?" she breathed.

"Yes, my little cherub?"

She looked up at him as he drew her to her feet and let

her gown and petticoats fall to the floor. He shrugged out of his shirt and she watched it land on the couch.

"Do you love me?"

"Oh! Can you doubt it?" He tugged her chemise over her head. "I am besotted with you!"

Lifting her, he carried her to the bed and tossed her across it. Climbing the bed steps, he took her shoes and hurled them away.

Jasmine wrapped her arms about his shoulders and responded to his languid, probing kisses with an ardor Michel had honed to perfection on long, passionate nights at Saint-Antoine. She shuddered as he trailed kisses over her breasts and then leaned away to remove his own boots and brown velvet breeches. When at last he lay beside her, she went eagerly into his arms.

"Giacomo?" she whispered.

"Yes, my own beloved?"

She hesitated as he moved over her and possessed her. "I . . ." She went on, "Oh, I've forgotten what I was going to say!"

She laughed and then sighed and, forgetting her questions, abandoned herself to the rapture he was only too eager to lead her toward.

Chapter 19

The sound of voices startled Jasmine as she awoke. The scarlet brocade curtains of the bed were drawn and she parted them only enough to peek out.

Casanova sat before the dressing table watching carefully while a young man circled him, examining his hair.

"Well have you finished?" he asked impatiently.

"Yes, Monseigneur," the young man replied. He toyed with his powder puff while his client surveyed his work.

Casanova poked at a horizontal curl over his left ear. His hair, ordinarily so black, was pomaded and powdered to a light blue-gray. Tied in the back with a black silk ribbon, it was in the height of fashion.

"It will do," he approved at last. "It will do."

"Thank you, Monseigneur," the young man said, helping him off with his long powdering gown.

"Giacomo?" Jasmine ventured from between the bed curtains. "Where are you going?"

Casanova smiled. "Good afternoon, my angel," he said. "Did you sleep well?" He noticed the young hairdresser staring at her. "That will be all, Basile," he said tersely.

The young man hurriedly packed his powders, pomades, combs and puffs and backed from the room.

Parting the bedcurtains, Casanova sat on the edge of the bed and took her into his arms.

Jasmine kissed him, carefully avoiding his freshly powdered hair. "Where are you going?" she repeated.

"I have calls to make—I told you I have many friends in Paris. As a matter of fact, I may say without boast that I am highly thought of by the Madame de Pompadour and the King himself."

"Are you going to see them?"

"Not this afternoon. I am going to start out with less illustrious personages."

"May I come with you?"

"What? And leave Madame Thibault without a client? You were to choose your wardrobe, remember? Madame Sauveur sent word that the mantua-maker had arrived nearly a half-hour ago."

Jasmine sighed. "Then I suppose I should get dressed." She drew her lone gown lying in a pile beside the sofa and groaned. "I suppose it is ruined. Now I won't be able to go out until Madame Thibault finishes a new gown." With a pout, she swung her legs over the side of the bed. "Giacomo, will you hand me my chemise, please?"

"Don't bother with it," he told her. "Madame Thibault will want to take measurements." He smiled. "I am tempted to remain here to watch the proceedings."

Leaving the bed, he went to the armoire and brought her his red-and-gold brocade dressing gown. Holding it out, he wrapped it around her as she stepped off the bed.

Jasmine watched as he slid his arms into a coat of green velvet. Its shade matched the embroidery on his cream satin waistcoat and his velvet breeches.

"When will you return?" she asked.

"I don't know, my darling. It depends upon how happy my friends are to see me." He tweaked her protruding lower lip as she pouted. "Now, now, let's have none of that. If you are good perhaps I will have a treat for you when I return."

"A treat? What kind of treat?" she asked eagerly.

"You will have to wait to find that out. In the meantime, I will send for Madame Thibault."

While Jasmine gathered her discarded gown and petticoats and hid them behind the bedcurtains, Casanova went to the drawing room and summoned the dressmaker.

Madame Thibault bustled into the room with a young girl in tow. Each bore cases filled with fabric samples and dressmaker's moppets—the small dolls which were outfitted in the latest fashions for use as examples of the dressmaker's art.

"Good afternoon, Madame la Marquise," she said, depositing her case on a table. "Good afternoon, Monseigneur."

"Good afternoon, Madame Thibault," Casanova said. "Madame la Marquise wishes to have a new wardrobe made. Madame Sauveur assures me that you are very good at your craft." Madame Thibault was obviously pleased. "You are to use only the best of materials. Madame la Marquise is to have anything she desires, do you understand?"

"Yes, Monseigneur, of course, Monseigneur," Madame Thibault assured him.

"Good." Coming to the sofa, he leaned over and

kissed Jasmine's cheek. "I will try to return as soon as possible, my seraph," he told her. "Enjoy yourself."

"I will miss you, Giacomo," Jasmine whispered.

"And I you," he assured her. Taking his Spanish-lace-trimmed tricorne from the dressing table, he bade them a pleasant adieu and left the apartment.

Madame Thibault, recognizing a pampered mistress when she saw one, eagerly opened her cases and spread her moppets and fabrics across the table.

"As you can see, Madame la Marquise," she said, "they are of the very latest fashion."

In spite of her pique at being left behind while Casanova went out, Jasmine leaned forward and picked up one of the moppets. Dressed in pale pink grosgrain, it wore a gown which was spread over a wide pannier. Flounces of delicate lace fell over the doll's wooden forearms and an exquisite underskirt of ecru chiffon trimmed with gold lace.

"This is magnificent!" she told a pleased Madame Thibault. "Could you make this for me in pale green?"

"Certainly!" the dressmaker agreed enthusiastically. The gown was the most expensive she had to offer.

"And perhaps also in periwinkle. Can you make it in periwinkle with white chiffon and silver lace?"

"Ah, Madame la Marquise! You have exquisite tastes!"

Jasmine smiled condescendingly. She'd been secluded at the Château de Saint-Antoine since her marriage and this first experience with tradespeople who made their living catering to the titled and moneyed nobility was a heady experience. She picked up another moppet. It wore a gown of white taffeta with sprays of flowers painted on it and outlined with silver thread. Ruffles of white lace fell nearly to the moppet's hands.

"Madame de Pompadour has a gown nearly as lovely," Madame Thibault sniffed.

"Nearly as lovely?"

Madame Thibault shrugged. "Made by Madelaine Rideaux. She is very fashionable but not very good. Her attraction at Court comes from the persistent rumors that she is an illegitimate daughter of Louis Quatorze."

"Is she really his illegitimate daughter?"

The pink-cheeked, middle-aged dressmaker laughed. "The closest that fool's mother ever got to Louis Quatorze was once when his coach was passing and she got sprayed with mud from the gutter. If she got pregnant from that, she's a better woman than you or I!"

Jasmine laughed and went back to the dressmaker's fabrics and moppets. As she ordered one gown after another along with the panniers, petticoats, chemises, and underskirts to go with them, Madame Thibault's compliments got more and more effusive.

By the time the door of the bedchamber opened and Casanova returned, Jasmine was having second thoughts about her purchases.

"Did you find anything to your liking, my darling?" he asked, placing his hat carefully on the dressing table.

Jasmine looked at the pages of Madame Thibault's ledger detailing her purchases. "I am afraid I found nearly everything to my liking, Giacomo," she said apologetically. "I will simply have to cancel some of these."

Taking the ledger from her, Casanova looked over the purchases. "They would seem to me to be in order. You cannot neglect your wardrobe, you know. It is by your appearance that you will first be judged." He looked at Madame Thibault. "I would be grateful, Madame," he told her, "if you could recommend someone to provide

204

Madame la Marquise with stockings, shoes, boots, gloves, fans, and so on.''

Madame Thibault nodded delightedly but Jasmine touched his sleeve.

"Giacomo! It's too expensive.''

He waved a dismissing hand. "Do not worry yourself about it. You will get wrinkles on that lovely forehead. Madame Thibault? I thank you for coming to us. I trust we can expect to see the fruit of your labors within a reasonable length of time?''

"I will begin work this very day, Monseigneur,'' she promised. She looked at her daughter, who had been silent most of the afternoon. "Are you sure you recorded Madame's measurements correctly?''

"Yes, Maman,'' the girl said softly.

"Well, then, it would seem we are finished.''

Jasmine smiled as the dressmaker and her daughter curtsied and left the room. Casanova saw them to the door and then returned to find her frowning.

"Really, Giacomo, I could have done without all those gowns. I ordered far too many.''

"A beautiful woman can never have too many gowns,'' he assured her.

"But the money . . .''

Reaching into the pocket of his overcoat, he drew out a leather pouch of considerable size. Untying the laces, he poured a stream of louis d'or into her lap.

Jasmine dipped her fingers into them. "But where did you get them?''

He sat beside her. "Did your grandmother or husband ever mention a man by the name of François de Bernis?'' She shook her head. "François de Bernis is the Abbé de Bernis. He is the Minister of Foreign Affairs.''

"And he is a friend of yours?''

"We met a few years ago when he was the French Ambassador in Venice. In fact, we shared a mistress."

"I don't want to hear about your mistresses, Giacomo," she pouted.

He laughed. "Very well. At any rate, he was recalled to France and has become Minister of Foreign Affairs. I went to him today at the Hôtel de Bourbon and he was most kind."

"And he gave you this money?"

"And the promise of more to come! So do not worry about your gowns, my darling, they will be paid for."

She helped him replace the gold into the leather pouch and then eyed him skeptically. "And now, Monsieur, where is my treat?"

"Your treat?"

"Giacomo! You promised me a treat if I were good."

"And were you good, my angel?"

"Oh! Very, very good!"

Leaning over, he kissed her forehead. "All right, then, you deserve a treat."

Going into the room beyond, Casanova returned with a rustling bundle over his arms. Motioning for her to get up from the sofa, he lay the bundle down carefully and unwrapped it.

Jasmine caught her breath. A gown of sea-green satin lay on the sofa. The décolletage was edged in silver ruching and silver bows were centered on the bodice. Silver ruching edged the base of the sleeves from which several ruffles of cream-colored lace fell. The skirt of the gown was open from the waist and, as Casanova lifted the gown, a cream chiffon underskirt trimmed with silver embroidered flowers lay beneath it.

"Well, Jasmine," he said. "Is it not beautiful?"

"It's magnificent!"

Smiling, he went to the salon once again and returned with a box in which she found several parcels containing cream silk stockings with silver clocks, and a silver ribbon to be worn about her neck. In an inlaid case she found a fan with a delicate pastoral scene painted on it. In another tiny box, she found a pair of diamond earrings.

"Giacomo! Where did you get this?"

"I have my ways," he assured her. "I have friends who know where one can obtain anything."

"But how did you know what size I needed?"

He made a circle with his arms. "I said, 'The lady in question is this big across her lovely bosom,'" He made a smaller circle, "'And this big about the waist . . .'"

She pursed her lips. "Surely not that big!" she protested.

"At any rate, I would wager it will fit you exactly. I have a good eye for feminine measurements, you know."

Throwing off her dressing gown, Jasmine held the beautiful gown before herself and peered into the mirror. "It is wonderful," she breathed. "But where will I wear such a gown?"

He appeared behind her in the mirror and leaned to kiss her ear. "I thought perhaps you would like to visit Versailles this evening," he told her.

"Versailles! Do you mean that, honestly?"

He nodded. "Indeed I do. The Abbé de Bernis is also a cherished friend of Madame de Pompadour and he has invited us to accompany him on a visit to that lady this evening. Would you like that, my darling?"

She stared at his reflection, unable to speak. But then, her astonishment faded to be replaced by a look of grave concern.

"What is it, darling?" he asked.

"Giacomo! I must have a bath! I must have a hairdresser and cosmetics. Oh, Giacomo! What shall I do?''

"Calm yourself, my angel, calm yourself. I will call for Madame Sauveur and order your bath and I don't doubt she will be able to provide you with whatever you need. Her son, whom you saw this morning dressing my hair, is equally talented with ladies' coiffures and will doubtless be available to perform his dubious magic for you.''

While Casanova went to summon the propriétaire, Jasmine poked through the treasures he'd brought her. She was going to Verssailles! She was going to meet Madame de Pompadour! On a whim, she pinched herself to be sure she was awake and not merely lying in her bed at Monsieur Brousseau's inn having a beautiful dream.

"Madame Sauveur should be here shortly," Casanova told her. "Shouldn't you put the dressing gown back on?''

Jasmine giggled and regretfully returned the gown to its resting place on the sofa. She wrapped the dressing gown about herself and sat down to await her bath.

"Oh, Giacomo," she sighed, leaning back in her chair, "I am so glad you found me at Brousseau's inn. How can I ever thank you for what you have done for me?''

He stroked a long finger down her cheek. "We will find a way, my dearest," he assured her. "Rest assured that we will.''

Chapter 20

Feeling grand in her new ensemble with her hair drawn into a stylish chignon atop her head, Jasmine rode beside Casanova in a fiacre he'd hired to take them to Versailles.

"I can hardly believe that I am going to see Versailles!" she said breathlessly.

"You will probably not see much of Versailles."

"But why not?"

"The Court has removed to Trianon, a small château in the gardens. It is much easier to heat than Versailles."

Jasmine frowned but then brightened. "Then we are more likely to see the King!"

"I doubt we will. Especially if the King knows that Monsieur l'Abbé de Bernis is there. He is not overly fond of his Minister of Foreign Affairs."

"Then how did the Abbé get the post?"

"As I told you, Madame de Pompadour is fond of him. Therefore, he is able to rise to a high office in spite of the King's dislike."

"Such power she has!" Jasmine murmured, impressed.

"A man in love is an easy beast to tame," Casanova said philosophically.

"Then you should be completely domesticated by now."

He laughed. "Easy, my angel," he warned. "I sense a touch of venom creeping from your honeyed lips!"

"If you insist upon reminding me of all your mistresses, you had better get used to venom!"

"Jealousy!" he said, feigning surprise. "Pure, unbridled jealousy! How delightful!"

Unwilling to admit that he was right, Jasmine snuggled deeper into her fur-lined pelisse and refused to speak for the rest of the fourteen-mile ride.

The immense palace of Versailles was ablaze with light as Jasmine and Casanova stepped out of the fiacre in the Place d'Armes.

"I thought you said the Court had removed to Trianon?" Jasmine asked as they began the long walk to the palace.

"Not the entire Court. Thousands of people reside in Versailles. Trianon could never hold them all. Those who are not especially invited must remain in this palace, uncomfortable or not."

"Why are we coming here then? Surely Madame de Pompadour goes to Trianon with the King."

"Oh yes, but the Abbé de Bernis was stopping to pay his respects to Madame Victoire, the King's daughter, who is confined to her rooms with a cold in the head."

They entered the palace and Jasmine was awed by the beauty of the galleries through which she passed.

"The State Apartments upstairs put these to shame," Casanova assured her, nodding to guards and minor courtiers they passed.

As they approached the Salle des Gardes they saw a double line of the King's Swiss Guard waiting.

"What does it mean, Giacomo?" Jasmine asked.

"The King must be in the palace," he informed her. "We had better wait outside . . ." He paused as he heard footsteps approaching. "Better yet, back up and curtsy. I don't believe we have time to get out before he arrives."

Jasmine's eyes widened. "The King is coming?"

She strained to see down the corridor but Casanova pulled her by the skirt until she was beside him, nearly pressed against the wall. With another tug, he forced her down into a curtsy while he bowed low.

The King, in a pale colored surtout and a black tricorne, walked toward them followed by the Dauphin and some other gentlemen Casanova did not identify for her. The moment he was past them, Jasmine rose and looked eagerly after him not noticing the gentleman who had been following the King but had stopped when he'd seen them there.

"Giacomo! So you have come. As you can see, I am most fortunate—the King arrived while I was visiting Madame Victoire."

"Then you were indeed fortunate," Giacomo told him. "It is never a misfortune here at Court to find yourself a part of a private gathering with the King, eh?" He drew Jasmine forward. "François, this is the Marquise de Saint-Antoine of whom I spoke this afternoon. Jasmine, this is Monsieur l'Abbé de Bernis."

Jasmine curtsied, "Good evening, Your Excellency."

The Abbé, a handsome man of forty-two, had lovely dark eyes which surveyed Jasmine with the practiced eye of a connoisseur of feminine beauty.

"Good evening, Madame," he said, raising her hand to his lips. "You are as beautiful as our Giacomo said

211

you were—even though I doubted he could be telling the truth this afternoon. But come, let us follow the King. My coach is waiting outside and we can ride in the royal procession back to Trianon."

They hurried toward the exit through which the last of the King's companions was passing and arrived in time to seem as though they had walked with them from Madame Victoire's suite. Appearances, so the Abbé informed Jasmine, were of the utmost importance at Court and if the small group of minor nobles and towns-people from Versailles who were gathered outside to watch the King leave thought they were privileged enough to accompany him, the word would quickly spread up the ranks and would add to their status.

By the time they were descending the steps to the wait-ing coaches, they were close enough that Jasmine caught a glimpse of a disheveled man who leapt from the crowd, pushed past the guards, and struck the King. As quickly as he'd come, he disappeared into the spectators and was hidden from view.

"Someone has struck me," the King murmured, his voice incredulous.

They stopped on the steps and, in the flickering torch-light, the King felt beneath his coat. When he removed his hand, Jasmine caught a glimpse of the glistening blood which covered it.

"I saw the man," one of the King's companions, the Duc de Richelieu, said. He motioned to the guards. "Come with me. I see him there."

"Do not kill him!" the King ordered. "Bring him inside."

"Papa!" the twenty-seven-year-old Dauphin said, his smallpox-pitted face alight with concern. "Come back inside."

Jasmine stepped back as the Dauphin and the Abbé de

Bernis took the King's arms and led him back into the palace. As she turned to follow the King and the men who were half carrying him, she glanced down. A small object lay on the snowy steps and she reached down to pick it up. It was a canif, a small, two bladed knife of which the smaller was open and spotted with blood. Closing her hand carefully about the weapon, she followed the others inside.

By the time they approached the King's private bedchamber in the Petits Appartements, the King was near to swooning and the Dauphin shouted to several astounded lackeys to run ahead and light a fire in the fireplace of the frosty room. As the King was carried through the splendid state rooms of his apartment to the smaller chambers of his private suite, a lackey hurried from the bedchamber.

"There is no linen on the bed, Your Royal Highness."

"Find some!" the Dauphin snapped.

"There are none of His Majesty's nightshirts."

"Find one or by God I shall see you broken on the wheel of the Place de Greve!" the Dauphin screamed.

The frightened men hurried away while they took the King into the bedchamber and divested him of his surtout.

Jasmine sank onto a chair in the Council Chamber outside the King's private bedchamber. It was a handsome room paneled in white and gold with blue silk hangings shot with gold. But she noticed none of the beauty of the room. She was stunned by what she had witnessed. As courtiers and lackeys rushed through the room she acknowledged none of them; her entire attention was focused on the weapon she held in her closed hand.

Casanova, the King's tricorne still held in his hand,

appeared in the doorway and came to sit beside her.

"How is he?" she asked anxiously.

"He fainted. When he regained consciousness he asked to see a confessor."

"Is . . . is he going to die?"

Casanova shrugged. "He thinks so. We will not know how serious it is until a surgeon can be brought. No one can tell how serious the wound is for no one saw the weapon."

Holding out her hand, Jasmine revealed the small knife. "I found it on the steps."

The Abbé de Bernis, who had just left the bed-chamber, hurried over to them and plucked the knife from her hand. Seeing the blood staining her hand, he asked: "Did you cut your hand or was that blood already on the blade?"

Jasmine shook her head. "It was already on the blade; it is not mine."

"Sweet Jesu!" The handsome Abbé sank onto a chair. "This is terrible! This is a calamity!"

Casanova nodded. "It could be too late for the surgeon already."

"What do you mean?" Jasmine demanded. "It is only a tiny knife. Surely such a weapon could do no great harm."

"This type of knife," Casanova informed her, "is commonly used by assassins. The blade is coated with poison. All that is needed is to insert the blade into the body. The poison does the rest."

Jasmine paled. "The King could be poisoned? How horrible! How . . ."

A tall, older man entered the room and the Abbé de Bernis rose to greet him.

"How is he?" the man asked breathlessly. "I have just arrived from Trianon."

214

"He is weak," the Abbé informed him as they went toward the bedchamber. "He has lost a great deal of blood. This is the knife."

"Oh, my! Oh, my!" the man fretted, taking the knife. "This is bad! This is very bad!"

"Giacomo, who was that?" Jasmine asked as the two men left the room.

"That was Germain de La Martinière. He is the King's first surgeon. The Dauphin summoned him from Trianon." He stood. "Come, Jasmine, we must leave."

"Leave? But why?"

"If La Martinière was brought from Trianon the news must be racing through the palace. Soon we will be hip-deep in royalty and we have not the right to be present should the King die."

"Do we have to go back to Paris?"

"We could not if we wanted to. François de Bernis was going to take us back with him. He is obviously not going to leave."

"Then where will we go?"

"Let us go out into the Galerie des Glaces."

Jasmine followed him out of the Council Chamber to the magnificent Galerie de Glaces.

The breathtaking Hall of Mirrors was dimly lit with a few candles burning in each of the silver candelabra which stood on tables along the wall. Dodging the courtiers and servants who rushed along the gallery in confusion, Jasmine crossed from one side to the other and watched the procession of coaches hurrying from Trianon. Occasionally, when a particularly important personage approached, Casanova would tug Jasmine into a curtsy and whisper the identity of the latest arrival.

She looked up as he took her hand. "Come. Let us go downstairs," he said.

"But, Giacomo, I want to see the Queen!" she

protested watching Madame Adelaïde, one of the King's daughters, being led in tears to her father's side.

He pulled her away from the windows and took her toward the end of the Hall of Mirrors. "I will take you to meet someone far more interesting than the Queen."

They passed through the magnificent state salons and descended a staircase to arrive on the ground floor just as the flock of chattering courtiers parted to allow someone through.

Jasmine looked out from behind Casanova as she heard a pleasant female voice cry:

"Jacques! Oh, Jacques! Have you seen him?"

The handsome woman, in a dark blue pelisse lined with sable, clasped Casanova's outstretched hands.

"Indeed I have, my precious Marquise," he replied softly.

As though just aware of the hordes of courtiers watching, Madame de Pompadour dropped his hands. "Come to my apartment, Jacques. I want you to tell me what has happened. No one seems to know—there have been so many rumors."

As Madame de Pompadour and Casanova started off toward her apartments, Jasmine hesitated. She'd not been presented to the Marquise—was it proper for her to accompany them to her rooms?

Her uncertainty was resolved when, after walking a few steps, Casanova glanced over his shoulder and, with a quick nod of his head, motioned for her to come along. She quickly fell into step with Madame du Hausset.

A maidservant rushed up to them as they entered Madame de Pompadour's beautiful apartment and took the Marquise's pelisse. Although the room was freezing, the newly lit fires not yet having had time to dispel the cold, the Marquise paced up and down, unmindful of the icy air.

"Where were the guards?" she demanded, barely pausing to accept a fur-lined robe Madame du Hausset draped about her shoulders. "Why was he not protected?"

"The guards were there, Madame," Casanova told her. "But the man took them by surprise."

"It should not have happened!" she cried, her agitation increasing. "It should not . . ." Pausing at the fireplace, she pressed a hand to her forehead.

"Monseigneur!" Madame du Hausset cried. "Quickly, catch her!"

In the barest fraction of a moment, Casanova was at Madame de Pompadour's side and swept her into his arms. With Madame du Hausset preceeding him, he carried her to the bedchamber and laid her carefully on the bed.

Jasmine stood in the doorway of the beautiful room and watched as Madame du Hausset administered a dose of the Marquise's medicine.

"Vivienne!" she called to the maidservant. "Take a footman or two and see if you can find Doctor Quesnay. Look upstairs; I've no doubt half the doctors in Paris are there right now!"

Discreetly, Casanova left the room as Madame du Hausset began unlacing the Marquise's gown.

"Pardon, Madame," she said, looking up toward Jasmine, who was about to follow Casanova. "Would you be so kind as to help me? The rest of Madame's maids are still at Trianon."

She looked uncertainly at Casanova and he replied with a barely perceptible nod and a look which said: "Go on, comforting the most powerful woman at Court in her darkest hour can do you nothing but good."

"Of course, Madame," she said, going to the bedside. Together they undressed the swooning Marquise and

Jasmine marvelled at the unblemished beauty of the King's mistress. At thirty-five, Madame de Pompadour's skin was as fresh and delicate as that of Jasmine, who had not yet reached her seventeenth birthday. While she held the Marquise in her arms, Jasmine waited for Madame du Hausset to return from the armoire with an ermine-edged velvet dressing gown. She looked down at the Marquise and found her looking up at her, her expression bewildered.

"Who are you?" the Marquise demanded, struggling to sit up.

"I am Jasmine de Saint-Antoine, Madame," she said shyly. She was uncertain of how to address La Pompadour for, although she retained the title "Marquise" out of habit, the King had long before raised her rank to that of Duchesse. "I am here with Giacomo."

"Saint-Antoine?" Madame de Pompadour seized upon her unexpected guest eagerly, anxious to divert her mind from the drama which was being played out in the King's apartment directly over their heads. "I had heard that the Marquise de Saint-Antoine had married. But you are only a baby."

Jasmine blushed. "I am nearly seventeen, Madame la Marquise."

"Nearly seventeen." She leaned forward to allow Madame du Hausset to slip the dressing gown about her. "Did you come to Versailles to meet the King?"

"No, Madame, I came with Giacomo to meet His Excellency, the Abbé de Bernis. We were then going to drive to Trianon to meet you."

"Jacques?" Madame de Pompadour summoned Casanova from the adjoining room. "Madame de Saint-Antoine here tells me you were on the way to visit me when . . . when this disaster came upon us."

"That's right, dearest Madame," he acknowledged.

"I thought . . . I thought perhaps she was the King's jasmine."

"The King's jasmine?" he repeated.

"Reinette, that is only a coincidence," Madame du Hausset insisted.

But the favorite's mind was fixed on doom. "No, it is too much of a coincidence." She looked at Casanova. "The King was bored a few days ago—he was yellow, you know how he turns yellow when he is bored? He spoke to one of his doctors about it—Doctor Quesnay as a matter of fact. The doctor suggested some small change in his habits to break the monotony. He said perhaps the King should change his scent—he suggested that the King try the scent of jasmine. Isn't that what he said, Louise? He said, 'I believe Your Majesty would greatly benefit from breaking your old habit and changing to jasmine.' " She looked accusingly at Jasmine but, as she was about to speak, Doctor Quesnay arrived and hurried to her bedside.

"Reinette," he said soothingly. "Everything will be well. I have spoken to La Martinière and he has assured me that the King will live."

Madame de Pompadour sagged against the pillows with relief. "Thank heaven!" she whispered. "Thank heaven!"

"His Majesty has confessed twice and, so I have heard, would have demanded extreme unction had we been able to find the Cardinal de la Rouchefoucauld."

"But you are certain that he will not die?"

De Quesnay nodded. "Had the knife been poisoned, he would be dead by now. He has lost a lot of blood but he has a ruddy complexion and that always means a surfeit of blood. He can afford to lose some."

"I wonder if he has promised God that he will give up his Maîtress en Titre as he did when he was ill at Metz. Then he promised to break with the Duchesse de Châteaurox. When he recovered, he kept his promise and never saw her again. Has he promised to forsake me, François?"

"Of course I am not privy to His Majesty's confessional, Reinette, but I doubt very much that the King would make such a promise. What would he do without you?"

Madame de Pompadour looked past him toward Jasmine who was sitting with Madame du Hausset. "Perhaps he could find something else to amuse him," she said softly. "Did you not tell him it would be good for him to try jasmine instead of his usual old habit?"

"Well, of course I did, Reinette, but what does that have to do with . . ."

Interrupting him, La Pompadour motioned for Jasmine to approach the bed. "François, I want you to meet a lady who has only tonight paid her first visit to the Court. This is the Marquise de Saint-Antoine's little bride. Madame, please tell the good doctor your name."

Jasmine blushed under their gazes. "My name," she said softly, avoiding their eyes, "is Jasmine."

Chapter 21

Jasmine yawned and blinked away the slumber which clung stubbornly to her eyelids. She groaned as she sat up. Having spent the night on the chaise longue in Madame de Pompadour's Red Salon, her muscles were stiff and sore.

She pushed away the fur-lined pelisse she'd used as a coverlet. The room was warm; a fire had been lit in the fireplace. Suddenly remembering where she was, Jasmine pulled the pelisse around herself. Madame de Pompadour's maid, Vivienne, had helped her out of her gown the night before and she'd slept in her chemise.

Going to the salon door she looked for the maid. A footman bowed to her.

"Could you please find Vivienne for me?" she asked.

He bowed again. "Yes, Madame la Marquise."

When the maid arrived, she helped Jasmine into her gown and combed her hair into a chignon atop her head.

"There is a bowl of fruit on the table, Madame," Vivienne told her, "if you are hungry."

"Thank you, Vivienne." Taking an apple from the

bowl she took a bite and only then realized how hungry she really was. "Do you know where Monsieur Casanova is?"

"No, Madame. Perhaps Madame du Hausset can tell you."

Leaving the Red Salon, Jasmine went to Madame de Pompadour's bedchamber in search of the older maid. She found her with her ear pressed against the Marquise's bedchamber door.

"Madame du Hausset?" she said. "Have you seen Monsieur Casanova?"

"He has gone to meet with the Abbé de Bernis. Now . . . shhh!"

She watched her curiously, taking another bite of the apple. "What are you listening to, Madame?"

The maid frowned. "The King is visiting Madame de Pompadour."

"The King? Then he is better?"

With an exasperated look, she nodded. "Yes! Now, with all due respect, Madame la Marquise, shut up!"

After a few moments, the Marquise de Pompadour called from within the room. "All right, Louise. You may come in."

"She knows you were listening?" Jasmine asked.

"Of course she does. I always listen."

Leaving Jasmine to stare after her in astonishment, Madame du Hausset swung the door open and entered the Marquise's bedchamber.

"Madame de Saint-Antoine?" Madame de Pompadour called, catching a glimpse of Jasmine through the open door.

"Yes, Madame?"

"Come in. I hope you did not find my chaise longue too uncomfortable."

"Not at all, Madame," she replied, entering the bedchamber. "It was fine. I hope His Majesty has recovered from his attack?"

The Marquise waved a hand while Madame du Hausset plumped her pillows. "Physically, he is not badly hurt. His wound is painful, of course, but not terribly serious. But his mood is very bad. He is in a fearful fit of melancholy."

"The attacker was captured, was he not?" Madame du Hausset asked.

"Oh, yes. His name is Robert Damiens. He is a butler or something of the kind from Artois."

"Why did he want to kill the King?"

"He didn't; if he did, he would have poisoned the knife blade."

"What will happen to him?"

La Pompadour shrugged. "He will be put to death, of course. After a trial at which he will certainly be found guilty, he will be put to death in Paris. The King showed me a proclamation to the effect that . . ."

Madame du Hausset held out a sheet of paper she'd retrieved from the floor. "This proclamation, Reinette?"

Madame Pompadour took it from her. "Yes. He must have forgotten it."

Du Hausset reached out for it. "Shall I take it up to him?"

"No." The Marquise shook her head. "Perhaps we should let Madame de Saint-Antoine take it to him."

"Oh, I do not think that would be wise," the maid said.

La Pompadour's eyes were accusing. "Why? Are you uneasy about their meeting one another, Louise?"

"Of course not, Reinette," she replied hurriedly.

"Then what could it harm? He will meet her sooner or

later. Perhaps this coincidence with her name and Doctor Quesnay's advice will amuse him."

Reluctantly, Jasmine took the proclamation from Madame de Pompadour. "I am not sure of how to get to His Majesty's apartment, Madame. There was so much confusion last night . . ." She looked over with dismay as Madame du Hausset opened a section of the paneling to reveal a handsome little staircase.

"That staircase," Madame de Pompadour informed her, "will take you directly to His Majesty's bedchamber. Simply tap on the door and deliver the proclamation."

Afraid to refuse and risk further antagonizing the King's powerful favorite, Jasmine started slowly toward the staircase.

"And, Madame?" La Pompadour called just as she was about to mount the first step. "Be sure to tell the King your first name. He will undoubtedly ask you who you are—do not merely give him your title."

"Yes, Madame," she replied meekly. She handed her apple to the maid and started up the steep staircase. Madame du Hausset closed the panel, leaving her to grope her way up in the darkness.

Arriving at the top of the staircase, she tapped lightly. From within the room came a dispirited "Entrez," and, gathering her courage, she fumbled with the latch and swung the panel open to step into the King's private bedchamber.

The room was seemingly empty but, from an alcove across which heavy draperies were drawn, a voice said, "Reinette? You should be resting."

Jasmine looked nervously around the grand room whose ivory paneled walls sported gilded carvings and exquisite tapestries.

"It is not Madame de Pompadour, Your Majesty," she

ventured shyly. "She sent me to bring the proclamation which was left in her apartment."

"Leave it on the table," he said. When he said no more, she placed the proclamation on a table and turned to leave. As she was about to step back onto the staircase, his voice stopped her.

"Wait. Who are you?"

She swallowed nervously. "I am the Marquise de Saint-Antoine, Your Majesty." Knowing that the Marquise de Pompadour would be angry if she did not tell him her name, she added: "Jasmine de Saint-Antoine."

There was a pause. "Jasmine?" he said at last. "That is truly your name?"

"Yes, Your Majesty. It is."

"How extraordinary! Why, only a few days ago Doctor Quesnay said to me . . ." His voice trailed off and she saw the draperies part a little. "Come here, Marquise de Saint-Antoine."

She approached the bed with trepidation and he pulled back one side of the draperies. Even clad simply in a linen nightshirt and a dressing gown of purple velvet with a collar of sable, the King was a handsome man. In fact, Jasmine realized as they took stock of one another, he was more handsome this way. In his public appearances he seemed awfully stern and forbidding— there, in private, he seemed somehow a little uncertain and shy. She curtsied deeply, sinking into her green satin skirts.

"I have never seen you before, have I?"

"No, Sire. I came to Versailles for the first time last night. His Excellency, the Abbé de Bernis, was going to take Jacques Casanova and me to visit Madame de Pompadour at Trianon."

"Jacques Casanova. So he has come back to France, has he? I find him most amusing." The King nudged one of his pillows into shape. "But tell me, Marquise de Saint-Antoine, why do you not share you husband's exile in the country?"

Jasmine dropped her eyes, fearing that he would be angry. "I . . . I was in the country, Sire. We were married there last summer. Unfortunately, my husband and I . . . that is . . . the situation . . ."

He waved his hand, silencing her. "Never mind, never mind, I am acquainted with the Marquis. He is a most disagreeable man. Whatever possessed your parents to marry such a delectable creature as yourself to such an odious man? His wealth?"

Jasmine nodded. "My grandmother is the Marquise de Mareteleur—my husband's stepmother."

"Oho! I am acquainted with that lady as well—a crafty woman. She seeks to control both your husband's and her husband's fortunes, I suppose?"

"I expect that is true, Sire," she replied.

"Well, Marquise, it would seem that you have been singularly cursed in your family." His slight smile faded into a look of melancholia. "As I have been cursed to rule a people who hate me."

"Oh, Your Majesty! Surely they do not hate you! Are you not called 'Louis le Bien-Aimé'?"

"When I was a young man I was indeed well-beloved. But now—" He shook his head. "If they loved me, they would not seek to kill me."

"But certainly that man was insane."

He shrugged. "Perhaps yes—perhaps no. Can we ever truly know the mind of the people?" He looked into her eyes and his expression was sad. "Tell me, Marquise, would you want to kill your poor King?''

"Of course not, Your Majesty!''

"I am glad I have a few loyal subjects left. Welcome to Versailles, Jasmine. Jasmine—how remarkable. Can it truly be a coincidence? I wonder.'' He patted the edge of the bed. "Sit down.''

Trying to avoid jiggling the bed, Jasmine perched on the edge and wondered what was about to happen.

Taking her hand, the King pressed it to his lips. He touched her face and, with a finger beneath her chin, drew her toward him. She made no protest as his lips touched hers. In spite of the fact that he was not many years younger than her husband, he was a superbly handsome man and the fact that he was the King awed her into silence. She felt his arms steal about her waist but, as he embraced her, a hiss of pain escaped him and he pushed her away.

Lifting one side of his dressing gown, they saw a dark red stain spreading on the linen of his nightshirt.

"Go to the Council Chamber,'' he told her, pointing toward the door. "Bring Monsieur la Martinière.''

Not bothering to curtsy, Jasmine rushed to the door and pushed it open. The gentlemen gathered in the room leapt to their feet and looked at the unfamiliar woman standing before them.

"Monsieur la Martinière?'' she said.

A tall, elderly man nodded. "Yes, Mademoiselle?''

"His Majesty has accidentally opened his wound.''

Both Doctor la Martinière and Doctor Quesnay, who had been seated across the large room, left the group and hurried toward the King's bedchamber. As Jasmine stepped back to allow them to pass, she heard the Duc de Richelieu, First Gentleman of the Bedchamber, whisper loudly to the Duc d' Ayen:

"His Majesty must be feeling much better this morning!"

Jasmine blushed as the men laughed. As Doctor Quesnay passed her, he said, loudly enough for them to hear:

"Good morning, Madame de Saint-Antoine."

"Good morning, Doctor Quesnay," she replied softly.

As she closed the door behind the doctors, she heard a buzz of conversation start in the room.

"Madame de Saint-Antoine? Is that what he said?"

"Isn't that Marquis still in exile?"

The Duc de Richlieu laughed. "Perhaps he was exiled to get him out of the way!"

Ignoring their speculation and coarse insinuations, Jasmine closed the door.

Uncertain of what to do, she decided the best course of action was retreat. She curtsied to the King even though he could not see her from behind the two doctors, and went back to the staircase and Madame de Pompadour's apartment.

"Well?" the Marquise de Pompadour demanded as Jasmine opened the section of paneling and stepped into the room.

"His Majesty has reopened his wound. Doctor La Martinière and Doctor Quesnay are attending him."

"How did he reopen the wound—Jasmine?" she asked, her dark eyes narrowing.

Jasmine looked at the floor. "I do not know, Madame," she lied.

Madame de Pompadour's cheeks flushed and she averted her eyes. "Good day, Madame de Saint-Antoine," she said coolly.

"But . . . I do not know my way around Versailles,

Madame," she reasoned. "I would not know where to find Jacques and the Abbé de Bernis."

Madame de Pompadour raised an eyebrow. "That is not my problem, Madame. Do not forget your pelisse on your way out."

Realizing that it would be better to leave an annoyed rather than angered Marquise de Pompadour behind her, Jasmine hurried from the room. She paused only long enough to collect her pelisse and a few more of Madame de Pompadour's apples and oranges and then made a hurried exit from the apartment.

The corridor was crowded and she stood there with no idea of where to go to find Casanova. After several attempts at stopping a courtier or footman to ask directions, she wrapped her pelisse around herself to ward off the chill of the corridor and set off on her own.

Chapter 22

With her pelisse pulled tightly about herself to ward off the chill and the fruit pilfered from Madame de Pompadour's salon stowed in its pockets, Jasmine set out in search of Casanova.

The galleries and salons of the palace were filled with courtiers but every one of them seemed to be in too much of a hurry to pause and give directions to a woman none of them recognized as anyone of any importance.

From Madame de Pompadour's suite she wandered to the magnificent Queen's staircase and climbed the stairs. Braziers did little to take the freezing chill out of the air and groups of courtiers gathered about them and around fireplaces in the rooms. None bothered to look up as she passed; no one was interested in her when there was the far more fascinating attack on the King to be discussed.

Eventually she found herself in the attics. In sharp contrast to the large and breathtakingly beautiful rooms below, the attics of Versailles were like rabbit warrens with narrow corridors lined with doors which gave onto rooms normally allotted to servants and minor nobles.

The corridors were without the braziers which burned on the floors below and Jasmine blew little puffs of steam out into the frosty air.

Surely, she told herself, the Abbé de Bernis was not likely to be found in such mean surroundings. In spite of the fact that the King was not overly fond of him, he was a Minister of France and a favorite of Madame de Pompadour. Such a man commanded better accommodations than a drafty cubicle beneath the snowy roof of the palace.

She was about to retreat to the relative warmth of the State Rooms downstairs when she heard a sudden burst of coughing from behind one of the doors. It was a horrible, hacking sound followed by a groan of abject misery.

After several moments of hesitation, she gathered enough courage to knock on the door.

There was a silence after which a small, female voice asked, "Who is there?"

"Are you all right?" Jasmine asked. "Shall I bring a doctor for you?"

After another silence, the door opened to reveal a young girl. Her blonde hair was lank and her cheeks were flushed. With one thin hand, she rubbed at her reddened nose. "Who are you?" she asked suspiciously.

"I am the Marquise de Saint-Antoine," Jasmine explained. "I heard you coughing. Is there anything I can do?"

The girl curtsied. "Did someone send you here?"

"No. I was looking for someone."

"Would you like to come in?"

Jasmine was about to refuse but there was a look in the girl's blue eyes that seemed to beg for companionship.

"Very well," she replied.

The girl stepped back and Jasmine entered the tiny room. Its dark walls made it seem even smaller than it was and the only grimy window gave onto a dull interior courtyard. Jasmine squeezed between the plain four-poster, whose hangings and coverlet were of brown velvet which had obviously seen better days, and a battered clothespress. She sat on a rickety window seat and smiled uncertainly at the girl who had crawled over the bed. Her feet, encased in thick woolen stockings, peeked out from beneath a worn velvet gown.

Jasmine pulled her hands into the soft fur lining of her pelisse. A small fire burned in the tiny fireplace but it could not overcome the blasts of wintry air which blew in around the window.

"Do you work for someone in the palace?" Jasmine asked. She smiled uncertainly as the girl buried a sneeze in the coverlet of the bed.

"I was brought here in case the King sent for me," the girl replied, her tone proud in spite of her surroundings.

"Why would the King send for you?" Jasmine asked with a shiver.

"Because I am his mistress."

Jasmine could not hide her astonishment. "You are the King's mistress? But you are so . . . so . . ."

"Common?" the girl supplied haughtily. "I may not be a Marquise, like you, but the King has loved me all the same! And I pleased him—else Monsieur Lebel would not have brought me from Parc aux Cerfs."

"I have heard of Parc aux Cerfs," Jasmine said, remembering Madame Giroux and the diligence ride to Paris. "Someone told me it is very beautiful."

"Oh, yes! I have a room there all to myself," the girl boasted. "And it is much larger and prettier than this. I expected Versailles to be wonderful but . . . but . . ."

She covered her face and sneezed violently.

"You should be where it's warmer with that cold," Jasmine told her.

The girl shook her head. "I cannot leave my room. Monsieur Lebel said that I would be sent for if I was wanted. Otherwise I was to remain here."

"How long have you been here?"

She shrugged. "I'm not sure. It must be nearly a week."

"A week! They left you here when the Court moved to Trianon?"

"Trianon! How long have they been there?"

"I'm not sure, a few days I believe."

"A few days! That must be why they stopped sending someone up with food."

Jasmine laughed but then, when the girl's expression remained serious, asked: "Are you actually telling me that no one remembered to feed you after the Court left for Trianon?"

"I expect Monsieur Lebel forgot to give instructions to the kitchens. One would think he would have taken me back to Parc aux Cerfs if the King was not going to be here."

Jasmine fumbled in the pockets of her pelisse and drew out the apples and oranges she had stolen from Madame de Pompadour's salon.

"You are welcome to these, if you would like them," she offered shyly.

With no pretense of reluctance, the girl snatched the fruit out of her hands and sank her teeth into one of the apples.

"Oh! That feels good, Marquise," she said, her mouth full. "I wish I could taste it!"

When she paused in mid-bite to sneeze, the girl shook

her head sadly. "Sometimes, Marquise, I think that if I sneeze one more time my head will fall off!"

"This is no place for you in your condition, Mademoiselle—er—Mademoiselle . . ."

"Beaujean, Madame. Henriette Beaujean."

"Mademoiselle Beaujean. When you are finished eating, I will thank you to pack your belongings. I am taking you out of here."

"Back to Parc aux Cerfs?"

"If that is where you wish to go. You are welcome to come home with me if you like. Once you are well you can return to Parc aux Cerfs."

Finishing the apple, Henriette began peeling an orange. "I don't know, Marquise. Monsieur Lebel might be angry."

"I will speak to Monsieur Lebel. If he will not listen to me I will ask the Abbé de Bernis to speak to Monsieur Lebel."

"The Abbé de Bernis!" Henriette was impressed. "He's a close friend of Madame de Pompadour!"

Jasmine laughed. "Those apples and oranges I gave you came from Madame de Pompadour's apartment."

Henriette paused, an orange section poised before her mouth. "Really? Imagine that." With added relish, she popped the orange section into her mouth. She looked at Jasmine curiously. "How did you come to be stealing fruit from the Marquise de Pompadour?"

"I slept in her salon last night. There was so much confusion last night after the King was stabbed . . ."

Henriette choked on her orange. "Stabbed! The King was stabbed? Is he dead?"

"Oh, no. He is quite all right. The wound was not serious. But the gentleman I came to Versailles with has gone somewhere to meet with the Abbé de Bernis and I cannot find them. We were supposed to ride back to Paris together, you see."

"This gentleman . . . is he your husband? There is a Marquise de Saint-Antoine, isn't there?"

"Yes, there is a Marquise de Saint-Antoine but he is not the gentleman I meant. I am sharing lodgings with another gentleman for the present."

Henrietta's eyes grew round. "Oh, yes? Why did you take a lover? Is your husband old and ugly and impotent?"

Jasmine smiled. "Something like that. Tell me, Henriette, how old are you?"

"Fifteen. I was fifteen just before Christmas. How old are you?"

"Sixteen. I will be seventeen in a few months. I . . ." She held a hand to her face and a hard sneeze shook her. "That's it, Henriette. If you want to come with me, I suggest you gather your belongings now. If I stay any longer I will have a cold like yours."

Henriette scrambled off the bed and pulled a copious carpet bag from the clothespress. Without ceremony she deposited a silk nightdress and dressing gown and a pair of mules inside.

"That nightdress is exquisite, Henriette," Jasmine said, surprised.

"Thank you, Madame. Monsieur Lebel said I must save it for the King." She dumped the brushes and combs from her dressing table and, after assuring herself that the stopper was secure, tossed in a scent bottle.

Jasmine watched as she pushed her feet into leather half-boots and pulled a pelisse from the clothespress.

"Don't you have any other gowns?"

"No. Only the one I was wearing. Monsieur Lebel said I wouldn't need any other since only the King would see me and then only in the nightdress.''

"I see. Well, shall we go?"

Henriette buttoned her pelisse and picked up her carpetbag. "I won't be sorry to get out of this room, Madame!" she said emphatically. "This is not what I expected Versailles to be!"

With Henriette staying a step behind her, Jasmine led the way back down the stairs to the State Apartment. Henriette drew a sharp breath as she entered the first of the grand salons.

"How beautiful it is!" she murmured to Jasmine. "This is what I imagined Versailles to be!"

They passed a small group of courtiers who gossiped as they warmed themselves before a fireplace. As they passed, they heard one of the young men ask another:

"Exactly who is this new maîtress?"

"The Marquise de Saint-Antoine," the languid, pale gentleman replied. "Surely you remember the Marquis; he was banished last summer for insulting La Pompadour's father."

"Is that you they're talking about?" Henriette whispered.

"So it would seem," Jasmine replied.

They paused near a brazier not far from the courtiers and listened for the conversation to continue.

"Yes, it seems I do remember him. Rather boorish fellow. But isn't he older than the King? I take it his Marquise is much younger than he."

A man whose black eyebrows seemed incongruous with his white-powdered wig leaned forward. "From what the Marquis de Belle-Isle heard from the Duc de Richelieu, she looks to be about sixteen or seventeen."

"The Duc actually saw her with the King?"

The man with the black eyebrows laughed. "She was

in his private bedchamber. She came for the doctor after the King reopened his wound."

The men laughed and Jasmine moved away before they could make their bawdy speculations as to how the King had managed to injure himself.

"Is that true?" Henriette demanded. "Were you with the King?"

"Not in the way they think," Jasmine assured her.

"You are not his mistress?"

"No. I am not his mistress."

Henriette smiled knowingly. "Pardon me, Madame, but that is your loss. I have been making my living catering to men since I was eleven and I have never known a man like the King! If you like, I will tell you about it."

Jasmine blushed. "Thank you, Henriette, but I think not."

Henriette shrugged. "Suit yourself, Marquise, but I tell you, no matter what kind of man your lover is, he can certainly not hold a candle to the King."

It was Jasmine's turn to smile. "You say that, Henriette, never having met Jacques Casanova."

"Jasmine!"

She turned as a male voice hailed her. From the adjoining Salon of War, Casanova came toward her accompanied by the Abbé de Bernis.

"Jasmine," Casanova repeated. "I have been looking all over the palace for you."

"I have been looking for you! I got lost in the attics," she replied. She noticed the eyes of the two men lingering curiously on Henriette. "This," she told them, drawing the girl forward, "is Henriette Beaujean. Monsieur Lebel brought her from Parc Aux Cerfs, lodged her in the attics, and then promptly forgot her. I would like to take her home with us until she is over her cold."

Henriette obliged her by sneezing and Casanova handed her his handkerchief.

"You would be welcome to come with us, Mademoiselle."

"This is the Chevelier de Seingalt," Jasmine told her.

Henriette curtsied. "Thank you, Monseigneur, you are most kind." She offered the handkerchief back to him but he waved it away.

"This," Jasmine went on, "is His Excellency, the Abbé de Bernis." As Henriette curtsied, she went on. "Do you think it would be all right if I took Henriette home with me, Your Excellency? I would not want her to be in trouble with Monsieur Lebel for leaving the palace."

"From what I hear, Madame de Saint-Antoine," the Abbé said, his dark eyes glittering with amusement, "you are in a position to do as you like at Versailles."

"What do you mean, Your Excellency?"

"Don't tell me you are the only person at Court who has not heard that the King's new mistress is the mysterious Marquise de Saint-Antoine?"

"I heard those gentlemen saying that but . . ."

"You were seen in His Majesty's bedchamber this morning, Madame. That is all it takes."

"But His Majesty will certainly tell everyone the truth!"

The Abbé smiled. "All His Majesty said on the subject was to ask repeatedly where his 'little Jasmine' disappeared to. That does not sound like a denial to me."

Jasmine pursued her lips. "Nevertheless, all this gossip is unfounded and I, for one, will be happy to return to Paris."

The Abbé consulted his watch, the cover of which bore a miniature of the King. "I am happy to be able to oblige you, Madame. I must return to my duties. There are a great many dispatches to be sent concerning His Majesty's condition. I have ordered my coach, which should be waiting in the courtyard. Shall we go?"

They started out of the salon and out of the palace. The Abbé, thoroughly enjoying the respect his position commanded, led them grandly, nodding to the right and left. Jasmine and Casanova followed him and Henriette brought up the rear.

As they left the palace and crossed the Cour de Marbre, Casanova whispered in Jasmine's ear:

"Jasmine, my precious angel?"

"Yes, Giacomo?"

"Exactly what were you doing in the King's bedchamber this morning?"

She tossed him an exasperated glance and quickened her steps. With a dazzling smile, she took the Abbé's arm and walked the rest of the way to the waiting coach in silence.

Chapter 23

Jasmine giggled as the silence of the night was broken by an explosive sneeze.

"I shouldn't laugh," she whispered to Casanova, who lay beside her, "but she really never stops!"

He laughed and pushed one of her curls back over her shoulder. "She's miserable. But it was kind of you to bring her home from Versailles."

She sat up, tucking the coverlet beneath her arms to cover her nakedness. "She might have died in that foul little room, Giacomo! How could the King have been so heartless?"

"The King probably knew nothing about it. Lebel doubtless brought her to him once or twice and then he assumed she'd been taken back to Parc aux Cerfs."

She shivered a little as he drew circles on her knee with one long, tapering finger. "Do you really think so? I would hate to think he could be so callous."

"You liked the King?"

"He seemed very kind. But his mood changed so suddenly. One moment he was . . . well . . . in an amorous mood, and next he was so melancholy. He actually asked me if I would want to kill him!''

''The King is a moody man. It is the Bourbon temperament. It gives him an air of mystery most women find utterly fascinating. Tell me, my naked angel, did you find the King utterly fascinating?''

She smiled hoping the rather forced air of levity in his tone betrayed a touch of jealousy. ''I found him attractive,'' she admitted.

''He may send for you, you know, When he is recovered. He may seek to make you his mistress.''

Jasmine snuggled beneath the coverlets and wrapped her arms about him. ''I don't want to be his mistress. I only want to be your mistress.''

He turned on his side to face her and kissed her. ''I am delighted to hear you say so, my sweet Jasmine; but I will not always be here.''

In her alarm, Jasmine did not even hear Henriette sneezing in the drawing room.

''Giacomo! What do you mean? You are not leaving Paris?''

''At some point it will become necessary for me to leave. Paris is not my home as it is yours. I am Venetian by birth. Venice is my home.''

''Then I will go to Venice. Oh, Giacomo, don't leave me!''

He held her closely as she buried her face in the hollow of his shoulder.

''I cannot take you with me,'' he said seriously. ''That is why you must be safe before I leave.''

''Safe? Safe from what?''

He pushed her a little away and his expression was serious. ''Your mother and grandmother are serious in their ambitions, Jasmine. They need you to complete their plans.''

"What are you saying?'' she demanded. "Do you imagine that they would try to spirit me out of Paris? All they want is a child to inherit the titles and fortunes of my husband and his father. Perhaps it could be your child, Giacomo. They would not care.''

"If you were to bear a child nine months from now, no one would believe it belonged to your husband. You must cohabit with him for some time at least. For that reason you must have a protector by the time I must go on my travels.''

He shivered a little and, climbing out of the big bed, went to the fireplace and pushed a few more logs into the fire. She watched him, an expression of uneasy curiosity on her face.

"What are you suggesting?'' she asked as he climbed back into the bed.

"I am suggesting,'' he replied, pulling her back into his arms, "that, should the King desire to make you his mistress, you should accept the position.''

Her eyes widened and she pushed away from him.

"Giacomo! You want me to be the King's mistress?''

He nodded. "What more powerful protector could you have? As the King's mistress you would be constantly surrounded by people. No one could do you harm.''

She gazed deeply into his dark eyes. "But I don't want the King. How can you imagine that I would want the King after I've been with you?''

He smiled, accepting the compliment. "If half of what I hear is true, you would not be disappointed in the King. Every woman who has been his mistress agrees that the King is tireless in love. It is well known that on his wedding night he made love to the Queen seven times. Surely no woman could ask for more than that. From what Henriette says he is still capable of making love four times or even five in a single night. It is for that reason that he keeps the villa at Parc aux Cerfs. Madame de Pompadour, though he loves her to distraction, does not possess the stamina to satisfy his physical desires. It is on a more spiritual plane that their souls meet and become united. But the woman who can slake the burning thirst of his passion could be a rich and powerful woman.''

Jasmine shook her head. "I don't want power and riches, Giacomo. I only want you.''

"With riches and power you can buy anything you desire.''

Smiling coyly, she nibbled his ear. "And what is your price, Monsieur?''

He laughed and stroked her cheek. "Delightful creature! I am jealous of the King already!''

They kissed but the fragile spell was broken by another shattering sneeze from the drawing room.

"Ahhh-choo!'' Casanova mocked, and Jasmine slapped him lightly on the bottom.

"You're terrible!'' she chided.

"On the contrary, Madame la Marquise, I've been told that I'm quite wonderful!''

"And not the least bit conceited.''

"Conceited!'' His tone was incredulous. "Am I to blame for the opinions of others?''

She giggled and then sighed as he took her into his arms.

"Well, my darling,'' Casanova said as he approached the bathtub in which Jasmine lolled contentedly. "It would seem that you are a sensation at Court.''

She raised an eyebrow as he brought a chair from the window and sat beside the tub. "What do you mean?''

He waved a sheet of paper. "This message has just arrived from the Hôtel de Bourbon. From the Abbé de Bernis, to be precise. He has been asked by the King to bring Madame la Marquise de Saint-Antoine to Versailles for an intimate supper with the King and a few selected friends."

'And are you one of the King's few, selected friends, Monsieur le Chevalier de Seingalt?''

He gazed at her for a long moment. "No," he said at last.

She sat up in the tub. "No? Giacomo, if you are teasing me . . ."

"I am not teasing you, my angel. Do you think that His Majesty would invite the lover of a woman he himself desires? With his temperament can you imagine that he would want to admire a woman and beside her see the man who has known her favors?"

"I won't go." Swinging her legs over the side of the gilded tub, she stepped down onto the bed steps which had been placed beside it. The tub, which was suspended between four caryatids, rocked and sent scented, soapy water over the carpet.

Casanova caught her as she walked away and, heedless of the fine embroidered satin of his suit, jerked her against himself.

"You will go, Jasmine. Don't you remember what we talked about the other night?"

"No! No, I don't remember what we talked about! I don't want to remember! All I know is that I will not be led into Versailles like one of the harlots of Parc Aux Cerfs!"

"The protection you must have . . ."

"Stop it, Giacomo! I do not, for one moment, believe

that there is some conspiracy between my mother and my grandmother. I think it is your conspiracy! I think you want me to become the King's mistress so that you will be rid of me! Is that it? Are you tired of me?''

''Of course not, don't be foolish . . .''

''Foolish! Now I am foolish? Am I foolish because I love you? I love you, Giacomo. When my mother took me away from Virginia and Barrett Paxton, I didn't think I would ever love anyone again but I love you!'' Her chin quivered. ''Or are you weary of hearing that? Have so many women said those words to you that you no longer listen to them?''

She turned away from him to hide her embarrassment and pulled a thick dressing gown about herself.

He came to her and, sitting on the sofa, drew her onto his lap. ''Of course I listen to them, Jasmine. But you must understand my concern for you. You may think I am exaggerating when I speak of a conspiracy to return you to your husband but believe me, I know about women. I have often met women like your mother and your grandmother. They would be most anxious that your husband think your child was his own flesh and blood. For that you must be induced to be his wife—in every sense of the word. And, as long as he is banished to the country, you must be returned to the country.''

''And so,'' she finished for him, ''if I am at Versailles, safe in the King's bed, they will be unable to force me back to my husband.''

''Exactly!''

She slid off his lap and stood before him, arms akimbo. ''Very well, if you want me to go to Versailles, I will! I will wear my most daring gown and should the King desire to make love to me before the entire Court, I will oblige him! Does that satisfy you?"

"You must not allow him to make love to you tonight."

"What! You want me to be the King's mistress but you do want me to make love to him. Will you explain exactly how I can accomplish both those things at the same time?"

"Jasmine. Any strumpet from Parc aux Cerfs will accommodate the King on demand. You must make him desire you. You must allow him only enough liberties to make his Bourbon temperament scream for more."

She looked away. "There is a name for a woman like that, Monsieur, and it is not a complimentary one."

"It may not be a complimentary name, Madame, but it often makes an impression where meek surrender fails. You are a great lady of the Court of Versailles. The King would not expect you to lie down like a paid whore."

She sat down and, crossing her legs, leaned her elbows on her knees and her chin in her hands.

"Ah! And now the knowledgeable Chevalier de Seingalt is going to teach me the fine art of aristocratic harlotry."

He frowned and stood. "I am trying to help you, Jasmine. A woman alone needs protection. I have tried to help you secure the best protection a woman can have in France. If you choose not to take advantage of my help, I leave the matter entirely in your hands."

As she watched, he drew on a surtout and clapped on a hat trimmed with fine Spanish lace. Without a backward glance or parting word, he left the bedroom and she heard him slam out of the apartment.

Jasmine stood alone in the bedchamber and shivered in spite of the crackling fire in the fireplace. It was up to her now—it was her decision to make. She retrieved the paper he'd left on the sofa. The Abbé would arrive at five to take her to Versailles.

In a muddle of indecision, she sank onto the sofa. Part of her was determined to refuse the King's invitation, knowing as she did what it would mean if she accepted, but part of her was exhilarated by the thought of being included in the most select group of people in France. It was well known that the King, being a shy man, rarely admitted newcomers to his intimate gatherings. Those ladies and gentlemen who frequented the private entertainments of his Petits Appartements were by and large old friends who had proved their loyalty over the course of many years. That she, after only one appearance at Court, should be invited was an accomplishment without equal. It was a personal triumph only slightly tarnished by the fact that it was not her wit and personality that elicited the invitation, but the King's lust for her person.

She stretched out on the sofa and drew her cold feet beneath the hem of her dressing gown. Immersed in her indecision, she did not hear Henriette enter the room.

"I couldn't help hearin', Marquise," she said. "You and the Chevalier had an argument. Is that why he stomped out of here?"

Jasmine nodded. "He wanted me to go to supper at Versailles tonight and I did not want to go."

"Great Jupiter, Marquise, why wouldn't you want to go?"

"The King wants me to be his mistress."

"And you don't want to? Pardon me for speaking frankly, Madame, but you must be loose in the head! Even if the King was a wizened old man who couldn't do justice by a woman nine times out of ten there would still be women eager to lay down their all for the honor of the position of royal mistress."

Jasmine waved a hand, silencing her. "You sound like Giacomo. Very well, I will go to Versailles; if only to escape the nagging I have been the target of here. Madame Thibault brought some of the gowns I ordered. Look through them and decide which you think the King would like. You know him better than I do."

The gown that Henriette chose was of periwinkle satin. Worn over an oval hoop, the periwinkle over-dress was open from the waist down and an underskirt of white chiffon was embroidered with silver thread. Flounces of silver lace decorated the center front of the bodice from the deeply pointed bottom of the edge of the low, wide décolletage. The elbow-length satin sleeves were edged with silver lace and, from beneath the edging, four wide flounces of heavy, white lace fell halfway to her wrists. Her slippers were of silver brocade, and a white lace ruffle threaded through with silver ribbon ran around her throat. Her hair was drawn into a chignon atop her head and diamond earrings completed the ensemble.

"Well, Henriette?" she asked, turning slowly in a circle. "Do you think the King will notice me?"

"He could hardly notice anyone else!" Henriette breathed. "You'll make Madame de Pompadour seem like an old hag!"

Jasmine frowned. "I'm not sure that would be wise. Madame de Pompadour may not be the King's mistress in the full sense of the word but she is first in his affections and, I sense, determined to remain first!"

A rapping at the outer door of the apartment interrupted them and Henriette went to answer it.

The Abbé de Bernis smiled as Henriette showed him into the bedchamber where Jasmine still stood before the mirror.

"You are ravishing, Madame," he said. "It is not difficult to understand the King's interest in you."

"Thank you, Your Excellency." She stood still while Henriette draped a matching pelisse of periwinkle velvet lined with astrakhan over her shoulders. She took her fan, whose painted pastoral scene she considered a bit more erotic than proper, and tucked it into her astrakhan-lined velvet muff. "It would seem," she told the Abbé, "that I am ready."

She took the Abbé's arm and they left the apartment and went to the beautiful gilded coach which waited in the courtyard to take them to Versailles. As the coach rolled out of the courtyard and through Paris, she wondered if she had made the right decision. She wished she could have spoken to Giacomo before she'd left—she wished they could have settled their differences.

The Abbé noticed her biting her lower lip and chuckled. "Nervous, Marquise?" he asked. "You need not be. In merely being invited you have won half the battle. The King is obvioiusly very attracted, some would say infatuated, by you. Smile, Marquise, your troubles are nearly over."

Jasmine smiled wanly but, as the coach entered the Avenue de Paris which would take them to Versailles, she had an uneasy feeling that her troubles were only beginning.

Chapter 24

Jasmine lowered her eyes as she passed through the magnificent salons on her way to the King's private entertainments. As they entered the Galerie des Glaces, she whispered to the Abbé de Bernis:

"They are all staring. Have they nothing better to do?"

Without a pause in his nodding and smiling, the Abbé replied: "They are here purposely. It has been a great many years since a lady of the Court threatened La Pompadour's position. They want to see the woman who succeeded where so many have failed."

"What must the Queen think of all this?"

"The Queen is in the happy position of ignoring it all. You have not been formally presented at Court and therefore, as far as she is concerned, you do not exist."

Pausing at one of the sets of mirrored doors, the Abbé gave their names to a pair of lackeys who opened the doors enough for them to enter. As they stood there, neither noticed the surprised eyes of her grandmother, the Marquise de Mareteleur, upon them.

The gentlemen in the room looked up from their discussions as Jasmine and the Abbé entered. They rose slowly as Jasmine sank into a curtsy.

The Duc de Richelieu, whom Jasmine recognized from the day the King had sent her for the doctor, bowed shallowly. She felt his cool eyes sweeping over her and experienced a feeling not unlike that she'd experience in her husband's company. Elegant in bottle-green velvet, his waistcoat was exquisitely embroidered in gold.

"Madame de Saint-Antoine?" he said, holding out a hand to help her rise from her curtsy. "May I extend my welcome to Court?"

"Thank you, Your Excellency," she murmured.

Relinquishing his hold on her elbow, the Abbé stepped back and watched in amusement as the Duc took possession of her. It was no secret at Court that the Duc hated Madame de Pompadour. In spite of her grand title and ever-growing wealth, he despised her for her bourgeois origins. In his mind, she was no better than the King's wantons at Parc aux Cerfs. It made no difference to him that she was a grand lady in the best traditions of the French Court; that she was cultured and possessed perfect manners mattered not the slightest. She had been born the daughter of a steward and no matter how noble her title or how large her fortune, a steward's daughter was what she would remain.

"Madame la Marquise de Saint-Antoine," the Duc de Richelieu said grandly, "His Excellency, the Duc d'Ayen."

The Duc d'Ayen, who—unlike the Duc de Richelieu—liked Madame de Pompadour, inclined his head politely and looked at Jasmine as though she were a curiosity brought back from an excursion to the mysterious East.

"Welcome, Madame," he said coolly. "I believe you have met Monsieur de Quesnay."

"Indeed I have, Your Excellency," she replied, smiling shyly toward the doctor.

As the two Ducs moved off to speak to the Abbé de Bernis, Jasmine shifted uncomfortably from one foot to the other.

"How is Madame de Pompadour?" she asked Doctor Quesnay. "I assume she is feeling better."

"Why do you assume so, Madame?" the doctor asked.

Embarrassed, she fastened her eyes onto the gold buttons on his claret-colored velvet coat. "I assumed so, Monsieur, because I did not think his Majesty would tax her strength with a dinner party unless she were feeling better."

"And you think she is going to attend?"

Her frown showed plainly in her eyes. "Isn't she?"

The doctor smiled, liking her better for the lack of eager ambition she displayed. "Yes, Madame, she is. She and the King will be host and hostess for the evening. As you can see, there will be only six of us. Four gentlemen and two ladies; admirable odds, don't you think?"

Jasmine was puzzled. "Four gentlemen? There are four of you here—the King would make five."

"His Excellency, the Abbé de Bernis, will not be joining us. He will pay his respects to His Majesty and then leave."

"But why? I thought Madame de Pompadour was fond of him."

"She is. But the Abbé is a priest and, by tradition, priests do not dine with His Majesty."

"Then I am to be abandoned by my escort?"

He smiled. "I am certain His Excellency, the Duc de Richelieu, would be happy to be your escort."

A lackey brought them champagne and Jasmine glanced at him over the rim of her glass.

"Monsieur de Quesnay, may I speak frankly?" She waited for him to nod. "I have heard that Madame de Pompadour and the Duc de Richelieu are, shall we say, less than boon companions. I take no sides; I do not intend to become the Duc's protegée. My attitude toward Madame de Pompadour before I came to Versailles was one of complete admiration. I never entertained thoughts of supplanting her. I have no designs on any part of the King's affections. I am flattered by His Majesty's attention and I will not deliberately spurn his friendship if it is offered to me; but I would appreciate it if you could tell Madame de Pompadour that I am not interested in becoming Maîtress en Titre regardless of the gossip to the contrary. Will you tell her that for me?"

The doctor looked toward the set of doors which were even then opening. As the men in the room bowed and Jasmine sank into a curtsy, the doctor whispered:

"Why don't you tell her yourself, Madame?"

The King, handsome in a suit of burgundy velvet with a waistcoat of gray satin embroidered in burgundy, entered the room with a smile on his face and Madame de Pompadour on his arm. They circled the room going first to the Duc d'Ayen, who bowed over the King's hand and kissed the Marquise's cheek, then to the Duc de Richelieu, whose greeting to the King was full of respect while his salute to the Marquise was as cool as he dared make it. The Abbé de Bernis smiled his charming smile as they exchanged greetings, and then it was

Jasmine's turn.

She curtsied before the King and kissed his out-stretched hand. Not daring to raise her eyes to their faces, she curtsied again to Madame de Pompadour.

"Marquise de Saint-Antoine," he said with his odd habit of addressing courtiers by their titles, "I am glad you could join us."

"The honor was mine, Your Majesty."

"May I say, Madame," the Marquise de Pompadour added, "that your gown is really quite lovely."

Jasmine looked up shyly. "Thank you, Madame, you are most kind. Of course, your own ensemble is far lovelier."

The Marquise pressed a hand to her taffeta gown which was painted with delicately beautiful oriental designs. She was acutely aware of the difference in their ages and the fact that she could have been, just barely, she reminded herself, the younger girl's mother. She knew the King's penchant for young girls and, until now, had been relieved that there were few, if any, at Court.

"Nonsense, Madame," she replied, pleased at the humble tone the girl adopted. "However, since we are the only ladies in this gathering of admiring gentlemen, let us settle on camaraderie rather than rivalry, shall we?"

Jasmine breathed a sigh of relief. "Gladly, Madame," she replied passionately.

The Abbé having departed, Jasmine found herself taken under the wing of the Duc de Richelieu. He seemed to have appointed himself her unofficial escort and the musky scent with which he perfumed himself filled her nostrils until she feared she would suffocate.

The evening progressed and it seemed a good one,

though Jasmine felt consistently left out of their conversation and jests. Not only was she unfamiliar with the people and events which formed the pivotal points of their anecdotes, she was so much younger than anyone else that she often felt like a child who is dragged along for want of a nursemaid. Of the six people in the room, the Marquise de Pompadour, at thirty-five, was the closest to her own age. The gentlemen were many years her senior, the Duc d'Ayen being the youngest at forty-three and the Duc de Richelieu and Doctor Quesnay the oldest being both sixty-three years of age. It made her uncomfortable to know that some of the events they discussed happened years before her birth.

She was relieved to see that the King did not intend to linger over dinner. When the meal was served it was eaten with a minimum of conversation for the food was delicious and if one desired to eat one's entire portion before the King signalled for the next course to be brought, one was obliged to direct all one's attention to the food.

Under the cover of a story the Marquise de Pompadour was relating, the Duc de Richelieu said:

"His Majesty is a bit edgy tonight."

Jasmine sipped her champagne thoughtfully. "What makes you say that, Your Excellency?"

"He hasn't demonstrated how deftly he can knock the top off a boiled egg."

She looked at the dish of boiled eggs which sat near the King's elbow and then back at the Duc.

"Is that generally the evening's pièce de résistance?" He nodded and the look of abject boredom on his face made her smile.

"Mesdames, Messeigneurs," the King said, "shall we retire?"

Offering his arm to the Marquise de Pompadour, the King left the dining room and went to a magnificent salon where sofas were placed near the fireplace and a few gilded tables were furnished with cards and backgammon sets.

"Jean-Louis," Madame de Pompadour said to the Duc d'Ayen, "you must play backgammon with me. You must give me a chance to win back all those thousands of livres you have relieved me of."

"I hope you are prepared to lose some more," d'Ayen warned her good-naturedly as he held her chair.

The Duc de Richelieu and Doctor Quesnay already occupied a table and the Duc deftly dealt cards.

As for the King, Jasmine was surprised to see him working diligently at a table pouring freshly brewed coffee into delicate porcelain cups.

Unsure of what was expected of her, Jasmine wandered about the room looking at the art works which decorated the walls. Holbeins and Raphaels, among others, adorned the walls and she studied them intently. When she reached the fireplace she was surprised to find a thick cushion of crimson velvet trimmed with gold braid upon which slept an enormous white angora cat.

Sitting on the Savonnerie carpet near the edge of the hearth, she stroked the cat's silky fur. Opening its golden eyes, the animal acknowledged her presence by stretching and resuming its former position.

"Madame?"

She looked up to find the King standing over her, a cup in his outstretched hand. Taking the hot cup gingerly, she sat it carefully on the tiles of the hearth.

Long days spent in the saddle worked to the King's advantage as he gracefully lowered himself to her side.

He raised an eyebrow at her astonishment. "Is something wrong, Marquise?'' he asked over the rim of his cup.

"You're sitting on the floor!" she said incredulously.

He smiled. "I can take that remark as a compliment reflecting your concern for my royal dignity, or I can take it as surprise on your part that I can still get around so well at my advanced age."

"I did not mean it that way, Your Majesty," Jasmine said, blushing.

"I am glad. Do you like my cat?"

She stroked the sleeping cat once more. "Oh, yes! He is quite beautiful!"

"Reinette's dog, Plon, used to chase him until one day several courtiers took it upon themselves to pour champagne down his throat. Apparently it endowed him with an unusual amount of courage for he promptly avenged himself on the unfortunate dog."

Jasmine giggled. Smiling at the King, she did not see the triumphant smirk which crossed the Duc de Richelieu's features, nor the tiny frown which touched Madame de Pompadour's. She picked up her coffee and sipped it, trying to hide her distaste for the bitter brew.

As a valet entered the room to remove the coffee set and replace it with a fresh one, a draft swept across the room. It passed Jasmine enveloping her in the heavy scent of the Duc de Richelieu's musky perfume. She wrinkled her nose and the King nodded.

"A bit overpowering, no?"

She nodded and he drew a small, stoppered bottle from his pocket. Drawing out the stopper, he held it beneath her nose.

Inhaling the sweet scent, she smiled. "It's lovely."

Using the stopper, he applied it to his wrists beneath his shirt ruffles and behind his ears near the edge of his powdered wig. Holding out the stopper, he offered it to her. She held out her hands and he touched the cool glass stopper to her wrists and just behind each of her ears. Then, oblivious to the presence of the others, he dipped the stopper into the tiny bottle once again and, looking deeply into her eyes, touched it to the valley of her breasts just above the edge of her neckline.

Jasmine drew a sharp breath and returned her attention to the cat.

"Do you know what the scent is?" he asked softly.

Still refusing to look at him, she shook her head. "No, Your Majesty."

"It is Jasmine. I have had it distilled especially from plants in the greenhouses." Lifting her hand, he kissed it. "It smells different on your skin than mine." Leaning toward her, he pretended to smell the perfume near her ear but she felt the slight touch of his lips on her earlobe.

Frightened that he might decide to smell the perfume he'd daubed on her breasts, she pretended to shiver and reached up and, crossing her arms over her bosom, grasped her shoulders.

"Are you chilly?" he asked.

She nodded in spite of the fact that she was sitting only a few feet from the fireplace. To her alarm, he pulled off his own velvet coat and slipped it around her shoulders.

"Is that better?"

She was stiflingly hot but only nodded. "Thank you, Your Majesty."

In an effort to turn his attention to something other than herself, Jasmine picked up a book which had been left on a sofa and idly flipped through it.

"What a beautiful binding this is," she murmured,

fingering the fine morocco binding with the royal coat of arms in gold.

"Are you fond of books?" he asked.

"Oh, yes. My father had a fine library."

Standing, he offered her his hand. "Come, I will show you my library."

Realizing that she had trapped herself, she put her hand into his and he pulled her to her feet.

"Sit, sit," the King told the others who had interrupted their games to stand when he stood. "I am merely going to take Madame de Saint-Antoine to see the library. Please, continue with your amusements."

Not daring to look at the Marquise de Pompadour, Jasmine left the room on the King's arm, draped in his velvet coat.

To her surprise, he led her out of the room and up a tiny staircase. The rooms into which he took her were much smaller than either the State Apartment or the Petits Appartements, but they were so exquisitely decorated as to be breathtaking.

"Do you like this apartment?" he asked.

"Oh, yes. It is magnificent," she replied.

"It used to be Reinette's, before she moved downstairs."

He led her into a little room which had filled bookcases lining the walls.

"I find that my collection of volumes grows faster than I can find space to store them."

Jasmine went to the first of the cases and examined the books it contained.

The King opened the case and drew out a volume. "Do you enjoy poetry?"

"Very much."

"This is a very fine volume of poetry." Handing it to her, he led her to a sofa which was near a candleabrum.

Jasmine opened the volume of poetry but did not look at what it contained. She looked instead at the fire which had obviously been burning for some time, making the room cozy and warm, and the candleabrum which had been burning on the table when they'd entered the room. She threw a suspicious glance toward the King.

Reading the look, he smiled. "No, Madame, I did not plan this. I was here earlier to find the book you noticed downstairs. The fire was kindled and the candles lit then."

Noticing the accumulation of melted wax at the base of the candles, Jasmine found it easy to believe him. Nevertheless, it seemed almost too fortunate for the King to be true.

She returned her attention to the poetry but it was not long before she felt his hand steal about her waist beneath the velvet coat he'd draped about her. She looked up and saw his face close to hers.

"Your Majesty," she said softly.

He pressed his index finger to his lips and then to hers. "Are you frightened of me?"

Her nod was barely perceptible. "A little."

"You've no reason to be frightened. The last thing I would want to do is hurt you."

His odd, husky voice and gentle tone stirred her and she was uncomfortably aware of it. When he took the book from her and laid it aside she looked away, unwilling to look into his dark eyes.

"Jasmine."

She drew a deep breath, knowing what would happen when she turned her face toward him. Without looking, she knew his face was only inches from hers. Slowly, apprehensively, she looked toward him.

Her lips nearly brushed his as she faced him and she shivered as he kissed her. Despite her vow to avoid just such a situation and despite her love for Barrett and infatuation with Casanova, she felt her heart begin to pound. She was unable to resist the strange attraction he held for her. It was more than his looks, which were superb; it was more than his royalty which awed her. There was a certain vulnerability mixed with an over-powering masculinity which crushed her resistance like a fragile flower.

Gently, he pushed her back against the velvet bolster of the little sofa. Her wide, oval hoops which jutted out on either side of her made it impossible for her to roll away from him and escape even if she'd wanted to. As he leaned over her, and his fingers worked at the hooks hidden beneath the silver lace of her bodice, she gazed into his black eyes enraptured.

The hooks yielded and she drew a long, hissing breath as his white-wigged head bent and his lips found her breasts. She knew it would only be a matter of minutes until he made her completely his own and she felt a growing eagerness for that moment to arrive.

She only vaguely heard the light tapping at the door of the little room and the King heard it not at all. When the tapping was repeated, slightly more insistently, she made a little disappointed sound and the King looked over her shoulder toward the door with a frown.

When they heard nothing more, they smiled into one another's eyes and she reached up to stroke the King's cheek and draw his lips toward hers. Neither heard the door-latch being depressed and neither noticed the Duc de Richelieu framed in the doorway watching them silently.

It was Jasmine who noticed him and her violent start made the King look in the direction of her gaze. The Duc bowed and, while Jasmine held her bodice together over her bosom, the King sat up, an expression of intense aggravation showing plainly on his face.

"What is it, Richelieu?" he demanded, his ommission of the Duc's title showing his displeasure.

"I am grieved to have interrupted Your Majesty's pleasure," he said, a smirk twitching the corners of his lips, "but Madame de Pompadour has fainted and been taken to her rooms."

"Fainted? What is wrong with her?"

The Duc shrugged. "She became more and more agitated until, finally, she collapsed. She was carried to her rooms in a state of unconsciousness."

Standing, the King straightened his clothing and took his coat from Jasmine.

"I will go to her. Duc du Richelieu, I hope I may depend upon you to show the Marquise back downstairs?" The Duc bowed his acquiescence and the King turned to Jasmine, who was blushing furiously. "I must go," he said softly. "I will look forward to our next meeting."

Jasmine nodded and, still clasping her gown together, curtsied as he left the room.

As the door closed behind him, her eyes met the narrowed blue eyes of the Duc de Richelieu and she turned away.

Chapter 25

The Marquise de Mareteleur paced the floor of her grand salon while Michel watched her, amused.

"Sofie, Sofie, calm yourself. I do not understand what you are so upset about."

"I told you when I walked through the door what I was upset about! It was Jasmine! The Abbé de Bernis was taking her to the King's apartment! Everyone at Versailles was speaking as though she were already his mistress!"

"Would it not be to our advantage for her to become the King's mistress?"

"Of course it would be to our advantage!" Sofie snapped. "Do you think I am unaware of the benefits which are available to the family of the King's Maîtresse en Titre? Madame de Pompadour is not getting any younger and her health is not what it should be. If the King were already in love with Jasmine when La Pompadour dies, she could step into Pompadour's shoes before her body was cold! But Jasmine is only sixteen— she has plenty of time to capture the King's affections.

Our first priority must be the matter of a child.''

Michel shrugged, smiling. "She could bear the King's child."

Sofie rolled her eyes heavenward. "You know Henri. He would no more accept the King's bastard than he would accept the bastard of that Italian adventurer she has taken refuge with. He has to believe the child to be his. And for that to happen, he has to spend time in her bed.''

"He can hardly spent time in her bed when he is in Saint-Antoine and she is at Versailles."

"That is precisely why we must take her back to Saint-Antoine."

"And then?"

Sofie smiled and patted his cheek. "And then, my darling Michel, we must see that she becomes pregnant."

He raised one blond eyebrow. "May I offer my humble services, Madame?"

"Ah, Michel, what a sacrifice for you, eh? Unfortunately, I do not intend to go to Saint-Antoine with our little Marquise. I will remain in Paris in order that I might keep an eye upon the situation at Versailles. Should another young woman appear at Court and threaten La Pompadour's position, we will bring Jasmine back to Paris just long enough to remind the King of her incomparable charms."

"But what about the child? Do you really think the Marquis de Saint-Antoine is capable of begetting an heir?"

"No. He bedded Jasmine for months and is still sleeping with Isabeau and neither of them conceived a child by him."

"Jasmine miscarried."

"True," Sofie agreed, "but she became pregnant only after admitting you to her bed. I'm convinced the child was yours."

"Then how will she conceive at Saint-Antoine?"

Sofie grinned. "Perhaps the ailing Marquis de Mareteleur could travel to Saint-Antoine for the fresh air in the care of his faithful, and so virile, valet."

Taking her hand, Michel kissed it. "But how," he asked, "do we lure our pretty little moth away from the flame of Versailles?"

Sofie smiled confidently. "We will find a way, Michel, I am convinced of it!"

As the King's steps faded away outside, Jasmine turned her back on Richelieu and began to fasten the tiny hooks up the front of her bodice.

"You should have made more of a show of resistance, Madame," the Duc said.

"I do not need you to instruct me, Your Excellency," Jasmine replied as she heard him approaching and caught a whiff of his musky aroma. "I already have two advisors."

"The Abbé de Bernis and the Chevalier de Seingalt, I presume? If they told you to resist the King, they were correct."

Grasping her arm, the Duc swung her around. Before she knew what was happening, one arm was about her waist, his free hand slipped into her still partially open bodice, and his lips were pressed against hers. She struggled against him, pounding his broad shoulders with her fists. It was only when she dug her nails into the hand which held her breast that he stepped away.

"That," he said, a smile playing about his lips, "is what you should have done with the King!" He glanced ruefully at the bruised flesh of his hand where the marks of her nails showed like little crescent moons. "Though a bit less forcefully."

She glowered at him as she finished hooking her bodice but her anger only made him laugh.

"I am only telling you the truth, Madame. I was the King's friend before you were born; I knew him very well. If you want him to desire you above all others, you must first make him remember you. If you yield too easily, you will be easily forgotten. When he merely wants a female body beneath him, he can send Lebel to Parc aux Cerfs for someone. But you, you must be more than merely a pretty receptacle. You must be different." Seeing that he had her attention, however grudging, he went on with the air of a professor. "Since there is doubtless nothing you could do for him in bed that some little whore with more practice has not done, and probably very well, the only route to memorability open to you is to be the first woman who ever said 'no.'"

She looked at him suspiciously. "Why are you telling me this, Your Excellency? Surely it is not because you are so fond of me."

He grinned. "I am entirely ambiguous toward you, Madame, although you are not without your obvious charms. What I am not ambiguous about is the fact that the position of Maîtresse en Titre, an honorable if somewhat irregular position, is being filled by a woman whose origins are only one step out of the Paris gutters. A King's choice of mistresses reflects upon him. When the Ambassadors of other countries see the King of France making his courtiers bend the knee to a bourgeois steward's daughter, their estimation of him is somewhat lowered. I would like to see the position of Maîtresse en

Titre filled by a woman of gentle birth and noble blood.''

''Me?''

He lifted his shoulders. ''You seem to be the King's first choice. Will you work toward that goal, Madame?''

''I don't like this game I'm being asked to play, Your Excellency,'' she replied coolly. ''Am I then to inflame the King's passions—and my own—and then deny us both release?''

The Duc pursed his lips. ''I wouldn't worry about that, Madame. The King can always find release. He could even go to Madame de Pompadour; she has never refused him. But he would not know satisfaction for you would be the woman he craved. As for your release,'' he followed the edge of her gown's neckline with one beringed finger, ''I would happily give my all for your benefit. After all, I am First Gentleman of the King's bedchamber and responsible for the Court entertainments.''

''How generous of you to offer, Your Excellency,'' she said with a sweet smile. ''But I would rather be left in my misery than be relieved through your offices.''

Laughing, the Duc offered her his arm. ''You are spirited, Madame. I concede you that. But I ask you to remember that I may be either a valuable ally or a most considerable enemy. A few words in the right ears and, in spite of the King's lust for you, you would have a hard time gaining admittance at Parc aux Cerfs let alone Versailles.''

Jasmine said nothing, admitting to herself that his words contained a great deal of truth. He had given her much to think about. As he led her back to the salon of the King's Petits Apartments where the Abbé de Bernis waited to take her back to Paris, she was lost in thought.

It began to rain as the gilded coach of the Abbé de Bernis sped along the Avenue de Paris taking them home from Versailles.

"And so, Madame," the Abbé said over the sound of the coach wheels and the hoofbeats of the horses drawing the coach and those being ridden by four outriders, "did you enjoy your evening in the King's inner sanctum?"

"To a point," Jasmine replied. "Until the King went to see to Madame de Pompadour and I was left in the questionable care of the Duc de Richelieu."

"Did the Duc annoy you?"

"He took it upon himself to advise me on the matter of ascending to the position of Maîtresse en Titre."

"And what was his advice?"

"The same as yours and Giacomo's. Arouse the King to a fury and then deny him the ultimate favor."

"Do you find the idea repugnant?" the Abbé asked.

"I find it odious! I will allow the King no liberties or every liberty."

"And which do you find the more attractive prospect?"

"I will not deny that I find the King desirable. Had the Duc de Richelieu not intervened tonight, I would undoubtedly be the King's mistress by now. But I do not covet Madame de Pompadour's position. I am content to remain with Giacomo."

The coach turned into the courtyard of the Hôtel de Sauveur and the Abbé clasped her hand.

"In spite of my allegiance to my King and my desire to see him happy in all respects, I must say that I am happy for my friend to hear you say so."

The Abbé helped her out of the coach and they

entered the hôtel together. When they reached the door of Casanova's apartment, Jasmine tried the latch but found the door locked.

"I wonder if Giacomo has returned home," Jasmine said as she pulled her key from her muff and fitted it into the lock.

"Probably. His temper can be quick but he forgives as quickly. You will likely find him waiting for you in the bedchamber with open arms and a bottle of champagne."

She laughed and entered the empty drawing room. "It would seem you are correct," she murmured.

The Abbé hesitated. "I think I will leave you here, Madame. I have no wish to intrude upon your reconciliation. Good night."

"Good night, Your Excellency," she replied, tilting her head to allow him to kiss her cheek.

As he left the apartment, she went on through the drawing room and dining room to the bedchamber. But, as she stood outside the door, she heard a feminine giggle followed by a hearty sneeze.

"Pardon me, Monseigneur," Henriette said coyly.

"Think nothing of it, my little seraph," Casanova replied.

Eyes blazing, Jasmine pushed open the door and stood, seething, in the doorway.

Casanova and Henriette lay on the bed, their skins glowing pink in the firelight. As Casanova bent his head to the pulsing hollow of Henriette's throat, the girl groaned and turned her head to the side. Her eyelids fluttered open and her mouth dropped when she saw Jasmine standing in the doorway like a wrathful avenging angel.

"Oh, my," Henriette whimpered.

Casanova looked toward the door and, seeing Jasmine, moved warily away from Henriette.

"You are home early, my angel," he said cheerfully.

"So it would seem!" Jasmine snapped. "Pray, don't let me interrupt your pleasure," she said with a bow reminiscent of the Duc de Richelieu's.

Backing out of the room, she pulled the door shut with a crash.

"Jasmine!" Casanova's voice was muffled by the door. "Jasmine, wait!"

Ignoring him, she left the apartment and hurried down to the courtyard. Her heels clacking on the wet cobbles, she ran across the courtyard as fast as her swaying hoops and heavy skirts would allow and pushed open one side of the tall, iron gates.

Standing in the Rue Croix des Petits Champs, she hailed a fiacre which was passing by.

Climbing into the hackney, she called: "Hôtel de Mareteleur. It is in the Faubourg Saint-Germain in the Rue de Lille."

As the fiacre started off she glanced through the gates of the Hôtel de Sauveur and saw Casanova standing just outside the doorway in the rain clad in a dressing gown and slippers. She leaned back against the grimy leather upholstery of the hackney and bit her lip to force the sobs down into her throat.

The concierge of the Hôtel de Marteleur leaned out of his lodge, angry at being disturbed from the first dozings of his night's slumber.

"What do you want?" he growled.

"Open up for the Marquise de Saint-Antoine!" the fiacre driver bawled.

The concierge peered into the darkness of the cab and,

recognizing Jasmine, stumbled out of his lodge and swung the gates wide.

The fiacre rolled over the cobbles of the courtyard and drew up before the grand front door of the hôtel. As she stepped out of the cab, Jasmine tossed the driver a louis d'or.

"I can't change this, Madame La Marquise," the driver told her after biting the coin.

"Keep it," she replied, already halfway to the door.

As though eager to leave before she could change her mind, the driver cracked his whip over his horse and rolled off into the night.

Jasmine rapped on the door and pulled the bell-chain. She waited impatiently and was about to pull the chain again when the door was opened.

A lackey stepped back in surprise as Jasmine pushed past him and entered the hôtel.

"Where is the Marquise?" she demanded.

"In the front parlor, Madame La Marquise," the startled lackey sputtered.

Marching along the corridor, Jasmine stopped before the closed doors of the parlor and tapped lightly.

"Entrez!" the Marquise called from within the room.

Jasmine opened the door and found her grandmother seated in an armchair while Michel stoked the fire.

Mouth open in astonishment, the Marquise got slowly to her feet while Michel nearly dropped the brass poker.

"Jasmine?" the Marquise whispered as though seeing a vision.

Safe in the familiar surroundings of her grandmother's home, Jasmine gave way to her chagrin and her chin quivered.

"Grand-mère?" she murmured. "I've left Giacomo. He . . . he . . ."

271

"Oh, my darling!" the Marquise exclaimed, flinging her arms wide. "Has he hurt you? The cur!"

As Jasmine rushed into her grandmother's embrace and buried her sobs in the Marquise's plump shoulder, Sofie looked over her granddaughter's shoulder toward Michel.

They exchanged a delightedly amazed smile. Their prayers had been answered; the golden pigeon had come home to roost.

Chapter 26

Jasmine sat on the sofa of the front parlor staring moodily into the fire. Claudette, who had entered the employ of the Marquise de Mareteleur after her dismissal from the Château de Saint-Antoine, had helped her out of her gown and into a nightdress of fine linen and a robe of lime-green velvet. Her hair was brushed out and hung in waves over her shoulders and she seemed completely unaware of the speculative glances her grandmother and the valet directed at her and one another.

"Jasmine?" Sofie said softly. When her grand-daughter failed to respond she leaned over and touched her arm.

Jasmine started. "I'm sorry, Grand-mère," she said quickly. "Did you say something?"

"I was only going to ask if you would like some chocolate. The cook has been dismissed but Michel is very good at making chocolate."

"Thank you, yes. I would like a cup of chocolate."

Michel bowed and left the room and Sofie moved closer to her on the sofa.

"And so, my darling. Did you enjoy your dinner with the King?"

Jasmine looked at her in surprise. "How did you know about that?"

"I was at Versailles tonight. I was standing in the Hall of Mirrors when the Abbé de Bernis took you to the Petits Appartements."

"I didn't see you."

Sofie chuckled. "No. I'd wager you didn't see much of anything! You were too busy looking at the floor!" Placing a finger beneath her granddaughter's chin, she lifted her face. "Hold your head up, Jasmine. It is no sin to be desired by a King. Women can be raised from the gutters to the highest place in the kingdom through a King's love."

Jasmine smiled sadly. "As Madame de Pompadour was raised?"

"That peasant!" the Marquise spat. "It is time she was returned to the gutters that spawned her!"

"The Duc de Richelieu said that very thing to me tonight—or something very like that."

"His Excellency!" Sofie was impressed. "He took an interest in you?"

"He took it upon himself to advise me in the matter of becoming the King's mistress."

Sofie clasped her hands over her bosom. "If His Excellency favors you, you will become exactly what he wants you to be." Her eyes glittered at the prospect. "Tell me, what did he tell you to do?"

"He told me to respond to the King's advances—to lead him to the very brink of ecstasy and then leave him there."

Sofie nodded. "I have always said His Excellency was a

very wise man. Such tactics would drive the King wild with desire for you.''

Jasmine smiled as she accepted her cup of chocolate from Michel. ''I should think it would make him hate the sight of me.''

''You do not understand men, my poppet. And especially men like the King. He has been spoiled from the day of his birth. When the measles epidemic took the lives of his parents and brother and he was the last legitimate descendant the old King had, he was treated as though he was made of spun glass. His every wish was gratified. I am not so very many years older than he but I can remember seeing him pushed about the gardens of Versailles and the Tuilleries in a wheeled cart lest he walk by himself and perchance fall. He became King when he was five years old and, since then, I doubt he has ever been refused anything he really wanted.''

''Until now,'' Michel said with a smile that was more a leer.

''He would not have been refused even now had not the Marquise de Pompadour fainted and the Duc de Richelieu come to inform the King.''

''Then for once I am grateful to the Marquise de Pompadour,'' Sofie declared. ''It would have been a tragedy if you had surrendered so easily.''

Finishing her chocolate, Jasmine stood. ''Frankly, Grand-mère, I am tired of discussing the matter. I will sleep with any man I please.'' Pausing at the door, she looked back at them. ''Or with any man who pleases me. Now, if you do not mind, I am tired of being discussed as though I were a commodity. Good night, Grand-mère. Good night, Michel.''

With the sound of her granddaughter's footsteps

fading into the distance, the Marquise arched an eyebrow at Michel.

"She has grown up in these past months, Michel."

"Indeed she has. She has more spirit; it becomes her."

"Yes. She is rapidly turning from a pretty child into a beautiful woman. We must get her back to Saint-Antoine and get this business of the child finished quickly."

Michel sipped his chocolate thoughtfully. "I could go to her tonight. Perhaps she is in a mood for revenge against her Italian lover."

Sofie went to where he sat near the fireplace and stroked his blond hair. Taking hold of his long, black-beribboned queue, she jerked his head back.

"Do not be so overeager for my granddaughter's bed, Michel. She will be yours in time. Meanwhile, I will remind you that your first duty is to me. I want you in my bed tonight. Look in on Alexandre and then come to me."

Michel pried her fingers away from his hair and stood. "Be careful, Sofie, or I will use your own advice against you. I may just drive you to the brink of ecstasy and then leave you there. There are many pretty—young—maid-servants in this house who wouldn't object to my finishing with them what I begin with you."

Pushing her aside, he strode from the room knowing, as he did, that she would be the more eager for him after his insolence.

Jasmine lay in her bed, her arms wrapped about a large feather pillow. She frowned in her sleep and then smiled for, in her mind, she had returned to Virginia and Belle Glade. Barrett Paxton was there—gentle, kind Barrett. There was no jealous Marquises nor scheming courtiers.

There was no black-eyed Casanova who could crush her heart in the twinkling of an eye. There was only Barrett beneath the willows on the banks of Mobjack Bay. In her dream they lay beneath the willows' boughs and her head rested on his shoulder while he tickled her cheek with a long blade of grass.

The sound of a door closing disturbed her and she opened her eyes. The soft, scented shoulder of Barrett Paxton had regained its true shape and, with an anguished cry, she pushed the plump pillow over the edge of the bed.

"Barrett," she whispered aloud in the empty room. "If only they had let me stay with you. If only they had made me your wife, how happy I would have been! If only . . ." Her words trailed off and, ignoring the hot tears which filled her eyes and overflowed to stain her pillow's case, she slipped back into a troubled sleep.

"Giacomo is very sorry about this misunderstanding," the Abbé de Bernis began.

"There was no misunderstanding, Your Excellency," Jasmine replied. "He and Henriette Beaujean were naked, in bed, making love. That leaves very little room for misinterpretation."

"Still, Madame, you are being a bit harsh, aren't you? After all, only an hour or so previously you yourself were in a state of some undress with a man other than Giacomo. You told me that you would have gladly become the King's mistress if not interrupted."

Jasmine leaned against the mantel in the front parlor of the Hôtel de Mareteleur. "I will have you remember, Monsieur l'Abbé, tha Giacomo himself counseled me to become the King's mistress. I gave him no such advice

277

concerning Henriette.''

Sighing, the exasperated Abbé leaned his chin on the gold head of his walking stick while, outside the closed doors, the Marquise and Michel leaned closer to hear everything.

"Jasmine," the Abbé said at last, his voice soft and persuasive, "you love Giacomo, don't you?"

"I love only one man, Monsieur l'Abbé, but I am very fond of Giacomo."

"Well, whatever your feelings, he needs you."

"Then why didn't he come himself and tell me so?"

The Abbé shrugged. "He's a proud man unused to pursuing women. You should consider it a compliment that he put forth the effort to find you."

Her laugh was scornful. "Come now, Your Excellency, it could not have been so difficult. Where else could I have gone? Who else do I know in Paris? Did he expect me to go back to Versailles and ask to sleep on Madame de Pompadour's chaise longue again?"

"Still, he might not have bothered."

"Why should he have? His bed is full."

"You underestimate his depth of feeling for you."

"No, I do not! If anything, I overestimated it. Now, Your Excellency, if you have nothing more to say to me, I will bid you good day."

The Abbé stood as she curtsied. "If you change your mind, do not hesitate to send for me or Giacomo."

She shook her head. "I will not change my mind."

The Abbé followed her out of the room and they found the Marquise and Michel standing at the far end of the corridor conversing with a hastily summoned maid-servant.

"You're not leaving so soon, Your Excellency?" Sofie

cried, hurrying toward him.

"Alas, Madame, business of state leaves me little time for socializing."

"Will you allow me to see you to your coach?"

He offered her his arm and, with another supplicating glance at Jasmine, left the hôtel.

"Well, Madame," Michel said as the door closed behind the Marquise de Mareteleur and the Abbé, "has His Excellency convinced you to return to your Chevalier de Seingalt?"

Jasmine lifted her chin and set her jaw stubbornly. "No! If he wants his little harlot from the Parc aux Cerfs he is welcome to her and she to him!"

"It will not be long before he realizes the enormity of his loss."

Jasmine smiled up at the handsome valet through lowered lashes. Casanova had hurt her pride and it was comforting to see such unconcealed admiration in a man's eyes. She smiled as Michel leaned over and pressed his lips to her throat. It was as much the thought of avenging herself on Giacomo as it was Michel's lips and ever-boldening caresses that titillated her senses.

When he whispered a decidedly improper suggestion into her ear, she giggled and nodded. Hand in hand, they climbed the stairs to her suite where, she assured herself, she would have her revenge on the fickle Chevalier de Seingalt.

As Sofie turned back toward the front doors of the hôtel, the sound of a heavy coach passing through the gateway made her look back.

A grand coach drawn by six matched black horses circled the courtyard and drew up before the entrance. Sofie pressed a hand to her bosom as she recognized the gilded coat of arms of the Duc de Richelieu emblazoned on the door.

She sank to the ground as a footman opened the coach door and lowered the steps. The Duc stepped down and critically surveyed his surroundings.

"Good day, Madame de Mareteleur," he said.

"Good day, Your Excellency," she breathed. "I am honored to receive you in my home."

"Of course." He followed her into the hôtel. "Was that the Abbé de Bernis just leaving as I arrived?"

"Yes, Your Excellency. His Excellency came to speak to my granddaughter. Won't you step into the parlor?"

The Duc went into the parlor and, refusing a lackey's offer to relieve him of his surtout and hat, sat on the recently vacated sofa.

"That is exactly why I am here. I was informed at Madame de Saint-Antoine's former lodgings that she was now residing here."

"Yes, Your Excellency, that is true. My granddaughter is in her rooms. If you will excuse me, I will get her."

As she hurried upstairs, Sofie's eyes glistened with a mixture of pride and newly born respect. That such illustrious personages as the Abbé de Bernis and the Duc de Richelieu should come to try to persuade her granddaughter to do anything suddenly made her realize the potential power that seemed within Jasmine's reluctant grasp. She entered Jasmine's suite and went to the bedchamber. Flinging open the door, she found her granddaughter and Michel locked in one another's arms. The greater part of their clothing was flung about the floor and Jasmine's flower-trimmed chignon was a shambles.

As her grandmother approached the bed, Jasmine smiled over her shoulder.

"Good afternoon, Grand-mère. Have you seen the Abbé off?"

Sofie snatched Jasmine's petticoat from the floor and threw it at her.

"Get dressed! The Duc de Richelieu is downstairs and wants to talk to you."

"I don't want to talk to him. Tell him to go away."

"Don't be a fool! Michel, take your clothing and get out!"

His passion considerably cooled, the valet slipped off the bed and struggled into his satin livery.

"Michel!" Jasmine contradicted. "You don't have to go."

"I think it would be wise if he did, Madame," the Duc de Richelieu said from the doorway.

Jasmine held the silk petticoat before her as the only garment she wore was her diaphanous chemise. The Duc dismissed the valet and the Marquise de Mareteleur with an imperious wave of his hand and, when they had gone, sat on the edge of the bed.

"Is this the best you can do, Madame?" he asked with an air of distaste. "Rutting with the servants?"

"I do not see where it should be Your Excellency's concern," she said haughtilly.

"It is my concern!" he roared. "The King desires to make you his mistress and I do not care to find myself bowing and scraping to a whore!"

Lashing out, Jasmine caught the Duc squarely across the cheek knocking his powdered wig askew. With a bellow of rage, the Duc seized her arm and threw her across the bed. Pinning her face-down on the satin coverlet, he thrust aside her chemise and brought his hand down forcefully across her bared buttocks.

Jasmine screamed and struggled but, in spite of the fact that she was nearly a half-century his junior, she was no match for his soldier's strength and her struggles did her no good.

"Let me go, damn you!" she wailed. "Stop it!"

When at last he ceased his blows and let her go, she rolled over and hissed:

"Don't you ever touch me again!"

"If no one else is going to discipline you, I will!" he growled.

"What I do is none of your business! I will choose my own bedpartners!"

He reached for her arm once again and she quickly slid to the opposite side of the bed. Standing, he straightened his wig.

"If I ever learn that you are cavorting with lackeys again, Madame, I will have you soundly birched! And, what is more . . ."

"Yes, yes, I know," she interrupted him. "You will see to it that I am not received at any noble home in France."

The aged Duc shook his head. "You need a good caning, Madame. You are naught but an incorrigible child."

"Tell that to the King and see what he says!" she shot back.

Clenching his fists, the Duc left the suite and returned to the parlor downstairs where a frightened Marquise de Mareteleur awaited him.

"Well, Madame," he said sternly as he paced the room. "Is this the way you encourage a young woman of noble blood to disport herself?"

"No, Your Excellency, but Jasmine is of a passionate nature."

"Do you realize that your husband's valet could easily destroy your granddaughter's good name and with it any hopes any of us might have of seeing her displace La Pompadour?" The horror in the Marquise's face answered his question. "I can see that you are not insensible of the benefits which stem from the King's favor."

"Of course I am not insensible of them, Your Excellency."

"I am happy to hear it! You must take care to see that your granddaughter does not yield to her passionate nature."

Sofie nodded and smiled slyly. "Not unless it is in the right bed, at any rate—no, Your Excellency?"

"Not even then, Madame. At least not for a reasonable length of time."

"I wonder, Your Excellency, if it might not be wise to make Jasmine unavailable to His Majesty for a period of time. After all, he does occasionally slip away from Versailles after his coucher, does he not? What would stop him from coming here and demanding to see her?"

De Richelieu pondered her words. "And what would you suggest?"

"She could be taken to Saint-Antoine for the remainder of her husband's exile. An absence of five months should whet the King's appetite."

The Duc considered it. He knew from experience that the Marquis de Saint-Antoine was a boor. But there was a certain element of truth in the Marquise's reasoning. What was more, the King disliked the Marquis de Saint-Antoine intensely. What could make him desire Jasmine more than knowing that she had been returned to her oafish husband's home and, more specifically, his bed?

"If she were ordered back to Paris, would the Marquis

allow her to come?''

"Of course!" Sofie assured him hurriedly. "My stepson is ever anxious to serve His Majesty."

The Duc smiled, knowing the truth about the loutish Marquis. "Perhaps it would be for the best, Madame, if your granddaughter were returned to Saint-Antoine until such time as the King orders her back to Court. In the meantime, I will remind His Majesty of what a delicious morsel she is."

The Marquise curtsied. "I will see that she leaves in the morning."

"Good." He drew on his surtout and placed his hat carefully atop his powdered wig. Returning to his coach, he paused suddenly in the doorway of the hôtel. "And, Madame," he added, "try to keep the amorous valet out of her bed, if you would."

"I will try, Your Excellency," she promised. She watched as the Duc's coach rolled away and disappeared through the gateway. Going back into the hôtel, she called out: "Michel!"

"Is he gone?" the valet asked from the doorway of a small anteroom.

"Yes, he's gone." She waited until he'd left his hiding place and come to her side. "Now, I want you to go to Jasmine's room and comfort her. By the sound of things, the Duc may have hurt more than her pride. However, knowing my granddaughter as I do, she may well be in the mood to defy the Duc in spite of a smarting bottom."

Michel smiled. "I will be gentle with her, and this time, I will lock the door!"

As he turned and started up the stairs, Sofie reached out and gave his satin-liveried bottom an appreciative pinch. It was more important that Jasmine bear a child than it was to follow the Duc's instructions. Sofie smiled as she heard Michel softly tapping at Jasmine's door— she had great faith in Michel; he could be counted upon to apply himself devotedly to his task.

Chapter 27

The gardens of the Hôtel de Mareteleur stretched from
the elegant garden facade of the hôtel down to the Sein.
Commissioned during the reign of Louis Quatorze and
executed by Le Nôtre, the creator of the gardens of Versailles, gravelled walks radiated from a fountain in the
center which depicted a great bronze dragon rising from
the pool.

But the dragon was mute and the pool was empty. The
manicured lawns and shrubbery were frosted with snow.
At the end of the garden the Seine was frozen over. As
Jasmine stood near its banks, she could see ruts in the
snow where Parisians had been driving their carriages on
the ice.

She shivered inside her sable-lined pelisse as a particularly icy blast of wind struck her. But it seemed, as she
started back toward the hôtel, that the coldest of the
winter winds could not be colder than the depths of her
heart.

Re-entering the hôtel, she paused as a maidservant
took her pelisse and pattens.

"Where is Madame la Marquise?" she asked.

"She went out, Madame," the maidservant replied.

"Where is Michel?"

"I believe he is in the drawing room with Monsieur le Marquis."

Going to the drawing room, Jasmine found the old Marquis de Mareteleur sitting near the fire petting a tiny lapdog.

"Cher Papa?" Jasmine said softly. One never knew, she reflected, whether to speak to him or not. Most of the time he'd just had a dose of his ever-present medicine and was incapable of communication.

"Who is there?" he demanded.

Jasmine looked at him sadly. He seemed to have withered from even the deteriorated condition he had been in when she'd met him seven months before.

"It is I, Cher Papa," she said, going to his side. She didn't even bother to stay out of his reach as she might once have done. "It is Jasmine."

He turned his gaze toward her and she winced. His blue eyes, which had once twinkled merrily in spite of his condition, were rheumy and dull.

"Sit down, little girl," he said. "Sit down. I thought you might be Michel."

"Michel will probably return soon, Cher Papa."

"He will want to give me my medicine." The old man's voice was strangely woeful.

"Shall I find him now, Cher Papa? Do you wish to have your medicine now?"

"No, no!" He started violently and the little dog fell from his lap with a yelp. "The medicine . . . the medicine . . . it is poison!"

Jasmine's mouth fell open in astonishment. "Cher Papa! Surely you cannot mean that! Why would Grand-mère seek to poison you? You cannot imagine that she wants to kill you!''

''No, not kill me,'' he agreed. ''As long as I am under the medicine's spell she can do as she likes with the money.''

She looked at the innocent-looking glass which stood on the silver tray nearby. The small bottle of medicine stood next to it.

''I'll speak to her about it,'' she promised.

They both started as Michel walked into the room.

''Michel,'' she began, but the Marquis touched her knee and shook his head. Confused, she laughed nervously. ''Oh, I seem to have forgotten what it was I was going to ask you.''

The valet laughed as he measured out a dose of the medicine and poured it into the Marquis's chocolate. He handed it to the old man and, to Jasmine's astonishment, the Marquis drank it without protest.

When Michel took the glass and the vial of medicine out of the room, she leaned over and said quietly:

''Why did you stop me from questioning him, Cher Papa?''

The Marquis de Mareteleur shook his head. ''I am afraid of him,'' he said softly. ''I believe Sofie has promised him great rewards if he helps her in her scheme. I think he is the one who desires my death.''

''Michel!''

''Yes, he is ambitious. He desires to become a rich man and perhaps marry a woman who can bring a title to him. In the meantime, he is happy to play the gigolo to Sofie.''

Jasmine paled. ''He is still Grand-mère's lover?''

''Of course he is.'' The Marquis's words were beginning to slur.

288

"But, Grand-père . . ." She stopped. The drug was beginning to take effect and further questions would be useless.

Leaving the Marquis to his drug-induced mumblings, she left the drawing room and wandered down the corridor.

"Good evening, Madame," Michel said as he emerged from the kitchens. "If you are bored, I am sure I could suggest something. Or are you still tired from this morning?"

He slipped his arms about her waist but she stepped away and slapped his face.

"Do not touch me!" she hissed. "I will not take my grandmother's leavings!"

"Is that what that old man told you?" Michel sneered. "He's mad—do not take the ramblings of a sick old man seriously."

Without a word, she turned and started into the little-used music room. Sitting at the clavichord she ran her fingers over the ivory keys.

Sitting beside her on the gold-tasselled, burgundy velvet bench, Michel tried to take her into his arms and melt her resistance with passionate kisses and seductive caresses. But, steeling herself against her body's betraying response, she remained cool and aloof.

"Jasmine, Jasmine," he murmured against the warm flesh of her shoulder. "How could you imagine that I could remain your grandmother's lover after having touched you? Why, the very thought turns my flesh to ice. How could I ever again make love to that aged, grim-visaged old harridan?"

"Indeed, Michel," Sofie said from the doorway. "How could you?"

"Madame!" he cried, jumping from the bench, "I

did not hear you enter the hôtel!''

''That I can well believe. Would you be so kind as to attend to the Marquis? That is, after all, why you are employed in this hôtel.''

''Yes, Madame la Marquise,'' he said meekly. Bowing deeply, he slipped past her and hurried up the corridor.

Jasmine swung around on the stool and smiled. ''He is an impertinent swine, Grand-mère. And, were I you, I would have him thrown into the street.''

The Marquise nodded and held onto one maid's shoulder while another knelt to untie her pattens. When the maids had relieved her of her pelisse and muff and had been dismissed, she came to Jasmine and stroked her upswept, auburn hair.

''You are right, ma petite-fille, he is exactly that; but he is also a magnificent lover—as you well know.''

Jasmine feigned surprise. ''You mean Cher Papa was telling me the truth? Michel is your lover?''

''Certainly!'' she said with a shrug. ''Your Cher Papa has been incapable for years.''

Jasmine looked out the window toward the frosty gardens and the frozen Seine beyond which were barely visible in the gathering darkness. ''I think, Grand-mère, that in spite of Michel's prowess in the bedchamber, he should be dismissed from Cher Papa's service.''

''Dismissed? Why?''

''Cher Papa is frightened of him.''

''Cher Papa is a very sick man. He has flights of fantasy which make him imagine . . .''

''No, Grand-mère. He is frightened of Michel. He believes that Michel means to kill him.''

''He told you this?''

''Yes!'' She was glad of the concern she saw in Sofie's

eyes. "He told me before Michel gave him his medicine."

"He should not have worried you with his baseless fears. Do not worry about Alexandre; I will speak to Michel. Right now, I have other things to speak to you about."

"And what would that be?" Rising from the clavichord, Jasmine walked to the gilded corner chair near the fireplace. Sitting down, she stretched her embroidered-velvet, diamond-buckled shoes with their tall "Pompadour" heels before her.

"I was talking to His Excellency, the Duc de Richelieu yesterday, as you know, and . . ."

"That bastard!" Jasmine growled. "There is nothing he could say which could interest me."

"Jasmine! His Excellency is a great man!"

"His Excellency is a great brute!"

"Whatever your opinion of him," Sofie went on with exaggerated patience, "he is a most powerful man. He has taken an interest in you for which you should be grateful." She held up a hand to silence the disparaging remark Jasmine was about to make. "At any rate, he says, and I agree, that it might be wise for you to leave Paris for a time."

"Leave Paris!"

"Jasmine, now listen to me. He thinks you should go to Saint-Antoine and . . ."

"Never!" Jasmine leapt out of the corner chair and paced the parquet floor. "I will never return to Saint-Antoine!"

"His Excellency says it would be best."

"His Excellency can go to hell!" Jasmine screamed. "If His Excellency wants someone at Saint-Antoine, His

Excellency can go!''

''And when do you intend to fulfill your duties to your husband?'' the Marquise asked coolly.

''I have fulfilled my duties to Henri,'' Jasmine snapped. ''I dutifully serviced him whenever he could tear himself away from my mother's bed!''

''You know that is not the duty I meant.''

''It is not my fault, Grand-mère, if Henri cannot produce children.''

''You were pregnant once,'' Sofie reminded her.

''I have my doubts as to whose child that was,'' she sneered. ''It could have been Michel's.'' When she saw the lack of surprise on her grandmother's face, Jasmine's eyes narrowed. ''You already knew that Michel was my lover at Saint-Antoine, didn't you. He told you didn't he —the filthy whoreson!''

''Jasmine! I will not have a granddaughter of mine using such language!'' Sofie was careful to neither confirm nor deny Jasmine's theory that Michel had bragged about being her lover. Had she admitted that she and Isabeau had planned to place the valet in her bed, she knew she could easily lose any trust the girl had in her.

''I don't care, Grand-mère!'' Jasmine continued. ''I hate Michel! And I will not go back to Saint-Antoine! I will go back to Giacomo first!''

''Jasmine,'' Sofie began as her granddaughter started out of the room, ''Jasmine, listen to reason.''

''No! If you persist in this, Grand-mère, I shall leave this hotel in the morning and go back to Giacomo!'' Pausing in the doorway, she threw her grandmother a sly smile. ''He is a better lover than Michel anyway.''

''Really?'' Sofie's voice had a tone of disbelief mingled with interest.

"Grand-mère!"

"I'm only teasing you, darling," the Marquise insisted.

With a skeptical glance, Jasmine left the room. She passed Michel in the corridor and, when he would have spoken to her, threw him a look of such venomous dislike that he moved away from her.

"Well, Sofie," Michel said as he went to the Marquise who stood framed in the music room doorway, "how are we going to beget a child now? She will never allow me into her bed again."

"I don't know, Michel," Sofie admitted. "We shall have to revise our plans. Is everything ready for her departure in the morning?"

"Yes. But I've the feeling we're in for the Devil's own time getting her there."

Claudette shook her sleeping mistress by the shoulder. "Madame! Please wake up!"

With a groan, Jasmine opened her eyes. "What is it, Claudette?"

"Madame de Mareteleur told me to wake you. Your bath is waiting for you."

"Did I ask for a bath?"

"No, Madame, but Madame de Mareteleur said to draw it for you. So you will be ready to leave for Saint-Antoine shortly after breakfast."

"I am not going to Saint-Antoine!" Throwing back the bedclothes, she slid off the bed and pulled her nightdress over her head. "I will take that bath but I will not go back to Henri. After my bath, I will tell my grandmother that!"

Dressed in a gown of yellow silk, Jasmine marched down the grand staircase and went in search of her grandmother.

Hearing voices in a small salon, Jasmine paused near the half-open door.

"You will give the Marquis this dose just after we leave," Michel was saying, "and this dose just before you put him to bed. Do you understand?"

"Yes, Michel," Du Brosse, the steward of the hôtel, replied.

Backing down the hall a little, Jasmine called: "Michel? Michel! Where are you?"

Michel hurried from the salon. "Yes, Madame?" he said meekly.

"Where is my grand-mère?"

"In the dining room, Madame. I believe she is waiting for you to join her for breakfast."

Setting her chin stubbornly, Jasmine went to the beautiful dining room where antique hand-painted wallpaper in a delicate blue with exotic birds which had been imported from China provided a background for the delicate, gilded furniture so much the vogue.

The Marquise de Mareteleur sat at one end of the gleaming dining table and motioned for Jasmine to take her place on her right.

"Good morning, darling," she said brightly. "I hope you are not too angry at my having you awakened so early."

"Of course not, Grand-mère," Jasmine replied sweetly. "But it was really rather a waste of time."

"A waste of time? I thought I told you that we would need to get an early start on our journey to Saint-Antoine."

"And I thought I told you I was not going."

"Don't be silly," the Marquise said tasting her soup. "Of course you are going."

"I am not!" Jasmine glared at the servant who was about to serve her soup. "Take that away! I don't want anything to eat!"

"Jasmine, eat your soup. You will get very hungry during the trip if you have no breakfast."

"I am not going on any trip!"

The Marquise sat back in her chair. "Jasmine, everything is ready. The coach is waiting in the courtyard. Now, eat your breakfast so we can leave!"

"I will not! I will not!"

"I knew you would be difficult," Sofie hissed. "I told Michel last night that you would put up a fuss."

"I do not care what you told Michel. I will not go. In fact, I will leave this hôtel. I will go back to Giacomo if I have to sleep with him and Henriette!"

"Very well, then, my grand lady," Sofie said scathingly, "the least you could do before you go on your merry way is share your Grand-mère's breakfast. You don't have to eat the soup if you do not wish to, but at least you could join your Grand-mère in a cup of chocolate."

"All right," she agreed grudgingly. She lifted the cup of chocolate which had already been poured when she entered the room and, with a mocking salute, downed the warm liquid in a single gulp. "There," she snarled, slamming the fine Sèvres porcelain cup onto the table. "Does that satisfy you?"

"It does indeed," Sofie replied, smiling.

"May I go now?"

"Of course, darling."

Without a goodbye, Jasmine left the dining room and strode purposefully up the corridor intending to go to her room, collect her pelisse, muff, and pattens and leave the hôtel de Mareteleur forever.

She was nearly to the stairs when the first wave of dizziness struck her. Gasping, she stumbled to the staircase and gripped the newel post.

"Something wrong, Madame?" Michel asked politely.

Jasmine shook her head trying to clear away the mist that befuddled her mind and clouded her vision. Over his arm, she noticed the lynx-lined pelisse and muff which matched the gown she was wearing. As she stared at him, her grandmother's face appeared over his shoulder. The Marquise was tying the silver ties of her pelisse while a maidservant waited, holding her wolfskin-lined muff.

"Oh, you are crafty," Jasmine said, struggling with the words. She felt Michel draping the pelisse over her shoulders, but was powerless to stop him. She put out a hand and pushed at his surtout-covered chest, but grasped the newel post once again to maintain her balance. "It was in the chocolate, wasn't it? Some of Cher Papa's medicine?"

"What a bright girl," the Marquise sneered. "I was Michel's idea. I wanted to put it into your soup but Michel said it would be easier to get you to drink the chocolate."

She looked at Michel whose face was blurred. "You bastard!" she snarled. She closed her eyes as the room began to whirl and a strange fatigue overcame her.

As her fingers involuntarily loosened on the post and she slipped toward the floor, Michel caught her and swept her into his arms. The maidservant held the door open as the Marquise left the hôtel for the waiting coach. Michel followed pausing only long enough to tell Du Brosse:

"Do not forget the Marquis's medicine."

"I won't," the steward promised.

Two footmen helped him lift Jasmine into the coach and, though she could hardly move, she was aware of being laid on one side of the coach while her grandmother and Michel faced her on the opposite seat. Michel put out a hand to steady her as the coach rocked and started in a wide arch toward the gateway.

"Don't touch me!" she mumbled, the hatred in her eyes clear in spite of the numbing effect of the drug.

"But I have to touch you," Michel said. Knowing she was powerless to stop him, he caressed her throat and bosom through her thick pelisse. "I have to touch you," he repeated. "After all, Madame de Saint-Antoine must give her husband a child."

She tried to scream but the sounds refused to form. As tears of frustration welled in the corner of her eyes, the Marquise and Michel laughed at her helplessness. The grand coach of the Marquis de Mareteleur left the hôtel's courtyard and entered the Rue de Lille followed by another, less grand coach carrying Claudette and Sofie's maidservant, Berthe.

As the two coaches rolled through the Faubourg Saint-Germain, beginning their trip to Saint-Antoine, Michel and Sofie shared a smile of smirking exultation.

Chapter 28

Jasmine struggled against the lingering effects of the drug she'd been given. Her surroundings seemed to slip in and out of focus. After several unsuccessful attempts, she gave up trying to sit up in her bed.

"He gave her too much," Isabeau said as she and Henri de Saint-Antoine stood by the side of the bed. "He should never have given her the second dose."

"She was fighting him; he had no choice."

"Maman?" Jasmine said weakly. She tried to sit up again but her mother's hands gently pressed her against her pillows.

"Lay back, Jasmine," she said softly. "You will only make yourself woozy."

"What time is it, Maman?" she demanded. "Have I been unconscious long?"

"It is nearly noon. You have been unconscious since yesterday morning."

"Yesterday morning!" She sat up, ignoring the effects of the drug.

298

"It was yesterday morning when you set out from Paris," Henri told her. He sat in a chair at her bedside, his feet propped on the bedsteps. "The drug began to wear off when you were nearly here and Michel gave you another, larger dose. Do you remember?"

Jasmine frowned. "I seem to remember trying to jump out of the coach."

"Sofie tried to stop you and you loosened two of her teeth." He ignored the chiding look Isabeau threw him and his tone of voice was grudgingly admiring.

"Where is she? I don't want her or Michel to come near me."

Isabeau took her hand. "Michel and your Grand-mère have returned to Paris."

Jasmine looked at Henri for confirmation and he nodded.

"A rider arrived from Paris this morning with some distressing news," Henri added.

"Distressing news?"

"Really, Henri," Isabeau scolded. "You could have given her time to eat something before you told her. Maman said she' eaten nothing but a cup of chocolate since yesterday morning."

"What is this distressing news?" Jasmine demanded.

"It is nothing that will not keep," Madame DuPré assured her daughter. "First I want you to eat some soup."

"Maman!" Jasmine cried, but her mother had already left the room. "Henri?"

He shrugged. "If I told you before you'd eaten your soup, there'd be hell to pay."

She laughed. "Maman has you firmly in leading strings, eh, husband?"

"Eat your soup, Madame, and then I shall show you how firm those leading strings are." Leaning forward in his chair, he brushed her auburn curls back over her shoulders. "You've matured during your absence, child," he said softly. The hated sobriquet seemed more an endearment now.

She threw him the look she'd practiced so often on Casanova. "Really, Monseigneur, I've only been gone a matter of weeks. How much maturing could I have done in that time?"

"Perhaps we will find that out later."

"Perhaps," she agreed. "But then, perhaps I shall suffer a relapse and be indisposed."

"You've gained some spirit," he observed. "Has your Italian lover taught you that?"

"Grand-mère told you about Giacomo, did she? Well, it's true, he has taught me to be spirited—in addition to other lessons."

"For instance?"

"For instance, he taught me that a man need not take a woman in the same manner he takes a fortress in a war."

"And that is how I take a woman?"

She shrugged. "You are a soldier, Monseigneur. Giacomo, on the other hand, is a lover."

"Did you enjoy his love-making?"

She smiled in rememberance. "Oh, yes!"

The Marquis de Saint-Antoine moved from his chair to the edge of the bed. The pale blue of his eyes was merely a ring around the dilated pupils as he pushed Jasmine's silk nightdress off her shoulders.

"Perchance you would be so kind as to demonstrate those attributes you found so attractive in your lover's technique?''

"Here is your nice warm soup!'' Isabeau announced as she barged into the room followed by a footman bearing a silver tray with a covered bowl on it.

Slowly, deliberately, Jasmine leaned forward and kissed her husband lingeringly. Leaning back against her pillows, she was amused at her mother's obvious vexation.

"Henri!'' she said, her voice shrill. "Please move so that Jasmine may eat her soup.''

Smiling at him through lowered lashes, Jasmine drew her nightdress up over her shoulders and turned her attention to her mother.

While the footman held the tray, a maidservant brought a bed table and placed it next to the bed. Jasmine leaned foward to allow Isabeau to plump her pillows and then began eating her soup. It was hot and good and she suddenly realized how hungry she was.

"Henri,'' Isabeau said, her voice strangely tight, "may I speak to you?''

He looked up from the chair to which he'd returned. "Of course, what is it?''

"Not here!'' Catching herself, she softened the tone of her voice. "In your room, if you please.''

Jasmine smiled as the Marquis and her mother retired to his bedchamber. Through the thick door which connected the rooms, she could hear them and, though she could not make out the words, she recognized the angry tones her mother used and the unconcerned ones in which the Marquis replied.

When they returned, the Marquis seemed amused while Isabeau's gaiety was forced.

"You've finished your soup,'' she gushed, giving the

bell-rope a tug. "What a good girl!"

The footman arrived and took the tray away. When the door closed behind him, Jasmine looked at her mother.

"All right, Maman, I have eaten my soup like a dutiful daughter. Now tell me, what was this distressing news you were speaking of earlier?"

Isabeau's smile disappeared and great crocodile tears suddenly appeared in her eyes.

"Oh, Jasmine! It's too, too sad!"

"If you are that distraught, Madame," Henri said impatiently, "you should go to your room and ask Lotte for a compress."

"But, Henri!"

"You may go, Madame," he insisted. "I will break the news to the Marquise."

Isabeau lifted her chin and stalked from the room giving each of the doors a vicious slam on her way out of the apartment.

The Marquis sat on the edge of the bed and propped one foot, encased in a blue morocco slipper, on the chair.

"Jasmine, I know you were fond of my father . . ."

"Were? What do you mean, Henri?"

He took a deep breath. "A messenger arrived from Paris just before noon this morning with the news that he died during the night."

"Cher Papa?" She sagged against the pillows. "He is dead? Oh, Henri! I should have known! How could I not have guessed!"

"Guessed what?" he asked, puzzled at her reaction.

"There must have been something I could have done!"

Grasping her by the arms, Henri shook her. "Jasmine! What are you talking about?"

"Yesterday morning I heard Michel instructing Du Brosse to give Cher Papa two doses of his medicine. And, the day before yesterday, Cher Papa told me he was afraid of Michel—afraid Michel wanted to kill him."

"I'm not surprised."

"You're not?"

"No. Your grandmother has long desired the use of my father's money without having to worry about my father."

"Michel is her lover."

He nodded. "None of this surprises me."

"Have you notified the police? Shouldn't Grand-mère and Michel be arrested?"

"It would serve no purpose, Jasmine. My father was old and not well even before he married Sofie. Now he is dead and to bring charges against her and Michel would do nothing but drag our family's name through the courts. I've no wish to revive the poisoning scandals of the last reign. What Paris does not need is another Chambre Ardente Affair."

"Then Michel and Grand-mère will escape punishment. They committed murder and yet they will go free."

"I will deal with Michel in my own way and, now that I have control of the money, I will keep our dear Dowager Marquise on a short lead."

"Dowager Marquise?"

"You forget, Madame, that since my father is dead, I am the Marquis de Mareteleur. Since you are now the Marquise de Mareteleur, your Grand-mère is the Dowager Marquise."

She wrinkled her nose. "I don't want to be the Marquise de Mareteleur, Henri. Can we not retain our present titles?"

"If you prefer. We will remain Madame and Monsieur de Saint-Antoine—until you give me a son to inherit this title." He stroked her cheek but then grasped her chin in a tight grip. "Tell me, wife, are you sure you are not pregnant by your Italian fortune-hunter?"

Blushing, Jasmine shook her head. "No, Henri, I am not pregnant. I am certain of it."

"Good." He relaxed his hold on her chin. "I do not care who you sleep with, Madame, so long as you are discreet. But I will not give my name—my estates—to another man's bastard."

"Not even the King's?" she asked slyly.

"Well . . ." He grinned. "Perhaps the King's. As long as a duchy went with it. But I would rather have a son of my own first."

Jasmine watched him warily as he slipped out of his coat and waistcoat.

"Henri, I really do not feel like making love. This news of Cher Papa's death . . ."

He removed his stock and began working on the buttons of his shirt.

"I am not asking you to be wildly passionate, Madame, I am merely asking you to oblige me. I want a son. You need not swoon in ecstasy; you need merely allow me to help nature take its course."

Realizing that he would not take no for an answer, she sighed and pushed the pillows away. Lying back on the satin coverlet, she waited for him to finish undressing.

Swathed in black bombazine, Jasmine and Isabeau

304

faced one another in the crepe-draped coach. Henri, in black shalloon, sat beside his wife. Their coach, drawn by four black horses, followed another in which rode Sofie in heaviest mourning.

At the head of the short procession which wound its way down the hill from the château, a hearse carried the coffin containing the mortal remains of the Marquis de Mareteleur.

"Henri," Jasmine said, "why is Cher Papa being buried in Saint-Antoine? Shouldn't he be buried in Mareteleur?"

"The d'Auboises were Marquises of Saint-Antoine before we were given the estate in Mareteleur. We have been buried in the crypt below the cathedral in Saint-Antoine for generations."

Jasmine and Henri followed Sofie down the cold marble stairs to the crypt of Saint-Antoine cathedral. Flambeaux lit the way and Jasmine shivered as they descended into the unheated depths of the crypt.

The tomb of the Marquises de Saint-Antoine and Mareteleur was lined with shelves. On each shelf a marble sarcophagus rested containing the remains of a long-dead Marquis. They ranged along one side of the tonb. Facing them, in identical sarcophagi, rested their wives. Jasmine noticed with a shiver that empty shelves awaited Henri and herself.

Henri noticed her uneasiness and slipped an arm about her waist in an uncharacteristically tender gesture. She leaned against him while the old Marquis's coffin was lowered into the sarcophagus.

When the ceremony was finished, she hurried up the stairs and left the cathedral. But even the cold February air could not clear the stale odor of death from her nostrils. She wondered, as Henri helped her into the coach for the return ride to the château, if she would ever be able to forget it.

Chapter 29

Jasmine lay across her bed lost in musings of Barrett. Both her mother and grandmother had denied having received another letter from him and she wondered, with growing dread, if he had married Miss Octavia Dashwood. Brushing away a tear, she looked up as the door to her husband's room opened.

"Are you coming down to dinner?" Henri asked.

"No, I'm not hungry. Perhaps you could send someone up with something a little later."

"Your mother would appreciate your presence."

Sighing, she sat up. "Is she still angry with me?"

He sat in the gilded chair at the bedside and crossed his right ankle over his left knee. "Yes. She thinks you should have been more cordial to Sofie."

She remembered the days the Dowager Marquise de Mareteleur had spent at the château and how, when she and Michel had taken their leave nearly a week before, she had refused to come out into the courtyard and see them off.

"I don't care if she's angry, Henri. Michel and Grand-mère murdered Cher Papa. If you do not wish to bring the authorities into the matter, so be it. But I will not behave as though it never happened."

"I didn't say you should. But I promise you that Michel shall be dealt with and, when the time comes, you shall have a share in his punishment."

She smiled, looking forward to the day when the valet should pay the price for his crime.

"And Grand-mère?"

"I will take care of Sofie," he promised. "But there is nothing I can do until I am allowed to return to Paris."

"But how . . ."

Jasmine's question was interrupted when Isabeau entered the room. Madame DuPré frowned at finding her daughter and the Marquis together in such a picture of domestic harmony. Henri had been spending more and more of his nights in Jasmine's room and had nearly abandoned her. She had begun to wish that she hadn't encouraged Sofie to secure her daughter's return to Saint-Antoine.

"Jasmine! Henri! Come downstairs quickly! We have visitors."

"I have to dress," Jasmine told her mother.

Isabeau scowled at her daughter's late afternoon dishabille.

"It does not do for the Lady of the Château to remain in her dressing gown all day, Jasmine. Call Claudette and hurry! Come down when you are ready. Henri, come along. At least the Master of the Château can be downstairs to greet his guests."

"Who is it?" the Marquis asked as they left the room.

The thick door closed before Jasmine could hear her mother's reply. Not that it mattered. The only visitors they had were burghers from nearby towns arriving to ask favors.

Climbing off the bed, she tugged the bell-pull. While she waited for Claudette to arrive, she slipped her damask dressing gown off and pulled her silk nightdress over her head.

"Yes, Madame?" Claudette said as she entered the room. "You rang?"

Standing before the fire to keep the chilly air from her bare skin, Jasmine nodded. "Maman tells me we have visitors. Find me something to wear, if you will."

Claudette brought her a gown of dark blue satin with robings and cuffs embroidered with silver thread. She helped Jasmine into the chemise, dome-shaped hoop, and petticoats, and then lowered the gown into place over the whole. While she sat at her toilette table for Claudette to arrange her hair, Jasmine pulled the lace ruffles of her chemise sleeves out at the ends of her gown's sleeves and fluffed them up.

Tying a ribbon sewn with a tiny pattern of diamonds into place about her throat, Jasmine picked up a painted fan.

"I hope," she said, examining herself in the pier glass, "that today's visitor is more interesting than that Bishop who arrived a few days ago."

"I saw them leaving their coach," Claudette offered. "Two very handsome men!"

"Handsome men, eh? Perhaps it will be amusing."

As she descended the staircase to the ground floor of the château, Jasmine could hear laughter coming from the Silver Salon. Pushing at the door of the salon, she tucked a few stray hairs into her chignon and smoothed a wrinkle from the tightly fitted bodice of her gown.

Entering the salon, she smiled politely at her husband, her mother, and their guests.

"Ah, Jasmine," Henri said, standing. "Come in. I believe you know our guests?"

Looking over as the visitors rose, Jasmine's smile dissolved to be replaced by a look of astonishment.

"Madame de Saint-Antoine," the Abbé de Bernis said, saluting her with his glass of champagne. "I believe you know my secretary, Giovanni Baletti?"

"I . . . I . . ." she stuttered. Standing behind the Abbé was Giacomo Casanova dressed in a suit of somber brown velvet with his own black hair unpowdered. He examined her through a quizzing glass which hung from a ribbon about his neck. She recovered herself quickly. "Of course I remember. Signor Baletti?"

He bowed deeply. "Madame is very kind to remember."

Accepting a glass of champagne from a lackey, Jasmine sat opposite Casanova. But every time she looked at him, he raised his quizzing glass and peered through it and she had to bite her lip to keep from laughing aloud.

"Don't you think so, Jasmine?" Henri asked.

She looked up. "I'm sorry. Don't I think so what?"

"Don't you think His Excellency should remain with us before resuming his journey to Paris?"

"Oh, absolutely!" she agreed. "You must stay."

The Abbé held his glass while it was being refilled.

"Your offer is most generous. Since it is growing late and beginning to snow, I will accept your hospitality. But only until tomorrow. We must resume our journey in the morning."

"If we cannot persuade you otherwise, Your Excellency," Isabeau said, "I suppose we will have to settle for one night's visit. For now, may I suggest that we all retire to the dining room for supper?''

"If you do not mind, Madame," Casanova said, exaggerating his Italian accent, "I will take a tray to my room. I have much correspondence to attend to for His Excellency."

"Oh, very well, Signor Baletti," Isabeau agreed.

As they left the Silver Salon for the dining room, Isabeau summoned a lackey.

"Please tell the cook to take a tray to Signor Baletti. He is in the north tower room on the first floor."

As Casanova stepped back to allow the others to pass on to the dining room, he ogled Jasmine through his gold-framed quizzing glass. Stifling a giggle, she threw him a broad wink and then followed the others, who were already taking their places at the long table.

She sat impatiently through the soup course and picked at the pigeon pie. When she could stand no more waiting, she lifted her glass of burgundy and, in lifting it to her lips, deliberately poured it down the front of her gown.

"Oh, no!" she cried, standing quickly and brushing at the dark stain spreading in the stain. "How terribly clumsy of me!"

"Oh, Jasmine!" Isabeau groaned. "Your dress will be ruined!"

"I must change. Excuse me, Your Excellency?"

The Abbé de Bernis's dark eyes twinkled with knowing amusement. "Of course, Madame. Shall we wait for you?"

"No, no. Do not wait on my account. I was not very hungry to begin with." She curtsied. "Excuse me, Your Excellency. Monseigneur. Maman."

Leaving the dining room, she hurried up the stairs. Pausing at her own door, she looked up and down the corridor to see if anyone was watching. The corridor was deserted. Lifting her stained skirts, she ran up the hallway to the tower room at the end.

Rapping lightly in case a lackey was inside serving Casanova his supper, Jasmine glanced nervously toward the other end of the long corridor.

The door opened and Casanova, his brown coat and waistcoat discarded and his quizzing glass abandoned, stepped back to allow her into the room.

"Giacomo!" she cried, throwing herself into his embrace. "Oh, Giacomo! How I've missed you!"

Feeling the wine in her bodice seeping through the fine lawn of his shirt, Casanova stepped away from her.

She looked down at the darkened stain. "It was the only way I could think of to get away from them."

"There is only one thing to be done," he said thoughtfully. "We must get out of those wet clothes."

She turned her back and he unfastened the hooks of her gown and pulled it over her head. Quickly stepping out of her petticoats and hoop, she kicked off her shoes and, climbing into his bed, eagerly held out her arms to him.

Discarding the rest of his clothing, he joined her in the massive bed and drew her into his embrace.

"Oh, Giacomo," she breathed as he began the tantalizing caresses she remembered so well, "I'd almost forgotten how glorious this could be!" She traced the edge of his jaw with a trembling finger. "Giacomo, how did you know where I was?"

"I'll tell you about it later, my angel," he murmured against the pulsing flesh of her throat.

"But . . . but . . ." she stammered. Her words died as he kissed her and were replaced by a shuddering sigh.

The nights she'd been forced to spend in the arms of her dispassionate husband had clouded the memory of the heights to which Casanova could take her. Lifting her chemise over her head, he covererd her with languid, searing kisses, his lips following his hands over her satiny skin until he felt her quiver and heard her softly call his name. Unable to hold his own desire in check, he knelt over her and, grasping her hips, drew their bodies together. Moving as one, their bodies and lips sealed, they made love with a ferocity that, once their passion was spent, awed them into silence.

She held her hair up as he hooked her gown.

"You still didn't tell me how you found me," she told him over her shoulder.

He smiled. "I paid a visit to your grandmother last week. She invited me in to dinner. She said you had mentioned me to her."

"And she told you that I'd been taken here?"

"Oh, no. She refused to discuss you with me."

"Then how did you discover my whereabouts?"

A slow grin broke over his face. "She talks in her sleep."

Jasmine's eyes widened. "You slept with her? You slept with my grandmother?"

"Jasmine, she seemed lonely."

"Lonely! She has Michel!"

"Ah, yes. The valet." He arched an eyebrow. "I believe that I may say without undue braggadocio that she will never be quite as happy with poor Michel again. Of course, I can only judge by her reaction. And the fact that she offered to marry me.''

"Marry you! She's been a widow only two weeks!''

He shrugged. "I can only tell you what she said.''

She looked at him askance. "If I didn't have to get back to my rooms and change . . .''

"Yes, Madame?'' he said, taking her into his arms. "If you didn't have to get back to your rooms?''

She kissed the warm flesh of his chest. "Oh Giacomo, if only I didn't have to get back to my rooms!''

Having changed into a gown of dark green silk, Jasmine rejoined the Abbé de Bernis and her husband and mother.

"Well, Jasmine,'' Henri said as she entered the salon, "you missed His Excellency's news.''

"Did I really? What news was that, Your Excellency?''

The Abbé smiled broadly. "It seems, Madame, that you are to be officially presented at Court.''

"Presented at Court? When?''

"Next week. In the meantime, you are to return with me to Paris to prepare.''

"How exciting!'' Isabeau cried. "My darling Jasmine to be presented at Court! How wonderful it would be to be able to witness that moment!'' She looked hopefully at the Abbé, but he only sipped his champagne.

"No doubt Madame de Saint-Antoine will be sure to write to you both and tell you all about it. Will you not, Madame?''

Stifling a giggle, Jasmine nodded. "Of course, Your Excellency.''

He put down his glass. "You seem vexed, Monsieur de Saint-Antoine. If you would like, I can show you the King's orders in which I was commanded to deliver the

Marquise to Paris."

"No, Your Excellency," Henri assured him hastily. "That will not be necessary."

The Abbé smiled. "Then, if you will excuse me, I will accompany the Marquise to her room. We shall be leaving very early in the morning and the hour grows late."

Leaving Henri and Isabeau in the salon, the Abbé offered Jasmine his arm and then walked up the stairs.

"What would you have done if he had asked to see the orders?" she asked.

The Abbé pulled a document from his pocket. "I would have showed them to him."

Taking the document, Jasmine opened it and saw the King's signature at the bottom.

"The King actually issued orders for my return?"

"The King doesn't know you ever left Paris."

She stopped at the head of the stairs. "But the signature?"

"I am Minister of Foreign Affairs," he explained. "There are occasionally trifling matters which require His Majesty's signature but are too insignificant to warrant his personal attention. For those occasions, I have a wooden stamp with a facsimile of His Majesty's signature embossed upon it."

"So you signed this document with your stamp?" He nodded and her face fell. "Then I am not to be presented at Court?"

"Oh, yes, that part is quite true. The King told me to notify you. I went to visit Giacomo and he told me that you had been taken to Saint-Antoine. And so, here we are."

Standing on tiptoe, she kissed his cheek. "Thank you,

Your Excellency. How can I ever repay you?"

"Listen to Giacomo's advice. He has only your well-being in mind."

"I will," she promised, standing outside her own room. "I will listen."

"Good. Now, go to sleep, we have a long journey ahead of us tomorrow."

Smiling contentedly, Jasmine went into her room. Claudette helped her into her nightclothes and, when the candles were extinguished and she was alone, Jasmine watched the flames dancing in the fireplace.

A soft click caught her attention and she saw the door of her bedchamber opening. Casanova, dressed in his velvet dressing-gown and red slippers, entered the room and approached the bed.

"Giacomo!" she said softly. "Are you mad?" She pointed to the light shining under her husband's door. "Henri is in there!"

Climbing over her, he bounced the bed and tugged at her hair.

"That makes it the more exciting," he whispered.

"Giacomi, you really shouldn't be here."

But his lips nibbled at her ear lobes and his fingers fluttered over her skin. She felt her own will bowing to his.

"Giacomo," she murmured. "I can see Henri moving about in his room. I can see his shadow beneath the door."

Reaching across her, Casanova drew the heavy draperies closed shutting out the rest of the château.

"Now, my angel," he breathed, "surrender to me. I have needed you so badly these past weeks."

She pushed his hands away. "What about Henriette

316

Beaujean?''

"She has gone back to Parc aux Cerfs. Forget her. I never cared for her. She was merely a tantalizing tidbit to be enjoyed and then forgotten.''

She drew in a breath in a long hiss as his caresses became more intimate. But, as she lay back against the rumpled satin sheets, she heard a sound that froze her blood. Peeking out between the draperies, she saw the door of her husband's bedchamber opening. The Marquis de Saint-Antoine entered her room and, closing the door behind him, approached the bed.

Casanova slipped off the bed and hid himself behind the draperies which covered the wall. Jasmine, trembling with fear lest his presence be discovered, straightened her nightdress and pulled the coverlet to her chin.

"Jasmine,'' the Marquis said, parting the draperies on his side of the bed, "are you sleeping?''

"I was almost asleep, Henri,'' she said, feigning great drowsiness. "Is something wrong?''

"No. I merely thought that since you are leaving in the morning, perhaps we could spend this last night together.''

Since her return to the château, she had not refused him. She knew that to do so now would be to arouse his suspicions.

"I'm really very tired, Henri,'' she said, hoping he would take the hint. "I don't believe I am equal to a night of lovemaking.''

To her alarm, he removed his dressing gown and knelt on the edge of the bed.

"Then I will not stay the entire night. Just once and I will be on my way.''

Unable to think of a plausible excuse, she moved over

in the wide bed and, blushing from the top of her head to the soles of her feet, allowed her husband to take her.

When the door closed behind the Marquis, Jasmine rolled onto her side and wept bitter tears of mortification. Emerging from behind the draperies, Casanova climbed onto the bed and cradled her in his arms.

"Poor little angel," he cooed gently. "Poor sweet darling. I can understand your tears. I would cry too if I were you."

"You would?" she asked as his fingers brushed a tear from her cheek.

"Of course!" he said seriously. "I would cry if I were married to the Marquis. The man has no technique. He has no finesse. He reduces the art of making love to a level with . . ."

"Giacomo, please! I wanted to die! I didn't want you to see . . ."

"What I saw, my little beauty, was that you were not satisfied. He did not even try to give you pleasure. He is not worthy of you."

Drying her tears, he retrieved her crumpled nightdress and helped her into it. With a tender kiss on the forehead, he took his leave.

"Good night, Jasmine, tomorrow we will return to Paris and then you will be out of your husband's reach."

"Good night, Giacomo," she whispered, sniffling. "I adore you."

He kissed her ear. "And I you," he murmured. "Until tomorrow; sleep well."

She lay back against her pillows and smiled sadly. Tomorrow she would return to Paris—and to Giacomo. As she drifted off to sleep, she thought about it, but the thought repeated in her mind with a nagging addition. Tomorrow she would return to Paris and to Giacomo. And, the thought continued unbidden, to Versailles and the King.

Chapter 30

The great, crested coach of the Abbé de Bernis left the Château de Saint-Antoine early in the morning. Inside the elegantly upholstered vehicle, Jasmine and Casanova faced the Abbé de Bernis across the wide, carpeted aisle.

Their hands clasped beneath a lap robe of bear-skin and velvet, Jasmine leaned her head contentedly into the hollow of Casanova's shoulder.

"You do not seem sorry to be leaving Saint-Antoine, Madame," the Abbé observed.

"I was not happy to be there, Your Excellency," she replied. "Why should I be sorry to leave? After all, I will be back in Paris with Giacomo."

"But not for long."

She glanced at Casanova and then back to the Abbé. "What do you mean?"

The Abbé paused as though gauging her likely response. "After your presentation at Court, you will be given an apartment at Versailles."

"Will I have to stay there all the time? Surely I could spend some of my time in Paris."

"Jasmine," Casanova said patiently, "the mistresses of kings do not spend some of their time with former lovers."

"Former lovers?" she asked fearfully. "Giacomo, do you mean to say that I will no longer see you once I become the King's mistress?"

"Of course you will see me, my angel," he assured her. "But we can no longer be lovers; the King would never allow that."

She looked at the Abbé for confirmation and, when he nodded, set her chin stubbornly. "Then I will not become the King's mistress! I will wait until you have to leave Paris!" She looked at Casanova hopefully.

But he shook his head. "No. You cannot wait. Even though I expect to be on my way to Amsterdam within a week of your presentation, it will still be too long a delay."

"His Majesty," the Abbé explained, "will expect to share your bed on the night of your presentation."

"So soon?" She stared out at the frozen countryside, frowning. "Can't I wait? You, yourself, said I should hold the King off for a time. The Duc de Richelieu said so!"

"The situation has changed," Casanova said.

"How has it changed?"

The Abbé and Casanova exchanged a glance and de Bernis said:

"Jasmine, since the death of your father-in-law, your husband has become the Marquis de Mareteleur. There is a great deal of business which must be attended to so he can take charge of the estates and business dealings in which his father's fortunes are invested. To properly attend to that business, he will be required to come to Paris."

"Henri is coming to Paris?" she asked nervously.

"Yes. So you see, it is important for you to be securely installed at Versailles before he arrives."

"If you are the King's mistress," Casanova went on, "the King will never restore your husband's entrée at Court. He will be unable to take you into his possession again."

"When will he be invited to return to Paris?"

The Abbé studied her closely. "The day after your presentation."

She hid her eyes in the soft cloth of Casanova's surtout. "Then I have no choice."

"There is always a choice, Madame. Yours is between your husband and the King."

She remembered the King's gentle eyes on the morning she'd met him after the attempt on his life. She remembered those same eyes alight with passion on the night of the dinner in his Petits Appartements. Then she remembered the icy blue eyes of her husband.

"No, Your Excellency," she murmured, "there is no choice for me. There is only the King."

As her gray-green eyes met the sparkling brown eyes of the Abbé, she asked suddenly:

"Your Excellency, might I ask a question?" She waited until he nodded. "I had thought you to be a friend of Madame de Pompadour."

"I am her friend," he acknowledged, "as well as her admirer."

"Knowing how much she loves the King, how can you claim to be her friend and yet work to provide the King with a mistress?"

His smile was somehow sad. "Do not take what I am about to say as in any way disparaging. I am working to place you into the King's bed because I know you pose

322

no threat to Reinette. That is not to say that you are not a very beautiful woman. It is merely that the woman has not been born who could turn the King completely away from La Pompadour. She will be his Maîtresse en Titre until the day one of them is dead. Unfortunately, it is very likely to be Reinette who is the first to die; she is not a robustly healthy woman. As you have no doubt heard, the King shares her bed but rarely these days—he looks to Parc Aux Cerfs for his physical gratification. It is my intention to provide him with a mistress who is fit to grace the salons of Versailles. In that way, he will always have a woman available to him and will not have to share Reinette's bed. She has suffered many miscarriages during her tenure as Maîtresse en Titre—I am afraid another will kill her.''

''And so,' she concluded, ''I am to satisfy the King's desires in order to spare Madame de Pompadour's health.''

''Exactly!'' Casanova agreed. ''In the process, however, you will be serving yourself by ridding yourself of your husband.''

''Everyone benefits,'' she commented.

''Absolutely!'' the men exclaimed in unison.

''No, not absolutely!'' she cried. ''What about my health? Giacomo, you told me that the King is practically insatiable!''

''After all, Jasmine,'' the Abbé said, ''you are not yet seventeen. His Majesty is thirty years your senior. You doubtless have more stamina than he.''

Seeing their smirks, she blushed and turned her gaze out the window.

The Abbé de Bernis waved to them as his coach rolled out of the courtyard of the Hôtel de Sauveur. Hand in hand, Jasmine and Casanova entered the hôtel and went to the apartment they'd shared since arriving in Paris. Claudette, who had ridden with the Abbé's valet in another, plain coach, followed them.

"Welcome home, Jasmine," Casanova said quietly as he led her into the drawing room.

"You cannot imagine how I've missed these rooms," she sighed, allowing Claudette to take her pelisse.

"But I can imagine, my angel," he said, enfolding her in his arms, "for I missed you as much."

She tilted back her head to receive his kiss and, parting, they both laughed to see Claudette blushing hotly.

"The bedroom and dressing room are through there," Jasmine told her. "I am afraid you will have to sleep on one of the chaise longues in the dressing room until we make other arrangements."

"Yes, Madame," Claudette said with a curtsy. She left the room quickly as Jasmine stifled a giggle.

"Claudette came with Maman and me from Virginia and I fear she is a bit bewildered by my changes of living quarters."

"Ohhhh! Madame!" Claudette's squeal filled the rooms and brought Jasmine and Casanova to the dressing room on the run.

Jasmine stopped in the doorway of the dressing room and saw what it was that elicited the maidservant's response.

On a headless dressform in the dressing room was the most beautiful gown she had ever seen. Of glistening white satin, it had robings and cuffs which were thickly embroidered with silver. The satin petticoat, which showed at the open front of the overgown, was embroidered in silver in an all-over pattern of flowers. At the ends of the elbow-length sleeves, three long flounces of silver lace fell to wrist length. In a box near the gown, she found white satin shoes embroidered with silver and adorned with buckles encrusted with diamonds. In another box lay a satin ribbon sewn with diamonds and three long ostrich plumes held together with a diamond hair clasp.

"Oh, Giacomo!" Jasmine breathed, not daring to touch the magnificent ensemble. "Where did this come from?"

"From Madame Thibault, of course," he replied. "She had your measurements from the gowns she made earlier. You needed a proper ensemble in which to be presented at Court."

With careful fingers, she lifted the embroidered train at the back of the gown. "I am to be presented in this gown? I hope I do not trip on the train!"

"I'm sure you won't," he replied. "Claudette? Please bring the blue lacquered box from the table there."

Jasmine looked up from her examination of the gown as the maidservant obediently retrieved a wide, flat wooden box from a shelf at the back of the dressing room.

"This is also for your presentation night," he told her.

Carefully lifting the top of the box away, Jasmine caught her breath as she saw what the box contained.

A nightdress of white silk covered with delicate silver lace lay inside the box and, as she lifted it out, she found a dressing gown of white velvet trimmed at the collar and cuffs in soft, silver fox fur.

"Isn't it beautiful, Madame!" Claudette sighed, extending a shy finger to stroke the exquisite fur.

"Yes, Claudette," Jasmine agreed. "It is very beautiful. But it looks like the attire of a bride on her wedding night."

She looked up at Casanova and found him watching her with a mixture of sadness and cynical amusement in his black eyes.

Wordlessly, she handed the garments to Claudette to replace in their box and stepped, trembling, into Casanova's embrace.

The days before her presentation at Court seemed to rush by and Jasmine, as though determined to ignore their passing, refused to discuss the approaching night which would mark the beginning of her life at Court and the end of her life with Casanova.

It was nearly midday and she and Casanova were still in bed. It was as if each was determined to get their fill of the other before they were separated.

She kissed his chin and throat, ignoring the rough stubble of his beard.

"Giacomo?" she whispered. "Please love me."

He smiled and wound a long tendril of her hair about his finger.

"Ah, my angel, at this rate I shan't have the strength to make the long journey to Amsterdam!"

"Good! Then you can stay here with me."

"How I wish I could." Reluctantly, he climbed out of the big bed and pulled on his velvet dressing gown. "But I can vaguely remember something about an appointment."

"Forget your appointment," she coaxed. "Come back to bed."

Sitting in an armchair, he put on his slippers. "Really, Jasmine, I was sure one of us had an appointment."

A shy tap on the bedchamber door made them look up.

"Yes, Claudette?" Jasmine called.

The maidservant opened the door slightly. "Pardon me, Madame, Monseigneur, there is someone . . ."

"Out of the way, girl," the Duc de Richelieu commanded. Prodding Claudette with his gold-headed cane, he pushed open the door and entered the bedchamber.

"Merciful heavens above!" he cried, seeing Jasmine clutching the bedclothes over her nakedness. "Do you never get out of bed? I cannot imagine how the King is going to find the time to govern the country after you've become his mistress!"

"That is the appointment I was thinking of!" Casanova exclaimed. "The Duc de Richelieu is coming to talk to you about your presentation!"

"Thank you, Giacomo," Jasmine snarled.

"If you will excuse me, Your Excellency," he said, bowing. "I will dress and leave. I have arrangements to make for my journey to Amsterdam. When I am finished dressing, I will leave by the other door so as not to disturb your discussions. And then I will go downstairs to have Basile Sauveur shave me and dress my hair."

Coming to the edge of the bed, he kissed Jasmine's forehead. With a grand bow to the Duc de Richelieu, he went into the dressing room and closed the door.

Removing his surtout and hat, the Duc laid them on a sofa and propped his cane against the wall. Coming to the side of the bed, he drew up a chair and sat down.

"Well, Madame," he said, propping his booted feet on the bed steps, "are you ready for your presentation?"

"Your Excellency," she said impatiently, "before we discuss my presentation, could you please hand me my nightdress?"

He grinned and toyed idly with one of his white-powdered curls. "You look exceedingly fetching just the way you are." His blue eyes swept over her bare shoulders and bosom over which she held the bedclothes. "I almost envy the King, Madame. You are an exceptionally provocative woman. I don't suppose you would consider . . ." Her cold glance answered his unspoken question. "No, I didn't think so. But I can assure you, you would not find me lacking."

"Please, Your Excellency . . ."

With an exaggerated sigh, the Duc left his chair and retrieved her silk nightdress from the floor at the bedside. Holding it out to her, he kept it just outside her reach.

"Your Excellency," she repeated, "please give it to me."

He held it out again and again, just as she reached for it, he pulled it away. At last, with an angry hiss of exasperation, she dropped the bedclothes and leaned toward him. Snatching the nightdress from him, she struggled into it.

"Are you a voyeur, then, Your Excellency?" she sneered. "Do you derive your pleasure from sneaking glances at women?"

Settling back in his chair, the Duc smiled self-satisfiedly. "I will not close my eyes when presented with the sight of a lovely woman in any state of undress, Madame, regardless of how that sight is obtained." Pursing his lips, he picked up a stray hair from the sleeve of his gray velvet coat. "But I believe we are to discuss your presentation. You will be taken to Versailles by the Abbé de Bernis. Once there, you will be taken to the King and then to the Queen. My daughter, Septimanie, the Comtesse d' Egmont, will present you. Do you know how to approach Their Majesties?"

"I think so, Your Excellency. I make three curtsies . . ."

With a wave, he silenced her. "Show me, Madame. Pretend I am the King."

Reluctantly, Jasmine climbed out of bed. Knowing that her thin silk nightdress hid few of her charms, she was aware of the Duc's eyes upon her. She walked to the opposite side of the room and, faultlessly, approached him making three perfect curtsies.

"Welcome to our Court, Madame de Saint-Antoine," the Duc said, trying to imitate the King's distictive voice.

"Thank you, Your Majesty," she replied in all seriousness. She knew that if she made a mistake, he would make her repeat the entire performance. "I am honored to be here."

With a quick kick to an imaginary train, she backed away from the Duc and, supposedly, out of the King's presence chamber.

"That was perfect, Madame!" the Duc told her. "Perfect! You are to be congratulated."

She turned her back on him and pulled a satin dressing gown over her nightdress. "Thank you, Your Excellency." She stiffened as she felt his hands on her shoulders.

"And now, Madame, shall we rehearse the other part of your evening at Versailles? You will be taken to an apartment above the King's Petits Appartements which will be yours if the King is satisfied with you. There your maidservant will undress you and you will be anointed with perfume. Then you will be dressed and left to await the King's pleasure. I know him well, Madame. I have shared some of his little trollops from Parc aux Cerfs and they have told me every detail of the King's technique."

His hands caressed her through the thin material of her dressing gown and nightdress. "Shall I show you what you can expect when you are alone with him at Versailles?"

She turned toward him and the smile on her lips was surprisingly seductive. "Of course, Your Excellency," she cooed, pressing close to him and caressing him as intimately as she dared.

His eyes widened in surprise and he caught her in a tight embrace. He kissed her lingeringly and then, with a strength unexpected in a man of his age, swept her into his arms and carried her to the bed.

She lay atop the rumpled coverlet and smiled sweetly. But, as he would have mounted the bed steps, she pressed a hand against his chest.

"Of course, Your Excellency, I will have to refuse His Majesty tomorrow night. But I am sure he will understand when I tell him that I am simply too tired after an afternoon of passion with his good friend, the Duc de Richelieu."

The Duc's blue eyes narrowed and his passion cooled immediately.

"You would do that, wouldn't you?" he said. But the fury in his tone was strangely tempered with grudging admiration.

"Indeed I would, Your Excellency," she replied. Rolling on her stomach, she tossed him a coquettish glance over her shoulder.

"You deserve another spanking," he observed, his eyes alighting on her rounded bottom.

She giggled and slid off the other side of the bed. "I think you enjoy those spankings entirely too much, Your Excellency."

He nodded with a chuckle. "I don't deny it." Going

to the sofa, he donned his surtout and hat and picked up his cane. "I will bid you adieu, Madame, until tomorrow night."

Going to the doorway, he paused thoughtfully. "You know, Madame, I believe we are going to be strong allies —or bitter enemies."

With another nod, he left the room and Jasmine stared at the closed door, frowning.

"I fear I know which it will be," she murmured to the empty room.

Chapter 31

"Are you ready, Madame?" the Abbé de Bernis asked as his coach stopped in the Cour Royale before the palace of Versailles. The late February night was bitterly cold and he was eager to be inside the relatively warm palace.

"In a moment, Your Excellency," she replied. She looked up at Casanova, who sat beside her. "Can't you come with me to the Duc's apartment?"

"How would that look, my angel?" he demanded. "Tonight I must be merely a face in the crowd. You must notice me no more than you would notice anyone else."

The Abbé consulted his watch. "Madame, it is nearly four o'clock. You're only two hours to dress."

"All right." She tipped her face up and Casanova kissed her briefly. Releasing his hand reluctantly, she climbed out of the coach and accompanied the Abbé de Bernis to the palace. Just before they entered, she glanced back and, with a tremulous smile and a little wave of her hand, bade adieu to Casanova, who stood beside the coach.

"Where will he go?" she asked as she mounted the staircase beside the Abbé.

"Probably to pay his respects to Madame de Pompadour. I understand she has suffered an attack of her usual malady and has taken to her bed."

Jasmine noticed a group of young men watching as they left the staircase. The Abbé looked away from them.

"Do not deign to notice them," he commanded. "They are of no importance."

She lowered her eyes and, for the rest of the long walk to the apartment of the Duc de Richelieu, all she saw of Versailles was the floor and an occasional skirt or pair of shoes.

The Abbé left her and Claudette in the magnificent salon of the Duc de Richelieu.

"Will you come back?" she asked anxiously.

"I will be present when you are brought to the King's rooms," he promised. With a nod, he left her.

"Madame de Saint-Antoine?"

Jasmine looked around and found Septimanie, the Comtesse d'Egmont, standing in the doorway.

"Yes, I am," she replied. "You must be Madame d'Egmont?"

Septimanie nodded. Only a few months Jasmine's elder, the beautiful girl had been married at a tender age to a Spanish Grandee nearly twice her years.

It seemed to Jasmine that there was a great sadness in the Comtesse's lovely blue eyes. The Abbé de Bernis had told her how the Duc de Richelieu had compelled Septimanie to marry the Comte, who was of an ancient and noble lineage but also of a stern and dreary disposition. She had been in love with the dashing Comte de Gisors with whom she had grown up. Though he was a heroic soldier and heir to the fabulous fortune of the Marquis de

Belle-Isle, the Duc had forbidden the match citing the fact that Gisors' grandfather had been Nicholas Fouquet, the first Marquis de Belle-Isle. That the unfortunate Fouquet had spent years in prison for using his position as Minister of Finances under Louis XIV to siphon public funds to build the exquisite château and gardens of Vaux-le-Vicomte bothered the Duc not a whit. What made young Gisors unaccaptable as a husband for Septamanie was the fact that Nicholas Fouquet had risen from the ranks of the bourgeoisie. Only the bluest of blood must run in the veins of the Duc de Richelieu's son-in-law.

"Please," the Comtesse invited, "come into the bedchamber. Your clothing has already arrived."

Under the watchful eye of the Comtesse d' Egmont and the ancient Duchesse de Sedgmont, who made it her business to be the first person to view any new arrival, Jasmine was stripped of her lavender satin gown. Then she was dressed, slowly, in the white and silver finery in which she would be introduced to what passed for polite society at Versailles.

Her stockings, of white silk with silver clocks, were fastened with white lace garters and her white and silver shoes buckled. Her white chiffon chemise with its silver lace trim was lowered over her head hiding her figure, if only barely, from the prying eyes of the old Duchesse, who would eagerly report to all who would listen on the intimate charms of the new Maîtress Déclarée. Her white silk stays were laced and her frothy petticoats fastened over wide panniers. And then, to her surprise, a gentleman entered the room.

She held her hands before her scantily covered breasts but heard Septimanie laugh.

"Madame, be at ease," she urged. "It is only Monsieur Benét, the hairdresser.''

The man removed his surtout revealing his blue-and-white striped taffeta waistcoat. Opening a case, he removed a great quantity of hair needles, combs, and brushes. He unfastened the latches of another lacquered box and, opening it, revealed a white wig on a carved, wooden block.

''Monsieur Benét,'' Septimanie explained, ''will fasten your own hair up and then put your wig on.''

Jasmine sat on a gilded stool before a grand toilette table. ''But why doesn't he dress my own hair?'' she asked the Comtesse d'Egmont, who carefully draped her own pale pink gown over a little stool and sat down beside her.

''The pomatum and powder would take too long to remove later.''

Jasmine blushed. ''I see,'' she whispered.

''I am leaving now, Septimanie,'' the Duchesse de Sedgmont announced. Coming to Jasmine's side, she peered at her for several moments and then, followed by two young maidservants, swept out of the apartment.

Jasmine raised her eyebrows. ''Where is she going?''

Septimanie laughed. ''To the Queen's rooms, I expect. She and Her Majesty are great cronies. The Queen will want to know what to expect.'' Seeing Jasmine's grimace, she smiled gently. ''You need not be nervous. If His Majesty did not think you capable of managing the situation, you would not be here.''

Toying with a silver hair needle which Monsieur Benét had dropped onto the toilette table, Jasmine asked shyly:

''Madame, may I ask a rather tactless question?''

Septimanie shrugged. ''Of course.''

''His Excellency, your father, has encouraged His Majesty to make me his mistress. He has impressed upon me time and time again that it is an honor and a privilege to serve the King in this fashion. Why, then, didn't he put you forward for the position?''

The Comtesse smiled again. ''Because His Majesty did not desire me, I suppose.''

''Otherwise he would have?''

''Undoubtedly so.'' Her smile soured a little. ''He would have ordered me into the King's bed in the same way he ordered me into my husband's bed.''

Jasmine said nothing but was relieved when her white wig, with its many ringlets and spray of sparkling diamonds holding three snowy ostrich plumes, was lowered into place diverting their attention.

''And now,'' Septimanie said, eager to change the subject, ''it is time for the gown.''

With Claudette and the Comtesse d' Egmont's maid working in concert, the Monsieur Benét and Septimanie giving often contradictory orders, the white and silver gown was lowered over her head.

''How lovely it is,'' Septimanie said, using one finger to wipe away a tiny smudge in Jasmine's rouge. She stepped aside and Claudette fastened the back of the gown. Jasmine examined herself in the toilette table's mirror.

With her white wig and the black velvet beauty spot placed just to the right of her mouth, she seemed some glittering stranger. When the diamond-trimmed ribbon was tied about her throat, it shimmered in the candle-light. She looked beautiful—and as cold as the snow-covered statues in the garden.

An ormulu and porcelain clock struck the hour and Madame d'Egmont thrust an ivory and lace fan and white kid gloves into Jasmine's hands.

''It is time, Madame,'' she said.

Closing her eyes, Jasmine took several deep breaths. Her ordeal was upon her. Steeling herself against her own fear, she followed Septimanie from the apartment.

The corridors between the Duc's apartment and the State Apartments were filled with people. It seemed to Jasmine that every nobleman in France must surely have descended upon Versailles to witness her presentation.

She kept her eyes staring straight ahead and tried to ignore the throngs which parted to allow her and Septimanie to pass. It was only when they started through the brightly lit Hall of Mirros that she noticed a familiar face in the crowd.

"Solange!" she said under her breath. "Solange Lancour!"

Septimanie tilted her head toward her. "What was that?"

"Solange Lancour. There, in the violet and white gown."

The Comtesse d'Egmont glanced toward the wall. "Ah, yes, the Comtesse d'Auligny. She came to Court nearly a month ago. Of course, one never knows much about these provincial nobles. They come to Court for a while, exhaust their finances, and retire to the country once again. Though, I must admit, that gown is lovely."

It should be! Jasmine thought. It was one of those Solange had stolen when she and Luc had abandoned her at the inn in Sommeville. She was about to tell Septimanie the truth about the "Comtesse d'Auligny" when they arrived at the King's Council Chamber. Her moment was at hand and the bogus Comtese was temporarily forgotten.

The King's Council Chamber was nearly as full of courtiers as had been the grand salons of the State Apartments and the Hall of Mirrors. As Jasmine entered, the nobles fell back allowing her a clear path to the King.

From the corner of her eye, Jasmine saw a few familiar faces. The Ducs d'Ayen and de Richelieu and the Abbé de Bernis surrounded the King, who stood near the council table.

Curtsying three times, Jasmine approached the King. Her cheeks, beneath the dusting of rouge, blushed hotly while his, though his complexion was naturally ruddy, turned to a deep, rosy pink. As she made the last of her curtsies, the King at last turned his eyes from the gold embroidery of his pale blue coat and looked at her.

"Madame de Saint-Antoine," he said, his words barely audible. "Welcome."

"Thank you, Your Majesty," she whispered in reply. With the toe of her shoe, she kicked the train of her gown to the side so that she could back from the room.

"That wasn't so difficult, was it?" the Comtesse d'Egmont asked wen they were once again in the Galerie des Glaces.

"No," Jasmine admitted. "The real test is yet to come."

They passed into the Queen's apartment and Jasmine tried to stop the trembling which she was sure was visible to the people they were passing.

"There is someone you know," Septimanie whispered.

Jasmine looked in the direction of the Comtesse's glance and saw Casanova standing near the door of the Queen's presence chamber. He threw her a wink as she passed.

Fantastic Goeblins tapestries decorated the walls of the salon and the ceiling was painted to represent the god Mercury protecting the sciences and arts. Of the wonderful Savonnerie carpet she could see little. It was nearly covered with elegantly shod feet and thickly embroidered skirts.

The Queen sat in a gilded armchair waiting to receive her. To her right stood her boon companion, the elderly Duchesse de Luynes, and to her left, having reported her findings, the Duchesse de Sedgmont.

Queen Marie Leszczyńska, daughter of the deposed King Stanislas I of Poland, was a handsome woman. Though seven years the King's senior, she looked no older. Her dark eyes sparkled beneath her powdered hair and her expression was one of mild curiosity as her husband's new mistress approached.

Jasmine curtsied the prescribed three times and studied the Queen closely. She found it odd that such a handsome, gentle-looking woman would, if rumor be true, have kept her priests busy searching out obscure saints in order to use their days as an excuse to keep her husband from her bed. That was the gossip and, from all appearances, the King had completely abandoned the marriage bed.

As she made the last of her curtsies, her eyes met those of the Queen.

"Madame de Saint-Antoine," the Queen said in her heavily accented French, "welcome to Versailles."

"Thank you, Your Majesty," Jasmine replied softly.

"May I compliment you on your gown? It is quite exquisite—and you, yourself, are very lovely."

"Your Majesty is too kind."

With a smile, the Queen nodded, dismissing her. Jasmine curtsied again and, removing a glove, took up the hem of the Queen's dark red satin gown to kiss. Her presentation hopefully completed, she once again kicked her train out of the way and backed from the Queen's presence.

"Are we finished?" Jasmine asked as they left the Queen's apartment.

"I fear not," Septimanie replied. "You have yet to meet Their Majesties' children. You must be presented to the Dauphin and Dauphine and to Mesdames, the King's daughters."

They descended the multicolored marble Queen's Staircase to the apartments of the Enfants de France. In short order, Jasmine was presented to the Dauphin, twenty-seven-year-old Louis, heir to the throne. He was handsome—much resembling his father—though his face was piteously scarred by a bout with smallpox. At the same time, Jasmine met the Dauphine. Marie-Josèphe was the second wife of the Dauphin, the first having died in childbirth. She was not pretty, being rather too robustly Germanic for French tastes. She had not been a tactful choice for Dauphine. Her father, the Elector Augustus III, King of Poland, had taken the throne of Poland from the Queen's father. But Madame de Pompadour had favored her to be the Dauphin's second wife and so the Queen's feelings were not considered.

From the apartments of the Dauphin and Dauphine, Jasmine was taken to the rooms of the Mesdames. Madame Adelaide, Madame Victoire, Madame Sophie, and Madame Louise remained at the French Court though all were of an age to be married. Of the King's daughters only the eldest, Madame Infante, was married. The others—from Madame Adelaide, who was twenty-five, to Madame Louise, twenty—could not bear to be separated from their father nor he from them.

Jasmine was presented to them and received, as she'd expected, a chilly reception. She was the woman with whom their father would be spending most of his nights and she was three years younger than the youngest of them.

"Now are we finished?" she asked wearily as they once again climbed the Queen's staircase.

"Now we are finished," Septimanie confirmed.

They returned to the Hall of Mirrors, where the crush of courtiers seemed to have lightened. The chief entertainment of the evening was over and many had gone elsewhere in search of other amusements.

As Jasmine entered the gallery, she was captured by the Duc de Richelieu.

"You did everything perfectly, Madame," he told her.

"Thank you, Your Excellency."

"If you do as well in the bedchamber, you will be Maîtresse en Titre very soon."

"Your Excellency," she said with a sullen tone she would not have dared use before, "if you will excuse me, I see someone I wish to speak to."

Ignoring the surprised look on his face, she left his side and crossed the gallery. A woman in voilet and white stood near the windows speaking to a gentleman in peach-colored satin.

"Solange?" she said.

The young woman whirled toward her and dropped her a profound curtsy.

"Come with me, Solange. I want to speak to you."

Taking the former maidservant to a corner of an adjoining salon, Jasmine whispered harshly:

"Are you mad coming here and pretending to be a Comtesse? The fine for impersonating a member of the nobility is two thousand livres!"

"Are you going to expose me, Madame?" Solange asked fearfully.

Jasmine sighed. "I should! If only for leaving me at that horrible inn! But I won't. It doesn't matter to me if you get into trouble. But do not expect me to save you if you are caught."

"Oh no, Madame!" Solange said gratefully.

"All right, then." Noticing eyes upon them, Jasmine took Solange's arm and returned to the Hall of Mirrors where they were immediately separated in the crush of courtiers.

"Madame de Saint-Antoine?"

She looked toward the familiar, and welcome, voice eagerly. Casanova, resplendent in crimson satin which accentuated his swarthiness and black eyes, bowed before her.

"May I claim a dance before you are stolen by anyone else?"

"Oh yes, Monsieur," she replied.

With scores of eyes upon them, they danced and their conversation was whispered beneath the strains of the music.

"You were beautiful tonight, my angel," he said. "I was very proud of you."

"Take me back to Paris with you, Giacomo."

His smile faded a little. "You must not speak so; though I insist you think of me constantly. You are a lady of the Court now and very shortly to be . . ."

"Do not say it," she begged. "Please do not."

"Very well, but still, you must be discreet. There are hundreds of eager ears waiting to hear something about which to gossip." He looked toward the mirrored doors of the King's suite which had been closed but now were opening. The music died and the entire assemblage sank toward the floor, the gentlemen bowing low and the ladies curtsying as the King emerged.

"Goodbye, my angel," Casanova whispered. Stepping away, he left her alone as the King approached.

"Marquise de Saint-Antoine," King Louis said, standing before her.

"Your Majesty," she replied.

He signaled to the musicians and, as they began to dance, the rest of the Court joined them beneath the thirty-two chandeliers of the Hall of Mirrors.

The Duc de Richelieu held Jasmine's hands as the dance ended. "It is time, Madame," he said.

"So soon?" she whispered fearfully.

They worked their way slowly from the Hall and passed through the beautiful salons and up a staircase to the second floor. The Duc entered a suite of small rooms and stepped back to allow her to pass.

The rooms were not so large as the grand apartment occupied by Madame de Pompadour, but they were so exquisitely decorated that they seemed unreal. She was taken through a salon decorated in pale blue and gold, an antechamber in light green and white, and into a bedchamber with walls of pastel pink with delicate, gilded trim. Ancient Goeblins tapestries decorated the walls and the parquet floor was covered with a Savonnerie carpet. Though the furnishings of all the rooms had been exquisite, the bedchamber was by far the loveliest. Against the pale pink of the walls, the dark rose brocade hangings on the large, high bed stood out startlingly.

"The bathroom is through there," the Duc told her, pointing to a door. "The dressing room is through there." He pointed to another doorway in which Claudette stood. "You remember, Mademoiselle," he said to the maidservant, "that you are to retire to your room as soon as Madame is ready for the King. Do you understand? You are not to be here when his Majesty arrives.''

Claudette curtsied. "Yes, Monseigneur.''

Taking Jasmine's hand, he kissed her and his lips lingered longer than necessary. "Good night, Madame,'' he said with a leer. "Pleasant dreams—though I doubt you will have time for many.''

With a shallow bow, he left the room pausing only long enough to say: "By the bye, Madame. The King requests that you wear no perfume. Remove any you are wearing, if you please.''

The bedchamber door closed behind him and Jasmine felt Claudette's fingers working at the hooks of her gown. With trembling fingers, she reached up and removed the heavy, white wig.

"Are you nervous, Madame?'' Claudette asked, seeing the way the wig shook as Jasmine placed it on the toilette table.

Jasmine's eyes met hers in the mirror and she nodded. "Terrified,'' she whispered.

Chapter 32

Divested of her glittering Court attire, Jasmine paused before donning her nightdress to remove the last vestiges of her perfume. She took a deep breath, drawing in a long whiff of the violet-scented orrisroot perfume Casanova had given her.

"Why does the King want you to take it off?" Claudette asked.

"I don't know." Sadly, she washed the scent from her skin. "But it is now my duty to do as he wishes."

Leaving the basin stand, she went to the fireplace and stood, shivering, clad only in her fur-lined mules while she waited for Claudette to bring her nightdress and robe.

The thin silk and lace of the nightdress did little to warm her chilled skin but the white velvet robe with its trimming of silver fox was thick and caressing.

She sat on the gilded dressing stool while Claudette brushed her hair until it gleamed in the candlelight.

"Well, Madame," the maid said, laying the gold

brush on the toilette table, "I will leave you now."

Jasmine caught at her hand. "Not yet, Claudette! Please, stay a little longer!"

"I mustn't. His Excellency said . . ."

"To Hell with His Excellency! Please, stay until the King arrives."

But Claudette was awed and frightened by the immense power wielded by the Duc de Richelieu and she couldn't be dissuaded.

"I am sorry, Madame," she insisted, already backing away, "but I must leave. My room is just beyond the dressing room. I will be there if you should require anything."

"I require your company!" Jasmine pleaded.

But it was too late. Retreating to her room through the dressing room, Claudette closed the dressing room door and turned the key in the lock.

"Claudette!" Jasmine called, rattling the door latch. "Unlock this door at once!"

There was no answer and Jasmine heard Claudette closing the door to her own room beyond the locked chamber.

Left alone, Jasmine paced the floor of her beautiful bedchamber nervously. Two tall tripod lights, each bearing three lighted tapers, flanked the door lighting the room softly. In addition to the large bed whose plumed finials brushed the painting ceiling, the room contained a toilette table with a canopy supported by chubby cherubs, several tables and chairs, a basin stand, and a brocade-covered chaise longue. Standing in the center of the room, Jasmine peered up at the ceiling which was barely visible in the weak light. Painted by François Boucher, it abounded with handsome young men and beautiful women in a variety of sensuous attitudes.

A barely audible sound in the silent room made her look up. It seemed to be a muffled thud-thud, as of someone ascending a staircase.

She went to the doorway of the adjoining antechamber and the sound seemed a trifle louder. Moving out into the green and white antechamber, she followed the sound, which seemed to be coming from an adjoining room. But, as she pressed her ear to the wall, she knew it could not be. Beyond that particular wall was only her own dressing room.

Leaning against the wall, she listened. The sounds seemed to be getting louder, their source coming nearer. When they reached their loudest point, the sounds abruptly stopped. Listening carefully, Jasmine heard only a soft click.

She started as a section of the paneling seemed to bulge. Stepping back, she gasped as the section opened and a man entered the room.

The King stepped back, startled, but then smiled.

"I didn't expect you to come through the walls," she replied.

Holding the panel open, he showed her the tiny staircase up which he had come from his own private bedchamber a floor below.

"My great-grandfather had many such passages built into the walls," he explained. "I find them most useful." Closing the panel, he handed her his candlestick. As she placed it on a table, he sat on the dark green velvet sofa near the small windows which overlooked the Cour de Marbre.

Shyly she joined him on the sofa and the white velvet

of her robe mingled with the rich purple velvet of his. Looking into his dark eyes, she thought that he looked much younger without the powdered wig he wore in public. His own dark hair was pulled back simply and tied with a black velvet ribbon.

"You did very well tonight," he said quietly. "Even the Queen was impressed with you."

"I'm glad," she replied. "I was so very frightened that I would embarrass you."

"Nonsense, you were perfect." Taking one of her hands, he kissed it gently. "You are trembling," he said, and endearing air of concern in his husky voice. "Are you cold?"

"A little," she admitted. "But mostly I am merely frightened."

"Frightened!" His tone was incredulous. "Of me?"

"After all," she reasoned, "you are the King."

"Not tonight, ma petite. Tonight I am merely a man. Respect and formality are fine for public, but for now, I would be simply an admirer of a delicious young woman." He stroked her cheek. "Do not be frightened. I would never harm you. As for being cold . . ." He held out his arms and Jasmine found herself cuddled closely to him. "Is that better, ma petite?"

"Yes, Sire, much better." She closed her eyes and enjoyed the comforting touch of his hand stroking her hair.

For several minutes they sat together in silence and it seemed to Jasmine that she could feel the King relaxing —it was as if the tensions and burdens of his never-ending labors were draining from him. She looked up and he smiled and leaned to kiss her forehead.

"Shall we go into the other room?" he asked.

It seemed to Jasmine that it would be all too easy to discourage the almost timid man. One sharp rebuke and she had no doubt he would be on his way down his secret staircase to the welcoming, familiar arms of Madame de Pompadour.

Standing, she held out her hand and found it clasped in his. They walked together to the pink and gold bedchamber and she smiled uncertainly as he closed, and locked, the door.

In spite of her chagrin at having been parted from Casanova, she quivered with anxious anticipation as he slipped the white velvet robe from her shoulders. Her head fell back as he bent to kiss her throat and the swell of her breasts above the deep, wide neckline of the silk and lace nightdress.

"I have brought you a gift, ma petite," the King murmured. "Get onto the bed and I will bring it to you."

While Jasmine climbed onto the high bed, the King removed his dressing gown and draped it over a chair. Before he came to the side of the bed, he reached into one of its commodious pockets.

"This is for you," he told her. "It was made especially from plants in the royal greenhouses. There are only two people in the world who will have it—you and I."

He came to the bed and held out his hand. A crystal flagon encased in gold filigree lay there.

"How exquisite!" Jasmine sighed. Taking the small bottle from his hand, she drew the tall stopper and held it beneath her nose. The heady scent of jasmine assailed her nostrils.

Gathering his long, linen nightshirt above his knees, the King climbed onto the bed and knelt beside her.

Taking the bottle and stopper from her, the King

applied it to her throat and breasts and then, as she raised her arms allowing the long sleeves of her night-dress to fall back, to her wrists and elbows.

She giggled as he thrust his nose near her and sniffed loudly.

"Now, Sire," she told him. "It's my turn."

She unbuttoned the front of his nightshirt and, taking the flagon, touched the stopper to his throat and chest. Looking up, she saw his dark eyes widen and was not surprised when he took the perfume from her and placed it on the bedside table.

Gently, he tugged her nightdress over her head and dropped it over the side of the bed. Jasmine blushed as his eyes swept over her in the faint candlelight. But her abashment was eased as she noticed that he was also blushing as he removed his nightshirt. He took her into his arms and she trembled as his hands fondled her tenderly.

She untied the velvet ribbon which bound his dark auburn hair that was not so different from her own.

"You will not be sorry," he whispered. "You will not be sorry that you have forsaken Monsieur Casanova."

Forsaken! She stiffened in his arms. Was that what he thought? Was that what Giacomo believed? That she had deserted him for the glamorous life of a royal mistress?

"Do not be afraid," the King told her, mistaking her sudden hesitancy for fear.

Jasmine bit her lip and buried her face in his shoulder to conceal her distress.

Mistaking her anguished shudder for passion, the King lowered her softly to the scented satin sheets.

The King of France was a skilled lover and most

women would never know his equal; but for Jasmine he could not compare with the man who would soon leave her to make his way to faraway Amsterdam.

She closed her eyes and imagined that the fingers that touched her belonged to Casanova, that the lips that kissed her were his; that the body that touched hers was his. It was only then that she felt the rush of passion building in her veins. She shivered and moaned softly but when she opened her eyes and found herself gazing into the brown eyes of the King rather than the black eyes of Casanova, a faintly puzzled look crossed her face. But the King, burying his face in the hollow of her shoulder, did not see the look nor the expression of sadness which replaced it.

When his passion was temporarily spent and he fell into a deep sleep, she lay beside him staring at the canopy above not daring to give vent to the melancholia which engulfed her. She slipped out of the bed and extinguished the guttering candles in the tall candlesticks near the door.

"Jasmine?" the King said faintly.

She went back to the bed. "I am here."

He held out a hand to her and she slipped beneath the coverlet and into his arms once again.

He made love to her four more times during the night and every time she found she had to conjure the image of Giacomo Casanova in order to respond to his caresses.

In between, he would sleep with his head nestled on her bosom while she, holding him in her arms, watched the fire in the marble fireplace die.

When dawn was breaking over Versailles and the King's valet tapped discreetly on the door to wake his master and take him back to the magnificent state bedchamber where his official levée would take place, Jasmine feigned sleep. Only when she heard the door close behind him did she sit up in the wide bed and, covering her eyes with her hands, give way to the tears which had hovered so near the surface all night long.

Wrapped in a hooded, pale blue velvet, sable-lined pelisse, Jasmine left her apartment and went down through the State Apartment. To avoid the gazes of the curious whose whispers followed her like a wake, she engaged Claudette in a deep conversation containing not the least bit of substance.

"Madame de Saint-Antoine?"

Directly addressed for the first time, Jasmine stopped. A man in black velvet approached and bowed.

"Madame, I am Dominique-Guillaume Lebel, the Concierge of Versailles. May I enquire as to whether you are leaving the palace?"

Jasmine and Claudette exchanged an apprehensive glance.

"I would like to go into Paris for a few hours," she told him. "Is that permitted?"

His smile was kind. "But of course, Madame. You are not a prisoner at Versailles. Quite the opposite, in fact. I merely inquired because, if you were leaving the palace, I would see that your coach is waiting."

"My coach? I was going to hire a fiacre. I have no coach."

"You have now, Madame." Summoning one of the pages who followed him around, Monsieur Lebel sent him to the stables to order Madame de Saint-Antoine's coch. "Your coach should be waiting in the Cour Royale by the time you arrive, Madame," he told her. "If it is not, please tell me and I will discharge those responsible for the delay.''

"Thank you, Monsieur Lebel," Jasmine said.

"Thank you, Madame," he replied with a bow.

Descending the Queen's staircase, Jasmine and Claudette left the palace and crossed the wintry Cour de Marbre. They were just over half way across the courtyard when they saw a grand coach leave the stables beyond the Place d'Armes and come toward them.

A footman handed them inside and, when they were comfortably settled beneath fur-lined robes, the coach started off on the Avenue de Paris.

As the coach entered the courtyard of the Hôtel de Sauveur, Jasmine chuckled.

"We shall have to take Giacomo for a ride," she told Claudette. "He will be very impressed with this coach."

The coach stopped before the door and she climbed out and hurried into the hôtel.

As the door of their apartment, she rattled the latch.

"Giacomo!" she called. "Giacomo!"

"He must be sleeping," Claudette speculated.

"It is too late for that. He must have gone out. Well, no matter. We'll wait."

Taking out her key, Jasmine let them into the apartment. She shivered as she realized that there was no fire burning in the drawing room.

"It's freezing!" she cried.

Passing on through the dining room, she found it equally as cold. A terrible fear began to gnaw at her and she thrust open the bedchamber door.

The room was empty. It was exactly as it had been on the morning they'd first arrived in Paris. Going to the clothespress, she opened the drawers and found them empty. The dressing room, from which her own belongings had been taken the previous afternoon for transportation to Versailles, was now completely bare.

"Madame?"

Jasmine spun toward the voice and found Madame Sauveur standing in the doorway.

"Where is he, Madame?" Jasmine demanded.

"He has gone," the propriétaire replied. "He left for Amsterdam at first light."

"Left for Amsterdam! But he said he would wait a week!"

She shrugged. "He said his business in Paris was finished, Madame."

"Finished? No, no! His business is not finished!" Her eyes filled and she waved a hand toward Claudette and Madame Sauveur. "Leave me, please. Leave me alone for a few moments."

The other two women withdrew, closing the door behind them. In the city bedchamber, she knelt on the bedsteps and buried her sobs in the velvet coverlet of the bed they had shared. He was gone—even then on his way across France. In her heart she knew that he had not only left Paris—he had left her life.

Drying her tears, she willed herself into some measure of composure. As she turned away from the bed, she noticed a piece of ribbon lying on the floor nearby, concealed by a fold of the coverlet. Picking it up, she recognized it as one of the ribbons Casanova had used to tie his impeccably powdered hair. Traces of pomade and white hair powder still clung to the ribbon and, as she pressed it to her lips, she could smell the faint odor of orrisroot.

Clutching the ribbon like some treasure beyond price, she left the apartment and the hôtel and climbed back into her grand coach to return to Versailles—and Louis XV.

Chapter 33

"Pardon, Madame?"

Jasmine paused in the War Salon before the great Coysevox medallion of Louis XIV.

"Yes?" She did not recognize the man who stood before her.

"I have a message for you, Madame." He held out a folded, and sealed, document.

Taking the document, Jasmine saw that the seal was that of her husband. "Is this from my . . ." she began, but the man was gone; he had melted into the crowd filling the adjoining Hall of Mirrors.

"Who was that, Madame?" Claudette asked.

"I don't know."

Taking the message to a window, Jasmine broke the seal. It was indeed from Henri and requested that she meet with him.

"You're not going to Paris, are you?" Claudette asked apprehensively.

"No, he wants to meet me here at Versailles."

"But he is banished from the palace."

"He doesn't intend to come to the palace. He wants to meet me at the Bassin de Neptune."

"Oh, Madame! You are not going, are you? It is secluded there and no one will be about in the cold weather!"

Jasmine frowned, looking out the window at the parterres and garden beyond. "I have to go, Claudette. He says it concerns Michel. If he has found a way to punish Michel, I must help him."

"At least tell the King you are going. If the Marquis tries to abduct you, his Majesty will know where to look for you."

"Claudette! Use your head! If I tell the King I am going to meet Henri, he will have guards there to arrest him for disobedience."

The maidservant shook her head stubbornly. "I don't like it, Madame!"

"You are free to remain here, if you wish," Jasmine replied, starting for her apartment. "As for me, I intend to change into something a trifle less noticeable." She glanced ruefully at the lemon yellow gown she wore and the matching pelisse which was draped over her shoulders.

"I could not let you go alone!" Claudette insisted.

"Then come along!"

Returning to her apartment, Jasmine changed from the eye-catching yellow ensemble to one of an unexceptional gray. When both she and Claudette were swathed in hooded pelisses of a nondescript fashion and hue, they slipped down the stairs and out of the palace.

Crossing the Parterres du Nord, they passed the Pyramid fountain and entered the Allée des Marmousets. Thirty-six bronze children supported twelve fountains along the Allée. At the far end was the Dragons' Pool and beyond that, the Bassin de Neptune.

They were at the edge of the garden now and the palace could be seen but vaguely through the trees.

"Where is he?" Claudette asked nervously. "I don't like this, Madame."

"Jasmine?"

Claudette jumped and Jasmine looked toward the thick growth of trees and shrubs behind the basin.

Clad in a gray surtout with its wide collar buttoned to hide his chin and his broad-brimmed hat pulled low, the Marquis de Saint-Antoine emerged from the thicket and came toward them.

"Where is your coach?" Jasmine asked.

He nodded toward the trees. "There—in the road just beyond the trees."

"It was very dangerous for you to come here. You could be sent to the Bastille for disobeying the King."

"I know it. But this is important. Do you still want to punish Michel?"

"You know I do."

Reaching into his pocket, the Marquis drew out two documents. He hesitated before handing them to her.

"Are you the King's mistress?" he asked, his tone indifferent.

"Do you mean to say that rumor has not yet reached Paris?" she countered cynically.

"Well, there are always rumors. There have been rumors to the effect that you are displacing La Pompadour. But those rumors began even before you were presented last month."

"For once, rumor is reasonably correct. I am not displacing La Pompadour—it would take an act of war to do that—but yes, I am the King's mistress. What has that to do with Michel?"

"You are going to need the King to accomplish our goals." Unfolding the papers, he thrust them at her. "These are lettres de cachet. Do you know what a lettre de cachet is?" She shook her head. "A lettre de cachet," he explained, "is, in effect, a warrant for imprisonment. The person named in the warrant can be arrested without formal charges and imprisoned indefinitely without trial."

"There is no name inscribed."

The Marquis smiled. "That is what makes them so dangerous—and so effective. The King signs the warrant before the name is inscribed. In that way no one, except for the unfortunate prisoner, knows who the warrant is for. If someone comes to His Majesty to request that the prisoner be released, the King can honestly say that he knows nothing of the matter."

The potential power she held in her hand astonished Jasmine. "No one is safe from a lettre de cachet?"

"Very few."

"Why are there two of them here?"

"One is for Michel. The other you may use for Sofie if you decide to punish her as well. Or you can keep it as protection. In your position, you may well find yourself with many enemies."

Folding the documents, she tucked them into a pocket in her muff.

"Once the King has signed them, and I have inscribed Michel's name, what do I do with it?"

"Give it to Godefroi Jaquot. He is a footman in Madame de Pompadour's employ. Very tall, with bright red hair."

Jasmine nodded. "I know the one. What has a footman to do with a lettre de cachet?"

"He is not really a footman. He is an agent of the

secret police. He will see that the document gets to Monsieur Berryer, the Lieutenant of Police, at the Châtelet in Paris.''

''Godefroi Jaquot is an agent of the police?''

''Madame!'' Claudette hissed. ''I thought I saw someone on the parterre!''

The Marquis stepped back. ''I must go. I cannot risk being seen. Goodbye, Jasmine.''

''Goodbye, Henri.''

She stood there for a little while watching him return to his coach. As he disappeared into the thicket, she turned back toward the palace. It was early March and the bitterly cold winter was giving way to a pleasant spring. But the air was still chilled. She realized, as she and Claudette returned to the parterre and to the palace, that she was really very cold.

''Good evening, ma petite,'' the King said as he entered her apartment by way of the little stairway.

It was after midnight and he had suffered through the elaborate ceremony of his coucher in which the highest nobles in the land helped put the King to bed in the drafty state bedroom. He habitually slipped out of the magnificent state bed, for he was uncomfortable sleeping in the grand, cold room. Sometimes he went to the smaller private bedroom in the Petits Appartements to sleep but, more often, he slipped up the little staircase to Jasmine's apartment.

''Good evening, mon cher,'' she replied.

Though she was not in love with the King, Jasmine was very fond of him. He was a kind, noble man whose air of majesty concealed an endearing vulnerability which, while it never interfered with his being a strong monarch, tempered his authority with compassion.

360

She drew the skirts of her satin dressing gown aside to make room for him on the sofa in the antechamber.

"You look tired," she told him. "You have not been getting enough rest."

"It is true," he admitted. "But the Court expects to be entertained. How would they feel if I deserted them at nine o'clock?"

"You should try it sometime and see." Looking away from him, she began tentatively:

"Mon cher, may I ask a favor of you?"

"Of course. What can I give to you?"

"There is nothing I desire in the way of material gifts." Leaving the sofa, she went to the desk and got the lettres de cachet. "I need you to sign these."

Coming to her side, the King examined the documents.

"You know what these are, ma petite? These are very serious business."

"Yes, mon cher, I know they are serious."

"The persons whose names you intend to inscribe, they are not of nobility?"

"No," she assured him, deciding not to try to explain about Sofie, "they are servants."

He chuckled. "I was afraid you were going to put Reinette and the Duc le Richelieu in the Bastille!"

"Oh, mon cher," she teased. "How can you imagine such a thing? I would never do that to Reinette."

"But what about the Duc de Richelieu?"

She shrugged noncommittally. "I will reserve judgment upon that gentleman."

"A wise decision. But tell me—what crime have these servants committed?"

"They murdered their master—a noble gentleman."

"You are sure of their guilt?"

"I myself heard them plotting their crime."

"Why do you not bring the matter to the attention of the police openly?"

"The victim was poisoned, Sire. When it happened I was advised that it would not be wise to resurrect shades of the Chambre Ardente."

The King nodded. "Yes, that would not be wise. Give me a pen—I will sign."

Jasmine watched as he signed the two documents and then replaced them in the desk.

"When they are completed," he told her as they returned to the sofa, "you can give them to the Abbé de Bernis, or perhaps to the Duc de Richelieu."

"I was given the name of an agent of the secret police here at Versailles."

"Really?" He leaned toward her. "Whisper his name to me—I will tell no one."

Jasmine giggled. "You are teasing me, mon cher. I know very well that you know all the agents of the police at Court." She got up from the sofa. "I will get you some chocolate—it is fresh and warm. It will help you to sleep."

The King watched her silently, his curiosity aroused. Monsieur Berryer wielded immense power through his secret police and even the King did not know which of the lackeys he passed every day reported back to the Lieutenant of Police in Paris. After Jasmine's giggles, however, he could not bring himself to demand that she reveal the agent's name.

She brought him a cup of chocolate and poured one for herself. Sitting side by side in the silent apartment, they sipped their chocolate and talked of trivialities. It was the part of their relationship Jasmine enjoyed the most. Although she knew that he was exceptionally amorous by nature and her chief attraction for him was that she was physically able to accommodate his prodigious desires, she suspected that he also enjoyed the relaxing prelude to their sensuous encounters.

"Madame," he said with a fond smile, "you have a chocolate moustache."

Leaning toward her, he kissed the sweet, warm liquid from her lip. Jasmine sat her half-drained cup of chocolate aside for she knew that this was the beginning of the almost timid courtship which would culminate in the adjoining bedchamber.

"Is my moustache gone now, mon cher?" she whispered softly.

"I am not sure," he replied. "Let me look again."

He kissed her leisurely, tenderly, while she went willingly into his arms. He stood and, taking her by the hand, led her into the bedchamber where the quilted satin coverlet had been turned down over black, jasmine-scented, satin sheets.

Jasmine smiled into his dark brown eyes as they climbed into the high bed. She no longer saw Casanova's face when she looked into the King's eyes; he was too expert a lover for her to remain indifferent to him. His lovemaking, while perhaps not so honed to perfection as Casanova's had been, was satiating as it was exhausting.

She sighed with fulfillment as the King drew her to him and began the slow, unbearably tantalizing caresses that always started the ritual which would last until the dawn was breaking over the gardens. By sheer force of will she had relegated the sadness of Casanova's departure to the back of her mind where it waited with the pain of Barrett's memory to slip into her consciousness in unguarded moments. The memories would linger along with the anguish they caused her; but for now, as the

King gathered her into his arms and she arched her body to meet his, she was impervious to them. For the next few hours, her entire life would resolve about the kind-hearted and impassioned King of France.

Chapter 34

Jasmine sat at her desk carefully inscribing the name of Michel Onfroi on one of the lettres de cachet. She looked down in annoyance as the tiny puppy which the Duc de Richelieu had given her began chewing on a frill of lace decorating her petticoat.

"Claudette!" she called. "Come and take this animal away from here!"

The maidservant scooped up the little dog, which could nearly fit into one of her hands, and shook her head.

"He has destroyed a pair of your mules and one of His Majesty's slippers already," Claudette reported. "And he shredded the hem of one of the bed draperies."

Melting sealing wax onto the folded document, Jasmine frowned.

"If His Excellency thought he was doing me a favor by giving him to me, he was sadly mistaken! He should have given him to the King, who has much more patience with animals; or the Madame de Pompadour, who dotes on little dogs as though they were . . ." She smiled slyly.

"Oh, Madame, you couldn't give him to Madame de Pompadour!"

"Couldn't I?"

"The Duc de Richelieu would be livid! You know how he hates her!"

Jasmine beamed. "Yes, he does, doesn't he? Find me a basket or something—no, wait—bring me the gold box with the filigree top His Excellency gave me last week. If we are going to make him angry, we might as well do a good job."

With the lettre de cachet tucked into a pocket of her pelisse, and the gold box containing the dog cradled in her arms, Jasmine left her apartment.

In a gallery on the ground floor, she noticed the Abbé de Bernis deep in conversation with a gentleman she didn't recognize. Seeing her, the Abbé smiled.

"How are you, dear Madame?" he asked as she approached.

"I am well, Your Excellency," she replied. "Have you had any word from—" she hesitated, not knowing how much she could say in front of the other gentleman, "from the Chevalier de Seingalt?"

"No. I've had no word. But Giacomo is not a great correspondent. I expect to have word from him when he has a need of me. Meanwhile, may I present Monsieur Nicholas-René Berryer?"

Jasmine looked at the grim-faced man who bowed before her. His unpowdered hair was drawn back by a black grosgrain ribbon with none of the elaborate curls of the courtiers. His clothing was unpretentious and his face, which reflected every one of his fifty-three years, was set in a stern expression.

"Monsieur Berryer? The Chief of Police?" she asked.

"The same, Madame la Marquise," he replied.

"Monsieur Berryer has come to Versailles to attempt to ferret out the source of the newest wave of poissonades," the Abbé explained.

Jasmine had read a few of the libelous pamphlets which Madame de Pompadour's enemies wrote and distributed. Insulting to the extreme and accusing her of every iniquity known to man in the coarsest of terms, they were called "poissonades" because they consisted in large part of puns on her maiden name—"Poisson."

"I have seen them," she admitted, "they are horrible." She looked at the Abbé. "I was going to visit Madame de Pompadour. Is she receiving visitors?"

"Yes, though she is understandably in low spirits." He kissed Jasmine's hand. "If you will excuse me, I have an appointment to see the King." He nodded toward Monsieur Berryer. "Good day, Monsieur. And good luck in your search."

"Monsieur Berryer," Jasmine said as the Abbé walked away. "May I speak confidentially?"

"Certainly, Madame," he replied. "Something to do with the poissonades, perhaps?"

"No. Those that I read were left beneath my apartment door. I've no idea where they may have originated. What I want to speak to you about is . . ." She stopped as a group of courtiers passed at a leisurely pace, undoubtedly trying to overhear what it was that the King's young mistress was discussing with the Chief of Police. Lowering her voice, she continued: "I was directed to give this to Godefroi Jaquot." Handing the gold box containing the puppy to Claudette, she took out the lettre de cachet and gave it to Monsieur Berryer. "It is for a servant at the Hôtel de Mareteleur. He was involved in the death of my father-in-law."

367

Taking the document, he slipped it into his pocket. "It is signed by the King, of course?"

"Of course."

"Very well, then, Madame. I am returning to Paris immediately. Your wishes shall be carried out at once; the person in question will be lodged in the Bastille before nightfall."

"Thank you, Monsieur. I appreciate your cooperation."

"I am at your service, Madame."

"If you will excuse me now, Monsieur, I will go to pay my respects to Madame de Pompadour."

He bowed. "Good day, Madame."

Moving on toward Madame de Pompadour's apartment, Jasmine whispered to Claudette:

"I hope Reinette agrees to see me. It would be most embarrassing to be turned away."

"Do you think she would dare turn you away?"

"She would—and could—dare anything. If the King demanded an excuse, she could say she was too ill to receive visitors. Her health is poor—who could say she had not been ill?"

Arriving at Madame de Pompadour's door, Jasmine asked to be admitted. The footman who had answered the door disappeared and, when the door opened once again, it was Madame du Hausset who stood there.

"Good afternoon, Madame de Saint-Antoine," she said coolly. Even though she knew that Reinette's health was the better for not having to try to accommodate the King's desires, she could not help but be jealous that another woman could accomplish what her beloved Reinette could not.

"Good afternoon, Madame du Hausset," Jasmine replied. "I would like to visit Madame de Pompadour if she is receiving callers. If she is not, perhaps you would be so good as to give her this small gift for me."

She took the exquisite gold box from Claudette and showed it to the maid. The puppy inside, apparently exhausted by his morning of destruction, was asleep and escaped Madame du Hausset's notice.

"One moment, please, Madame. I will see if she is receiving callers."

Jasmine and Claudette waited in the corridor for several moments longer and then the door was opened and Madame du Hausset beckoned them into the apartment.

They were shown into the red lacquered salon where Madame de Pompadour, fragile and beautiful, reclined gracefully on the chaise longue upon which Jasmine had slept her first night at Versailles.

"Come in, Madame," Reinette invited. "Sit down."

The room was kept warm, for Madame de Pompadour suffered from perpetual chills, and Jasmine let her pelisse slip from her shoulders. Claudette, ever solicitous of her mistress's elegant wardrobe, picked the garment up and draped it carefully over a chair.

"I was not sure that you would be admitting callers," Jasmine said. "I spoke to the Abbé de Bernis outside and he said you were in rather low spirits."

The Marquise waved a translucent hand. "Ah well, there are always matters which tend to lower the spirits."

"At any rate, I brought you a little gift. I hope it will raise your spirits."

She extended the box toward the Marquise who took it with a little cry of delight.

"How lovely it is!" she exclaimed. She was an avid collector of anything rare or precious and her apartments in the royal palaces as well as her numerous homes were filled with priceless treasures. She lifted the delicate filigree lid and her eyes filled with tears. "How adorable!" Gathering the puppy gingerly, she took him out of the box and set it aside. Laying her cheek against his fur, she chuckled happily as he extended his pink tongue and licked her cheek. The coolness in her voice had disappeared as she smiled at Jasmine and said:

"Thank you, Madame. You were right, I feel much better already."

Jasmine smiled, watching the Marquise cuddle the tiny animal. Madame de Pompadour cherished her many pets. They lived far more comfortably than did many people in Paris. The general consensus was that they in some small way took the place of the children she'd always wished for. She'd suffered many miscarriages and the two children she'd borne her husband, Charles-Guillaume Lenormand d'Étoiles, were both dead—a son had died in infancy and her daughter, Alexandrine, had died two years before at the age of ten.

Jasmine stood. "I will take my leave now, Madame," she said. "I've no wish to overtax your strength."

Reinette looked up from the puppy, which had begun to chew on the satin bows of her bodice. "His Majesty will be arriving shortly for lunch."

"All the more reason for me to leave."

The Marquise studied her for a moment and then looked down at the puppy. "No, Madame," she said at last. "I insist you stay."

Happily agreeing, Jasmine sat down again. Word would spread that the King had spent the afternoon with both his mistresses and the news of their reconciliation would send enemies of both women scrambling for cover.

Her dressing gown lying open over her black brocade, lace-trimmed corset and frothy petticoats, Jasmine dozed on the chaise longue in her bedchamber. Supper was over and it would soon be time to dress for the evening's entertainments, but she was grateful for an hour or two of rest before then.

She groaned as she heard someone knocking on the outer door of her apartment.

Claudette, who had been working in the dressing room, went out to ask the footman at the door who was there.

"Madame?" she said, returning to the bedchamber. "It is His Excellency, the Duc de Richelieu."

"Oh, no!" Jasmine moaned. "Well, show him in."

She fastened her dressing gown and sat up on the chaise longue.

The Duc de Richelieu, already clad for the evening in oyster-colored satin liberally embroidered with gold, stormed into the room.

"What is the meaning of this, Madame?" he demanded angrily.

"I was about to ask you the same thing, Your Excellency," she replied languidly, not bothering to rise.

Lifting the skirts of his coat to avoid crushing them, the Duc sat on the foot of the lounge.

"Do not take that tone with me, Madame," he warned. "You are not indispensable. Versailles—nay, all of France is full of women who would gladly take your place. Women of a better quality than you, I might add. Why, I've a mind to place my own mistress in the King's bed—I doubt not she would prove more grateful than you!"

"Do as you like, Your Excellency."

Infuriated by her indifference, the Duc turned red beneath his white wig.

"How could you give the gifts I gave you to the guttersnipe downstairs?" he raged.

"That 'guttersnipe,' as you call her, was most grateful for the puppy. I, on the other hand, was tired of finding his teeth embedded in everything he could reach."

"If you ever do such a thing again, you little imbecile, I swear I will . . ."

"You will what, Duc de Richelieu?" the King asked from the doorway. Having come up the little staircase in the wall, he had arrived unheralded.

The Duc paled and, standing, made a profound bow. "Why, Your Majesty, how good to see you. Madame de Saint-Antoine and I were merely visiting."

"Do you threaten everyone you visit?"

"I fear your Majesty did not understand . . ." the flustered Duc began.

"I understand only too well, Duc," the King interrupted. "It was most kind and generous of Madame de Saint-Antoine to make the Marquise de Pompadour a gift of the puppy. You should be happy that your gifts have been put to such a good use."

"Of course, Sire," the Duc agreed.

His expression pleasant, the King asked; "Tell me, Duc de Richelieu, how long as it been since your last visit to the Bastille?"

The Duc blanched. "Several years, Sire," he whispered nervously.

"Take care, Duc, or you will find yourself organizing entertainments for the rats."

With another deep bow, the Duc hastily took his leave. As he slammed out of the apartment, Jasmine giggled.

The King smiled and, sitting on the lounge, lifted her silk-stockinged feet into his lap. "It was really most kind of you. Reinette is delighted with the puppy."

"I'm glad, mon cher. She desperately misses her little girl, doesn't she?"

"Yes. She would have liked to have been the mother of many children but," he shrugged, "it was not to be." His fingers traced the clocks embroidered on her stockings. "You know, ma petite," he said softly, "we have more than an hour until supper."

"Yes," she said noncommittally, "I know." She was amazed at his capacity for lovemaking. Sometimes she wished Monsieur Lebel would find a delectable new prostitute to lure him to Parc aux Cerfs for a while.

They both started as a loud pounding sounded on the apartment door.

"His Excellency, perhaps?" she suggested.

"If it is," the King replied grimly, "he will find himself in the Bastille before midnight!"

"Madame?" Claudette said, peeking shyly around the bedchamber door. "It is Madame de Mareteleur and Madame DuPré."

"Maman?" Jasmine asked in surprise. "And Grand-mère?"

Climbing off the chaise longue, Jasmine straightened her dressing gown. The King took her place, reclining on the lounge.

"I will wait," he told her.

Jasmine found her mother and grandmother waiting in the blue and gold salon beyond the antechamber.

"Maman! Grand-mère! Good evening, I was not expecting . . ."

Her words were cut off and she gasped as her grandmother's hand lashed out and caught her across the face.

"You little bitch!" the Marquise de Mareteleur growled. "Who do you think you are?"

Her hand pressed to her cheek, Jasmine backed away from the raving woman.

"What are you talking about?" she demanded.

"Do not pretend," Isabeau snapped. "She is talking about Michel! They came tonight and took him away—they had a lettre de cachet! For that one must have the King's signature and you are the only one in a position to get it!"

"Michel deserved to be put into prison!" Jasmine cried. "He murdered Cher Papa!"

"That is a lie!" Sofie hissed.

"It is not a lie! You know it is not! You and he conspired to kill him to get control of his money!"

Sofie's eyes narrowed. "And what if we did? You would benefit too! Henri inherited the estates—you are a very wealthy woman. You would be wealthy even if you were not the King's whore!"

"Get out!" Jasmine snarled. "I will have you thrown out!"

Isabeau came to her and Jasmine cringed. "Don't speak to your grand-mère like that, you miserable little ingrate!" Taking her daughter by the shoulder, Isabeau pushed her against the wall.

"I brought you to France so you would have opportunities. Now, you have risen to heights even I never imagined! And how do you pay me back? By obtaining warrants against our friends!"

"Michel was no friend! He is a murderer!"

Sofie sneered. "That did not keep you from admitting him to your bed!"

"That was before I knew what he was! Now I know he is a murderer—and so are you! I have another lettre de

374

cachet, you know, Grand-mère. Would you like to join Michel?''

Both Isabeau and Sofie were momentarily stunned into silence but then, maddened, they came at her.

''How dare you speak to us that way!'' Isabeau spat, raining blows on her daughter.

Jasmine cowered against the wall protecting her head with her arms. When her mother attempted to pull her away from the wall, she cried:

''Louis! Louis, help me!''

The drawing room door was thrown open and the King stared, astounded, at the sight of his young mistress being beaten by the other two women.

Dumbfounded by the sudden appearance of the King, Isabeau and Sofie backed away from Jasmine and sank to the floor and curtsied.

Entering the room, the King went to Jasmine, who knelt on the floor her face buried in her hands.

''Are you all right, ma petite?'' he asked.

She nodded and let him take her into his arms. Standing, she sobbed into his shoulder and he turned a terrible gaze on the women.

''What is the meaning of this, Marquise de Mareteleur?'' he demanded, his royal dignity summoned to its fullest.

''A misunderstanding, surely, Sire,'' Sofie replied fearfully. ''A matter of a lettre de cachet.''

''Was the lettre de cachet signed by me?''

''Yes, Your Majesty.''

''Are you, then, questioning my authority?''

''Of course not, Sire!''

He turned his icy look toward Isabeau. ''Who might you be, Madame?''

''I . . . I . . .'' Isabeau stuttered.

"She is Isabeau DuPré," Jasmine told him. "She is my maman."

"Do you question my authority, Madame?"

"Oh, no, Your Majesty," Isabeau breathed.

"Then why are you here? How do you dare beat this child!" He looked toward Sofie. "Marquise, be so kind as to describe the château at your estate of Mareteleur."

Sofie blenched, fearing what she knew would follow. "I cannot, Sire," she admitted. "I have never been there."

"No? Well then, may I sugget that you pay it a visit? I am sure Madame DuPré would be happy to help you pack what you need for the journey."

"How long a visit would you suggest?" she asked anxiously.

"Oh, I don't know. Let us just say that I will notify you when you are free to return."

Sofie felt herself on the verge of a swoon. The King was notorious for sending nobles to the country and then forgetting them. A suggestion for an extended trip to the country was, in effect, permanent banishment.

"When should I leave?" she whispered, clutching Isabeau's arm for support.

"There is no hurry," he said pleasantly. "Tomorrow morning would be fine. Good evening to you, Madame DuPré. Good evening to you, Marquise de Mareteleur. I expect you will be leaving the palace immediately; after all, you have much to do tonight."

As the women bustled out of the apartment, the King led Jasmine back through the antechamber to the bedroom.

"Undress your mistress," he told Claudette. "And put her to bed." He dried Jasmine's tears with a lace-edged, cambric handkerchief. "There, there, now, ma petite. They are gone. Shall I have Doctor La Martinière come to examine you?''

"Not, it won't be necessary. I'm all right," she replied sadly.

"You are excused from the evening's entertainments. Spend the evening resting.''

He looked around as a light knock sounded on the bedchamber door. ''Entrez!'' he called.

Louis-Dominique Bontemps, the King's valet-de-chambre—a member of the famous family who had occupied the influential position of valet since Louis-Dominique's great-great grandfather, Alexandre, had been valet to Louis XV's great-great grandfather, Louis XIII—entered the room and bowed.

"Pardon, Your Majesty," he said. "It is time to dress for the evening.''

"Very well." The King kissed Jasmine's forehead. "I shall look in on you after my coucher, ma petite.''

"Thank you, mon cher," she replied.

The bedchamber door closed behind the King and the valet and Jasmine leaned back on the pillows, drained by the emotional episode in the drawing room.

"None of this would have happened," she told Claudette dejectedly, "if Maman had allowed me to stay in Virginia and marry Barrett!" A sob catching in her throat, she wished desperately that she had the portrait of Barrett that had been left behind at the Hôtel de Mareteleur when she'd been taken to Saint-Antoine.

Chapter 35

The good ship Saint-Brieuc rode at anchor in the harbor of Le Havre. The lone passenger, leaving the crew to their business, took his baggage into the town and inquired as to the departure time of the next diligence to Paris.

"The next diligence," the man at the inn told him, "will leave in an hour—or perhaps two hours—depending on when it arrives here."

"If I go into the taproom, will you let me know when it arrives?"

Estimating the amount of wine he was likely to sell the young man in the next hour, the innkeeper nodded. "Certainly, Monsieur."

"Thank you." Carrying the leather-bound trunk that was his only baggage, Barrett Paxton went to the taproom and ordered a tankard of ale.

His ale arrived and, taking a sip, he reached into his pocket and drew out the letter he'd received over a month before.

After the letters Isabeau had written telling him that Jasmine was madly in love with her husband and wanted no more to do with him, he had nearly given up hope of ever being reunited with her. But then he'd received the letter from Jasmine herself and had known that Isabeau had deceived him. When Jean-Baptiste DuPré had decided to send a ship to France to sell a load of the dried tobacco from the previous harvest, he had asked permission to go along.

"Monsieur?" The barmaid stood beside him.

He looked up. "Yes?"

"Monsieur LaValle, the innkeeper, has asked me to tell you that the diligence has arrived. It will depart for Paris as soon as the horses are changed and the driver rested and fed."

He tucked the well-worn letter back into his pocket. "Thank you, Mademoiselle," he said.

He looked out the window and saw the large, rickety-looking diligence waiting to set out for Paris. Soon he would be on his way—soon he would be reunited with Jasmine.

The Marquis de Saint-Antoine seethed with barely concealed rage as the pile of gold louis d'or in front of him diminished and that before the Prince de Vaurigny grew. They were the lone players left in the game and the Prince's obvious glee at his good luck made the Marquis more determined than ever to recoup his lost gold.

"You had better consider whether you can afford to play any more, Marquis," the Prince said. He looked about with pride as the nobles standing around the table laughed appreciatively.

Beneath the gold and crystal chandelier in the gaming room of the Hôtel de Vaurigny in the Faubourg St. Germain, not so very far from the Hôtel de Mareteleur, the Marquis de Saint-Antoine shrugged his indifference toward his losses.

"Deal the cards, Your Excellency," he told the Prince. "It matters not to me if I win or lose. As you know, I have recently come into an inheritance. I have doubled my fortune."

"True," the Prince agreed, "your luck of late has not been all bad. It pays well to be the husband of the King's whore, does it not?" The assembled nobles snickered and the Prince, emboldened by their approval, went on: "You're lucky, Monsieur; it takes a special kind of woman to be the King's trollop."

The Marquis waited until the titters died away and then leaned across the table. "You should know about that, Your Excellency. After all, your grandmother was a royal whore."

The courtiers grew silent as the Prince's ruddy cheeks flushed. Being the grandson of Louix XIV and his flamboyant and beautiful mistress, the Marquise de Montespan, the Prince was notoriously sensitive on the subject. That only a marriage ceremony separated his family from that of his cousin, Louis XV, was a source of constant, gnawing irritation. That his rank and wealth was the result of his grandmother's adultery was an ever-present thorn in his side.

He stood, his dark eyes never leaving the Marquis's face. "You, Marquis, will apologize for that remark and then get out of my home!"

The Marquis stood, his gaze never wavering. "I will not apologize, Your Excellency, for speaking the truth. My wife does not deserve less respect than you allot your grandmother. If my wife is a common harlot, then so was your grandmother."

"You will pay for this, Marquis!" the Prince hissed.

"I am at your service, Your Excellency," Henri replied coolly.

The courtiers began to whisper among themselves. The scene was not a new one—the Bourbons were legendary for their tempers and in no branch of the family was this more true than among the sons and daughters of Louis XIV's legitimized children. Less than ten years before, the King's boon companion, the Comte de Coigny, had been killed in a duel by another Bourbon, the Prince de Dombes, for exactly such a comment as that made by the Marquis.

"Then I will be at my château near Saint-Cloud at daybreak. If you would care to present yourself there, we will settle the matter."

"Daybreak it is, Your Excellency," Henri agreed.

"Then I shall await you near the Mars fountain at the end of the garden."

Bowing his acquiescence, the Marquis called for his surtout and his coach and left the hôtel.

The young Comte de Clavignon and the Marquis de Ragnier returned to Versailles with a coach full of courtiers. They often found the entertainments at Court did not compare to those offered in Paris away from the watchful eye of the King and Madame de Pompadour.

Climbing the stairs to their attic apartments, the Comte de Clavignon nudged the Marquis de Ragnier and nodded toward Jasmine, who was mounting the stairway to her own apartment. Dressed in black velvet and silver lace, she was followed by Claudette, who was fast becoming more of a duenna than a maidservant.

"Madame de Saint-Antoine looks well in black, does she not?" the blond Comte demanded of the brunette Marquis.

As was intended, Jasmine heard the comment and smiled as Claudette prepared to ward off the attentions of the young courtiers.

"It is well that she does," the Marquis replied, "since she is very likely going to be wearing it for the next year."

Curious, Jasmine turned around at the head of the stairs. She waited until the young men had joined her there.

"Since I was obviously supposed to hear you," she told them, "perhaps you would care to explain your remarks."

"Here, Madame, in the corridor?" the Comte de Clavignon asked.

"Very well, Monsieur le Comte . . ." she began.

"Louis-Alexandre, dearest Madame," he said, seizing her hand and kissing it loudly.

"Louix-Alexandre, then," she agreed, "and Monsieur le Marquis . . ."

"Charles, lovely lady," he corrected, capturing her other hand.

"Louis-Alexandre and Charles," she said at last, "would you care to step into my drawing room?"

"Delighted!" they agreed.

Elated at their good fortune in being the first to bring the news to the King's mistress, the young courtiers followed Jasmine, and a disapproving Claudette, to her apartment.

Ensconced on her sofa, a glass of the King's finest champagne in their hands, the Comte and Marquis were reluctant to reveal their news and end their moment of favor from one of the most influential people at Court.

Jasmine sat in an armchair across the room trying impatiently to bring the rambling conversation around to the comments they'd made on the stairway.

"Gentlemen," she said at last, "I must warn you that I expect the King momentarily. He will not find it amusing to discover me here with two young gentlemen unless I can give him a good reason for your presence. Now, will you give me a reason, or will you take your leave?''

The nineteen-year-old Comte and the twenty-year-old Marquis exchanged an uneasy glance and smiled nervously at the sixteen-year-old Marquise.

''Actually, Madame,'' the Comte began, ''we were speaking of an incident which took place at the Hôtel de Vaurigny tonight.''

''The Marquis de Saint-Antoine and the Prince de Vaurigny became involved in an argument,'' the Marquis added. ''The Prince made some disparaging remarks about you and the Marquis countered with remarks about the Prince's grandmother.''

''The Prince,'' the Comte finished, ''challenged the Marquis to a duel.''

''A duel!'' Jasmine cried. ''Henri did not accept the challenge, did he?''

''Yes, Madame,'' the Marquis replied. ''They are to meet at daybreak at the Château de Saint-Hyacinth—near the Mars fountain.''

Jasmine sagged in her chair. ''Oh, my! They must be stopped!''

Claudette entered the drawing room. ''Madame, the King is coming! I can hear him on the stairs!''

The Comte and Marquis leapt to their feet, their nerve suddenly deserting them. They had suddenly decided that it was not wise to be discovered alone with the King's young mistress.

''Good night, Madame,'' the Comte said, bowing.

''Thank you for the champagne,'' the Marquis added.

''Why don't you stay? You can tell the King what you have told me.''

"No, no, Madame," they said nearly in unison. "You may tell him. Good night."

She smiled as she closed the door behind them. At almost the same instant, the panel of the antechamber opened and the King entered the room.

"Ma petite," he said coming to her. "Three glasses of champagne?"

"Only one of which was mine, mon cher," she replied. "I have had visitors who told me a most interesting story."

It was still dark when the elegant but unadorned coach left the courtyards before Versailles and turned into the Avenue de Saint-Cloud accompanied by a contingent of armed guards.

Inside the coach, Jasmine clasped the King's hand. "Thank you, mon cher, for coming with me. We have to stop this duel."

"I do not intend any insult to your husband, ma petite," the King replied, "but this is no duel. This is murder. The Prince de Vaurigny is one of the best swordsmen in all Europe. Your husband is no match for him."

"I, for one," the Duc de Richelieu said from across the coach, "will be glad to get back to the palace. I do not enjoy rising at this early hours."

"After we return and go through the formalities of the levée," the King told him, "you can go back to bed. I fear you are getting old, Duc."

The Duc bit back an impudent reply remembering the King's words about the Bastille. "My mistress will be interested to hear that, Sire," he replied instead.

The King laughed, his good humor restored. "I understand you've a new mistress."

"Yes, Sire, a lovely girl. I discovered her at Versailles—like a wood nymph in the gardens."

"Good for you. Ah, here we are."

The Château de Saint-Hyacinth had been designed by Le Vau, who had been the architect for Vaux-le-Vicomte and Versailles, and, in fact, it resembled nothing so much as a miniature Versailles. The gardens behind the château stretched for nearly a mile and the Mars fountain, where the confrontation was to take place, was at the far end.

Skirting the château, the coach bearing the King, de Richelieu, and Jasmine rolled out on the wide walk toward the furthest reaches of the garden. In the distance, silhouetted by the breaking dawn, Jasmine could see a group of a dozen or more men with their horses tethered nearby.

"They're already there!" she cried. "They've already begun!"

The coach careened along the gravel path but, while the pace was already dangerous, Jasmine urged the driver to whip the horses into a faster gallop.

"You will kill us all trying to save your husband," de Richelieu commented apathetically.

Jasmine ignored him and, as the coach reached the end of the path, flung open the door and jumped to the ground without waiting for someone to help her.

The crowd of noblemen gathered near the fountain turned to watch Jasmine hurry toward them followed by the King and the Duc. Bowing to the approaching King, they parted ranks and allowed them through.

"You are too late," the Prince de Vaurigny informed her haughtily. He wiped his dueling saber on a silk handkerchief which he then threw contemptuously to the ground.

385

Ignoring him, Jasmine went to the supine form of her husband. A surgeon, provided by the Prince, knelt beside him examining the surprisingly small wound in his chest.

Kneeling opposite the surgeon, Jasmine took her husband's hand. "Henri?" she whispered.

His pale blue eyes opened and he drew a long, rasping breath. "Good morning, child," he said.

His eyes fluttered shut and she looked at the surgeon who shook his head.

"He is dead, Madame," the surgeon said.

The Duc de Richelieu took the Marquis's velvet coat from an onlooker and covered the dead man's pale face. Taking Jasmine's wrist, he drew her to her feet.

"Come back to the coach, Madame," he said. "We can do nothing."

The King frowned at the Prince de Vaurigny. "You had no business challenging this man to a dual, cousin."

"The man insulted our family, Sire," the Prince replied, appealing to the King's Bourbon pride.

"After you insulted his wife as I heard it."

In the background, the Comte de Clavignon and the Marquis de Ragnier exchanged a glance. They were thrilled to have played a part in the drama.

The Prince bowed his head. "I may have gotten carried away in my remarks," he admitted.

"May have? Are you not certain?"

Humiliated at being reproved before the nobles, the Prince drew a deep breath. "I am not completely sure of it, Sire. I had, perhaps, too much champagne."

"I see. Well, then, you will see to the return of your victim's body to Paris and then remain here, at your lovely château, until such time as you are able to decide upon a suitable compensation for his widow."

The Prince bowed. "As you say, Sire."

Passing among the excited courtiers, the King returned to the coach where the Duc de Richelieu and Jasmine awaited him.

"I am sorry, Jasmine," he said softly as the coach started out.

"There is nothing to be sorry for, mon cher," she replied. "You tried—but we were simply too late."

As the coach passed the château and re-entered the Avenue de Saint-Cloud, Jasmine leaned against the King thoughtfully. She was a widow—when she returned to Versailles, she would dress in mourning for the husband she had never loved.

Chapter 36

It was late evening when Barrett Paxon rattled the locked iron gates of the Hôtel de Marteleur.

"Go away!" the concierge shouted, leaning from his lodge. "There is no one here!"

"I must speak to Madame de Saint-Antoine!" he called through the bars.

"She doesn't live here—she lives at Versailles!"

"But, I was told . . ."

"Monsieur, Madame de Saint-Antoine lives at Versailles! Now, go away!"

"But . . ." Barrett sighed with exasperation as the concierge slammed the window shut. Turning away, he returned to the fiacre standing at the edge of the Rue de Lille. "How long would it take to get to Versailles?" he asked the driver.

"An hour, perhaps more," the driver replied. "But it will do you no good to go there anymore tonight, Monsieur. Unless you have been invited."

"Well, then," Barrett said, climbing back into the fiacre, "take me back to my lodgings. I will have to wait until tomorrow to go to Versailles.''

Swatched in black silk mourning, Jasmine stepped out of her coach in the Cour Royale and wearily made her way to the palace.

She'd been absent from Versailles for two days, having made the journey to Saint-Antoine for her husband's funeral. It had been a nightmare. Her mother and Sofie, who had been allowed to travel from Mareteleur for the funeral, had not allowed her a moment's peace. Now that Henri was dead and there was no heir for the estates of Mareteleur and Saint-Antoine, they had spent the entire time trying to convince her that she had to give the King a child. She had fled from Saint-Antoine the moment Henri was laid to rest, leaving her mother to make her way back to Paris the best way she could.

Followed by Claudette, Jasmine entered the palace and climbed the Queen's Staircase. Passing through the Queen's rooms, she curtsied to the Queen and Mesdames, who were playing cards, and to the Dauphin and Dauphine, who were holding court nearby. Then, leaving the Queen's suite, she went on into the State Salons eager to reach her rooms.

She ignored the whispers and stares that followed her along the Hall of Mirrors. The mirrored doors of the King's rooms were closed and she supposed he was meeting with his ministers on the subject of the war which was going badly.

''Madame?''

She turned and found the inseparable Comte de Clavignac and Marquis de Ragnier standing side by side.

''Good evening, gentlemen,'' she said.

The Comte, who seemed the bolder of the two, said: ''We wished to tell you how sorry we were about the death of your husband.''

''Thank you, Monsieur,'' she said, ''and you, Monsieur.''

''Since His Majesty is occupied with his ministers,'' the Marquis added, with a nod at the closed doors, ''we thought, perhaps, you would care for company until he is free.''

Claudette frowned but Jasmine smiled. ''Very well, gentlemen, come along.''

Breaking into delighted grins, the young men fell into step on either side of her leaving Claudette to trail along in disgruntled silence.

Entering her apartment, Jasmine was pleased to see that the fires had been lit and the candles were burning.

''Help yourself to some wine if you like, gentlemen,'' she told her guests. ''If you will excuse me for a few moments, I would like to change my gown.''

The Comte and Marquis bowed and Jasmine left them to go to her bedchamber.

''Madame!'' Claudette hissed as she unhooked Jasmine's gown. ''You should not have invited those two up here!''

''Why not?''

The maid pulled the gown over her mistress's head and carried it to the dressing room. ''Suppose they begin telling people that you have allowed them liberties!''

Jasmine stepped out of her petticoats and began unlacing her corset. ''Suppose they do,'' she said, unconcerned. ''The King won't believe it and it does not matter what anyone else thinks.''

But Claudette would not be dissuaded. ''I still don't like it, Madame,'' she clucked as she helped Jasmine into a gown of aqua satin.

"Ah, that feels better," Jasmine breathed. Lightly boned, the aqua gown was not so constricting as her ordinary Court attire. "If you don't like it," she told Claudette as she left the room, "then I suggest you stay in here and unpack my trunk."

With a significant lift of her eyebrows, Jasmine left a sputtering Claudette behind her.

The Comte and Marquis jumped to their feet as she entered the salon.

"Sit, sit, gentlemen," she invited, "and tell me what I've missed during my two days in the country."

The ormulu clock in the salon struck midnight as the Marquis de Ragnier drained the fifth bottle of wine.

"And then," he said, finishing a story about the previous night's supper, "the Duc's quizzing glass fell right into the soup!"

Though the story was not terribly funny, Jasmine and the Comte de Clavignac roared with laughter. The Marquis, who was somewhat shy and tended to let his friend take the spotlight, flushed with pleasure at his own wit.

A knock on the door made both young noblemen start with fright.

"It is the King!" the Comte cried.

"Oh, no!" the Marquis groaned mournfully. "We will be banished!"

"No, no, no," Jasmine assured them. "It is not the King—the King never comes to the door."

Waving away a footman, she went to the door and swung it open.

"Your Excellency!" she said to a surprised Duc de Richelieu. "Come in, we are having a little wine."

Entering the salon, the Duc took stock of the empty bottles on the floor and the two young men standing sheepishly before him.

"It would seem, Madame," he said, "that you are having more than a little wine."

"That may be true," she admitted thoughtfully.

"Yes, it very well may." The Duc eyed the Comte and the Marquis. "Gentlemen, it is after midnight. Do you not think it is time you were on your way?"

"Absolutely, Your Excellency!" the Comte agreed. Kissing Jasmine's hand, he hurried from the room followed by the Marquis, who was frightened into silence by the frown the Duc de Richelieu directed at him.

"You should be in bed, Madame," he told Jasmine as he took the glass from her hand.

"I was waiting for the King," she told him.

"The King has retired. He is not aware that you have returned and he has made other arrangements for tonight." Taking her arm, he led her toward her bed-chamber. "Come, let your maid put you to bed."

"The King has made other arrangements?" she asked, leaning on the Duc's arm. "Has he gone to Madame de Pompadour?"

"No, I lent him my mistress during your absence."

The Duc sat on the chaise longue while Jasmine stepped behind a folding Savonnerie screen. Claudette brought her a nightdress and dressing gown and began unhooking the aqua gown.

"The King likes your mistress?" she asked over the top of the screen.

"Apparently so. He requested her again tonight."

"I suppose," she said, her chin quivering, "the King will not want me any longer."

"Oh, Madame!" the Duc groaned. "Do not get maudlin, I beg you!"

"But it always happens," she complained, her words muffled as Claudette pulled the nightdress over her head. "I am always abandoned by men! My husband . . ."

"Madame," the Duc reminded her, "your husband is dead."

"Yes," she agreed. She sniffed loudly. "Oh, Claudette, poor Henri is dead!"

Claudette rolled her eyes and disappeared into the dressing room with Jasmine's aqua gown and her petticoats and chemise.

Crossing the room, Jasmine sat beside the Duc and leaned her head on his shoulder.

"No one loves me," she whined. "My mother and grandmother hate me because of Henri and Michel. Giacomo left me to go to Amsterdam—can you imagine why anyone would want to leave Paris for Amsterdam?" she demanded suddenly.

"At this moment," the Duc said wearily, "I can think of only one reason."

"And then there was Barrett," Jasmine continued. "He never answered my letter. By now," her chin quivered, "by now he's probably married to Octavia Dashwood!"

"Jasmine," the Duc said pleadingly, "why don't you go to bed."

She shook her head. "I can't sleep."

"You have not even tried!" the Duc roared.

To his dismay, she burst into tears. "Don't shout at me!" she sobbed.

With exaggerated patience, he took her arm and

393

pulled her to her feet. Taking her dressing gown, he helped her into bed and pulled the coverlet up to her chin.

"Why didn't Barrett answer my letter?" she asked softly.

Totally confused, he shook his head. "I don't know, Jasmine. Perhaps he didn't receive the letter."

"Didn't receive it!" She sat up. "Claudette! Didn't you post the letter to Barrett?"

"Never mind, Jasmine!" the Duc shouted. "Doubtless you will get an answer tomorrow."

"Do you think so?" she asked hopefully.

"Yes, I think so." Tucking the coverlet beneath her chin once again, he patted her cheek. "Now, go to sleep."

"Good night, Your Excellency," she murmured, suddenly drowsy.

"Good night, Marquise," he replied, amused. With a grudgingly fond smile, he shook his head and left the apartment.

"Oh, Claudette!" Jasmine groaned. "Must you stamp your feet when you walk?"

"I was not stamping my feet, Ma . . ."

"And do not shout!"

Claudette sighed and hooked Jasmine's black silk gown.

When she was dressed, Jasmine surveyed herself in the mirror. Her clothing was entirely black from the black brocade slippers that peeked out from beneath her skirts to the black ribbon about her throat.

Claudette fluffed out the black lace trimming of her sleeves. "It would be much more striking with white powdered hair."

"I cannot bear to have my hair pomaded this morning and the wig is much too heavy!" She patted her own auburn hair, which was drawn into a chignon. "This will have to do."

Draping a black silk pelisse over her shoulders to ward off the early spring chills that still pervaded the palace in the mornings, Jasmine and Claudette left the apartment.

The Hall of Mirrors was filled with petitioners awaiting their turn to ask the King for favors. Jasmine hurried past them, determined to clear her head with a walk in the budding gardens.

"Madame de Saint-Antoine?"

She turned and found the Comte de Clavignac and Marquis de Ragnier smiling at her.

"Do you gentlemen ever part?" she asked.

"Occasionally, Madame," the Comte admitted, "but not often. We wanted to tell you that we hope the Duc de Richelieu was not angry with you because of our presence in your apartment."

"No, he was not angry with me—nor with you."

On the other side of the gallery, nearly lost in the crowd, Barrett Paxton paused in his conversation with a young courtier who was waiting to ask the King for a commission in the army.

"Will you excuse me, Monseigneur," Barrett said. "I believe I see a lady with whom I am acquainted and whom I have not seen in many months."

"Really? Who would that be?" the Chevalier asked.

Barrett nodded toward Jasmine. "There—Madame de Saint-Antoine."

The courtier was impressed. "You know the King's mistress?"

"The King's mistress? I thought Madame de Pompadour was the King's mistress."

"La Pompadour is his titular mistress. She satisfies the desires of his mind. Unfortunately, she is quite unequal to the task of satisfying his other appetites. For those he has Madame de Saint-Antoine. For which one cannot blame him—she is an exquisite creature, is she not? And only sixteen years old. She must be a welcome change from La Pompadour who, though still beautiful, is past the first blush of youth." He shook his head. "The privileges of royalty! What I wouldn't give to spend one hour with that delicious creature! But then, perhaps you can tell me what I am missing. You know her well, do you not, Monsieur Paxton?"

Watching her flirt with the two young noblemen, Barrett shook his head. "No, Monseigneur, I fear I must be mistaken. That is a lady I do not know at all."

As though feeling his eyes upon her, Jasmine turned. Her eyes widened in astonishment as she saw him but, as she would have called out to him, he whirled on his heel and walked away.

Desperately, Jasmine tried to push her way through the crowd that separated them. Her wide hoops made it more difficult and hampered her progress. When she was at last past the greatest portion of the mob, she found her arm imprisoned in the grasp of the Duc de Richelieu.

"Let me go!" she cried, struggling. "Please, Your Excellency!"

"Where are you going?" he demanded. "What has happened?"

Freed from his grasp, she started away. "You were right, Your Excellency!" she called back over her shoulder. "Barrett has answered my letter!"

Leaving the Duc to stare after her in puzzlement, she hurried down the stairs.

By the time she reached the courtyard, Barrett was

nowhere to be seen. She stopped a lackey who was passing.

"You there!" she cried. "Did you see a man pass by? A man with dark hair and wearing a blue satin suit?"

Recognizing the King's mistress, the man bowed. "Yes, Madame la Marquise. He seemed to be greatly vexed."

"Where did he go?"

"He had a fiacre waiting, Madame. He left in it."

"Try to find him! Follow him to Paris if you must, but find out where he is staying! If you bring me the information, I will give you five—no, ten—louis d'or!"

The lackey's mouth dropped open. Ten louis d'or! It was more than ten times his yearly wage. Without pausing to bow, he started off toward the courtyard.

"I will bring you the information, Madame!" he promised over his shoulder. "If I have to walk to Paris, you shall have the information you desire!"

397

Chapter 37

Jasmine chewed her lip nervously as her coach rolled toward Paris. In her hand she held a piece of paper, damp and wrinkled from her anxious fidgeting and the tense perspiration of her palms, which contained the address of Barrett Paxton's lodgings.

It was an inn run by Monsieur and Madame Faivre in the Rue de Saint-Regis.

As the coach entered Paris, she thought about Claudette's disapproval when she'd told her she planned to go into the city and find him—alone. In fact, she realized, Claudette had disapproved of her going to find him at all. The maidservant was very proud of her mistress's position as maîtress to the King and resented any threat to it. And she knew, as did Jasmine, that Barrett Paxton was the strongest threat there was.

The coach entered the Rue de Saint-Regis and she smoothed her black skirts for the hundredth time. She hadn't bothered to try to hide her identity. Though most of Paris knew by then that the King had a mistress named Jasmine de Saint-Antoine, only those who frequented the Court had ever seen her. If she did not reveal her name, no one was likely to know who she was.

The coachman reined in the horses in the courtyard of a small inn and one of the footmen leapt from the back of the coach and came to help her out. There were a few ragged children playing near the gate and they hurried over to see the grand coach and the beautifully dressed lady whose like they did not often find in their midst.

Reaching into her pocket, Jasmine pulled out a handful of francs. She handed them to the footman.

"Distribute them among the children," she directed.

He bowed and she walked on toward the front door of the inn where a rather blowsy looking woman stood waiting for her.

"You are Madame Faivre?" she asked as she reached the door.

"I am," the woman replied. "And who might you be?" Her dark eyes took stock of Jasmine, whose black mourning was obviously of quality materials and whose handsome coach and horses and liveried footmen gave the impression of great wealth.

"I am . . ." She hesitated, knowing it would not be wise to tell the truth. The general population of Paris resented the money the King spent on his mistresses and Madame de Pompadour's coach had been stoned on several of the rare occasions that she ventured into the city. "I am Mademoiselle DuPré," she said at last. "I was told that Monsieur Barrett Paxton was lodging with you."

"He is, Mademoiselle," Madame Faivre acknowledged, relaxing a little. In the absense of a title, she took Jasmine to be the daughter of a wealthy bourgeoisie whom she could tolerate more than the profligate courtiers. "Come this way."

Jasmine followed the woman into the building. The dining room was empty and the taproom, on the opposite side of the central corridor, had but a few customers. None bothered to look up as she passed. At the foot of a stairway, Madame Faivre stopped.

"Top of the stairs, Mademoiselle," she said, "second door on your left."

"Thank you, Madame," Jasmine replied. She dropped a livre into the woman's outstretched hand.

The hallway at the top of the stairs was lit only by a grimy window at the far end. Jasmine's black skirts trailed over a worn rug whose pattern was nearly invisible through the accumulation of dirt left by muddy and dusty boots. She paused at the door Madame Faivre had directed her to and then, gathering her courage, knocked.

Her heart leaped as she heard Barrett's voice answer from inside the room:

"Who is it?"

"Barrett?" she called breathlessly. "It's Jasmine."

It seemed an eternity before the door opened and he stood before her.

"How did you find me?" he asked.

"I sent someone to follow you this morning. Barrett, please, can't I come in?"

Stepping back, he opened the door and allowed her into the room. Alarmed, she noticed that a trunk lay open on the bed.

"Are you packing?" she asked.

He returned to the bed and continued his work. "Yes," he replied, his back to her. "I'm going back to Virginia."

Almost shyly, she went to him and sat on the edge of the bed. "Take me with you," she asked quietly.

He refused to look at her. "What about your husband?"

She lifted a fold of her black silk skirt. "My husband is dead. He was killed in a duel."

Still he concentrated on the clothing he was folding and laying in the trunk. "What about the King?"

"What about Octavia Dashwood?" she countered.

"She went home with her parents; I expect she got tired of hearing about you. But you are the King's mistress—could you leave him?"

"Of course I could."

"Don't you love him?"

"No, and he does not love me. I serve a purpose, but I am far from irreplaceable."

A slight smile softened the grim line of Barrett's mouth. "You're wrong," he said, looking at her at last. "You are irreplaceable. Else I would not have come halfway around the world for you."

Jasmine made no attempt to halt the flow of tears that flooded her eyes. Standing, she fell into his embrace. "Oh, Barrett, Barrett!" she cried. "Say you will take me with you. Take me home, Barrett, please!"

He crushed her to him. "I will!" He put her away from him. "Will the King allow you to leave?"

"I'm sure he will. Come back to Versailles with me— I think I know someone who can help us."

While a footman took Barrett's trunk to Jasmine's apartment, Jasmine took Barrett to Madame de Pompadour's apartment.

"Madame du Hausset," Jasmine told the maid. "We must see Reinette immediately!"

"One moment, Madame," the maid replied.

She returned after several moments, the door was

opened, and Jasmine and Barrett were shown to the Marquise's beautiful library.

"Jasmine," Madame de Pompadour said, standing behind her desk, "Louise said you wanted to see me?" Her eyes swept over Barrett but she asked no questions.

"Reinette," Jasmine said, crossing the room to place her hands in Madame de Pompadour's. "I need your help."

"Well, sit down. You too, Monsieur, and tell me what this is all about."

Sitting beside Barrett on a sofa, Jasmine began the story of their separation and the events which had brought her to Versailles. When she finished, Madame de Pompadour said:

"And now you have found one another again and you wish to be together?"

"Oh, yes," Jasmine replied. "We want to return to Virginia and continue as though this last year had never existed. That is why we need your help. Will you speak to the King, Reinette? Will you help us secure his permission to leave France? You know him so much better than I."

Her vanity appealed to, Reinette nodded. "Yes, I will speak to him." She looked at Barrett. "You have said very little, Monsieur Paxton. Do you as eagerly desire Jasmine's return to Virginia? If you receive permission to take her away from us, will you promise to care for her?"

"There is nothing, Madame," Barrett replied quietly, "that I desire more than to care for Jasmine."

"You love her very much; I can see it in your eyes." Reinette stood. "Very well, then, I will speak to the King. He is coming to have supper with me tonight—I will raise the subject then."

Hurrying from the sofa, Jasmine embraced the frail

Maîtresse en Titre. "Thank you, Reinette!" she cried, nearly weeping with relief. "How can I ever repay you?"

Madame de Pompadour stroked her cheek. "By being happy," she replied. "You are young—marry your Monsieur Paxton and give him a houseful of children." Her eyes were sad as she allowed Barrett to kiss her hand. "And you, Monsieur, be kind to your Jasmine. We have become very fond of her."

"I can promise you that, Madame," Barrett said.

Reinette sat behind her desk once again. "Run along, then, and pack your belongings. I believe I can assure you of the King's permission."

With copious thanks, Jasmine and Barrett took their leave. As she leaned back in her chair, Reinette's gaze was a little wistful for the years when her happiness was as unquestioning and complete.

Walking through the Galerie Basse, Jasmine giggled happily.

"Oh, Barrett! We have so much to do! We have to go back to Paris!"

"Back to Paris? Why?"

"To get Maman! She will want to go back to Virginia too!"

Going to the courtyards before the palace, Jasmine summoned her coach·and, for the second time that day, begain the long ride into the city.

The coach drew up before the Hôtel de Mareteleur and Barrett climbed out and helped Jasmine down.

Without bothering to wait for a footman to answer the door, she entered the hôtel and called out:

"Maman? Maman, where are you?"

"Jasmine?" Isabeau's voice echoed down the stairs. "Wait there, I'll be down in a moment."

Clad in a dressing gown of scarlet satin, Isabeau appeared on the landing at the head of the stairs.

"Barrett?" she asked, her face ashen with surprise. "Barrett Paxton? Is that you?"

Barrett smiled and bowed. "Indeed it is, Madame."

"What are you doing here?" she demanded angrily as she started down the stairs. "Why have you come to France?"

"Maman!" Jasmine reproved, astonished at her mother's rudeness. "Is that any way to . . ."

She was interrupted by a masculine voice which said: "Good afternoon, Madame de Saint-Antoine."

Looking up, she saw the elderly Duc de Beaupré—one of Versailles more notorious roués—leaning over the balustrade. He was clad in one of Henri de Saint-Antoine's dressing gowns and his pomaded, powdered hair was in wild disarray.

Instinctively, Jasmine curtsied. "Good afternoon, Your Excellency," she replied. "Maman," she said under her breath, "what the devil is he doing here?"

"Go into the salon," Isabeau commanded. Looking up, she smiled. "I will return shortly, Antoine. Help yourself to some wine."

While the Duc disappeared into the suite from whence he had come, Isabeau herded Jasmine and Barrett into the salon.

"Maman," Jasmine demanded again, "what is the Duc de Beaupré doing here? Are you his mistress?"

"Yes!" Isabeau hissed. "He is rich and, what is more, he is a widower. I hope to be able to induce him to marry me."

"Marry you!" Jasmine cried. Isabeau shushed her and she lowered her voice. "But you are already married! What about Papa?"

"What about Papa? Can Papa make me a Duchesse? Can Papa give me a château and jewels and beautiful gowns?"

"No, Maman, but . . ."

"Jasmine," Isabeau cooed, "don't you see? The Duc can give me everything I should have had! I have a right to such a life as he can offer—it was not my fault that my father died penniless!"

"Of course it was not your fault, Maman. But it is wrong!"

"It is wrong for me but it was not wrong for you? You were married to Henri when you gave yourself to the King. Not that you should not have given yourself to him. Part of the reason the Duc wants me is because I am your maman." She touched Jasmine's hair lovingly. "My beautiful baby; how proud I am of you. My lovely Jasmine—the King's mistress. You will send the slut Pompadour back to the gutters, won't you, my darling?"

"No, Maman," Jasmine replied. "I won't. That is what I came to tell you. Barrett has come to get me. I am going home to Virginia with him."

Stunned, Isabeau looked at Barrett. "Is this true?"

Barrett nodded. "Yes, Madame, it is true."

"Bastard!" Isabeau screamed. "Why did you come to France? Why couldn't you mind your own business?"

"Maman!" Jasmine cried, shocked.

"And you!" Isabeau turned to her, her eyes blazing. "I gave you everything! I gave you a rich husband! I gave you the opportunity to be everything I could not be! And now you are going to throw it away!"

Jasmine cringed as her mother raised her hand to strike her. But the blow was stayed as Barrett caught Isabeau's wrist in a cruel grasp.

"Maman," Jasmine pleaded, trembling. "I came to

ask you to come with us. Please, come home to Virginia —come home to Armand and Papa and Belle Glade."

"No!" Isabeau screamed, tearing herself from Barrett's clutches. "I will never return to Virginia! And if you go, you are no longer my daughter!"

"Maman!" Jasmine implored. "Do not say that! I beg you!"

"Get out!" Isabeau hissed. "Get out, you ungrateful little bitch! And take your precious lover with you!"

Tears nearly blinding her, Jasmine stumbled from the room and fled the hôtel. Climbing into the coach, she broke into heart-rending sobs.

Barrett followed her into the coach and gathered her into his arms. Leaning from the coach window, he called up to the coachman:

"Back to Versailles!"

Night had fallen and Jasmine stirred from the exhausted slumber which had overtaken her. She had spent nearly six hours riding to and from Paris and the emotional events of the day had taken their toll. She smiled as Barrett sat on the edge of the bed in her Versailles apartment.

"Is it late?" she asked softly.

He nodded. "You missed supper. A tray was delivered hours ago."

"I'm not hungry." She looked at the cluster of trunks in the corner. "Doesn't that look wonderful?" she asked. "Tomorrow we will leave for home." Barrett smiled and she touched the soft magenta silk of the dressing gown he wore. "It looks better on you than it did on the King," she told him. "I think you should take it with you."

"Perhaps I will," he agreed. "Is there anything at the

Hôtel de Mareteleur or the Château de Saint-Antoine that should be sent for?''

She shook her head. ''I don't want anything from either of those places. What I have here is more than enough.'' She looked around. ''Where is Claudette?''

''I dismissed her for the evening.''

''So there won't be any interruptions?''

He laughed. ''I haven't forgotten that night beneath the willows.''

''Nor have I. If only no one had found us. If only there had been no one else about.''

''No one else is here tonight,'' he whispered. Leaning over, he kissed her with all the tenderness she had remembered during their separation. ''I dreamed of this moment, Jasmine. I lived for this night.''

Jasmine stroked his cheek. ''Let's not wait any longer, my love. We belong only to one another now.''

Discarding the dressing gown, Barrett climbed into the bed and took her into his arms. That for which she'd defied her mother—that about which she'd dreamed for nearly a year—was about to be hers. And there was no force in heaven or earth that could have kept her from it.

She cried out as he touched her for it seemed that, in that moment, her senses had become excruciatingly acute. As their bodies, freed from the separation of their clothing, touched and interwined, she abandoned herself to him with a ferocity that would have amazed the King and even Casanova, and it seemed to her that at the height of her passion she could hear the whisper of the breeze through the willows on Mobjack Bay.

The fire in the fireplace was dying and the candles in the tall candlesticks were guttering out when the panel in the antechamber opened and the King emerged.

His slipper-shod feet making no sound on the thick carpets, he entered Jasmine's bedchamber and approached the bed. Having just come from Madame de Pompadour's, he was not surprised by what he found.

Clasped in one another's arms, Jasmine and Barrett slept and, as the King watched, the corners of her mouth turned up in a tiny, contented smile.

Pressing a finger to his lips, the King bent and touched her cheek. Then, smiling sadly, he left the apartment as quietly as he'd come.

Epilogue

A wagon piled high with Jasmine's belongings waited in the Cour Royale as Jasmine and Barrett bade adieu to the King and Madame de Pompadour. Settling into the coach, they waved once again and, followed by the wagon, started away from Versailles.

They were nearly out of the Place d'Armes when another coach drew alongside and the Duc de Richelieu stuck his head from the window.

"So you are leaving us, eh, Marquise?" he called across the narrow space separating them. "Good riddance to you!"

"And to you, Your Excellency!" Jasmine replied happily.

"I wish you a pleasant journey!" he continued. "Of course, accidents do happen."

"No accidents had better happen, Your Excellency," she warned. "Or you will answer for them."

He sneered. "You dare insult me, Madame? Might I remind you that your influence with the King is at an end while my influence remains strong?"

"My influence may be ended, Your Excellency, but the King's never ends."

"And what does that mean?"

Reaching into her pocket, she drew forth the second of the two lettres de cachet Henri had given her. The Duc paled as he saw his own name inscribed on the document which bore the King's unmistakable signature.

"I might have known!" he hissed. "Go then! It matters not to me! I have already chosen your successor!"

"Really? And who would that be?"

"My own mistress! She has already proved that she can please the King. Moreover, her impeccable breeding will prevent her from being as ungrateful and common as you!" He motioned to the lady beside him in the coach. "Madame, come and bid your rival farewell."

The woman leaned forward, emerging from the shadows of the grand coach. With seeming reluctance, she pushed back the concealing hood of her pelisse.

"Solange!" Jasmine cried in disbelief.

"Madame la Comtesse d'Auligny will be occupying your apartment within a sennight," the Duc predicted smugly.

Solange's eyes pleaded with her and Jasmine laughed. "Good luck, Solange," she said. "Make His Excellency proud of you."

Solange grinned. "That I will, Madame!" she promised. "That I will!"

Jasmine rapped on the wall of the coach and the vehicle rocked as it started them on their long journey home. Leaning out the window, Jasmine waved to Solange and then, unable to contain her mirth any longer, threw herself into Barrett's arms.

As the coach rolled away, the Duc de Richelieu looked after it in uneasy puzzlement while her peals of delighted laughter wafted back on the scented spring breezes.